OPERATION FOOLS MATE DEADLOCK

M.L Baldwin is a former Tank Commander who joined the Second Royal Tank Regiment in 1996 and served with them on operations in Northern Ireland, Kosovo, Iraq and Afghanistan over a 19 year career. He was awarded a Mentioned in Dispatches (MiD) during his last tour of Afghanistan. After leaving the forces he decided to try his hand at becoming an author, which is where you join him now in his journey. Inspired by the likes of Clive Cussler and Tom Clancy, he wrote his debut series of books for Operation Fools Mate back in 2023 which he hopes people will enjoy reading as much as he enjoyed writing them. This is book three in the series, following on immediately after the events of the second book Operation Fools Mate 48. Using his own first hand experiences of life on the front line of combat operations, he hopes to bring a level of realism and excitement that will both shock and excite his readers. After all, the modern battlefield is full of technology but ultimately, it's the human element and a certain degree of luck that play its part the most. His expertise in his field have garnered widespread acclaim and featured interviews on BBC Radio, whilst his articles in leading publications such as The European, NationalWorld, MSN, the Daily Star (UK), The London Economic and others, have helped solidify his reputation as a sought-after authority in the field. Keep watching for more exciting titles. In his own words, "I'm not finished yet, I'm only just getting started."

Also by M.L Baldwin

The Operation Fools Mate Series

Operation Fools Mate 24

Operation Fools Mate 48

Operation Fools Mate Deadlock

OPERATION FOOLS MATE

DEADLOCK

By M.L Baldwin

www.mlbaldwin.co.uk

Contents

Dedication

The true soldier fights not because he hates what is in front of him, but because he loves what is behind him.

G.K. Chesterton - Illustrated London News, Jan 14th 1911

Dedicated to all the brave men and women of this great country who in their lifetime have ever had to put on a uniform and put the needs of the country before their own selves.

For all the sacrifice, the hard work, the blood, sweat, and tears,

Thank you.

May you all find peace and happiness in whatever life you choose to settle into.

1

Breakout

Cerne Abbas

Mike reached over the breech as Baz passed the thermal mug to him, steam wisping away out of the hatch.

"Sorry boss, but you guys were out of milk. Black coffee is all I can manage."

Mike smiled gratefully, not caring one jot as he thought to himself, it was caffeine, it was warm, and it was welcome. He looked over at the loader's side as Baz passed the other two mugs down to the gunner and through the cab to Bill, who reached out under the gun. He was happy, now he had a full crew, he'd forgotten just how important the loader could be, even without the loading. At least that wouldn't be a problem now as he cast his eyes over the dull blue rounds positioned in the loader's rack. They'd already loaded the gun with DST, the coax was loaded, the RWS was loaded, and the main engine and GUE were fired up and online. They were as ready as they'd ever be. He stood up on his seat, his elbows resting outside the hatch as he looked behind him, everyone was ready, eager for the go, like hunting dogs straining on the leash. All he had to do was give the command over the troop net and they'd burst out of the woodline. But before he did, they were waiting on one last piece. Gunslinger Two-Three. He had no idea who they were, or what they were, but his orders had to been to wait for them. It was 06:40, only ten more minutes and he'd know. He saw that Baz had finished with his mothering duties and he quickly beckoned over the I/C.

"Baz, just check again for me that the HF (High Frequency) set is on and set to 67.375." Baz smiled as he did so, this was the third time that Mike had asked.

"All good boss, HF set is on, and frequency checked."

Mike nodded to himself, taking a sip of coffee, almost burning his mouth. He picked up his binoculars, looking over again towards the Russian artillery positions, which were a hive of activity as soldiers moved around the guns, removing cam nets and moving artillery rounds, looking like they were preparing to fire. They'd watched as the artillery soldiers were woken up at 06:15 by the Non-Commissioned Officer's, shouting and kicking as they struggled from the effects of the night's festivities. It was only after the Russians had started their engines that Mike had finally given permission for his own unit's engines to be started, the noise being drowned out by the Russians. With their engines running they were finally able to use the Boiling Vessels, or BV's as the crews called them to heat water, which had allowed for everyone to at least have had a hot breakfast and was how Mike now found himself enjoying the cup of coffee. Whatever happened in the next ten minutes, at least they wouldn't be grumbling about cold food. Now they were poised to go, engines idling lazily, waiting for H- Hour, the name given to the time to attack.

He looked ahead, beyond the lead Warrior sat the two Talons, providing them all with an early warning, they were in surveillance mode and Rachel was in the rear vehicle monitoring what they were seeing and more importantly what they were listening to. Mike checked his watch, it now read 06:49. Spider's voice came over his right earpiece, excitedly, as he announced over their troop radio.

"Tango One-One, this is Tango Two-Zero, Talon is picking up helicopters coming in from the northeast, range four miles and closing."

Mike raised himself up, lifting his earpiece, hearing nothing but the squawking of the early morning crows over his own tank's engine, as he settled back down, realising quickly the Talon would hear better than he could. What the hell were helicopters doing there? So much for the Colonel telling him not to worry about the enemy's air power. He looked behind him nervously at the Hornet, contemplating using it early on.

Baz reached over to him, lightly patting him on the shoulder and disturbing him from his thoughts, giving him the thumbs up sign as he answered up for them on the troop net, leaving Mike free to listen in on the HF set.

"Tango One-One roger that. Out."

No sooner had he sent the message than Rachel's voice could be heard on the radio, she was in the back of Spider's wagon using his callsign.

"Tango Two-Zero, continuing, they're Apaches! They're ours!"

Mike looked over, punching the air excitedly in relief, as Baz again acknowledged the message, energy clear to hear in his voice, as in Mike's left earpiece, he heard the HF set finally hiss to life, the voice composed and calm.

"Hello, Whiskey Three-Zero, Whiskey Three-Zero, this is Gunslinger Two-Three, over."

Mike beamed as he keyed the pressel. *They* were the ones with air support; the Colonel had managed to get them attack helicopters!

"Gunslinger Two-Three, Whiskey Three-Zero, damn glad to have you with us!"

On board the lead Apache the pilot smiled; he could almost hear the relief in the commander's voice. Trying to make light of it, he added.

"Ahh Whiskey Three-Zero, you didn't really think we'd let you have all the fun without us did you?"

"Roger that," Mike replied jovially, his fears subsiding as he continued, "Gunslinger Two-Three I have you to my northeast, about four miles away, is that correct? Over."

The pilot looked astounded as he heard his gunner remark, "Bullshit! There's no way they know where we are!"

He had to agree with him, it did seem impossible. They'd set off from Middle Wallop at 02:40, using the darkness, lack of enemy air activity and their years of experience of low level flying skills to slip in behind the lines, the area ahead being checked and cleared by drones, the feed being fed through to the pilots displays. After a fraught hour of slowly moving forward, they'd pushed on, the plan being to get as far behind the Russian lines as they could, flying at almost ground level the whole way. It had been the first time he'd ever flown that low, and so fast, that he had to watch out for livestock and was sure they'd find the remains of some of the slower cows in his attack helicopter's landing gear and 30mm cannon if, that was, they ever made it back to base. They'd found a landing site just as the sun had begun to rise, checking it from afar, using the helicopter's superior optics and thermal cameras to see the woods were clear of enemy, before going in and landing, each helicopter facing the opposite way, giving the best chance for all round defence as they waited for 06:50. Then with ten minutes to go, they'd fired up the engines and were now hiding behind a wooded area, hovering mere feet above the ground, their longbow mast deployed above the trees and painting the picture in front of them. They'd already identified the woodline where the artillery were positioned, and could just make out in the distance the woods where Whiskey Three-Zero were hiding. Up to now, they'd kept their electronics off, they didn't want the Russians knowing they were there. They were fully expecting to have to explain to Whiskey Three-Zero who they were and where they were hiding. To have been unmasked so quickly and easily, especially with all their sensors and electronics off, almost made a mockery of the effort and work both pilots had done so far.

Ignoring his gunner's outburst, the pilot simply replied. "Roger Whiskey Three-Zero, so do you have eyes on us then? Over."

Mike could hear the disbelief in the pilot's voice, quickly reminding himself that the Talons capabilities were not public knowledge.

As if to answer he replied, "Negative, we don't have eyes on you, we've got *ears* on you, prototype tech that can hear and identify you. It's all good, your whirlybird secret's safe with us."

The pilot smiled to himself, as he thought, Ahh, so they already knew what they were flying. The constant race and development of warfare. The AH64-E he was flying was considered state of the art, his Squadron only receiving it last year, but he knew it had been designed and developed some five years ago, already some might argue obsolete, before ever firing a shot in anger. Satisfied they hadn't given away their position foolishly, he looked through his monocle at the terrain around him, before looking over to his wingman, who gave him the thumbs up. They were ready.

"Whiskey Three-Zero, we're set, when you're ready, call us in."

Mike closed his eyes, taking a few seconds to compose himself, preparing himself for what was about to happen. Looking at his watch, he could see they had ten minutes to go, just ten more minutes. Keying the radio, he simply replied.

"Tango One-One, roger. Out."

Unit 163, Electronic Warfare Wing, Dorchester.

"There it is again, strong signal on the HF band."

The operator leant forward, tapping away at the console as he tried to pinpoint the location. After only a few moments the computer had worked out the position, relaying it onto the map overlay.

The Sergeant standing over him, looked over to the map at the position they were given. It looked like a woodline, near Cerne Abbas. He called over to his Lieutenant, who was sat lazily smoking a cigarette. The Lieutenant sighed irritably, putting the cigarette down, resting it on the table's edge, walking over to see what all the fuss was about.

"What is it?" he asked, glancing at his watch, "it's nearly 7am and our relief will be here shortly."

The Sergeant ignored the comment, pointing to a map on the wall.

"Sir, we're picking up HF waves, on this bandwidth at this position here, by this woodline."

The Lieutenant leaned forward, nodding as he looked.

"Of course you are, look here." he explained, as pointing to another woodline close by he continued. "That's one of our artillery positions, it's what, no more than 400 metres from the other woodline?"

"But Sir, shouldn't we report this in?" the Sergeant asked quizzically.

The Lieutenant looked at him, displeased with being questioned in front of the operator. He pointed over at the clock, the Sergeant's head following as he replied.

"What time is it, Sergeant?"

"Sir?"

"The time, what is it?" he asked again, slowly this time as if speaking to a child.

The Sergeant stammered as he replied. "Er it's 06:52"

"And what time are the assaults going in?"

The man stammered again, unsure of where the Lieutenant was going with this as, impatiently the Lieutenant answered for him.

"It's going to begin in three minutes. Now don't you think that it stands to reason, that three minutes before the attack goes in, that the commander of the assault might be sending and receiving orders to the artillery over the radio?"

The Sergeant replied half-heartedly, "Yes Sir, I understand that, but the grid for the artillery is incorrect, this is in another location."

"400 metres, that's all!" the Lieutenant shot back, his voice rising, quickly lowering again as he continued to explain.

"Now, they've either moved location to the other woodline without telling us, or our equipment is not as accurate as we think."

Satisfied with his explanation he sat back down, carefully picking up the cigarette before unceremoniously flicking the ash onto the floor, taking a long drag and blowing smoke circles, watching them drift lazily away. "And Sergeant, have the day shift calibrate the signals array again, just to be sure."

Sensing the displeased tone, the Sergeant merely nodded, keeping his own thoughts to himself, as he looked to the operator, both sharing a look. Both thought the officer was wrong, but what could they do? They were only conscripts; he was supposed to be the professional. Silencing the alarm, the operator cancelled all the frequency alerts. Now whoever it was would be free to talk.

Hill 254 on the outskirts of Yeovil

Golgolvin paced irritably in front of the command vehicle; a nasty, familiar feeling came over him. He'd been here before, only the other day, but it was different then. Then he hadn't been planning the assault. He looked at his watch, two minutes to go until the artillery barrage. Two minutes, two bloody minutes, he muttered. He quickly thought through the plan, was there anything else? He'd had the remainder of the 344th Tank Regiment allocated to him, the tank commanders visiting him as soon as they arrived, demanding revenge for the massacre of one of their Companies. Their tempers had cooled when Golgolvin had told them they would be the first to go in, to seek retribution for the humiliation they'd had heaped upon them. As well as the 344th, Yuri had been given the 126th Infantry Regiment, bolstering the troops under his command to nearly 4000. With that amount of manpower, he was certain he should be able to break into the town. Behind him, eight miles away, were two artillery regiments, in pre-planned positions ready to fire. They would flatten the forward edge of the town with a creeping barrage, preventing anyone from attacking the assaulting units, until it would be too late. Then they'd be in, and the infantry and his own airborne troops would show them what cold hard Russian revenge looked like. Speaking of his own troops, he looked back to where they were positioned, ready to go on their newly acquired BMP3's. The vehicles had belonged to units that were killed in the port attacks and now they'd been redistributed, his troops having taken delivery of them throughout the night. He was confident they'd quickly adapt to them, after all wasn't that one of the founding principles of the VDV? To be able to adapt to any situation? Even so, with the vehicles new to his men, he'd wisely decided to keep them back as a force reserve, ready to exploit any breakthrough if they had to.

He looked back over at one of the closer assault groups, lined up in their forward positions and ready to go. The mistakes of the past would not be repeated he swore, as he saw with satisfaction that the infantry were now loaded into the vehicles, not clinging to the top of them, and all the hatches were closed, the crews confident, now they understood their enemy.

He looked at his watch again, twenty seconds to go. He looked over to his artillery officer, who was nearby, his headset on and connected to one of the command vehicles, the long curly black lead stretched out and coiled around his leg. The man looked at him, reporting back.

"Sir, Hammer One-Zero and Two-Zero, reporting guns cleared and ready to fire on your order."

He nodded, pleased they were ready, and simply replied, "Begin." The artillery officer spoke into the radio and a few moments later he could hear a dull thudding in the distance, the guns having already begun firing, the flight time of the rounds being taken into account as at precisely 06:55 the first rounds began to land amongst the buildings, the smoke and debris being flung far and wide. The shock waves were horrific, the ground seemed to pulse and vibrate around him as the massive 152mm shells smashed the ground. He'd brought up the largest guns they had, and within a few moments, the edge of the town had disappeared into a cloud of dust, smoke and flame, as the creeping barrage began to take hold, the houses collapsing, streets being covered by rubble, far more powerful than yesterday's bombardment. After a minute he could see the barrage began to creep forward, smashing more houses and buildings, like a man-made earthquake it began to chew further into the town, paving the way for the assault group. With luck, there would be nothing left for them to fight, only corpses. The General had been clear to him when he spoke last night, he wanted Yeovil to be flattened to the ground, a lesson to anyone else foolish enough to try to stand and fight. They were here to stay, they meant business, and God help anyone who got in the way.

Around him, his men began to cheer, fists pumping into the air as each round slammed home. He grinned savagely, being swept along in the heat of the moment, the defeat and misery of yesterday already forgotten.

Good, he thought to himself, now let's see how the bastards react to that!

Headquarters Yeovil Town Centre

Fergus looked over at the assembled officers, quickly outlining what he wanted to happen. The shock waves and vibrations caused dust to shake from the ceiling, coating the maps with a fine layer of dust that he kept having to wipe away. The civilian radios they'd been using were no longer working, the Russians had been jamming all sixteen of their frequencies since 4am, playing the same music over and over repeatedly. Fergus had remarked it wouldn't have been too bad if it was something uplifting, but it was a horrible wailing screeching tone, spoken in a foreign language, and after hearing it a few times, the only course of action was to switch off the radios. Instead, they'd now had to rely on runners to carry the messages, and already five of them were waiting patiently for orders. The bombardment had begun a few minutes ago, but they were expecting it, thanks to the phone box, they now had their link to the outside world. They'd been warned about the build up of troops, they knew what the Russians were planning, and Fergus waited patiently as the shock wave of another closer blast resonated through, before he continued speaking.

"So, there you have it. Again, just to confirm, one long blast means you are to go forward to your defensive positions. Two short blasts means that they're coming. One short and one long blast means fall back to your secondary positions. If they do punch through somehow, one long continuous blast means get everyone back and rally here. Now, questions?"

There were none, as the officers shook their heads and keen as anyone to get out of the confines of the basement and back to their positions. With a look of confidence, he dismissed them, adding, "Good luck everyone." As they picked up their weapons and body armour, he turned to the drones' screens, watching the devastation that was raining down on the town's outskirts, two miles away. God, he thought, how can anyone survive in that? Thankfully the houses were empty. Fergus's plan had pulled everyone back, the same as yesterday, using the drones to provide an overwatch, relying on them, instead of trying to defend the whole town. Now he could push troops into the areas he wanted to defend, reacting to the incursions, instead of wasting manpower where it wasn't needed. Because they'd lost the radios, he'd resorted to using the town's antiquated cold war alarm system, which surprisingly still worked. Now at least he could co-ordinate the defence, using a series of blasts of the system. Basic, but hopefully, it would suffice, just like the buglers back in the days of Waterloo. All they could do was hang on; the rumours were flying already as to what troops they would get. Secretly he'd hoped to see his old airborne regiment, but he knew the chances that they'd be sent in were slim to none, no doubt the Paras were already guarding a town closer to home.

He looked up towards the ceiling again as another blast hit nearby, dislodging years of dust. The barrage was getting closer. The Russians were going to try to flatten them. He saw the young soldier next to him flinch as the shockwave shook the building, looking towards the stairway. He put out his arm, to steady him, reading the man's mind.

"Trust me son, you're better off down here, than up there."

The man's jaw hardened looking back at him, before finally he smiled and nodded in acknowledgement, before getting back to work. He'd seen what the Colonel could do, If Colonel Young said it would be okay, then fine, he knew it would be.

Turning his back to the man, Fergus himself looked up, keeping his own fears hidden, looking up to the ceiling. He hoped whatever the army were planning, they'd do it soon.

Cerne Abbas

Mike could see the flash of the guns up ahead, through the trees as the artillery had begun to fire. The shock waves passed through the tank and seemed to bury deep in his chest. It reminded him of his youth, when he'd go to the car shows and see the converted vans with the huge speakers setup in the back, the bass thumping through his inner body. He thought at first that the Apaches had launched early, then reminded himself the artillery were getting ready to fire. Perhaps Yeovil was the target. It wouldn't matter, not long now and they'd be silenced forever.

Mike checked his watch, watching the second-hand tick by, less than thirty seconds to H-hour. He looked down into the turret, speaking over the tank's intercom or I/C

"Ok everyone thirty seconds, let's look alive. Bill, you ready to go?"

"Ready boss."

"Smudge, you ready?"

"Ready boss."

Mike looked over to Baz, who was standing in the loader's station staring back up at him, his arms outstretched and holding onto the grab handles installed in the turret roof, ready for the bumpy journey.

"Baz, ready?"

"I'm ready boss, let's do this."

Mike smiled, before looking back up, his head peering out over the top of the cupola. Behind him he'd slung his AK12 on the hatch, if he needed to grab it quickly it was ready. He checked his watch, fifteen seconds to go. He keyed the radio.

"All callsigns, standby, ten seconds....."

He stared at the second hand as it ticked over, with three seconds to go, he began the countdown.

"All callsigns move in, three...two...one...MOVE NOW!"

He felt the tank jolt as it began to move forward, quickly looking behind to make sure the Warriors behind were following. He flicked across to the HF Set, simply saying,

"Gunslinger Two-Three, you're clear to engage."

"Whiskey Three-Zero, Roger, clear to engage, attacking now."

He flicked back to the troop net, leaving the Apaches to do their worst. The pilots knew what they were doing.

Looking ahead, he saw daylight break through, as the shadow of the lead Warrior broke through the cam netting and out of the woodline, accelerating away through the open ground.

Mike knew once they were out of the cover of the woods, they faced a 600-metre dash across open countryside to the next hill. It had a small, wooded copse on it that he'd already looked at that morning, selecting it for his next fire position. Once they got there, he'd choose his next fire position, but for now, all his concentration was on was making it through this first dash. It all depended on what the Apaches could do. Ducking to avoid a low branch, he looked back up as the tank smashed out of the trees, the open countryside seeming alien to him after the past few days in the woods. Quickly checking the turret was clear of the trees he reported back, the excitement making him loud.

"Gunner! Clear to scan!"

"Scanning!" was the simple reply, as he felt the turret start to jerk left and right as Smudge began to look for the enemy. It wasn't long before he found them, as his gunner reported back excitedly, "I've got them! COAX INFANTRY ON!"

Mike jumped down, his head leaning forward into the CPS, as he felt the excitement and fear begin to build on the crew, as Baz shouted back, "Okay everyone, here we go! LOADED!"

On the rear vehicle, Tango Two-Zero, Spider was watching the truck ahead as it bounced and juddered along the track. The passengers in the back were all looking out of the back, hanging on grimly to the frame as it navigated over the ruts, the thick black exhaust belching out smoke, clearly never designed to pass an EU emissions test. He smiled and looked over to his gunner, hiding his fears.

"Right Jenks, when we're clear of all this shit you're clear to engage yourself, don't wait for me to give the order, okay?"

The Fusilier looked back, his body moving against the motion of the Warrior as he nodded.

"No probs Spider, I'm clear to engage."

"And remember we've got six rounds of HE (High Explosive) loaded, I've got another six on a clip ready if you need it."

Jenks nodded, as he lowered himself down into his station, getting himself comfortable next to the 30mm cannon, stretching out his neck and back. It was going to be a long day.

Spider's headset burst to life, as the vehicles ahead began to report they were in contact. Someone was firing at them.

Spider looked forwards, trying desperately to see what was going on. The truck was going far slower than the Warriors ahead of it, and already there was a gap forming. The narrow track and thick treeline meant he couldn't cut past them. Cursing to himself he asked over the I/C

"Rachel, they're in contact up ahead, can you see what's going on? This fucking truck's being driven by Miss Daisy!"

In the back of his Warrior Rachel was watching the camera feed from the Talons on her display, as they were already out in the open and racing away, clearing the ground ahead.

"Sorry Spider, I haven't got time to turn them round, I've got to clear the next ridgeline."

He nodded, keeping his frustration in check as slowly they made their way down the track. Suddenly Linda's voice came over the intercom.

"Spider, what's happening up there? Tell me will you, I can't see anything down here."

He rolled his eyes, damn that reporter! Mike had placed her on his wagon that morning, telling him that now, she was his problem to deal with. Ever since she'd come on board, it had been question after question. He quickly bent down in the turret looking behind him at the troop compartment, which appeared a brilliant white thanks to the lighting. Linda was sat wedged between the burly frame of Fletch and Rachel, and she'd taken one of the spare headsets. She looked back at him, her face aglow from the screen of Rachel's control tablet. Fletch was sat simply watching on amusedly, his own tablet sat nearby, until he launched his Wasp there was nothing to do but sit and wait.

"Linda, I've told you already to stay off the I/C, you can listen in, but you're not to speak."

She smiled disarmingly, trying to use her charm, but Spider ignored it as he continued irritated. "Look, if I can't see what the hell's going on up ahead then how can I tell you?"

Ignoring her he stood back up, cursing the truck as he urged it on.

After what seemed like agonising minutes, he finally saw the truck pull clear, the daylight making him wince at the sudden brightness. Finally! He looked about; they were clear of the woodline.

"Right Jenks, turret's clear, now find me some fucking bad guys…"

The words were lost on his lips as his eyes adjusted to the scene in front of him. The turret began to traverse, as Jenks replied.

"Fucking Hell! Look at that!"

Spider had seen explosions before, he'd seen gunfire before, but nothing could have prepared him for the sight of an entire artillery regiment being decimated before his eyes. He stood open mouthed, ignoring the battlefield as he took in the magnitude of what he was seeing. The whole treeline was on fire, thick black smoke was billowing upwards, explosions going off in its centre. The colours of some of the explosions ranged from deep oranges, yellows, some flashed brilliant white, the sparks of the phosphorous arcing outwards, like a macabre fireworks show as clouds mushroomed skywards. He could feel the heat, even from this distance, but couldn't see any of the artillery vehicles or any of the crews. Had they just disintegrated? He wasn't sure how long he'd stood there for, was it seconds, was it minutes? He was jarred from his shock as the driver's voice burst through the I/C

"Spider! Where we going?"

Spider looked ahead across the open terrain, his two other Warriors were sat 200 metres away, on opposite sides of the open ground, their turrets scanning outwards, one of them was firing short, controlled bursts with the chain gun, into the treeline that was on fire. As the red tracer rounds shot into the trees, they were answered with green tracer rounds shooting back out. Someone was still alive in there, firing back.

He looked up ahead, the tank was about 400 metres away and already climbing a small rise heading for the copse. The first fire position. Shit, he was supposed to keep up with them!

As if to answer him, Mike's voice came over the radio.

"Tango Two-Zero, Tango One-One, you coming, or did you stop for coffee?"

Fuck! That fucking truck! he cursed, as he replied.

"Tango One-One, we're on our way."

Then he answered his driver. "Ping, can you see the Chally up ahead? We need to get there quick as we can. Put your foot down mate."

"Righty ho, hold on!"

They began to accelerate away, the vehicle jolting backwards as it bounced on its suspension. He heard Linda cry out as she struggled to hold on, the movement of the armoured vehicle catching her off guard. He ducked low, as green tracer fire began to come out of the wood line towards them, hitting the side of his vehicle in a shower of sparks.

"Fuck! Traverse right, coax, suppressing fire, get it in that tree line!"

He felt the turret smoothly turn, watching through the periscope as their machine gun began to bark out in return, the tracer rounds now beginning to arc out towards the unseen enemy. Linda's voice came over the I/C again, as the bombardment of rounds increased against their vehicle, sounding like a hammer beating a metal drum.

"What's that noise? Spider? Are we being shot at?"

Ignoring her outburst, he carefully watched where the other vehicles were, the last thing he needed was to drive into one. He could see he was about to drive through the middle of the other two Warriors, which were now firing on the same woodline as he was. Not wanting to get hit by his own troops he quickly reported up,

"Tango Two-One, Tango Two-One-Alpha, check fire, check fire, Tango Two-Zero coming through."

He cautiously peered through the periscopes; his elbows braced for anything as his Warrior raced between the other two. Both had stopped firing, their turrets still scanning the wood line. They waited until he was through them before they resumed firing, trying to silence the small arms fire still coming their way.

Spider could see their turret was almost pointing backwards as the gunner kept firing at the position, now almost behind them as they raced forwards.

"Right Jenks, that's enough, leave it to the others, let's get gun front and concentrate on what's ahead of us."

His body and head twisted with the motion of the turret as they now faced the direction of travel. Behind him Rachel reported over the I/C.

"Spider, tell One-One the next position is clear, I'll keep pushing on to the next bound."

"Roger that," he replied as keying the radio he passed on Rachel's message.

He could hear Baz's voice on the radio answering up for One-One, Mike must be chatting on the HF set he thought as the cockney voice replied.

"Tango Two-Zero, Tango One-One, roger that's understood. When you're alongside, can you push another hundred metres south of us, orientate yourself south, south west over."

"Roger that, south, south west." Spider replied, as he passed on to his driver. "Ping, start to bring us more over to the left please mate, let's get us in those trees."

His Warrior began to slow as they approached a road running across their front, he leaned forward, checking for any telltale ground sign that the ditch to the other side wasn't mined. It never hurt to be too careful, he thought. The Warrior pushed through the hedge and dipped as its nose dropped down into the culvert, before raising back up, the engine revving as the forty-tonne vehicle hauled itself up and over the road. After a few seconds they were through and up the other side, pushing through the small copse, the driver slowing as they were almost parallel to the tank. He looked over, watching as the tank slowly crept forwards, towards its next fire position, its long gun poking over the hill menacingly.

Looking across to his gunner he asked. "Jenks, same as the tank, let's creep forwards, let me know when you can see clearly over the hill mate."

Ping kept the vehicle in low gear as it trundled forwards, listening to the gunner's directions, mimicking what the tank crew were doing. After a few moments he heard the gunner shout out.

"Stop! That'll do us there!"

Spider looked about, checking the area behind him. If anything happened, he'd need to be quickly out of there, reversing off the slope. You never went forwards out of a fire position, that was a sure way to get yourself killed. Happy with what his gunner could see, and where he was, he confidently reported back.

"Tango One-One, Tango Two-Zero, set."

Mike's voice was now back on the radio, as he replied, "Tango One-One, roger, out to you Tango Two-One, move now."

He listened in as Patty's voice came on the net.

"Tango One-One, Tango Two-One, be aware we've still got troops left alive in the wood line."

"Tango One-One, roger, leave them, we'll deal with that now."

Behind them the Warriors stopped firing and began to move, racing away as they began the choreographed routine 'fire and manoeuvre.' As Spider and Mike's vehicles now provided the protection, looking out for any threats, the other two Warriors were now free to leapfrog through them to their next fire position, a further 400 metres ahead of Mike. Rachel already had the Talons there, listening in and observing, ready to report anything waiting to attack them. Once they were in position and set, they'd take over, providing the overwatch, freeing up Mike and Spider to leapfrog through them. This process would continue, over and over, each pair supporting the other. There was no textbook distance for their next position, it could be 100 metres, other times almost 700, it was always down to what the terrain and the situation on the ground dictated. The key to it all working was teamwork and flexibility, something the British Army had spent years perfecting on the training areas of Salisbury and Canada.

As his gunner scanned ahead of them, Spider kept a watchful eye out behind him, conscious of what Two-One had just reported. People were moving in the wood line in the distance, and the last thing he wanted was a die-hard fanatic coming at them from behind with an anti-tank weapon. Until they'd put enough distance between the artillery position and themselves, there was always still a threat.

He saw dust and smoke whip up next to him, and the trees sway violently as if a mini tornado had suddenly appeared above him. Confused, he glanced up as the shadow passed overhead, blocking the sun before smiling. Overhead one of the Apaches was hovering mere feet above him, its gun trained on the woodline. He hollered excitedly as the 30mm chain gun began to bark out, the gunner accurately taking out those still alive in there. He looked up, to see the pilot looking back down at him, an amused expression on his face, the huge cockpit giving him great all-round visibility. He waved up, enthusiastically, the pilot responded in kind, giving his own gesture. Spider was impressed, to have the control to keep the huge helicopter hovering mere feet above him as the pilot gave him the wanker sign was a feat in itself.

Linda's voice came over the I/C, as he watched the helicopter, almost groaning as she exclaimed. "Spider, I feel sick....I think I need to-"

"Fucking hell!" Fletch cried out from the back, as the reporter, not used to being locked in a steel box and thrown about, began to show him what she'd had for breakfast.

Laughing aloud at the Engineer's protests and the sound of the reporter throwing up, Spider ducked back down into the turret, his earlier fears beginning to subside. It had been a good start, let's see what the rest of the day would bring.

Wonderland Operations Centre (WOC)

The Chief of the Defence Staff (CDS) stood watching the map onscreen, tapping his glasses against his mouth in thought as he watched the marker for Whiskey Three-Zero finally begin to move westwards. He looked over to Colonel Stephens, who seeing the prompt began with, "We estimate they'll be in contact with the Russian rear echelon units in about thirty minutes time."

"Very well," the CDS nodded, "Have our LEWT teams begin transmitting in thirty minutes. I want the Russians to think they have a full battlegroup on the move in that area."

The Colonel nodded, keeping his own doubts and feelings hidden as he walked back to his own ops room.

The CDS watched him leave before looking across to another Colonel, himself in charge of another area of the south of England.

"Has General Boswell replied yet?"

The Colonel reached for the report nearest to him, reading aloud,

"General Boswell reports all units are ready to move on your orders."

"Good." the CDS replied, stepping closer to the map again. Now it all rested on what the Russians would do next..

Hill 254 on the outskirts of Yeovil

Golgolvin's eyes narrowed, something had changed, something was wrong. He looked on in confusion as the barrage seemed to lighten, rounds were still landing, but not in the same frequency as before. Already his forward units were advancing, but they needed the barrage to cover their advance. He looked over at his artillery officer, who seeing the same thing, had come to the same conclusion, both men shared a look. He walked over to him.

"Why has the firing slowed? Tell the guns to keep firing."

"I'm on it Colonel," he replied as he began to rapidly talk into the radio.

After a few moments, he saw the officer's eyebrows crease in confusion as his head continued nodding as he listened to what he was being told. Finally, he removed the headset, looking up at the Colonel.

"Well? What is it?" Golgolvin demanded impatiently.

"Sir, we're having trouble raising Hammer Two-Zero."

"We've got the attack going in! Get them firing now!" he ordered. He turned to Sasha, his second in command who sat, shaking his head angrily, with a map and headset, his arm and chest still freshly bandaged. "Order all units to hold position, until we find out what the hell is going on back there."

The Major nodded, quickly barking out the orders as ahead of them nearly two thousand of their soldiers stopped, suddenly confused, wondering why. Soon the airwaves were alive as section commanders began to ask platoon commanders, who then asked company commanders, who began to ask the regimental commanders, who in turn would be calling up the Command Post. Having no answers available, all the senior commanders could do was send the reply, "Wait out," leaving their soldiers confused and angry. The one thing you didn't do during an attack was stop and give your enemy time to prepare defences. All Golgolvin could do for the moment was pace angrily, looking over to the Captain of artillery, himself as confused as the others. After a few minutes he looked up towards the Colonel, a brief look of triumph suddenly dashed, as whatever was being said over the radio sunk in.

"Sir, Hammer Two-Zero are reporting...they're reporting they're under attack."

"What?" Golgolvin shot back demanding, "by who?"

"We don't know, they've gone off the air again."

Golgolvin chewed his bottom lip, staring at the map and then back at the town. Thinking through the options he turned to his air operations officer.

"Any reports on air activity?"

"Negative sir, no activity to report."

"Good, then get me an aircraft over that position, I want to know what's going on over there."

The officer looked back uncomprehendingly, "But Sir, I can't, all of our aviation assets are being used in the assaults on Winchester and Salisbury."

Golgolvin nodded in frustration, turning to one of his staff officers. "Which of our units is nearest to that position?"

After a few seconds of scanning the map the young officer fired back. "Sir, the nearest unit is the 127th Infantry regiment. They're dug into positions three kilometres to the south.

He looked over as the young officer indicated on the map the area he was talking about. He had a few moments to think before quickly replying.

"Get hold of the commander of the 127th. Have him detach one of his companies north to Hammer Two-Zero's location. Find out what the hell is going on over there!"

Nodding as he wrote down the message, the staff officer began to speak into the radio, as Golgolvin continued addressing the other staff officers, "Tell Hammer One-Zero to cease firing for now, save the ammunition, all units are to continue to hold current positions. For now, we wait."

2 Miles north west of Cerne Abbas

Mike was watching through his sight, trying to wipe away the sweat and cam cream that kept smearing against it. Occasionally he pulled his head out from the sight and checked around the tank. Keep checking your flanks Mike, keep checking your flanks, he kept reminding himself. It wouldn't have been the first time a tank would've been taken out at close range. He looked over at the Battlefield Management Display Screen (BMDS) seeing what the Talons were seeing and more importantly hearing. He'd had Rachel push them south, now if there was anything south of them, it would flash up on his display. The way their unit was now operating reminded him of a caterpillar, the forward units, the two Warriors of Patty and Changa would check ahead of them using their Wasps, checking there were no enemy waiting in ambush. Once they'd checked it was clear they'd push on to their next fire position, securing the route ahead. Then the rear callsigns of Mike, Spider and the Apaches would move up, covered by the lead two vehicles. The rear callsigns would then setup new positions near to the lead vehicles, but instead of looking forwards, would look back the way they'd just come, making sure nothing was trying to follow them. Then the whole process would repeat, over and over, allowing the unit to move as safely as it could through the hostile territory, whilst giving 360 degrees of protection. With the Apaches now watching out to their north and the Talons to the south, Mike was confident they'd see any threats coming in to get them.

Seeing it was all clear to the south, he went back to scanning his front. After the initial attack on the guns, it seemed to go quiet, he'd imagined a countryside full of enemy armour and vehicles in every tree and hedge, but since leaving the position from the initial attack, he'd seen nothing of the enemy, apart from the cattle and livestock, and the occasional civilian vehicle driving through. He remembered the surprised look on the face of the elderly driver of one of the cars, as she'd been forced to stop when the tank was crossing over the road. Had she recognised the vehicle for what it was? he'd thought. As she'd sat there, mouth agape, he'd smiled and waved, all he could do really, as once over the road he was back to scanning again. He looked over the mapping, seeing the Russian units they were to find and destroy were still some 5 kilometres to their west.

His earpiece burst to life as Tango Two-One reported they were now set in position.

"Okay prepare to move." he barked out, feeling the tank judder into gear. Above him the shadow of one of the Apaches passed low overhead, the downdraft, causing him to duck instinctively.

He looked behind him, checking out of habit before reporting back, "Move!"

The tank rolled backwards, off the slope, the same repeated procedure as before, get into the dead ground, out of sight, before advancing forwards, around the slope though, never go above it. Mike looked over, seeing Spider's Warrior repeating the same manoeuvre, as they both gathered speed and began to advance to the next position, speed was important, but they couldn't go too fast, they'd kick up too much dust and give away their position. It was always a fine balance, between stealth and speed. They were halfway there when they heard Spider's voice over the radio, his tone urgent.

"Tango One-One, threat warning from Talon, we've got ears on hostile armour approaching from the south, looks like BMP 3's. No eyes on yet, over."

Mike looked at the map display, as it updated with the new units, showing the enemy were still in the dead ground about four kilometres to the south.

He looked over to his loader.

"Baz, get Bill over to our next fire position, you see where it is?"

"I got it." he replied, watching through the RWS screen.

Leaving them to it, he quickly switched over to the HF Net.

"Gunslinger Two-Three, we've got enemy ground units inbound about four kilometres south of us, number unknown, over."

Both Apaches were hidden from view beyond the next hill, staying low in the depression, hovering near the two lead Warriors. The lead pilot quickly replied, "Roger that Tango One-One, you certain about that? Our systems aren't showing anything yet."

"Yes I'm certain, I need you to re-adjust to get eyes on."

"Roger understood, we're adjusting position now. Wait out."

Mike ignored what the tank was doing and began to focus on the map of the BMDS, looking at the best place to attack from. It looked like the enemy were heading for the artillery position that they'd just attacked. He really needed to get an idea on their numbers. He watched as the Apaches appeared momentarily as they flew over the ridgeline before sinking down from view again.

After a few moments the pilot's voice came through.

"Whiskey Three-Zero, Gunslinger Two-Three, we've got eyes on fourteen BMP 3's, heading northeast, looks like they're investigating the smoke. No signs of heavy armour, over."

Mike looked behind him, seeing the huge pall of smoke must have risen to at least 3000 feet into the sky, turning the area black. There was no getting away from it, surely the Russians would know now something was amiss.

As if reading his thoughts, Gunslinger Two-Three continued, "Whiskey Three-Zero, do you want us to engage the vehicles or remain with eyes on?"

"Negative, Gunslinger Two-Three, do not engage. I want you to continue to observe, let me know if you see them heading towards us."

"Roger that," the pilot simply replied, as Mike added, "Whiskey Three-Zero continuing, Gunslinger Two-Three what's your time left on station over?"

Mike knew as long as the helicopters remained where they were, they'd stay undiscovered by the Russians, they were so low to the ground that radar shouldn't pick them up, and they couldn't be seen, the longbow sensors were able to raise and lower like a submarine's periscope, keeping the rest of the helicopter hidden behind the trees. Aside from the noise of their engines, nothing would give them away. He wanted the Russians to keep guessing at where they were for as long as they could. However, the only thing that could limit that time was the amount of fuel they had on board. Mike had no way of knowing how long they could count on the helicopters and was now asking the question.

A few seconds later the pilot came back. "Whiskey Three-Zero, we have sixty, I say again, six-zero minutes of fuel remaining before bingo."

He quickly pulled one of the permanent markers from his assault rig and made a quick note on the turret. Now at least he knew how long they could loiter for.

He felt the tank begin to slow, as the gunner and driver began talking to each other, working together to get the tank hull down. After a few moments he heard Baz proudly send over the troop radio.

"Tango One-One, set."

He smiled and looked over at the loader appreciatively, giving a thumbs up, before looking about him, checking the route behind the tank was clear. Check the flanks Mike, check the flanks, he said again, always the same routine, looking through the sight out to their front. He checked the map, seeing they were almost two miles now away from the artillery positions. It was good, but Mike needed to go further if he was to follow his orders and find those logistic units.

On the lead Warrior of Tango Two-One, Patty was talking to his Wasp operator who, sitting in the back, had his eyes glued to the screen.

"What we got up ahead Wrighty? Does it look clear?"

He heard the young Sapper clicking his tongue in thought, the noise coming through the headset. At first it was an annoying habit that Patty had told him to stop, but now, with everything going on, he'd forgotten about it. If it helped the lad to think then it was a fair price to pay, he'd reasoned.

A few clicks later and Wrighty's voice came back.

"Looks good Corporal, treeline and hilltop to our front look clear."

Patty was watching his own BMDS, mirroring the feed from the drone, smiling as he heard how the young lad addressed him. He'd already said not to call him Corporal on the wagon, again another thing the young Engineer seemed to not take on board.

"Okay Wrighty, if you're happy, then Whippet, let's move."

He felt the Warrior jolt into reverse, looking across to the other Warrior, seeing Changa hunkered low in the hatch give the thumbs up sign as his callsign now began to move. Patty watched behind him, having to correct the driver when he got too close to a telegraph pole, missing it by inches. Suddenly the vehicles were on the brakes and going forward, the acceleration causing the vehicles to rock on their suspension as they shot forwards and began to race away to their next fire positions. Within minutes they were both at the next bound, the gunners already scanning ahead, they knew it was clear thanks to the Wasps, but it never hurt to be careful, you never knew what could be waiting ahead, and the adrenalin, excitement and fear was always there, adding to the soldier's heightened tension.

Patty hung on as the vehicle slowed to a halt, he'd already told Whippet to go more carefully on the brakes, usually the Warrior would bounce up onto its nose as the brakes were so good, but with the people in the back, one of which was using a tablet to fly a drone, Patty had decided to be more careful. No sooner had he stopped than he could feel the turret smoothly scanning left to right, expecting any second to hear his gunner reporting back there were targets.

Where the hell are they? he thought, as he keyed the radio.

"Tango Two-Zero, set."

He looked behind him, watching as the tank and Spider's Warrior began to move.

His gunner Sid asked, "How much longer do you think we can keep doing this for?"

"I don't know Sid, but I'm not complaining, every minute we're not firing at someone, means a minute they're not firing back, and that's a minute we're closer to our own lines."

His gunner nodded in acknowledgment, replying, "I can't wait till we get back, first thing I'm going to do is-"

"Hey!" Patty quickly cut him off, "Concentrate on now, not fucking later! We're not back yet, and until we are you're to think of nothing except firing that fucking gun!"

"Okay. Sorry." the gunner replied, his voice low. Patty felt angry with himself, he hadn't meant to snap at Sid, but it was the not knowing what was to come that was grating him. It was grating all of them. It was now twenty minutes since they'd left their positions and apart from the artillery there was still no sign of the enemy. What the hell were they doing?

Onboard the tank, Mike squinted his eyes against the wind that blew up as the tank was moving, pressing the pressel, struggling to hear what the Apaches had just reported.

"Say again, Gunslinger Two-Three, your last message was unworkable."

In the valleys and the hills, as they pushed on, the terrain was now beginning to work against them. The steep sided hills and valleys now began to block radio signals, and as the range increased between the tank and the low flying helicopters, the signal began to weaken. On flat open terrain they could expect anything up to 25 km of radio range, but here in the bottom of the valleys, with the radio's on low power, they were lucky to get 3 km. Ideally, Mike would have just moved the tank to higher ground, but that would mean advertising his position, and he didn't feel like doing that right now.

"Whiskey Three-Zero, I say again, we have eyes on a lone truck, believed to be *ours*, moving west, following your tracks."

Lone truck? Ours? That didn't make any sense, Mike thought, replying quickly.

"Gunslinger Two-Three, I don't understand what you mean by ours? Is it British Army?"

After a few seconds of static hissing over the earpiece the pilot's voice came back.

"The *truck* you left behind, the one with the orange marker tape on it, it's coming towards us and heading west, it's now following your tracks."

Shit! thought Mike, that morning before they'd left the wood line, Mike had placed dayglow orange marker tape on the bonnet, roof and sides of the truck, easily identifying it to the Apache pilots. He'd been worried about them mistaking it in the initial attack and shooting at it as it made its escape. He'd already spoken to Catherine and the police officer driving it, they were supposed to be heading east, getting as far away from them as they could. Instead, for reasons unbeknown to him, they were now heading west, back towards them.

"Gunslinger Two-Three, can you give me their grid."

He grabbed the marker pen, jotting down with difficulty the six-figure grid as he was bounced around in the turret as the pilot replied. Looking at the map and working out where they were, he saw the location put them about 1 kilometre west of the artillery strike.

Mike thought quickly, the truck was far slower cross country, it wouldn't catch up to them unless they waited for it. And, even if they did, it wouldn't be long before the enemy were following their tracks, and they'd easily catch up to the truck. And when they did, they'd assume its occupants had killed the original soldiers from the truck and execute them on the spot. He balled his fists in anger. They could keep going, just ignore the truck and keep pushing west, but if they did, it was a death sentence to everyone on board. Catherine, Joanna, all the police officers and the two civilians, all killed on the spot for what he'd done. And if they did that, then what had been the point in saving them all in the first place?

He pressed the pressel to talk.

"Gunslinger Two-Three, from where you are can you give me an estimate on how long before the BMP's catch the truck?"

"Whiskey Three-Zero, The BMP's are at the artillery site now, some of the infantry are dismounted, If they leave now, they'd be with the truck in less than ten minutes."

"Roger understood, let me know when the BMP's begin to move. Out!"

"Fucking hell!" he shouted out, causing Baz to look over. Shaking his head out of frustration, he switched over to the troop net and quickly began to outline the problem over the radio, finishing up with,

"So, now you know. I want your thoughts, if we keep pushing west as per our orders, we may make it a lot further before getting into a fight, but if we turn back to pick them up now, we'll get in a shooting match for sure and then everyone will know exactly where we are. We won't have the Apaches for too much longer, what do you all think?"

As he waited for the replies on the radio, he quickly looked around the turret.

"What do you think guys, you happy to go back? Is it worth the risk?

It was a unanimous decision, all three of them quickly replied they wanted to go back.

Mike smiled as the radio hissed.

After a few moments Changa's voice came back on the net.

"Tango One-One, Tango Two-One-Alpha, it's a go from us, let's go back and get them."

Spider and Patty followed close behind.

"Yeah, Tango Two-One, we agree, let's go get them."

"Tango Two-Zero, agreed, let's get them."

"Ok, all callsigns listen up, this is how we're going to do this..."

2

Boomerang

The Truck

"Ma'am, I don't think the engine's going to last much longer!" the police Constable shouted in warning, the noise of the engine revving as the truck slowed to cross the road junction. His eyes were scanning the warning lights on the dashboard, he didn't need to read Russian to know something flashing yellow and red wasn't good.

Catherine braced herself as the truck dipped down and then jolted over the hump, crossing the road before replying "Just keep it going for as long as you can Arnie!"

Looking out over the broken, shattered windscreen Catherine looked across at the terrain expectantly, hoping to see the others. She half expected to have caught up with them by now, and shook her head angrily, hoping this had been the right decision after all. She leaned out looking behind them at the flat tyre on one of the axles, the flat tyre seemed to be almost humming to her as it gyrated on the rim, threatening to tear away at any moment. Thankfully it was a run flat, designed to run when deflated, but for how long? That was the question that kept playing over in her head.

Behind them in the cargo bed of the truck the others stood, holding on as best they could, bouncing and jolting as the truck's frame and canopy swayed to and fro as it negotiated the terrain, watching the daylight streaming in through the newly acquired bullet holes.

This wasn't how it was supposed to have happened she thought angrily, thinking back to the past twenty minutes. It had started off well, they'd left the woodline and the sounds of battle behind as they made their way along the dirt track and into Cerne Abbas, heading south on the A352. They'd only gone two miles along the road when they'd blundered into the back of a Russian convoy that was travelling slowly along it. The troops sat in the back of the trucks had at first ignored them, sat lazily smoking and pointing out at the countryside to the rising smoke and sound of battle in the far distance. Then almost as one they began to take notice, some had looked up pointing, exchanging looks of bewilderment and surprise as they saw her and Arnie, the ARU officer in the cab, wearing their dirty, dishevelled police uniforms. Catherine could do nothing but smile and wave in response, and after only a few moments there were angry shouts, then they were banging on the cab of the truck, urging it to stop as they began to grab for their weapons.

Arnie had simply shouted to hang on, as he'd jammed on the brakes, and swerved the wheel hard over, the twin axles locking up, causing the whole chassis to shake and jolt as the wheels slid along the tarmac. The truck swerved around on the road, before juddering to a stop at a right angle to it. She'd thought at first that they were going to tip over, but thankfully the truck had stabilised as it stopped, bouncing on the suspension as the troops now began to fire at the truck as it began to try to finish the turn around. She'd watched as the windscreen had begun to shatter, then upon instinct had held up her arms to protect her face as the glass had begun to fly around them. She'd remembered how she'd heard the pinging and thudding as the rounds tore into the truck's engine, then suddenly with a squeal of rubber the heavy tyres scrabbled for grip and they were away, heading back up the way they'd come. The shouts from the back told them miraculously everyone was okay, as she'd quickly shouted back to explain what had happened. She'd had a quick look behind her, pleased to see the trucks weren't following them, for now it looked like they had managed to get away with it.

They continued to head north, slowly passing back through Cerne Abbas, forced to stop as a man had suddenly crossed the road in front of them. The scowl on his face turned to astonishment as his eyes looked over to the bullet riddled truck and the police officers inside the cab, sweating.

He'd begun to walk away when, for some unknown reason he'd stopped, as if something held him there, turning around and walking up to the passenger side. Catherine had leaned out, smiling in greeting as the man quickly spoke, his face serious.

"If I was you lot, I'd get off the bloody roads and as far away from here as you can. There's roadblocks north and south of the village. They're stopping everything."

Before she could thank him, he'd walked away, his head down, as if he'd never spoken to her. She'd looked back up at Arnie both astonished and angry. Now where the hell where they supposed to go? she'd thought, as like a punch to the gut, it finally dawned on her.

"Right Arnie, this isn't going to work. Let's turn around and head back, we've got to catch up with the others." she'd said to the driver.

"What about the people in the back, some of them wanted to get back to Weymouth." he'd shot back, glancing in the direction of the cargo area.

She'd shook her head and sighed. "We can't risk the roads, and this thing won't keep going forever. We've been captured before, and I don't know about you, but I don't fancy paying another visit to the Russian prisons."

He'd nodded in response as she'd continued.

"Let's catch up with Captain Faulkes, I'd feel a lot safer knowing we were on the right side of all this."

"Absofuckinglutely." he'd replied smiling, as he'd begun to turn the truck around. Within a few minutes they were back at the road junction, taking the off-road track that would now lead them back along the woodline. As they'd bounced along their old tracks she banged the truck's roof, leaning out and shouting through to the others, telling them the plan. After the excitement of the past few minutes, they'd all agreed, happy to be back with the safety of the soldiers.

Open mouthed, they'd quickly driven past the battleground from earlier, the woods ablaze, the heat intense, and this time they watched as the survivors of the attack were sitting on the ground in shock, looking back at the burning woodline, not believing what their eyes were telling them. Seeing the truck approaching, some of them stood up hopefully, one man had run towards them, shouting in Russian at them to stop, holding his injured arm as he had stood defiantly in the middle of the track. Catherine had guessed he was an officer, she remembered the confident, almost arrogant look on his face, as Arnie had put his foot down, watching as the man's face changed suddenly as he'd flung himself aside as they'd sped by. Looking in their wing mirrors they watched him get back up, gesticulating wildly to the others, some had remained seated, others had stood and began to pick up rifles and point them in their direction.

"Fuck! Here we go again!" Catherine had shouted in warning as the rounds had begun to shoot past. She heard a loud bang and had felt the truck lurch lazily to the right, as Arnie had fought manically with the steering wheel, struggling to keep the truck straight as one of the lights had now illuminated on the dashboard, followed by another. Looking behind her, her hair billowing in the wind she'd shouted back.

"One of the wheels has been shot out, looks like its deflating."

Arnie had cursed as he kept his grip tight on the wheel, grimacing as he'd replied.

"Not a problem, it's on run flats, should get us out of here. Just means it's a bitch to keep straight."

She'd nodded and sat back in, as the incoming fire had stopped as quickly as it had started. Perhaps they'd ran out of ammunition she thought hopefully, as the truck continued up and over the next rise in the hilltop, following the telltale tracks of the tank.

And that was where she found herself now, bouncing along, following the tank tracks as they wound through the valleys and hills. She noticed they never went over the top of a hill, clearly Captain Faulkes' units preferred the longer route, keeping them hidden from view as they instead contoured around the hill. They crossed another road and then drove through a small river. She held her breath in anticipation as Arnie shifted into a lower gear and the truck plunged down the shallow sided embankment and into the water, she thought it would be deeper, and looked with relief at the water that only came up to the middle of the truck's huge tyres. They made it to the other side, the engine revving loudly as the front wheels scrabbled in the mud, the rear wheels beginning to slip in the riverbed as the truck stopped and juddered back and forth, refusing to climb out. Arnie swore loudly, his frustration beginning to show, as he leaned out of the cab and urged the truck on.

"Come on you bastard! Come on!" he urged, the engine racing louder as slowly the rear tyres began to spin up and sink into the riverbed. Catherine quickly reached over, tapping him on the shoulder.

"Arnie, go easy on the gas, you're just digging us in. The flat tyre isn't helping. Reverse us back and have a run at it. "

He looked over at her, the revs dying away as he took his foot of the accelerator and nodded in understanding.

"Yes Ma'am." he replied simply as he shifted into reverse.

Looking at the embankment, she added, "Let's see if we can try over there, the bank's not chewed up as much, might be better going."

He slowly reversed the truck backwards carefully as it bounced over the smaller rocks. Now at least he had a ten metre run up.

"Hang on in the back! This will be a little bumpy!" she shouted in warning as he accelerated forward, the truck accelerating lazily, held back by the mud and the damage to the engine as it began to slowly pick up speed, bouncing as its front wheels hit the bank, catapulting it up and onto the other side. Within seconds they were up and away, crossing the fields to the other side and making their way up the small hill to the valley beyond, the cheers from the back telling her they were alright, as smiling she looked over to Arnie and clapped him on the shoulder.

"Good work." she smiled proudly as he shook his head and replied, "Not my doing, Ma'am, if you hadn't had suggested that, I'd have got us dug in."

She looked out of the window at the tracks. Wondering how much longer the truck could run for. The engine seemed to be running okay for now, but those warning lights must mean something. Silently she hoped that somehow Mike and his unit were held up, perhaps then at least they'd have a chance at catching them. For now, all they could do was keep going.

Hill 254 on the outskirts of Yeovil

"Sir! we've got units now on the ground at Hammer Two-Zero's location."

"Good! Update?" Golgolvin asked impatiently, his hands resting behind his back, his knuckles white with tension.

The officer's face creased into a frown as he listened to the report, the Colonel becoming more irritated as he waited, raising an eyebrow in response.

"Well?"

"Sir, they're reporting that Hammer Two-Zero has been destroyed, survivors have reported seeing...tanks and armoured vehicles with helicopter gunships in support pushing through and heading west."

Upon hearing the news, he rubbed his chin, looking over at his 2I/C who seemed to straighten up, his face concerned as he asked unbelievingly,

"Could this be a counteroffensive?"

He walked over to the map, looking at the position of the attack, confused.

"If it is a counter offensive, how did they get the forces assembled to do it? And how the hell have they got there without any of our forward units reporting on them? How did they manage to break through our front lines without ever firing a shot? They're what? Ten miles behind our lines? That can't be true. And why has no-one else reported them? They can't have just appeared there."

Adding to the confusion, the officer now reported, "Sir, one more thing, survivors reported seeing one of our own trucks driving past, after the attack, carrying civilians and being driven by what looked like...British police officers?"

"What the fuck is going on over there?" Major Lenosky replied angrily, walking over to stand beside his CO, both looking intently at the map.

Golgolvin scratched his head in thought. If what they were reporting was true, if there were tanks and armoured vehicles where they'd reported them, then they'd be in the middle of their units. He looked over to Sasha, pointing to the map.

"Look Sasha, here, the 346th Supply regiment, here, the 23rd Tank repair regiment, and here, the 76th Medical wing. All of them within five miles of striking distance from Hammer two-zero's position."

"You think this is a strike force? That their mission is to take out our supply lines?"

"Why else would you have that amount of firepower behind the lines? Gunships and tanks?" he replied shaking his head still unbelieving, looking over the map thinking. "But how? How did they get there?"

As if to explain Sasha replied. "Perhaps the men were confused? Perhaps they're reporting on spotting our own units during the attack. Maybe the truck was what attacked them, a squad of insurgents or spies maybe? That's who they saw escaping? These are after all artillery soldiers we're talking about.

"Perhaps..." he replied in thought, the joke lost on him. He turned to the officer that had sent the report.

"Get the units we sent to Hammer Two-Zero to chase down this truck, I want those people captured alive, *not dead*, alive. Find out who they are and if they were responsible. We need answers."

He looked back over to his 2I/C, thinking aloud. "I can't take the chance there's not enemy armour behind us."

Looking up to another staff officer he barked out, "Recall our troops, I'm postponing the attack for now. Have our units prepare to move immediately. And get me the General's headquarters..."

The Truck

Catherine was looking out at the countryside rolling by, wondering how much further they'd have to go. She was interrupted from her thoughts as she heard urgent banging on the rear of the cab. She leaned out, looking through the torn fabric of the canvas at the face of the police Sergeant.

"What is it?" she yelled above the noise of the engine.

"Behind us! We've got company!"

They were just cresting over one of the hills, deciding it would be quicker to catch up by taking the shorter route, when she looked to what the Sergeant was excitedly pointing over at. On the far rise of the other hill, she could just see the dark black shapes of vehicles coming over the other hill, chasing after them, she'd seen them before when they'd attacked her police station. She had no idea what they were called, but she knew they were tracked and moving faster than they were. She counted four of them, two now disappearing from view into the dead ground as she saw a flash from the turrets of the other two, seconds later the ground erupted next to them as the rounds hit the ground, covering the truck in mud and dust. She yelled at the others to hold on in the back as she quickly jumped back into the seat, yelling over to Arnie.

"Gun it! Get this bloody thing moving!"

Without waiting to be told, Arnie mashed his foot to the floor, as the truck now began to lazily accelerate down the other side of the hill, the flat tyre swaying the truck violently. For now, they were out of sight of the enemy, but they still had another hill to climb, and she knew it was only a matter of time before they caught them. Looking up, she saw that the tank tracks had followed the valley round to the right and could be seen on the far hill further along, disappearing off into the distance some two miles away. There was nothing else for it, all they could do was keep going and hope that Mike and his unit wasn't too far ahead.

She'd felt it before he said it. She'd felt the engine beginning to sound lumpy, almost knocking itself against the mounts as the revs began to die away. Her suspicions were confirmed as Arnie warned.

"Engine's beginning to die, not much left in it now." She looked around them, they were in the bottom of the narrow valley with a small river and some farm buildings running through its centre. Ahead of them a copse crowned the top of a hill. If they could make it there, at least they would find cover, perhaps even escape on foot. She looked hopefully at Arnie, pointing up to the area.

"Arnie do whatever you can and get us up to those woods."

He ducked low, looking up at the steep incline and the river between them before shaking his head sadly.

"I'm sorry Ma'am but we're not going to make that, not now."

She looked forcefully back at him. "We can at least try can't we?"

She was cut short as with a cough and sound of screeching metal against metal, the engine finally died. The truck was still going downhill, and Arnie quickly selected neutral, allowing the truck to keep freewheeling. Looking up she replied dejectedly, "Okay, fuck it, get us down to the river, at least we can try to take cover in the barns."

Arnie nodded, his face strained with concentration as he attempted to guide the heavy twelve-tonne truck down amongst the trees and bushes. With the engine off, there was no power steering, and within seconds sweat was pouring off him, as he fought to keep the truck on course. They ploughed through two sets of fences and bounced through another hedge, getting closer as the truck kept building up speed. At the last second, the wheel was torn out of his hands as finally the run flat tyre came away from the rim, turning the truck into the path of a medium sized tree. They both braced for the impact, which was lighter than they thought as the truck seemed to almost slide up and over the trunk as the tree uprooted and stopped the truck gently, its mass sliding along the tree and coming to a stop, it's front axle now feet above the ground.

Catherine looked over unbelievably at Arnie, both police officers sharing a look of surprise, before they were brought back to reality as smoke began to pour into the cab.

"Everyone out of the truck!" she shouted, as she reached for the handle and pushed the door open, yelling in surprise as she fell from a greater height into a gorse bush.

Swearing, she stood up, as the small branches and twigs tore at her arms and legs, the pain quickly forgotten as she heard the sounds of the vehicles following echoing in the distance. Figures began to jump down from the back, as she reached over to help them down, Thankfully, apart from a few more bruises, the group were uninjured, and she quickly took stock of their predicament.

Everyone looked to her for direction as the sounds of the vehicles approaching began to get louder. The only weapons they had were the two Russian pistols that Mike had given them, her Sergeant carried one, and Arnie the other. They'd never be able to fight off the armoured vehicles with those. She looked around her before barking out.

"Everyone! Run for the riverbank down there, we'll use it for cover and make our way to the barn."

As the others began to run, one of the civilians, Tim, stood up, complaining. "And then what? This was your idea, and now you don't know what you're bloody doing! I'm waiting here, I'm sick of all this fucking about! You're the ones they want, not me!"

He was manhandled by the police Sergeant, who nodded to Catherine in understanding, grabbing his arm and remarking forcefully, "This way *sir*, if you'd kindly like to follow me."

With a yelp of protest, they were both away, leaving her to follow closely behind, running as fast as they could, each person yelling in shock as they plunged down the riverbank and into the cold water, sinking up to their chests. The river wasn't fast flowing but had been deeper than she'd thought. They all lay there panting and breathing heavily, their heads close to the embankment for cover, as she slowly raised her head to see what was happening. She could hear the noise of the approaching vehicles echoing off the trees and buildings, making it sound as if they were already surrounded. She quickly looked behind them at the wooded area, before shaking her head. No, they couldn't be surrounded, not yet, she'd thought, instead she reasoned, her mind was playing tricks on her. She turned back, looking the way they'd come from, watching for any sign of the enemy stalking them. She was looking in one direction, expecting them to come over the hill, when she was shocked to see a vehicle appear lower down and off to her left, slowly coming around the hill, not over the top of it. Without realising it she gasped, and ducked lower, as the others in the group all gave muted gasps as some covered their mouths instinctively with their hands, as if the smallest breath would give them away. She slowly raised her head again, watching as the lone vehicle was joined by a second, its turret looking left and right as slowly, almost calmly, they both meandered down the valley. They'd seen the truck, as both vehicles now headed towards it, the turrets looking at the barn and the high ground behind them. They were coming to look for them.

She looked across to the barns, realising that from where they were hidden in the river, they should be able to sneak along the riverbed and towards the cover of the barns, then at least they could plan the next move. She was about to tell the group to move, when another small movement caught her eye, she looked back up at the hilltop. Another two enemy vehicles were now positioned on the high ground looking across the valley. Her heart sank as she realised that from where they were, they'd see them if they attempted to move. For now, like it or not, they were stuck there. She looked around her as the sound of the two vehicles coming towards them began to get louder, everyone looking to her for the answer. She looked around desperately, trying to think of something to do. It was Tim, the angry civilian, who seemed to read her thoughts.

"Well now what?" he asked, the tone sarcastic.

She said nothing but looked on as he continued, "You don't bloody know do you? You've led us all down here and now *you* don't have a bloody clue how to get us out!"

He was right, she was out of ideas. She tried to hide the desperation in her voice as she looked around at the group, asking, "Well, anyone else have a plan? If so, I'm all ears."

No -one answered. Making her mind up, she turned to the police Sergeant, reaching out for the pistol. "Sergeant, I'm going to stay behind and provide a distraction, when I say so, I want you to get everyone over to those barns."

The police Sergeant shook his head in defiance pulling the pistol away and replying, "No Ma'am, there must be another way. If you stay that's suicide. We've made it this far, let's roll the dice one more time.

Arnie stepped forward interrupting, "Ma'am, I've got the other pistol, I'll stay here and try to draw their fire, buy you the time you need to get to those buildings."

She was about to reply when the young fiery Constable also stepped forwards, adding, "Arnie, you're not doing that on your own, give me the other pistol and I'll stay with you. Two targets buy you double the time. You never know, the others might even make the woods."

Suddenly what appeared to have been a sole decision had all the police officers arguing amongst themselves as to who would stay. She almost laughed at the situation, but she could have hugged them all for their bravery. She looked around at them all, proud to be with them. She was about to speak when a new noise reached them, above the noise of the vehicles. She could hear shouting. She risked another look over the parapet, seeing both vehicles were now stopped at the truck. Infantry were being offloaded; some were checking over the truck as others now began to fan out with shouted orders from their commanders towards their direction. She counted at least twelve of them, split into two groups, far too many for any single person with a pistol to hold off for long. She looked on in despair as the left-hand group now split away and began to jog towards the barns, cutting off their escape. Three soldiers were in fire positions on one knee, weapons raised and looking over their sights, covering the advance of the other three, any attempt to flee in that direction and they'd be shot. The other group were walking towards them slowly, weapons raised and pointed in their direction, almost as if they knew that's where they were hiding. She balled her fists in anger, they'd left it too late.

She was disturbed from her angry thoughts as Joanna now spoke, breaking her daily silence.

"What's that?

She looked up to where the reporter was pointing overhead. She glanced up, shielding her eyes from the sun's glare as something black passed high overhead, she dismissed it at first as a bird, but then realised it was larger than that, and faster. Was it a drone? she wondered inquisitively. But why no noise? Suddenly it dawned on her, that's how the Russians knew they were there. They'd been watching them with the drone. Angrily she looked up as the drone passed, raising her middle finger, and mouthing the words silently. "Fuck you!"

Her police Sergeant laughed suddenly, causing those around him to look at him as if he'd lost his marbles. She looked over angrily, the joke lost on her. Seeing her rage and the looks of those around him, he quickly shot back, his hands raised defensively.

"Hey, that's not who you think it is."

"Oh, no?" she looked on, her face red with anger. "Then who the hell is it?"

He smiled, "That Ma'am is the cavalry about to arrive." Without explaining further, he ducked lower into the water until his head was just above it, urging the others to do the same. Without understanding why, or knowing why, they all followed suit, the water chilling them further. She looked over, about to demand what the hell was going on when suddenly the gunfire erupted all around them.

3

A Bitter Pill To Swallow

Catherine hunkered lower into the stream, coughing as the cold water hit her mouth and nose, the water disturbed, as everyone moved to stay as low as possible. Joanna was screaming, covering her ears and trying to stop the noises, as the two civilians were holding each other in shock, their eyes wide in disbelief. All of them could feel the explosions tearing at the ground above as the bullets whizzed and thudded into the opposite side of the bank. Someone was firing at them. More explosions, more shouts, more screams. What the hell was going on up there? She looked over to her police Sergeant who shouted over the noise, "The drone! I recognised it as one of the drones that Captain Faulkes had delivered last night. We weren't supposed to see, but when he opened the box, I couldn't help but sneak a look."

She smiled and closed her eyes in thanks, so that's what was happening she thought, as she raised herself a few inches to peer over the edge. Her Sergeant placed a warning hand on her shoulder, she ignored it, slowly raising herself up, wanting to see what was going on overhead. She could see flames and smoke drifting skywards; her eyes following as slowly she drew level with the ground. In front of them the first of the enemy vehicles was engulfed in flames, the yellow and orange colours licking out greedily from where its turret was supposed to sit, as she watched on, the rear door was opened and one of the crewmen jumped out yelling, his arm on fire as he rolled around in agony on the floor. Where had the second vehicle gone? she wondered, as up on the higher ground the two enemy vehicles sat in overwatch were now firing their larger cannons, the guns firing quickly, sounding like jack hammers, as the green tracer rounds shot into the woodline behind them on the opposite hill. She looked back up, seeing nothing but red tracer rounds flying back out to answer, but instead of firing into the enemy vehicles the rounds were flying down towards her, hitting the river embankment just feet from her. Why were they firing at her? She watched the dust and earth flying upwards as more bullets thudded into the ground. Suddenly her eyes were drawn to more movement around the burning vehicle. She looked over in shock as she saw five figures all wearing camouflage, were lying in cover, slowly crawling towards her position. One stood up, attempting to run the short distance, when the bullets came tearing past her and slammed into him, throwing him back down amongst the others screaming. She could see the anger on their faces, as they glared back at her. They were coming for them, that's why whoever was firing on the friendly side was firing close to her. They weren't firing at her; they were trying to stop the infantry from getting to her. If they made it to the safety of the river then they could do what she was doing, take cover from the bullets, and worse, shoot at them. She ducked again as more bullets thudded past, closer than before, causing her to duck low and wipe away the mud as it spattered onto her face.

"God damit Rachel, that's far too fucking close!" Spider warned over the I/C as he watched the rounds being fired through his display.

She replied angrily, "Well you go down there and tell her to keep her bloody head down. I don't know how many more hints she needs. It's not like I'm a fucking sniper with this thing!"

He ignored her outburst, she was right of course, she was doing her best, and considering she'd never used anything like the Talon before, she was doing well.

They'd arrived at the far side of the hill after their mad dash back, just as the truck had crashed, watching the feed from one of the Talons, which had raced ahead and was hidden in the amongst the trees. They'd left the other Talon with Patty and Changa's Warriors, guarding their old positions for when they returned. They'd watched as the occupants had bailed out and made it to the safety of the river, the plan being then to wait for Captain Faulkes to catch up in the tank before making their move. However, the Russians had called the shots when they sent their vehicles forward with the infantry dismounting. Spider knew then that Catherine and her truck party would have minutes before the Russians were on them. Deciding not to let that happen, he'd acted quickly, using Rachel to engage the two BMP's closest to the group with the Talon's Javelin systems. The first missile she had fired had hit dead centre, the missile arcing up and coming down into the turret, the perfect top attack, smashing through the metal and exploding inside, vaporizing the turret in a white flash of hot searing metal that shot outwards across the ground, fragments landing tens of metres away. She'd quickly lined up the sight onto the second BMP, the missile firing almost as soon as she had a lock, but by a twist of fate, or just good luck, the BMP crew had been quick to react and had quickly reversed their vehicle behind the dead truck. She'd swore loudly as the missile had come down, glancing off the truck's roof and exploding meters from its intended target. She could only watch in frustration as the BMP had accelerated away through the smoke and dust, its turret now rapidly firing high explosive rounds indiscriminately into the area where the Talon was as she'd already moved it away. The Javelin launcher tubes were now useless, empty of missiles, they'd need to be reloaded later by hand. After a few moments it was Spider's voice she heard warning her of the danger to the truck party as the infantry now stormed forward, guns blazing, trying to get to the safety of the riverbed. She'd switched over to the minimi machine gun and began to pour fire onto the infantry, who were forced to take cover, and it was this that Catherine had seen earlier, firing short, controlled bursts in her direction. Already the gunfire was drawing the attention of the other two BMPs sat in overwatch, who couldn't see the Talon yet, but were firing at the area, hoping to pin down whoever they thought was in there firing onto their own troops.

She cursed as she lined up the sights of the Talon again, trying to keep the infantry pinned down. The police Chief seemed to have a death wish, raising her head into the line of fire again. Twice now she'd had to readjust her aim onto the infantry, for fear of hitting her. The other group of infantry, heading for the farm buildings had already been taken out by Fletch using the Wasp. Two carefully placed fragmentation grenades had left them all lying, either dead or injured, leaving the other group to her. They were already too close to the group hiding in the river to risk using a grenade from the Wasp, leaving them no choice but use the machine gun. She'd already managed to take out two of the soldiers, but she couldn't move the Talon yet, or the infantry would get up and charge towards the group in the river. Stuck between a rock and a hard place all she could do was keep the Talon in position and continue firing, hoping that the Wasp could get eyes on again.

She looked over to Fletch who was controlling the Wasp.

"You got eyes on that second BMP yet?"

His tongue stuck out in concentration as he looked at the control tablet, he simply nodded before replying. "Yep, just sorting that out now."

On his display he could see the top-down view of the BMP slowly navigating around the back of the barns, the commander was low in the cupola, looking over to his left side, locating the firing point of the Talon. Unbeknown to the Russians, Rachel had driven the Talon through the trees and lowered its profile, making it much harder to identify and hit. Now as the Russians engaged what they thought were dug in enemy, they were hitting a decoy, as Spider's Warrior now began to slowly come around the side of the hill, hidden from view from the other two vehicles on the hill.

"Okay Spider, he's hiding behind the northernmost building with the black corrugated roof," Fletch reported, as slowly the Warrior's turret began to scan the area.

His gunner was quick to locate the enemy vehicle, as suddenly Jenks shouted out the fire order. "Enemy BMP, HE, seven-hundred, close range! Load AP!"

Spider slid down into the turret, his hands automatically picking up the three-round clip of Armoured Piercing, ready to feed it into the magazine housing as Jenks quickly adjusted onto the target. Spider looked through his own sight, seeing the enemy vehicle was hiding behind the barn furthest away, but the enemy vehicle had chosen poorly, the walls they were hiding behind were already crumbling, and the building too small to conceal the vehicle. Jenks was about to fire when Spider quickly shouted. "Wait! Gunner, target the wall with the HE, Six rounds automatic...Fire!"

Spider watched the BMP disappear in a cloud of smoke and dust, as the 30mm cannon fired quickly. No sooner had it began to bark out than he quickly loaded the Armoured Piercing clip into the feed tray and picked up another ready to load. After the sixth HE round had been fired Spider quickly shouted out the order.

"Target go on, three rounds, AP fire!"

Without pausing, Jenks had re-sighted the gun back onto the BMP, now clearly visible in amongst the rubble of the wall. Spider saw the commander looking over shocked, not understanding what had happened as their cover had fallen apart around them. There was just enough time for the BMP to begin to move backwards, as the gun began to bark out again, the red tracer rounds skipping through the target, hitting the BMP just behind the commander's cupola. As the third-round tore through they saw a flash, then the vehicle was out of sight to them, hiding behind another of the outbuildings.

"Target not observed!" Jenks shouted, as Spider looked over to his BMDS, seeing what the drone overhead could see.

"Looks like you've got it," Fletch reported, as they both looked at the same image. The BMP had stopped, smoke pouring out of its engine decks as the driver and commander now jumped off the vehicle carrying assault rifles and began diving for cover.

"Fletch, get back onto the BMP's on the hill, if you can, take them out, if not, keep eyes on them, watch where they go." Spider replied, watching as the drone flew on it's new course. The enemy vehicles hadn't moved and one was stubbornly firing into the woodline, still trying to hit the Talon. The other BMP was firing at the riverbank, trying to keep Catherine's group pinned down as the enemy infantry slowly advanced towards them.

"Ok Ping, we're going to keep going round this hill until we get eyes on those two BMP's. We've got to stop them from firing. "

His driver replied simply, "Roger, ready to move."

"Ok let's go, nice and slowly..."

He felt the Warrior slowly creep forwards around the base of the hill, the turret pointing over to the right as the vehicle leaned slightly to the left. Spider now stood up in the cupola, leaning over to identify the enemy positions, before his vehicle came into view of them.

"That's it Ping, nice and slow around this hill...Jenks, be ready with three rounds of AP, we'll target the first one. If we get time we'll-"

He was interrupted by a flash off to his left, down by the barns. He looked over, seeing the smoke and flame as a missile tore towards them. He had just enough time to duck down and shout in surprise as the anti-tank missile exploded prematurely, hitting one of the trees, showering the turret with wood and metal fragments.

"Shit! What the fuck?" he shouted.

He felt the Warrior lurch forward as his driver reacted quickly, mashing the accelerator to the floor in unknown panic, as the vehicle shot forwards around the hill exposing its position.

"No! Ping, don't do that!" he shouted in warning, but far too late. Now they were in full view of the enemy.

Seeing the explosion, then the sudden movement on the hill off to their right, both BMP commander's eyes were drawn to the area as the Warrior came into full view, charging forwards. Quickly, they turned their main guns onto it and began to fire away, the 100mm rounds hitting the ground all around it as the fast-moving vehicle began to jink left and right to throw off the gunners' aims.

"Shit! Now we're in trouble! Hang on back there!" Spider shouted in warning to those in the back, as Ping raced away down the hill towards the barns.

"No! don't head down there!" he exclaimed, as Ping quickly countered, "But the buildings, there's cover-"

Interrupting his driver, he shot back, "That's where the bloody missile came from!" As more rounds hit the ground, showering them in stones and dust. "Oh, fuck it! Just get us down there!" he exclaimed, preferring the cover and risk of a missile, to being stuck out in the open and fired on, as he braced himself in the turret, expecting to be hit at any second.

Rachel had wedged herself against her seat, her feet planted firmly on the Warrior's rear door as she tried to keep the Talon firing, holding onto the tablet with one hand and her other hand on the controls. Now recovered from her earlier bout of sea sickness, Linda, looking paler than before, reached over with her free arm, helping to wedge Rachel in position. Fletch was left to his own devices, as his head smashed into the roof, thankfully wearing a helmet, as he fought to keep control of the drone and prevent the tablet from smashing about.

Moments later and they were amongst the outbuildings, Spider quickly ordering Ping to halt as the Warrior screeched to a stop behind the cover of two barns, the dust and smoke billowing behind it, quickly overtaking and covering it in a thick cloud that caused both men in the turret to cough and wheeze. The BMPs continued to fire, the rounds tearing into the farm buildings as they sought to locate them. After a few seconds the incoming fire stopped, as, losing sight of the Warrior, they waited patiently for it to re-appear. Spider waited for the dust to settle before he shook Jenks on the arm and urged him up, both stood up, grabbing their assault rifles and began to scan the area close by for any threats. Seeing it was clear for now, and without taking his eyes off the weapon sight he reported over the I/C.

"Everyone okay? Rachel? Fletch? Linda?"

It was Linda who answered up first.

"What the hell just happened?"

He ignored her question as he asked again. "Rachel, Fletch, you both ok?"

"All good Spider," Rachel replied, as Fletch could be heard to groan, "Fuck me, I thought a roller coaster was bad enough! What happened?"

"Anti-Tank missile, fired from the outbuildings. My guess is the crew of the BMP we destroyed decided to get payback," Spider replied, slowly scanning around them.

"Okay so now what?" Linda replied.

Ignoring her again, Spider now took charge, issuing orders.

"Ping, Jenks, I want you both out on the ground in firing positions protecting the vehicle. Be aware of where the BMP's are located on the high ground, be careful not to show yourselves to them."

Both soldiers acknowledged and began to dismount, as he continued,

"Rachel, keep the suppressing fire going on the infantry."

"I'm on it," she replied simply, as he continued, "Fletch, I need you to get the Wasp back over here, quick as you can, we need to find those bastards with the missile launcher and quickly."

"Roger," the Engineer replied, as Linda asked again,

"Spider, forgive me for stating the obvious, but we're in an armoured vehicle, they're just two people on the ground with a rocket launcher. Why are you getting the troops out of the safety of the vehicle and onto the ground? Can't we just stay in the vehicle and go looking for them, and shoot at them like before?"

He kept his focus on the buildings, as he finally replied to her. Speaking slowly as if explaining to a child.

"Linda, right now those BMP's on the hill know where we are. They out gun us two to one, have the high ground, and they have 100mm guns, compared to our poxy little 30mm. The only advantage we had was surprise, which we've now lost. If we attempt to move from cover and hunt down the missile team, they'll easily destroy us. Likewise, the missile team now know we're here and will now be trying to get close enough to have another shot at us, meaning if we sit here thinking we're all safe and secure and just close the hatches up, they'll come along and slam a rocket up our ass. Now, if we do try to escape and drive back up the hill to find some cover, then both the BMP's and the missile team will have a perfect chance to shoot at us. All they've got to do right now is keep us pinned down and let the missile team do the rest, which is why I'm *not* doing that. With our guys out forming a perimeter, we can at least get a better chance of hunting them down and stopping them from taking the shot in the first place."

Linda looked on open mouthed at the rear door, expecting any second to see a rocket firing through it as his words sunk in. After a few moments she replied almost in disbelief.

"Hang on, are you saying that we're stuck here? And our only course of action is to sit and wait for them to attack us? I thought *we* were meant to be doing the rescuing?

"Well now Linda, until those BMP's and the missile team are taken out, *we're* the ones needing to be rescued."

Leaving her with her thoughts he flicked over to the radio.

"Tango One-One, Tango Two-Zero, I've got a problem over here..."

In the water shivering, Catherine and her group had watched in awe as the Warrior had begun its mad dash down the hill, disappearing in amongst the buildings. She'd felt sure that it would get hit and couldn't believe it when the vehicle finally made it to the safety of the buildings, untouched. She'd been so distracted, that she hadn't noticed that the suppressing fire keeping the Russians at bay, was beginning to slow. Already she could hear the confident shouts, as the Russian commander also realised, and was beginning to rally his troops, urging them forward as he began to take back control. She looked up again at the two enemy vehicles on the hill, they were pre-occupied with where the Warrior had gone. Now they had their chance to move. She looked over again at the group.

"Right come on, we can't stay here. We need to keep moving."

"Where to?" the police Sergeant asked, as he raised his pistol and fired two rounds in the direction of the enemy. He wasn't trying to hit them, just to keep them in cover for longer.

She pointed over to the barns again. "Instead of waiting for them to come to us, let's make it easier and go to them."

"I'm not going anywhere!" Joanna cried out fearfully, her eyes wide in shock. Already she'd managed to say more in the past twenty minutes than she had in the past twenty hours.

Catherine pointed the way to her officers, urging them to lead on as they began to walk past the hysterical Joanna and wade through the deep water, closely followed by the civilians. Catherine waited for the last of them to leave before she stepped closer to Joanna, moving her head closer to look her in the eyes.

"Joanna, if you stay here, you'll die. It's not safe here."

"I don't care...I don't care!" she kept repeating over and over, her eyes wide in shock. She was shivering, but Catherine didn't know if that was because of the water, or if the events of the past forty-eight hours were finally beginning to play out.

She reached out to hold her, instantly recoiling as the woman screamed out.

"Don't fucking touch me! Don't you fucking touch me! Stay away! Keep your hands off me!"

Catherine stepped backwards, holding her hands up in mock surrender as she tried to talk calmly to her. She'd been through hell, Catherine could see that, they all had, and of all the places for the demons to surface, this was not the place nor time. It was as if the gunfire had finally unlocked the door and now it was all pouring out. She thought back to all her experiences as a police officer, trying to find a way to talk to her, to reason with her, all the while looking upwards, hearing the voices of the Russians as they crawled ever closer.

"Calm down Joanna, calm down, you're amongst friends here. I'm your friend, I'm here to listen."

Joanna looked around her, as if suddenly she didn't know where she was. As if it were all a dream that she'd just woken from, as she spoke, surprised.

"Who are you? What am I doing here? How did I get here?"

Catherine knew the young woman had probably shut down that part of her brain, choosing to forget rather than explain what had happened. Not caring why, or how, she was just thankful to have the calmness back as she smiled and tried her best to look as reassuring as possible. It was as if she was talking to a child.

"Joanna, I'm Chief Superintendent Catherine Stokes. I'm a police officer, I'm here to help you, and I need you to come with me."

As if in a trance, Joanna mumbled meekly, "Police officer...am I in trouble? Have I done something wrong?"

"No love, you've done nothing wrong, but there's bad people coming who want to do bad things to us. We need to move now."

"Bad people?" the journalist replied meekly, cocking her head.

"Yes, *very* bad people," Catherine replied, her eyes not leaving the riverbank's edge, expecting any second to see the enemy soldiers. She began to wish now she'd kept a pistol herself.

"Okay." Joanna replied quietly, as Catherine held out her arm, guiding the way. She breathed a sigh of relief, finally they were moving, when suddenly she saw shadows above her and heard the splash of water as the heavy weight of boots landed amongst them. Someone landed heavily on her back, pushing her deep under the water. She opened her mouth to yell in surprise, quickly stopping herself as she was forced under, inhaling the clear water and almost choking as rough hands now pulled her back up onto her feet. She stood there, her vision blurred as the mud and water ran from her face, blinking in surprise, as she felt a rifle barrel digging into her throat uncomfortably. There were four of them, all heavily armed in combat gear and weapons, faces painted in dark green cam cream, the murderous looks on their faces, barely kept in check. Two of them were stood ready, weapons pointing down the riverbed towards where the others had already escaped. The one who looked to be the commander began shouting at her, she couldn't understand what he was saying and could only stand, hands raised in mute surrender, as the rifle barrel continued choking her. Joanna was standing off to the side, looking distant, her hands in the water, as if nothing concerned her. Catherine felt the rough hands of the commander as he searched her for weapons, and once satisfied she had none he turned his attention to Joanna, who looked over at her as he approached.

"Catherine are these the bad people you warned me about?"

She tried to answer, hoping the young reporter would realise the danger and not do anything stupid. Unable to speak with the rifle at her throat, all she could do was nod slowly as she gasped. "Yes!"

The commander approached Joanna, his rifle raised, demanding she raise her hands. His eyes opened wide in alarm, as without any show of fear or anger she raised her hands, the grenade in her right hand clear to see, the pin in the left, her hand holding the strike lever closed. They couldn't shoot her, all she had to do was release the grenade and it would go off within seconds, killing everyone. Catherine could only wonder where she had managed to get the grenade from. The soldier holding the rifle to Catherine's throat forgot all about her as all four men began to shout and turn inwards, pointing their weapons at Joanna, shouting and gesturing that she put the pin back in. The commander slowly dropped his weapon, shouting at the others, as slowly they all lowered theirs too. It looked like Joanna was in charge now. Catherine watched, as the commander put his hands into the air, smiling disarmingly as he began to talk in broken English.

"Okay...all good....all good...no kill...no kill."

Catherine could see the subtle movement in him as he moved slowly towards Joanna. She didn't know whether to warn her or try to let the Russian stop her. If the grenade went off, she'd be as dead as the rest of them.

Joanna looked over at her innocently, as if a child inside had been awakened, smiling. Without the others seeing it, Catherine began to slowly move backwards, all the soldier's attentions now on Joanna and the grenade in her hand.

She watched on as the commander continued to talk to her in that low non-threatening voice, all the while moving slowly forward.

"Preety girl, no kill…no kill preety girl, we like preety girl."

Catherine saw it, like a switch had been flicked inside her, Joanna's face changed as the Russian said the words. Perhaps someone had said something similar when they'd raped her. She had no idea, but within the blink of an eye, the child like face was gone, instead replaced by one of rage, her eyes burning fiercely as she spat out, her voice rising.

"Pretty girl? PRETTY GIRL! So, you like fucking pretty girls do you?"

The Russians began to look at each other confused as she continued to rant, mocking their attempts at English.

"Yes, that's right, come closer, come closer! Look at the *preety girl*, come and have a taste, you fucking rapist bastards! You aren't doing that to me again!"

Not understanding as to why there was a sudden change in the woman, the commander suddenly changed tact, speaking quickly in Russian, his eyes never leaving her. All of them nodded subtly at what was being said. They were going to try to rush her.

She looked over to Catherine, her breathing heavy, and eyes filling with tears as the rage quickly began to turn to sorrow as she said.

"I can't go back to that…not again…I'm so sorry…"

"Joanna, NO!" Was all she had time to shout as she saw the reporter release the strike pin and pull the grenade to her chest, as if it were some kind of salvation. Time seemed to slow as she watched the Russians leap towards her yelling, all trying to get the grenade out of her hands. Without waiting to see the outcome, Catherine turned and tried to run, counting down the seconds, the water slowing her down, ignoring what was going on behind her as she leapt forwards into the water, diving down as deep as she could go. She knew that bullets wouldn't travel far underwater, but she had no idea about grenades. All she knew about them was from what she'd seen on films, and all she knew, was that they were bloody deadly…

Over towards the barns, Jenks ran forwards, his heart racing in his chest as he held the rifle in one arm, the other pumping furiously across his body as he raced towards cover. Rounds were already zipping past him, coming closer, causing him to trip and stumble on the loose gravel as he fell towards the small brick wall. He smashed painfully against it, his adrenalin helping to numb the pain as his shoulder screamed in protest. He lay there trying to control his breathing as the rounds now began to hit the brickwork, covering him in a fine red dust, as to his horror he watched them slowly begin to crumble. The shooter must have seen the same thing, as the firing seemed to increase, causing the young Fusilier to duck lower down as the wall began to crumble inch by inch. He was pinned down and could only lay there cursing as he looked back towards where he'd just ran from.

"Come on Ping, come on!" he murmured to himself, all the while ducking lower and lower as the wall became smaller and smaller. In another few seconds and it wouldn't be providing any cover at all, and he desperately looked around for another form of cover, across from him to his right sat an abandoned tractor, its tyres deflated and the weeds and grass already trying to claim it as its own. It was only five metres away, but with the amount of incoming fire, it may as well be five miles away, he fumed, if he tried to dash across, he'd be shot for sure.

"Whose bloody stupid idea was this?" he shouted loudly, already knowing the answer. It had been his.

After he and Ping had dismounted from the Warrior, they'd heard Spider relaying to them, over their Personal Role Radios (PRR), where the missile team were lurking. The Wasp had eyes on the enemy, but they were hiding in the farmhouse. Fletch had already dropped two of the grenades through the large building's roof, but every time the smoke cleared, they seemed to emerge unscathed, still carrying the missile launcher. Now, they'd been seen working their way around the back of the building, the enemy knew where the Warrior was located, and were getting into a position to be able to finish it off. Spider had kept them under surveillance, the Wasp hovering about 300 feet above them, relaying the information both men needed to hunt them down. They'd approached the courtyard for the farm, hiding behind its walls, knowing the enemy were now across from the courtyard in the farmhouse in one of the rooms on the upper floor. One looked to be in the process of stabbing out one of the walls with his bayonet, trying to create enough of a gap to fire the launcher from, while keeping themselves hidden. The second soldier was covering the first, in a perfect fire position by a window, covering the approach across the courtyard to the building's back door. Anyone trying to cross the courtyard to get to them would have to run through the volley of fire. Annoyingly, the two Fusiliers couldn't go around to the front of the building, this would put them in line of sight to the two BMP's on the hill. Even now, they'd hear the thud and explosions as both enemy vehicles kept firing into the unknown, trying to get Spider to reveal his position.

Spider's voice had rung over their personal radios, the urgency clear to hear.

"Guys whatever you're going to do, you need to be quick, it looks like they're nearly through the wall."

Ping had looked over to Jenks, muttering.

"If we had another four guys here and some fucking smoke grenades we could flush the bastards out."

"Yeah, but we don't have that do we?" he'd replied, quickly thinking to himself. What would Spider do?

A thought entered his head suddenly, as he'd laid down and looked around the courtyard cautiously, remembering to keep his head far below where someone's head would emerge. Taking in the scene he'd quickly replied.

"Right, there's a wall running through the courtyard, big enough for cover, about fifteen metres past this wall."

"Ok, what you thinking?" Ping had asked.

He'd looked behind them, pointing to an old wooden outbuilding.

"If I create a distraction, and run like fuck to the wall, reckon you could follow me in and get yourself in over there and put some fire down on the fucker?

"Hang on, how do you know he's going to shoot at you, and not shoot me first?

"I've heard the Russians always shoot the ugly fuckers last."

Ping had stood there open mouthed, in mock indignation as Jenks had got himself ready to move, checking his magazine was secure to his rifle and his pouches were closed.

Taking deep breaths, he'd steadied himself against the wall, as he looked back at the sniper. "Ping, if you fucking miss him and I get shot, I'm coming back to haunt you."

Ping didn't smile, stepping behind him, ready to move himself, clapping the Fusilier on the shoulder as he readied himself.

"Okay, ready?" Jenks had asked, looking behind to him.

"Ready wanker, let's move."

Taking another deep breath to steady his nerves he'd said softly,

"Okay in 3...2...1..." There was no shouting go, within seconds of each other, both soldiers burst through into the courtyard, because Jenks was first through, he drew the first shots, the gunman choosing him as he was the one running towards the building. Ping was free to run through and had disappeared into cover behind the shed.

This was how the young Fusilier now found himself lying in cover that was rapidly diminishing, urging his mate on. He felt a pause in the firing, the shooter must be reloading. He looked up again at the tractor, tensing his muscles about to lunge, when suddenly the firing resumed, causing him to jerk back down. He'd delayed too long. He buried his face into his arms as the brickwork now began to hit him in the face, causing him to wince as he tried to get himself lower. He was contemplating pulling out his bayonet and digging himself a hole, when he heard a lone gunshot from the direction of the shed, then silence.

He lifted his head slightly, hearing over his PRR,

"He's down! Now, move your ass to the building, I'll cover you from here."

Needing no more encouragement, Jenks got up, the smashed brickwork falling off him as he ran in a cloud of dust towards the back door. Without waiting, he smashed through in a pile of glass and wood, falling into a heap on the floor, the doors white lace curtain wrapping itself around him. Cursing, he clumsily fought to extract himself, wasting seconds as the fabric clung stubbornly to him. He knew stealth was no longer an option, anyone upstairs would have heard him crashing through the door. He kept his weapon up, selecting automatic on the change lever as he looked through the sights and made his way through the kitchen, the glass crunching uncomfortably underfoot. He came out into a darkened hallway, a set of stairs led up to the second floor. He paused, letting his eyes adjust to the light, hearing nothing upstairs but the light sound of wind as it blew through the farmhouse. A few seconds later and he heard boots crunching on the glass behind him, he turned to look, his weapon moving with him, now an extension of his arm, to see the red-faced figure of Ping join him, his chest heaving heavily after the run to the house. Both soldiers moved cautiously through the hallway, weapons pointing upwards, expecting to see hostile forces looking down. Jenks signalled for Ping to cover him as he went upstairs, the sniper nodded in response, his face set and firm as he looked through his sight, finger resting lightly on the trigger. Jenks slowly approached the first step, then the second, his heavy boots causing the staircase to creak as he advanced upwards. His face began to come level with the top floor as he took in the picture. It was a landing with four doors all leading away from him. Three of the doors were closed, the fourth was open, a pair of legs in combat trousers and dirty boots were sticking half out, the carpet already staining red as the blood flowed around the body. Jenks stopped moving, using the stairway for cover as he looked at the open doorway. He was about to continue forward, through the door, when something stopped him, his senses held him there. He looked again down at the carpet, and down towards the stairs, seeing the muddy footprints of the enemy soldiers' as they'd made their way upwards. Two sets of muddy footprints went into the open doorway and room beyond, but then another seemed to come out of the open doorway, through the blood and disappear behind one of the closed doors. He narrowed his eyes as he pictured what the ground sign was telling him. Someone had come out of the room *after* the soldier was shot and was now waiting in ambush behind the other closed door. He looked down to Ping, indicating for him to come up silently, urging him to hurry up with a wave of the hand. Ping drew level to him, his weapon trained on the open door and watching as Jenks quickly indicated what he'd seen using hand signals. Ping nodded in understanding, shifting his aim to cover the closed door, as Jenks now walked prominently towards the open doorway, his own weapon up and looking in as he concentrated on clearing the room. He stepped over the corpse, avoiding the blood as he walked through the doorway. The room was large, painted in a garish pastel pink, and at the far side against the far wall sat a tripod, with a missile in its tube ready to fire. The daylight was pouring through the hole that was cut into the wall, still only half finished, the creator being disturbed in his work. He turned as he heard the door behind him crash open, the look of triumph on the face of the enemy soldier, quickly turning to pain and disbelief as Ping's rifle barked in anger, the automatic burst smashing into his chest, sparks flying off him as the rounds hit the metal of his magazines. He fell backwards against the far wall, his face taking on a strange, surreal look as his legs collapsed from under him, jerking in spasms as the life quickly left his body. Jenks turned to Ping and nodded in thanks before quickly running into the room, checking there were no other surprises waiting in there. Seeing the room was clear, both soldiers ran back to the missile system, it looked similar to the Milan system they were used to, but the writing was all in Cyrillic. After a few moments of looking it over, Ping looked up to Jenks.

"Any idea how to fire it?"

The young Fusilier shook his head, biting his lip in concentration as his hands felt around the launcher.

"Fucked if I know, it would help if we could bloody read it."

"Rachel speaks Russian, let's drag it back to her." Ping answered, looking back through the hole in the wall, seeing the Warrior a hundred metres away.

Jenks quickly sent a sitrep over the PRR, pride clear to hear in his voice.

"Corporal, two hostiles KIA, and one missile system captured, do you want us to bring it back?"

Spider answered quickly.

"Good work, no, leave it there, deny it if you can, and get your asses back here."

Jenks creased his eyebrows at the order as he looked at Ping. "Deny it? We've just fucking busted our asses getting it, and now he wants us to destroy it?"

Not fully understanding the dismissive tone, his pride bruised, he keyed the PRR again.

"But don't you want us to use this against the vehicles on the hill?"

Spiders voice cut back in, almost laughing at them.

"Why don't you take a look up on the hill and see for yourself."

Both soldiers crawled cautiously to one of the windows facing towards the hill, peering slowly through the net curtains, looking like nosey neighbours as they adjusted the netting to see. Up on the hill, two large plumes of smoke were rising upwards, the final indication that the enemy vehicles were destroyed. Confused, they looked over to the west, seeing the tank in a fire position, its gun slowly traversing the landscape.

They both shared a look before Jenks replied, "Corporal, how long ago were the BMP's destroyed?"

"About two minutes ago."

Both soldier's looked at each other dumbfounded, had they known that, then the mad dash through gunfire and clearing the farmhouse could have been avoided. As if to add to their misery, Spider now replied impatiently.

"Come on you two, stop fucking about, we've got people in the river to save, get that missile system destroyed and get your asses back here."

Both soldiers shook their heads in disbelief, sharing the same thoughts, as Ping added, "This fucking army, you couldn't make this shit up, could you?"

Smirking and nodding in agreement, Jenks replied. "Come on, let's get this fucking done and get back. I don't fancy having Spider raging at us all day."

Both soldiers wore grim looks as they set about the missile system, ripping out the cables and carefully removing the missile, before smashing up the firing handle. The missile was taken outside with them and dumped by the old tractor, marked with orange minetape, they didn't want the farm's owners to come back and accidentally set it off. Within minutes they were out of the farmhouse and running back to the safety of the Warrior, their achievements and bravery quickly forgotten about, for them it was simply all in a morning's work...

Catherine felt she'd held her breath for long enough, her heartbeat was pounding loudly in her ears as a dull thud sounded above the water. She felt something hit her legs, but no pain as she kept herself down for as long as she could possibly manage, her lungs bursting, as finally she came back up for air, her heart feeling like it would explode from her chest, not knowing what to expect. She came up, the water running down her face as she took in the scene. The water was already beginning to settle back down as four bodies lay close by in the shallows, three were face down, the fourth was on its back, she could see it was the commander. His eyes were open and glassy, staring skyward, but she could see from the pools of crimson spreading outwards from his missing arms that he was dead.

The fifth body was hanging halfway out of the riverbank at an unnatural angle, its head missing. She tried not to look at it, tried to ignore it, but she recognised who it once was from her clothes. She stood there in stunned silence, unable to move, almost rooted to the spot. She'd seen plenty of bodies before, attended plenty of crime scenes, but this was the first time she'd seen someone take their own life in front of her. The way in which Joanna had been willing to end it all, rather than go on, saddened her. How desperate she must have been, she thought as a bullet whizzed by overhead, making her head jerk as she ducked slightly, snapping her back to reality. Suddenly she was back, her thoughts turning to her own survival and those of her group. She waded up to the other bodies, quickly turning them over to see if any still carried weapons she could use. One of the bodies still had an assault rifle slung to it, without any care or remorse she rolled it over, ignoring the blood that pooled around her as her hands, now numb from the water, heaved on the rifle strap. After a few tugs it was free from the body and water poured out of the barrel as she freed up the rifle, checking the working parts still functioned before slinging it over her back. It had been a few years since her last firearms proficiency check, but she felt confident enough to handle it, besides, it wasn't like anyone would be arresting her for carrying it. She removed three of the magazines from the assault vest, stuffing them into her trouser pockets and turned, about to wade away in the direction of the others when she heard a sound behind her. She turned, just in time to see one of the soldiers had stood up, not as badly injured as she had first thought, the blood of his companions covering him, clearly making him look far worse than he was.

She froze, unsure of what to do as the soldier shook his head groggily, his eyes taking in the scene quickly as he became more aware, seeing the bodies of his comrades lying half submerged nearby. Suddenly, his face turned from pain to rage as he reached for his rifle lying in the mud, his fingers pulling it free and pointing it at her. It took a few seconds for him to realise the barrel was bent upwards, the grenade blast rendering it useless, as snarling, he threw it aside and rushed towards her. He reached out, his hands grasping onto her, as she stepped back, her own hands trying to pull her rifle free from her back, slipping on a rock and falling with the man on top of her, splashing under the water. She tried to fend him off, but he was strong, and together they both fell into the deeper water of the river, the weight of his assault vest dragging them both down as they wrestled, her rifle now lying useless, still on her back. She fought desperately, her hands and legs trying to remember the muscle memory from the years of arrest and restraint, as she struggled with him. She could feel his hands move upwards, going for her throat, trying to choke her, which seemed silly given they were both underwater, the lack of oxygen would kill her anyway. She let him, as her own hands scrabbled on the riverbed floor, finding what she was looking for as they closed around a small rock. She could see his head close to hers, his eyes wide open, bubbles escaping his open mouth as, even underwater, he was yelling at her in manic rage. She brought the rock up as hard as she could, the water seeming to slow her actions down. She struck once, then twice, the blood floating out of the head wound as the soldier's grip loosened and his eyes seemed to blink in surprise. She kicked him off her, his body sinking to the floor as she staggered back to her feet, her hands massaging her throat as she watched him underwater. He was struggling to get back up onto his feet, weakened now by the head wound, his face emerged on the surface, and on shaky legs, he stood, looking over at her, rage replaced with fear as he struggled to keep himself in the shallower water of the bank as the slow river current began to pull at his weakened legs, trying to pull him into deeper waters. He reached out an arm desperately towards her, the look of fear etched on his face as she reached out, the police officer in her answering the call, ignoring his earlier attempts to kill her. He smiled in thanks as she grasped him strongly, pulling him towards her, towards safety, repeating over and over weakly in Russian "Spasibo...spasibo..."

As she pulled him closer, she could see the flap of skin hanging from his head wound, she'd caught him good with the rock, already the blood was flowing freely and a lump the size of a golfball was beginning to form. She held him there, looking down at the soldier as his chest heaved quickly, hearing him drawing breath before looking back over at Joanna's body. Joanna wasn't breathing anymore, she didn't deserve what happened to her, she never wanted to be part of this, none of them did. All this was because of them. Suddenly the anger she'd felt when the soldiers had burst into her police station, began to resurface, she tried to stop it, but the more she tried to stop it, the more it seemed to blaze away. All the thoughts of the past forty eight hours flooded through her mind, the radio message of the execution of her officers on the bridge, the takeover of her police station, the humiliation of her capture, the treatment to the other prisoners, the rape of Linda and Joanna and her tragic death, the risk to her family, her country, her friends, all the people she'd seen suffer, all the pain *she'd* suffered. All because of these people, all because of *him*. Her eyes focused back on the soldier, he was lying on his back against the embankment, looking up at her, his eyes were wide with shock and fear as he could see the anger coursing through her, as if he could read what she was thinking.

She hardened her jaw, firming her resolve, as her anger burned brightly and coldly, slowly, she began to push the soldiers head back under the water, his hands scrabbling weakly at her as he pleaded.

"Net, NET! U menya yest' deti! U MENYA-"

Ignoring him, she pushed harder, cutting off his yells midsentence in a gurgle as his head disappeared under water, his legs thrashing weakly against the bottom, as his hands scrabbled weakly against her grip, her rage giving her almost inhuman strength as she clenched her jaw together, her thoughts dark as she sought her own justice. The policewoman in her was shouting to stop, but the anger was too deep, too painful, and as if to justify it, she looked over at Joanna's body, angrily, drawing resolve from it. She had no idea how long she was stood there, was it minutes? Was it hours? The cold water seemed to numb her senses as she snapped out of her reverie. She looked down at the water, the lifeless eyes of the soldier were looking back up at her, his mouth open, his arms and legs lifeless, moving with the current of the water. She looked up shocked, suddenly aware of what she had done as the anger seemed to melt away, replaced with a feeling of numbness as she let go of the body, the current pulling it into the deeper water as the weight of the assault vest caused it to disappear, the river helping her cover her crime.

She knew she should be feeling sick, holding her hands up to her face as she looked at them in astonishment, realising she'd just killed someone with them. She'd spent her whole career chasing people who did exactly what she'd just done, and she was supposed to be a police officer, a *senior* police officer, able to pull fact from fiction and replace the most primitive human behaviour with justice and law. And now, finally, she'd failed. How could she call herself a police officer now? She was supposed to represent the highest standards of law and values, and now she'd broken one of the most serious laws. She'd just murdered someone, all to satisfy her own primeval feeling for vengeance.

"Ma'am!"

She looked up startled, seeing the two British soldiers coming around the bend of the river, holding assault rifles, the weapons trained on her, closely followed by Arnie who was shouting wildly at her. Recognising her, both soldiers lowered their weapons and ran past her, she recognised them as Ping and Jenks, both of them nodded in recognition, water splashing up their legs as they took firing positions nearby, providing security detail. Arnie ran forward smiling, the smile vanishing as he saw the look on her face. She looked ashamedly at the water, as if he'd somehow sensed what she'd done, her guilt plain to see. His eyes took in the scene in a moment, looking first at the bodies lying nearby and then settling on Joanna, his eyebrows creased together.

"Is that-"

"Yes." she cut him off.

He looked sadly at the floor, shaking his head and speaking slowly.

"Those bastards. Why the fuck did they do that to her? What happened?"

"She did it to herself, she had a grenade hidden and set it off."

"Why? Where'd she get the grenade from? What made her do that?" he asked quizzically.

"NOT HERE ARNIE!" she snapped, her guilt and anger still simmering on the surface as the two soldiers looked around at her. Realising she'd shouted, she lowered her voice, her tone more soothing. "I mean, not here Arnie, I'll talk later, but not now, not here."

Seeing the look on her face, and the blood floating on the water's surface, he decided not to press the issue, as he turned to the two soldiers.

"Ping, we safe to head back now?"

Without taking his head from the weapon sight the young soldier replied, "Sure thing, but keep yourselves low, you two go first, we'll stay behind to cover you."

They were about to move when Ping called back over.

"And Ma'am..."

She turned to look at him as he pointed to the weapon slung across her back.

"Those things usually work better when you point them at someone, not have them slung across your back."

She was about to snap at him, to shout, when she saw him smile, something about the cheeky smile brought her back from the brink. With everything going on around them, all the death and devastation, this young man, who'd risked his life again to come back for her, could find it in him to crack a joke. Without knowing why, she smiled, and nodded in understanding as she unslung the rifle, holding it properly as the soldier went back to watching his arcs. Lightly tapping Arnie on the shoulder, she motioned for him to lead the way, relieved to be finally wading away from the carnage of the river. She turned one last time to look at Joanna, her eyes filling with tears as she thought of what she had gone through, the sorrow didn't last long though as anger surfaced, causing her to look back over to where the body of the soldier she had killed, had disappeared. Did she feel remorse, she asked herself. It didn't feel like she did, and although she was angry at what she'd just done, she didn't feel pity or regret, guiltily she felt almost justified. Nodding to herself in understanding, she waded through the water to catch her colleague, leaving the demons of Joanna behind her, and feeling somehow as if she herself was leaving a small part of herself behind in the river too. Perhaps she was, perhaps back there under the water somewhere, trying to get back to the surface was Chief Superintendent Stokes...

Mike looked away from his sights, glancing down towards the farmyard in the valley, silently urging the Warrior and its crew to hurry up and get moving. He'd only arrived a few minutes ago, quickly taking out the two enemy vehicles on the far side of the valley. The enemy vehicles had been so fixated on Spider's Warrior, they hadn't even noticed the tank approaching on their right side. Had they been doing what Mike was doing, and checking their flanks every once in a while, they might have seen him. As it was, he'd been able to bring the tank into the perfect firing position, almost broadside onto the BMP's at a range of 800 metres. Training ammo or not, at this range they weren't going to miss, and he'd watched as the two vehicles were quickly dispatched, patting his gunner in congratulations. Some of the infantry from the vehicles had escaped into the woods, and after loading the main gun, he had Baz use the RWS to provide suppressing fire into their positions. Now it was all about keeping their heads down, whilst the truck survivors ran towards the safety of the back of the Warrior.

It wasn't the infantry that was worrying him though, Gunslinger had reported the other ten BMP's were now on their way towards them, in battle formations, spread out and fully alert. Initially the company commander had only sent a small force of four vehicles to chase down the truck, but upon hearing them under attack had now sent the rest of his force. Mike was tempted to get the Apaches to fire at them, but knew if he did, they'd give away their own positions, playing his trump card early on. The BMP's could be carrying anti air missiles, more than a match to bring an Apache down. For now, he was happy to have Gunslinger hold fire and monitor their progress. Although not a tank, the BMP still carried some fearsome weaponry, including anti-tank guided missiles that could be fired from its main gun, over 4 km away, more than capable of disabling the tank, and the thought of ten of them waiting in an unknown ambush for him made Mike shudder.

He left his crew to it as he looked back down, watching as the final two crew members finished cramming everyone into the back and mounted onto the Warrior, Spiders voice, out of breath came over the radio.

"Tango One-One, Tango Two-Zero, that's everyone aboard and us ready to move now."

"About fucking time!" Mike said to himself quietly, as he keyed the radio, his voice though not relaying any of his concerns.

"Roger, good work, now let's get going. Out."

Without waiting for acknowledgment, Mike then transmitted out to Patty who he'd left with Changa 2 kilometres to their west, overwatching their route back.

"Tango Two-One, how's it looking in your sector?"

"Tango One-One, Tango Two-One, all clear so far."

"Roger, understood, keep your eyes open, there'll be coming for sure now they know we're here."

He looked back down, glad to see the Warrior negotiating the hill and making its way back up to his position. Already the second Talon was whizzing past him at speed, its electric motors and stabilisers keeping the body dead centre as the tracked chassis bent and torqued beneath it, the machine gun and launcher stowed away. If they got the chance to stop, then Mike would reload the Javelin launchers, the spare Javelin missiles were safely tucked away in the tank's armoured rear bin. Mike kept the tank where it was, the machine gun still firing, as the Warrior and Talon both made their way past them, and down the other side of the high ground. Only when he was sure they were clear did he finally give the orders to the crew.

"Baz, cease fire, Bill prepare to move...okay driver, reverse!"

Quickly checking behind, out of habit, he watched as the driver reversed back off the slope, using his cameras to see. Whilst the gunner was scanning their front, ensuring there would be no surprises for them as the heavy tank rumbled out of view. Only once they were sure they out of sight of the enemy, did Mike give the order to turn the tank around and follow the Warrior.

As the tank began to pick up speed, Mike ducked back down, looking over at the BMDS, watching to see if the first Talon further north was reporting anything. Nothing, all quiet.

Where are you, he thought to himself, looking over the mapping. The only unit being shown were the BMP's coming at them from the east. Somewhere out there, ahead of them lay a whole Russian Division in wait, ready to strike. Having those BMP's closely following them, reporting his every move, just wouldn't do. He had to eradicate them. Finally, sighing and taking a deep breath, he made the decision. He flicked his pressel over to the HF set, and set his jaw firm, as he reported.

"Gunslinger Two-Three, Whiskey Three-Zero, clear to engage BMP's."

He'd just played their ace card. Now let's see what the other side were holding.

Wonderland Operations Centre WOC

"Where the bloody hell is he going? He's supposed to be heading west!" the CDS barked angrily, watching as the GPS signal from the modified HF radio on the tank showed Whiskey Three-Zero had about turned and was now heading back the way it had come.

He looked angrily over at Colonel Stephens, who had his own look of surprise as the CDS ordered, "We've waited long enough. Start transmitting now."

"But they've still got another 5 kilometres to go before-" the Colonel tried to reply as the CDS interrupted.

"I don't care, we've waited long enough. We need to start moving ourselves. Send it NOW!"

Colonel Stephens looked over to the LEWT team Captain, whose own face was wracked with regret and guilt at what they were about to do. There was after all, one of his own team in the unit. Closing his eyes and muttering a silent prayer, he gave the order. "Do it."

Two Sergeants began typing on their keyboards, within seconds it was done. Now, unbeknown to Mike on the tank, his own HF set would now begin randomly transmitting as if it were a Battlegroup in that area. Now the Russians would know exactly where they were...

4

Tied To The Post

6th Div Headquarters Bovington

General Kuzmin stood amongst his command group, reading the reports, the words jumping out of the pages at him.

'*07:01 - Hammer Two-Zero reports contact with the enemy in grid square 31,87. Hammer Two-Zero now off the air.*'

'*07:15 - Rhino One-Three reporting, engaged by the enemy, grid square 33,87. Four vehicles destroyed. Still in contact. Rhino One-Three now off the air.*'

'*07:19 – Rhino One-Zero reporting enemy contact in grid square 34,87. Rhino One-Zero now off the air.*'

'*07:20 - Unit 163 reports enemy transmissions in grid squares 31,87 and 34,87 Estimates are that enemy are possibly battlegroup strength, moving southwest, intentions unknown.*'

Possible Battlegroup strength? The General re-read the words becoming increasingly angry. If that were the case then how the hell had the British got them in there undetected? And where the hell did they have the manpower to get a Battlegroup from? All of the messages stated contact with the enemy, but with what, and in what strength? The reports were vague and confusing and threw up more questions than they did answers.

He looked up, his face scanning the assembled officers as the reports were passed amongst them to read. All had the same look of disbelief after they'd finished.

Keeping his anger hidden he merely asked, "So Comrades, thoughts?"

"This can't be true!" an Infantry Colonel objected, "are all our soldiers sat at the front asleep? Are they drunk? Why this sort of breakthrough would have been reported already!"

Another Colonel of Artillery argued, "If it's not true then who the hell is fighting our units? And why have those units now all gone off the air?"

Another infantry Major added, "And why would unit 163 be reporting enemy signals in the same area consistent with a Battlegroup? Something must be there!"

"Comrade General!" Another Staff officer interrupted, holding a radio. "Forward command units want to know if they are to continue the assaults."

The General looked over and nodded in acknowledgement, altogether they had nearly 100,000 men on the offensive, assaulting all over the south coast, with attacks on the towns and cities of Yeovil, Winchester, Salisbury, Petersfield and Horsham all happening simultaneously. It was risky to have all the frontal assaults going in at once, but it was also necessary if they wanted to be in London quickly. Already Moscow was growing impatient, with his President now demanding immediate results, or face the consequences. But in concentrating his forces on these attacks, he'd been forced to weaken other key areas, areas where the enemy were not supposed to be, like right where this god damned phantom Battlegroup had now magically appeared. He couldn't defend against the enemy counterattack and mount the offensive simultaneously, something had to give. But what if this wasn't a counterattack at all, what if he was being fooled.

He strode over to the maps, his officers all following as he addressed them, highlighting the areas on the map of 34,87, the frustration clear in his voice.

"These co-ordinates cover nearly 5 km of terrain, and if this is an enemy counterattack as we are being led to believe then why the hell don't we have any eyes on them?"

The Colonel of Artillery replied, "General, the terrain in these areas is wooded and very hilly, and with our forces spread as thinly as they are, it's a lot of ground to try to keep eyes on. If this were an enemy Battlegroup, then it's the perfect terrain to hide them in."

Sensing he had more to say the General urged him to continue.

The Colonel stepped forward, pointing to the map.

"Comrade General, we have rear echelon units here, and here. The 346th Supply Regiment is only 5 km to the south and the 23rd Tank Repair Regiment 5 km to the southwest. These are key logistical units, any attack on them could threaten our future offensive capability. If this is an enemy attack then I believe their mission is to attack now where we are weakest, with most of our forces concentrated on the assaults to the east. If this attack is proven to be correct then we should not risk losing these units for a pyrrhic victory, especially not this early on in the offensive."

"Does anyone disagree with the Colonel's assessment?"

The Infantry Colonel stepped forwards, voicing his concerns. "Comrade General we must not stop the offensive! There is no attack, this is merely a ruse to draw our forces away."

"A ruse? The Artillery Colonel argued, "Then who the hell is fighting Rhino One-Zero?"

The two senior officers began to argue as the tension rose between them, deciding he'd heard enough the General yelled.

"COMRADES!"

A Captain entered the ops room, ignoring the standoff, barging through the group with another report held aloft. The General took it, quickly reading it before looking back and pointing on the map.

"Unit 163 are still reporting enemy transmissions at this grid square. Given the size and amount of transmissions they're certain it's a Battlegroup." Sensing the hesitancy in the General's voice the Artillery Colonel enquired, "You're still not convinced Comrade General?"

He thought through the logistics of such a move. It was a bold plan, but to what purpose? What on earth was so important in that area that the British would be attacking there? The frustration was beginning to tear at him, should he stop the offensive and reorganise for this new threat? He needed to know for sure what was there. He needed human eyes there, not more damn reports. He stared at both Colonels, weighing up the options, each soldier offering a different opinion, but ultimately it would be his decision, his mistake if he called this wrong. Putting away his doubts he looked up to one of his Airforce Captains.

"Get an aircraft to overfly those positions. I need to confirm what's there before we commit to anything."

After a few moments of speaking on the radio the Captain replied, "I've got two Mig 31's returning from a bombing mission, but they're out of ordnance."

"I don't care about the bloody ordnance!" the General snapped back, "I just need them to overfly that sector. Find out what the hell is going on there!"

Ignoring the rebuke the officer nodded and passed on the order as the General returned back to the map, thinking aloud as he continued. "Right, now we wait."

Whiskey Three-Zero

On board the tank, Mike took a final swig of coffee, tipping his head back, letting the cold remnants of the drink sooth his dry throat, before reaching behind to hang the empty cup on one of the many electronic cables behind him to use later. He leaned forward into the sight, checking where the gunner was scanning as the turret continued to track slowly left and right as Smudge looked for more targets. Baz was using the RWS thermal sight to keep an eye closer to home, checking the small cluster of outbuildings nearby, as the driver kept the reverse camera on, checking for anyone trying to sneak up behind them. Between them all, Mike was confident they had all their arcs covered, and there shouldn't be any surprises heading for them, not from the ground at least, now his unit were finally back together. After picking up the truck survivors, Mike and Spider's vehicles had made great progress, the terrain ahead already being cleared by Patty and Changa's Warriors as they'd caught up. Mike had them all stop briefly to transfer some of the passengers into Changa and Patty's warriors, hearing how crowded Spider's Warrior had become wouldn't have helped Rachel and Fletch trying to use the drones, and the last thing they needed were more injuries from being thrown about as people were forced to sit on the vehicles' floors. At least now everyone had a seat and could be strapped in with the vehicle's harnesses. Not that any were complaining, news had already filtered through of Joanna's death, so everyone knew how lucky they were to be alive, cuts and bruises be damned. Mike had also used the opportunity to reload the Talon's launchers, now at least the machine guns and launchers were all fully loaded and ready for round two.

It was Baz who broke the silence.

"Boss, something's not right with this bloody HF radio."

Mike looked over, watching as his loader stepped behind the gun and began checking the cables.

"Whats up Baz? What's wrong?"

"I think we're on permanent send. Look, the transmission light keeps coming on!"

Mike leaned over, looking to where Baz was pointing. After a few seconds he saw for himself the small TX symbol light up in the display, the radio *was* transmitting.

Quickly Mike ordered over the I/C, "Everyone check your pressels."

Mike checked his own pressel, tapping it gently against the cupola, wiggling the cables and blowing into his microphone. Sometimes pressels had been known to 'permanent send,' by accident, allowing everyone to overhear over the radio what was being said in the tank.

After a few moments everyone came back, confirming all their pressels were working correctly. Whatever was happening with the radio, it wasn't crew related. After a few more moments of checking cables Baz replied.

"Nothing's loose. Fuck knows what's causing it, but I'm pretty sure we're sending.. .wait...oh, it's stopped now."

Shrugging his shoulders, Baz went back to using the RWS as Mike sat chewing his lip in thought about the radio. He'd never been known as a signals guru on the tank when he was back in the Army, so now, with so much time off tanks, he struggled to think what could be causing it. Knowing they needed the radio to talk to other units, and seeing it was no longer transmitting, he pushed his concerns aside.

The radio problem was quickly forgotten as the pilot of Gunslinger Two-Three suddenly burst over the air excitedly.

"Tango One-One, Gunslinger Two-Three, Critical information! We've got two aircraft inbound on radar coming our way. Range is 30 miles and closing fast. ETA, two minutes!"

Shit! Mike thought, quickly replying, "Gunslinger Two-Three, any chance they're friendly?"

"Not a chance, One-One, they're enemy all right. We're shutting down our radars."

"Okay understood, but you can take them out though, right?"

"Negative Tango One-One, we're loaded for ground attack, not air to air. Sorry."

"Fuck!" Mike exclaimed loudly. Any attack from the air and they'd be sitting ducks. So much for Colonel Stephens saying not to worry about enemy airpower. Knowing his options were limited he knew now was the time to use the Hornet. Risky or not, they needed it.

Looking around he quickly saw the ground he wanted to use.

"Bill, see that high ground off to our left, take us up to it.

"Boss, we'll be visible. You sure about that?"

"Yes, do it now, quickly!"

He held on as the tank pulled away and to the left, slowing as it hit the rise of the hill. Less than thirty seconds later they were in the open on the small rise, with a commanding view of the area. Seeing the tank had moved position, it wasn't long before Spider asked, "Tango One-One what do you want us to do?"

Not wanting to waste time explaining Mike quickly fired back over the troop net.

"All Callsigns hold your position, we've got enemy air inbound. Tango One-One will be off these means for two minutes. Out!"

Leaving them to digest the news Mike ignored the explosion of chatter on the troop radio as he concentrated on the immediate threat.

"Bill, put the handbrake on, and engine in neutral. Then rev the engine up to 1200 rpm and keep it there no matter what happens."

Without waiting for an explanation Bill did just that, Mike heard the engine revs climb as he looked at the BMDS and selected the Hornet, watching behind him as the armoured doors of the second case opened, and a large mechanical arm began to pivot upwards, sat atop of it was what looked like an oversized cinema projector, about the size of a briefcase. When the arm reached its full extent, it began to telescopically extend upwards, rising to a height of 3 metres. After a quick visual inspection Mike was satisfied that all was in order. It had to be, they only had one chance at this.

He jumped back down into his seat, watching as the display now flashed green showing it was fully charged. He tapped the screen to activate it, the display flashing red in response. Almost immediately the lights inside the turret began to dim as a crackling sound now began to be heard over their headsets. Smudge pulled his head out of his sight, looking over to Baz as they both looked at each other in wonder. What the hell was happening? Only Mike knew, and he was keeping quiet, his eyes glued to his screen as the Hornet now began to scan 360 degrees around them, searching for the incoming threat.

"Come on...Come on..." Mike urged, as the Hornet began to search the sky, the time seeming to drag as he counted down the seconds. Any moment now and he was expecting to have a laser guided bomb drop down on him.

Onboard the Apaches the crews were silently watching on, with both helicopters keeping hidden low to the ground with all their electronics and search radars shut down. With no air to air missiles it was all they could do really, now at least the enemy aircraft wouldn't be able to track them, but now they couldn't track the enemy either. For now, the tank really was on its own.

One of the pilots remarked morosely to his gunner "I'll give you 5 to 1 odds we'll be going home without our little friends down there."

The gunner said nothing, both watching on in morbid curiosity wondering what was going to happen next...

Kestrel-Six

Flying in at 10,000 feet Captain Mikhail Vasilev checked his threat warning screen again for the third time that minute. Even with their control of the air, he knew it paid to be cautious, the RAF were not a foe he intended to underestimate ever again, especially after nearly being shot down by them on the first night. In the back his navigator and weapons officer, Lieutenant Nikolai Egorov was scanning using the high-powered cameras from the weapons pod to check the ground ahead, searching for the enemy activity they'd been warned about. Both pilots were still feeling in high spirits, having just completed a successful bombing run of the enemy positions in Salisbury. Mikhail having remarked how beautiful the cathedral looked, even with the smoke rising from its torn structure. Perhaps when this was all over, if there was anything left of the old city he could still visit it with his family. He'd already made up his mind to bring his wife over after the war had ended. Russia was no longer the country he remembered. Perhaps a new life awaited him and his family here, after all they'd need good patriots to teach the British the Russian way of doing things. He was torn from his thoughts of home and his future as Nikolai reported back.

"The signals we picked up earlier have gone. Looks like whoever was down there has shut their systems down. No matter, we'll have eyes on them in 60 seconds."

Mikhail glanced across at the switches for the chaff and flares, their own defences, ready to deploy it if need be. It felt uncomfortable to be flying into battle unarmed, and after the success of their mission he imagined they'd be back and on the ground in ten minutes, refuelling and re-arming ready for another sortie. Instead they'd received orders to fly over another piece of countryside and locate signs of an unknown enemy force. He doubted they'd find any, they were after all behind their own lines! But, he had to admit, things had changed these past 24 hours. All the pilots had noticed the ready-made supply of bombs and rockets they'd carried over on the transport planes were dwindling far quicker than they'd imagined. And this last mission had called for two sets of cluster munitions on four targets, but a lack of bombs had left them only hitting two. Secretly he wondered what was going on back at headquarters to warrant such havoc with their logistics.

He was drawn to movement overhead as a shadow appeared over his cockpit, he looked up and shouted in alarm as the nose of his wingman's Mig 31 began to loom above him, the pilot clearly concentrating more on watching his displays than his formation flying. Mihail quickly put his own aircraft into a dive, shouting over the radio.

"Kestrel-Eight, Kestrel-Six, you're too damn close! Back off and watch where you're flying!"

"Sorry Six, backing off now." the young pilot replied. Mikhail finally releasing the breath he'd held as the distance increased.

"Fucking rookie pilot!" Nikolai yelled angrily at the sudden commotion that had distracted him from his scanning.

He was about to say something else when suddenly he yelled excitedly.

"Shit! I've got a target!"

"What! Where?" Mikhail exclaimed, looking at his own display that mirrored his navigators.

"There! Look it's a fucking tank! There are enemy down there!"

Mikhail cursed his empty weapons racks.

"Okay, lets look for the rest of them." He ordered as keying the radio he began to send his report.

Whiskey Three-Zero

Back on the tank Mike held his breath whispering, almost as if the pilots could hear him. "And there they are!"

Onscreen he could see the image of two aircraft at altitude coming towards them, identifying them as Mig 31's, they looked huge as they filled the screen. The Hornet was locked onto one of them, the targeting reticule bracketing the target. Even though the aircraft were travelling at speed the Hornet was now easily tracking them.

Pulling his head from the sight he looked around the turret at his crew, keeping his voice as calm as he could given their circumstances. The next ten seconds were vital. "Right, everyone just stay calm, I need us all to sit here and do nothing. Nobody move. Smudge, I want you to keep the turret still for now, no more scanning please."

A strange eerie calm descended over the tank crew as everyone waited silently, not knowing what was going to happen next, but knowing that whatever plan their commander had in his head, for now, that's where he was keeping it. Smudge and Baz exchanged puzzled looks from across the turret, Baz merely shrugged his shoulders in response, looking up at Mike who was back to looking at the BMDS again.

Mike began to count down loudly.

"Okay everyone and here we go, fingers crossed, in three...two...one... FIRING!"

The turret crew were watching on, wondering what was about to happen as Mike pressed the button, holding his breath as the air around them seemed to fill with a sudden energy. Mike could feel the hairs on the back of his neck and arms begin to rise as a loud whining noise seemed to emanate from the Hornet, suddenly there was a crack like a lightning strike and the smell of burnt hair seemed to waft down into the turret.

Kestrel-Six

Mikhail had just finished sending his sighting report when his wingman's panicked voice came over the radio.

"Mayday! Mayday! Mayday! We're going down!"

"What?" he exclaimed, wasting precious seconds as he scanned behind him, trying to locate the aircraft. Behind him and to the left he could just see the fiery wreckage as it began to plummet towards the ground.

"What the-" Nikolai yelled confused as upon instinct Mikhail began to throw the aircraft into a series of manoeuvres, hoping to throw off whatever the hell had targeted his wingman. The dull pop of chaff and flares sounded as the countermeasures began to deploy.

"WHERE DID IT COME FROM?" Mikhail yelled, the fear of being caught without warning making him shout.

Nikolai tried to fight the G-forces as the fighter bomber tore through the air as he scanned his own screens, confused.

"Threat radars are empty, no EW, no Radar, no missile lock, I...I don't understand."

"NIKOLAI! Come on think! What's engaging us? There must be something out there!"

"I'm telling you now, there's nothing onscreen!" Nikolai replied fearfully.

"Goddammit!" the pilot yelled frustratingly. He rolled the aircraft over into a dive and leant on the throttles, as they began to scream earthwards, building up more speed before turning around and heading back the way they'd come from. Whatever was in the area, it was dangerous, and he wanted to be as far away from it as he could. Headquarters would need to know of the threat. He began to send the transmission when suddenly Nikolai shouted in alarm.

"Okay I've found it...Shit! Laser warn-" he got no further. Whatever Nikolai had found or wanted to say, died on his lips.

Whiskey Three-Zero

Mike punched the air delightedly as he watched the second aircraft disintegrate onscreen into a fireball.

"YES! Fucking YES!" he exclaimed, the tension finally being released. The rest of the crew all looked at him confused, only Baz had seen the two fireballs in the sky in the distance from his open hatch, not truly understanding what he'd witnessed he'd watched on open mouthed, until finally he asked.

"Boss, what the fuck was that? Did we just do that? Did we just shoot those planes out of the sky?"

Smudge was next to exclaim, "We shot them down? They're gone? What the hell is that thing boss? Is it a missile launcher?"

Mike ignored the questions for now, quickly flicking to the HF net.

"Gunslinger Two-Three, Tango One-One, I need you to fire up your radar, tell me if there's any more aircraft incoming."

The Apaches were 1 km to the north of the tank, both air crews were speechless at what they'd just witnessed. It took a few moments for Mike's words to sink in before Two-Three replied.

"Err Roger One-One We'll do that now, wait one."

After a few fraught seconds finally the pilot replied, the relief was clear to hear.

"One-One looks clear. I don't know what the hell you just did, but it looks like we're good to proceed."

"Roger understood. Give me two minutes to sort myself out then we'll continue as planned."

Mike closed his eyes in relief, muttering a silent prayer of thanks to the engineers back in Aurora. That had been close, too bloody close. He was certain the enemy aircraft must have seen him. Perhaps a few more seconds later and the outcome could have been different. He looked behind him as the Hornet began to slowly sink back into it's armoured case.

"Okay Bill, you can cut the revs now."

As the engine whined down Mike saw the crew's stares, looking to him questioningly. Knowing they'd want answers, and that he couldn't move the tank until the Hornet was safely stowed he finally relented.

"High Optical Radiation Emitting Transmitter, or as we like to simply call it, Hornet."

Seeing the blank faces he continued, "It's a laser beam, a very powerful and highly focused laser beam."

"Fuck! A laser!" Smudge shot back as Baz shook his head in disbelief.

"I had no idea we even had that!" he exclaimed as Mike continued,

"We designed it originally to protect tanks from guided missiles, but the missiles were always too fast and too close to the ground to give it the time it needed to hit. Instead we found it was better suited to targets coming in at longer distance and from the air."

"But I thought lasers had to have huge power sources and the smallest we had were the size of trucks!" Baz stated, as Mike replied.

"Not this one Baz, the Hornet's strength is its optics, it's fitted with special lenses that magnify the output of the beam."

Baz stood with eyebrows raised waiting for Mike to explain further, but realising he'd already said too much Mike countered.

"Let's just say it doesn't need quite as much power as a standard laser to fire. I can't say anything more than that."

Baz nodded in understanding and went back to using the RWS muttering "Fair enough, ask no questions, get no lies."

"Boss why don't we just leave it out and shoot at the enemy tanks? Why bother with the main gun?" Bill enquired, Smudge nodding in agreement as he piped up.

"Yeah Boss, why you putting it away, lets keep it out and just blast at every one that tries to get near us."

"Because guys it's not without its limitations. It uses a hell of a lot of power and is prone to overheating and catching fire, and has to be stowed away when we move, the violent movement of the tank, coupled with the weight of the sensor head will snap it's frame. We'd be wasting too much time if we kept stopping to deploy and re-stow it, plus when we've tested it in the past the best it can manage is five to ten shots before it overheats. Then it needs at least three hours to cool down."

"Oh." Smudge exclaimed as finally Mike saw the Hornet was stowed.

"Right then guys, enough of the lecture, let's get back into it. Smudge clear to scan, Bill, reverse, let's get off this bloody hilltop."

6th Div Headquarters Bovington

Captain Lunyou was stood in the corner of the ops room smirking to himself as he watched on, the officers reminding him of a troop of meerkats, all seeking approval of the General. All were either nodding their heads or shaking them, depending on which

Colonel they agreed with. His smirk turned to a grimace as the pain shot up his leg again as unknowingly, he shifted the weight onto his injured foot.

"Damn it!" he muttered through clenched teeth. "That fucking woman!" He reached into his pocket, quickly swallowing the pain killers as he waited for the pain to subside slightly. After a few minutes the sharp pain seemed to dull enough and he could watch the calamity unfolding before him again. He watched as the General was interrupted by the Air force Captain manning the radio who shouted over.

"Comrade General!"

"Well? What is it?" he demanded.

"We've got confirmation from Kestrel-Six, enemy armour has been sighted in grid square 35,87!"

"Any idea on numbers? Dammit I need to know how many!" the General demanded, waiting as the officer continued speaking into the radio. After a few more moments the officer looked up, shocked.

"Our aircraft have been shot down!"

"Do we have enemy aircraft in that sector?" the Artillery Colonel demanded, the Captain replying almost immediately.

"No, nothing at all, that sector is clear. It must have been ground to air missiles."

"We shouldn't have sent them in unarmed!" the Colonel complained, looking at the Infantry Colonel angrily.

"Right that confirms it!" the General barked, suddenly forced into action. "I want all of our attacks to stop for now. Have all attacking units in those areas pull back to this morning's defensive positions."

"But Comrade General!" the Infantry Colonel argued, "some of our units are already two or three kilometres from their start positions! Let's at least try to fortify what we have already taken!"

The General waved his concerns away with his hand as he continued.

"I don't care for your arguments Colonel. I won't waste more time holding untenable positions. Before we proceed further we must control and hold the ground that we have now. I want these vultures behind our lines destroyed before they can exploit their breakthrough and cause us yet more damage!"

Ignoring the Colonel's arguments he turned to another Captain nearby waiting for orders.

"Get me Colonel Golgolvin on the radio and then order all logistical units without armoured support in these areas to withdraw southwest, back towards Dorchester."

The Captain darted away as the General turned to the ready board, on it were listed the units already off loaded and deployed on the ground. Most of those unloaded were already committed to the fighting at the front lines, he dare not pull them back, weakening their front lines might be after all what the British were trying to get him to do

Thirty seconds later and the Captain returned, handing him the radio.

"Comrade General, Colonel Golgolvin on the line."

Without taking his eyes from the map the General began, "Colonel I need you to cease the attack on Yeovil and be prepared to move south."

The command group had no idea what was being said at the other end and could only listen into the General's replies.

"Yes that's right, yes, yes, yes, I KNOW THAT NOW!" he replied testily before his voice calmed down again.

"Good! Very good. Right. Yes, that's what we're considering as well. Yes, well in that case, get yourself going immediately...No don't wait for us, get moving now!"

He handed the radio back to the Captain, addressing the officers.

"I want the 75th and 77th Tank regiments moving northeast within the next few minutes, have them setup blocking positions north of Dorchester."

One of the Majors interrupted. "Sir, the 75th and 77th are still unloading. They only have half of their combat power ashore and won't be operational for at least another two hours."

"I DON'T CARE!" he snapped back, "I want them ready to move within the next ten minutes! I will not lose support units because the commanders of the 75th and 77th wanted to hang around and unpack their fucking suitcases! Get them moving! NOW!"

The Major nodded in defeat, knowing better than to argue further. Sensing no further objection, the General continued, waving his hands around the map.

"Now, Colonel Golgolvin is dispatching two companies of T-80's south, back down the A37, into blocking positions, here, around the village of Stockwood. If the enemy thrust continues pushing west or turns south, he will be the chopping block on which our enemy will place its head. The tanks of the 75th will be the axe which will chop through this thrust, then we'll gut the bastards from the south using the 77th and cut off their retreat to the east. With luck, we can stop this advance before it really begins.

The enemy don't know it yet, but the bastards have just put their head, hands and balls into the mouth of a waiting, hungry tiger."

Captain Lunyou smiled as the old man blustered away, always with animal quotes, he felt sure that some of the Divisions callsigns were all the Generals idea, Rhino, Tiger, Jackal, Wolf. Clearly the General had a thing for animals. He checked his watch, it was time for an update, his boss General Terekhov would want to know how things were progressing with project Houdini. He walked past, leaving them all to it, let them play their stupid games, he had other, more important matters to be getting on with. As he limped past the map he glanced up, finally paying attention to where the enemy's last location was reported. He stopped and stared, quickly taking in the names of the area, why did they sound familiar to him? Suddenly as it dawned on him, he gasped in surprise as he realised where the enemy were heading. Quickly he pulled his phone out of his pocket, dialling the number from memory and limping away from prying ears. Keeping his voice low but shielding an ear from the noise of the busy ops room, he waited, urging the person on the other end to answer quickly. Finally, after about ten rings it was answered, the voice on the end of the phone gruff.

"Yes?"

"Where are you set up?"

"What kind of stupid question is that? You know our location; I gave it to you yesterday."

Lunyou was not in the mood to play games, as he angrily hissed back.

"Just answer the fucking question, Vikram! I want your location, NOW!"

There was a pause as the person on the end of the line took in the Captain's tone, finally relenting, they replied.

"Alright, we're set up in a woodline, four miles northeast of a pissy little village called-"

"Godbury..." Lunyou interrupted, his voice trailing off into the distance as he remembered the name on the map.

"Well if you knew that already, why the fuck-"

"Shut up and listen!" he interrupted, trying not to be overheard as two officers looked over at his outburst, lowering his voice he continued.

"We may have a problem; how soon can you be ready to pack up and leave?"

"Leave? Are you fucking crazy? We've only just finished setting up here! I'm halfway through our second batch now!" the voice argued. "I'll need at least four hours to finish-"

Lunyou cut the call mid-sentence, his heart beginning to race as he realised what was at stake. Ignoring his foot that screamed in protest, he half ran, half limped to the door, bursting through at great speed, almost knocking an officer over as he ran down the corridor. He needed to speak to his boss, he needed to speak to General Terekhov.

Ten minutes later and Colonel General Terekhov burst through the doors into the ops room, Captain Lunyou, hot on his heels, sweating, as fresh blood now seeped through his bandaged foot. Seeing the head of the FSB in their midst caused some of the officers to flinch and look up, already wondering what had got the man who they'd nicknamed the lizard, out of his lair. Only General Kuzmin looked up amusedly, although both men were the same rank, as Commander in Chief of Southern forces, (CinCS) he outranked the FSB commander, and as such had nothing to fear. Not so for the rest of his staff, and all looked on uncomfortably as he strode up to the CinCS, who smiled thinly at him, the barest trace of cordiality in his voice.

"So, despite the rumours the FSB do occasionally come out of their offices. To what do we owe the pleasure *General?*"

Ignoring the barb, General Terekhov pointed to the map, his finger resting near Godbury.

"We have military units of a highly classified and sensitive nature in those woods. I want you to place that area under the highest priority and dispatch units to protect it at all costs."

General Kuzmin raised an eyebrow at the tone, looking at where the FSB commander was pointing, before replying forcefully.

"Highly sensitive nature? Classified? And if they are that important, then why is it that I am unaware of their existence?"

The FSB General smiled back venomously, clearly the CinCS was paying him back for withholding the shipping manifest earlier and was now fishing for information. Trying not to rise to the bait, he answered the question with another question.

"I was assured by your staff the location would be safe and secure. Now I find it is not. May I ask what has happened in the meantime? Are we not after all on the offensive? Or are we no longer following the orders of our superiors?"

General Kuzmin clenched his jaw in irritation, it was a dangerous game to play, the FSB could make his life difficult back home, and the last thing he needed was Terekhov gunning for him. But he was in charge, and the way the FSB commander had strolled in and barked out an order had rankled. Plus, his soldiers would see it, nobody followed a weak leader, and already he was aware of the eyes of his subordinates watching him closely awaiting his reaction. Firming his resolve, he doubled down.

"I'll ask again General Terekhov, what is in those woods that is it so important? We have no record of any units there, so please enlighten me as to what it is that you would *like* me to protect?"

Terekhov looked around the room, seeing everyone looking back at him. Inwardly cursing as he knew he'd already said too much, he should have approached the fool in his office, now everyone in the room knew something was there. Angrily he shot back.

"Will you allocate me the resources or not?"

"No, I will not." the CinCS replied firmly, his resolve hardening. He stepped forward and lowered his voice as he continued. "My priority is to stop this counterattack, not to waste the lives of our soldiers defending empty woodlands. Perhaps if you'd seen fit to tell me in the first place about Project Houdini, we might not have had this problem."

"But there are vital units there!" Terekhov shot back, his voice rising as the anger and tension began to surface.

"Fine! Tell me what type, and who they are and I'll listen!" the CinCS shot back, his own voice rising. The tension in the ops room had suddenly risen, now even with the emergency going on around them, soldiers, sailors and airmen had all stopped what they were doing to watch. Seeing he was not going to win, Terekhov looked around angrily at them all, his face finally coming back to the CinCS.

"You're a bloody fool!" he snarled, loud enough for only the CinCS to hear. He turned and stormed out of the ops room, leaving Lunyou open mouthed. The CinCS glared back at him, waiting for him to go. After a few uncomfortable seconds it was the General who broke the silence.

"Usually when the master pulls on the lead, the dog follows."

Captain Lunyou took the hint, throwing up the sloppiest of salutes, with the barest trace of respect as he hobbled from the room to chase his boss.

Out in the corridor, the FSB General was already halfway down the corridor, speaking rapidly into the phone as Captain Lunyou painfully stepped into pace beside him. He stopped suddenly, catching Lunyou off guard as he almost ran too far forward, turning to the Captain his face filled with fury, he held the phone to his chest, whoever was on the other end could wait.

"Project Houdini, I want it all shutdown for now, the whole operation. Get Vikram to pack up what he can and get out now. Anything he can't take with him he's to destroy. We can't take any chances."

Saluting, Lunyou turned and hobbled away down the corridor, stopping suddenly as the General Terekhov quickly added, his voice threatening. "And Lunyou! If this does comes back to me, it'll come back on *all* of us...your father won't protect you from this."

Both men looked at each other, the threat clear as with renewed energy Captain Lunyou nodded and limped away. There was still time, he could still stop it...

Headquarters Yeovil Town Centre

Fergus looked up as the runner burst into the ops room, breathless and sweaty. Seeing the Colonel he rushed up to him, saluting quickly before bursting out excitedly,

"Sir, Major Christie told me to tell you that the enemy are falling back in their sector, it looks like they're giving up!"

Fergus shook his head, damping the young man's optimism. "I doubt that son, more likely they're withdrawing to hit us elsewhere. Was there anything else in Major Christie's report?"

The young man shook his head, the words deflating him slightly as he remained standing to attention.

"Very well, report back to Major Christie, there's no change, she's to remain in her position for now, be prepared for a counterattack, these bastards can come at any time. Understood?"

The runner nodded, repeating the order out of habit before throwing up another salute and quickly dashing out and up the stairs.

Watching him go, Fergus couldn't help but remark how young the soldier had looked, feeling his age almost immediately. Smiling at the enthusiasm of youth he glanced back over the map, looking over to his Sergeant Major who seemed to read his thoughts as he asked,

"You're still thinking that they're going to attack again?"

"Yes, they must, they've already committed, otherwise why waste time and resources pulling back and allowing us the time we need to breathe? It doesn't make any sense."

"I don't care for the reason," the Sergeant Major countered, "all I care about is that the fucking artillery has stopped. Already half the town's blown to hell up there." He nodded to the stairway and Fergus realised he hadn't been up to look yet since it had begun. Guiltily, he wondered if his own home was one of those that had been flattened in the bombardment. Without working radios, he had no true way of knowing just how bad the artillery strikes had been, only that they had seemed to peter off and cease. Perhaps the Russians had ran out of ammo? he thought, quickly dismissing the idea as nonsense. He'd learned a lot about the Red Army, and the one thing they always had was lots of artillery. Like his Sergeant Major had said, for now, they'd stopped, and that was all that mattered.

Fergus looked over to another of his soldiers, a Sergeant, who was now in charge of keeping the chain of runners going between the HQ and the forward units. One of them had been stationed around the phone box, their only lifeline to the outside world. The Sergeant was busy applying a first field dressing to one of the runners' arms, who was injured by shrapnel in the last bout of running through the bombardments. The runner would live, it wasn't a life changing injury, but it would leave a nasty scar. The young lad grimaced against the pain, Fergus wondering himself how many of those under his command would live to carry the scars into later life. Pushing the dark thoughts from his head he looked to the Sergeant.

"Still no more updates on when these reinforcements will arrive?"

The Sergeant looked up glumly, pausing in his work.

"Not yet Sir, all we know is to have the radio on and listening out on the given frequency."

Fergus looked over to the High Frequency Radio that had been dropped off by motorcycle last night. It was already on and another of the soldiers trained in its use was sitting with the headset on, patiently waiting to hear something over the constant hiss of the static.

The Sergeant continued, "The callsign we're to listen out for is Whiskey One-Zero, should be coming through sometime today. We're to answer up as Whiskey Zero."

"Whiskey One-Zero..." Fergus repeated to himself softly, before looking over to the radio operator.

"Anything on the frequency?"

The operator lifted the headset from her ear, the hiss of static clearly heard as she shook her head.

"Nothing yet Sir, I can hear a lot of radio traffic, but it's scrambled, so all I'm hearing is white noise."

Fergus looked back to the Sergeant, remarking, "Of course, it's encoded. If we don't have the right code, how are we to hear this Whiskey One-Zero?"

"That's simple Sir, we were told they'd be transmitting in clear, once they get to us, they'll give us the codes."

"If they get to us," the Sergeant Major replied laconically, everyone turning to look at him. Fergus smiled confidently, his voice booming out.

"Now, now, Sergeant Major, let's think positively, shall we?"

Sergeant Major Macdonald looked guiltily at the map, not having intended for his private thoughts to have been said so loudly.

Fergus looked back to the Sergeant. "Make sure that all our units know to identify what they're firing at. If we do have friendlies coming in, the last thing we need is a blue on blue."

Nodding, the Sergeant waved over another two runners, writing out orders on paper before sending them away with a confident smile and pat on their shoulders. Already he'd sent three of them to their deaths through the barrage, the cost of which he had yet to think about. For now, like everyone else, he was concentrating on his task at hand, the grief and pain could come later, much later.

Operations Room Three, Southwest Division, Wonderland Operations Centre (WOC)

Colonel Stephens was busy marking the latest progress of Whiskey Three-Zero on the mapping when he turned to see the CDS stood in the doorway, watching the organised chaos as everyone worked around him. The LEWT team were busy, it's four operators were typing away on their computers, sending the fake transmissions that a battlegroup was to transmit if it existed and in battle. Each message would be sent in code via powerful antennae arrays to Whiskey Three-Zero's tank, where it's modified HF radio would secretly resend out the message on high power, easily identifiable by the enemy.

He stopped what he was doing and asked, "Everything okay CDS?"

The CDS smiled, replying, "Yes, Colonel, I just wanted to come down and let you to know we've received word that enemy forces are halting their attacks and pulling back. Intel is showing a redeployment of units into the southwest. It's working! The plan is working!"

Colonel Stephens remained tight lipped. Sensing his doubts the CDS continued.

"Didn't you hear me man? I said it's working! The attacks have stopped. We can finally get reinforcements into those areas! It's buying us the time we need! Well done!"

It had only been that morning that the CDS had finally revealed the plan to Colonel Stephens.

It had been two days since General Boswell and General Kew had flown out from the WOC to assume command of the defence forces, with General Boswell in the north and General Kew in the south. In the north, the enemy were already pushing deep inland, threatening to decapitate Northern England from Scotland, with General Boswell salvaging what he could from the Catterick garrison and mounting a series of delaying operations, trying to buy the time he needed for other units to form defensive positions. In the south General Kew was forced to scrape together 15 Air assault brigade out of Aldershot and what was left of 2 Mechanised Brigade from Tidworth but could ill afford to wait. Already a huge offensive was underway stretching from Yeovil all the way across the south coast of England to Worthing. The Russians were pushing towards London, and with the capital already under control of the Quisling government everyone knew the capital would fall without putting up much of a fight. General Kew's only option was to try to stop them where he could. And that's exactly what he was trying to do, his units were desperately rushing forwards to reinforce the defences of Winchester, Salisbury and Horsham, but had been delayed by the huge log jams of refugees who were streaming north out of the beleaguered cities. If the Russians had been allowed to continue unopposed with the assaults then they would have overrun the cities defences long before General Kew could have made a difference. Now, with Whiskey Three-Zero acting as a diversion, it was buying the CDS and General Kew the time they so desperately needed. In sacrificing the few, the CDS had hoped to save the many, including London.

"If it's all the same to you CDS, I'd rather not go pat myself on the back just yet. I understand why we're doing it, I know it's for the greater good and I'm glad it's working. But I'll be honest with you, it's still a hell of a bitter pill to swallow."

The CDS nodded, the smile vanishing as he replied. "Come now Colonel, we both knew there was going to be a price to pay. We're at war and there'll be more blood to shed before it's over!"

The Colonel pointed to the mapping.

"Well they're not dead yet CDS, they're still in it, in fact we have their current location here, on the three-six Easting."

"Lasting longer than I gave them credit for," the CDS remarked, the smirk vanishing, quickly replaced with unease as he realised what he'd just said.

"CDS seeing as the plan has worked, perhaps we can stop the radio messages? Perhaps even give Whiskey Three-Zero a chance to get out of there?" Colonel Stephens asked hopefully.

The CDS began shaking his head before the Colonel had finished speaking, replying, "Afraid not Colonel, there's still a chance the enemy could discover the ruse, turn back around and carry on as before. No we've tied our goat to the post, like it or not, we now have to wait for the lion to eat it."

Sensing the sudden discomfort between them the CDS excused himself.

"Right, I have to go, the PM has his new cabinet flying in shortly. Inform me immediately if there's any change to the situation."

Colonel Stephens watched him leave, the feelings of bitterness and regret eating at him. Quickly he scolded himself. "Come on man, pull yourself together! You're a bloody senior officer! You have to make the tough choices! You don't even know those bloody soldiers. Get a grip!"

Steeling himself to the task he continued to work, ignoring his doubts. The CDS was right. The goat was already tied to the post. There was nothing he could do about that now.

Whiskey Three-Zero

Mike was sad to see the Apaches leave as they finally reported they were bingo fuel, with just enough to make it back to wherever they were going home to. Mike waved overhead as they flew low and slow over the tank a mere 5 metres above them. The downdraft was immense, even Smudge felt it, sat in the confines of the gunner's station as they passed. Mike watched them fly northwards, wishing them luck, not totally certain of their chances of making it back. They still had a gauntlet of enemy positions to fly through. Gunslinger Two-Three had made him smile, the pilots reporting back jovially that out of the two units, they knew which one they'd rather be on, and wished him luck all the same, adding that they thought *his* chances of making it back were probably worse.

Ten minutes later and the tank was sat in another fire position overlooking one of the many sleepy small Dorset villages in the distance, as Patty and Changa pushed northwest through a large thick forestry block. They'd been forced to push further north than they would have preferred thanks to the terrain, and they needed to cover distance quickly. Mike had constantly been badgering everyone since they'd lost the Apache cover with the mantra, "Don't get fixated, just get moving." With the two Talons behind them covering them from the east, Patty and Changa were now their northernmost callsign. Mike's unit was approaching the Easting that he'd been ordered to get to, shortly he'd swing them all north, towards the safety of Yeovil.

It was Smudge who broke the silence.

"Boss! I've got eyes on a convoy of trucks coming towards us out of the woodline."

Mike leaned forwards, his head in the sight, seeing three familiar olive drab trucks appear into view, identical to the one they had captured. They were pushing out of the woodline that Patty and Changa were pushing through, about 600 metres away and heading across the tanks front. They were heading at speed, trying to race away, the cloud of dust being thrown up behind the lead truck was making it difficult for the trucks behind to follow.

"Want me to engage them?" Smudge asked, already laying the gun sight onto the lead truck and tracking it, selecting the coax machine gun. All Mike had to do was give the order and he'd fire.

"Not yet." Mike replied, seeing there was no cover for the truck to hide in for at least another mile down the road, they still had a few minutes to spare. He keyed the radio.

"Tango Two-One, Tango One-One, be aware, I've got eyes on three trucks exiting the woodline at speed, looks like you've got enemy units in that woodline, proceed with caution, over."

Mike waited for a response, as he followed the progress of the trucks, wondering who they were and what they contained. After a few moments of silence, he keyed the radio again. Perhaps Patty was in a comms blackspot.

"Tango Two-One, Tango One-One, acknowledge my last."

Still silence, nothing. Mike followed the progress of the convoy, they were now halfway down the track, still at least a minute away from disappearing into cover. Seeing he had the time, he looked down, pressing the pressel to check the radio was transmitting, the earlier HF radio problems still fresh in his mind. Seeing the small TX light flick on, he stood back up, just as the radio burst to life, Changa's voice coming through, the Fijian sounded different somehow.

Tango One-One…Tango Two-One-Alpha, Tango Two-One is currently on the ground."

What? Mike thought to himself, what the hell is Patty playing at? We need to keep moving!

Seeing the trucks were now almost out of sight, he ignored the message and looked down to Smudge, tapping him onto the shoulder.

"Okay, fuck waiting any longer, clear to engage, coax, truck!"

"ON!" the gunner replied.

"Loaded!" Baz shouted, checking the L94 chain gun was ready to fire.

He was about to order fire, when Patty's voice came back over the radio, his tone urgent.

"Tango One-One, check fire check fire! DO NOT ENGAGE THOSE TRUCKS!"

"DISENGAGE!" Mike yelled, not meaning to shout as loudly as he did, the confusion and surprise of the message had thrown him.

He looked over at Baz, who wore the same confused expression.

"What the fuck?" Baz exclaimed, as Patty's voice now came through loud and clear.

"Tango One-One, Tango Two-One, I need you at our location immediately."

Confused, Mike replied immediately, trying to hide the frustration at not knowing why he'd stopped, or why he'd called the check fire.

"Tango Two-One, no, we need to keep moving, we don't have the time to stop."

"Tango One-One, you need to see this, you *really* need to see this."

Mike could hear the desperation, almost sadness in the Corporal's tone, whatever it was, it must be important he thought, as finally he replied.

"Ok, we're on our way now, out."

He was about to get Bill to reverse when Patty added.

"Tango Two-One continuing, and bring Linda, she needs to see it too."

Now Mike was really baffled, why would Patty want the journalist there?

Keeping his confusion hidden, he looked across to Spider's vehicle, seeing the commander looking over in the turret, his arms raised in bewilderment. Mike nodded in response as he answered over the radio.

"Tango Two-Zero, I'm as confused as you are, let's get the Talons and Wasps in overwatch on our positions, then join us at Two-One's location, let's see what he's found in the woods today."

He heard Spider acknowledge, and disappear back into the turret of the Warrior, as Bill began to sing, "If you go down to the woods today..."

"Knock it off Bill!" Mike snarled, as turning, he guided the driver backwards, taking them off the high ground and turning around to follow the Warriors tracks. He hadn't meant to sound angry with his driver, he just didn't like surprises, and from the sounds of it, Patty had one lined up right now...

5

It's Not What You Think

Wonderland Operations Centre (WOC)

General Catmur busied himself pouring another glass of water and sat back, listening to the conversation as the cabinet meeting continued on around him. The General hadn't wasted any time, as within hours of the new PM's cabinet being chosen, he'd had the military race out and pick them up, bringing them all back, some came with their families, some alone, to join them at the new HQ. The irony wasn't lost on him, he'd spent years planning Wonderland to be the country's best kept secret, and now within 48 hours, almost all the new cabinet knew of its existence. Now, the newly assembled government was holding its first Cobra Meeting, not that any of them had any answers, as for now, the fledgling government seemed to be struggling just to keep its head above water. Following the attacks at Chequers and Downing Street, with some of the MP's siding with Samuel and his illegal premiership, the PM had found the normally large pool of MP's in his party now almost empty. Struggling to fill the senior roles, he'd been forced to ask members of the opposition to form a temporary alliance. Some had questioned it's validity, "Didn't this need to be ratified in the House of Commons?" they'd argued, to which the PM had replied, "The House of commons is now nothing more than rubble and dust, as will this country be if we all sit idly by and do nothing." That simple answer had been enough to galvanise them into action, without hesitation. He sipped at the water, listening in, waiting for his cue to re-join if needed and re-reading his notes.

Already the Chief of Police had briefed them on the situation in London. It didn't look good. He'd told them that his contacts in the Met had warned him that the Quisling government, as it was now being called, had come down hard on anyone not accepting the belief that this was anything other than a terrorist attack, perpetrated by rogue factions of the military. Already the Met was tearing itself apart, having officers arrested or relieved from duty, if any disagreed, or questioned the situation too much. The government that everyone had become used to seeing on their TV screens, or hearing on their radios, was now all gone, replaced by faces they'd hardly seen, or voices they'd never heard. With the lack of available information, and fear rife on the streets, people were listening to even the tiniest of rumours, facts be damned. And, even with the rescue efforts in central London still ongoing, the Quisling PM and his phantom government were already urging members of the public to take to the streets and voice their displeasure at what had happened. Attacks on members of the military around London were increasing, with the police doing little, and in some cases nothing, to stop them. The barracks at Horse Guards had been attacked, a large group of protesters had smashed through the gates and set fire to some of the buildings, making the most of the fact the barracks were empty, almost all the soldiers were at the various attack sites helping the rescuers.

Now a large anti-monarchy protest was planned for later that afternoon, no doubt hoping to harness the fear and turn it to anger, galvanising the people into action. The anti-monarchy voices were getting louder, and already the PM could see the problems coming over the horizon. The CDS had to admit, it was a masterstroke of planning. With nearly 9 million people in London, if they were convinced these attacks were the King's idea all along, then no number of soldiers would be able to contain the anger and uprising that would surely follow. The simple truth was that they were losing control of London, and with everything else going in the country, they would soon be faced with a cold choice. Concentrate on trying to stop the riots with troops they didn't have or concentrate on trying to save the country and leave the capital to sort itself out. The CDS looked up, jarred from his thoughts as the Foreign Secretary stood to brief the room on his recent meeting at NATO. He'd only just arrived back from Brussels, flying in on one of the RAF's two-seater Typhoons, still wearing the flight suit.

"I'm afraid the news isn't good Prime Minister, NATO are still refusing to take sides, at the moment all they're demanding is that both sides end the hostilities."

The PM sat stone faced listening on, as the new Defence Secretary scoffed, "Refusing to take sides? End the hostilities?" His voice rising as he added, "Dammit Simon, did you explain to them that we're the ones being invaded? And they just want us to cease hostilities, and simply let the bastards walk on in? Dammit, we're one of the founding fathers of NATO, we bloody helped to start it! What was the bloody point of it all if not for this? We need their help NOW!"

The Foreign Secretary nodded, barely concealing the irritation in his voice.

"Of course, I bloody well said that Bob, why the hell do you think I offered to fly there straight away? But look, as far as they're concerned NATO was set up to defend against attacks from non-NATO members, not settle what they see as an internal struggle between two competing governments. They're dealing with two UK governments, both of which swear they have legitimacy. So, which one do *they* listen to? We're calling for assistance from NATO, whilst that bloody turncoat in London is saying that they've asked for assistance all along from Tumat, a NATO member, and that *we're* the aggressors! As far as they're concerned the UK is in the midst of a civil war."

The Defence Secretary shook his head angrily at the mention of civil war.

"And of course, the Americans haven't helped our cause." All eyes now turned to look at the Chancellor, as she continued. "What with their President going silent on us, and refusing to condemn Tumat, it's almost giving NATO a green light *not* to listen to us."

"Bloody Americans! Happy to start all this off, then sit across the Atlantic and watch us fight amongst ourselves from a distance!" the Defence Secretary growled.

"Well, if we'd have spent more on the military budget to begin with, as my party were constantly suggesting, then perhaps we wouldn't now be reduced to standing with the begging bowl out!" the Home Secretary blurted out.

More people voiced their thoughts, until the room was alive with people arguing and shouting across from each other, the tension in the room rising as the different party policies and historic rivalries began to be dredged up again, each blaming the other for the current state of the country.

The PM said nothing, watching it going on around him, the tension reminding him of the earlier meetings when he was the Defence Secretary. Now, he was the PM, this was his ship, and it was down to him to steady it. Hearing enough, he stood up to address them all, attempting to calm their tempers and nerves.

"Everybody please, let's just quieten it all down for a second."

The conversations stopped immediately, all eyes turning towards him. Inwardly he smiled to himself, thinking that he'd never been able to have that effect on his previous cabinet meetings, but now things were different. Now people were scared. Clearing his throat, he continued,

"The US President was always going to be in a bit of pickle over this. If he agrees with us and condemns Tumat, then he's admitting that one of the most powerful leaders in the world was fooled by a foreign power, ignoring all along his own intelligence services, that's not the sort of thing that gets you re-elected. I don't think we can expect him to comment any time soon."

He saw the heads nodding in agreement as he continued.

"We have to be honest here, the Russians so far have outsmarted us at every turn, to have infiltrated NATO and taken it apart from the inside was a smart move. They've incapacitated all of our NATO defensive agreements and bought themselves the time they needed to invade, all whilst under the pretence of helping us. The world's underestimated them, we've underestimated them, and unless we do something quickly, we'll pay the price for it."

He looked over at the CDS, sharing a knowing glance. Before the meeting, both had already agreed not to divulge any details of how Operation Fools Mate had come about to the new cabinet. For now, they could all think the plan had been conceived by the Russians.

"So, what are you recommending Prime Minister?" the Defence Secretary asked, eyebrows raised.

The PM leaned forwards, hands resting on the table as he addressed them.

"I haven't called you all in today so that we can sit here and look for someone to blame, or moan about countries and organisations that *won't* be coming to help us." He paused, letting the words sink in before continuing,

"Instead, I've assembled you to help us fix the problems we have, and right now as I see it, amongst the insurmountable list of problems we face, there are two that stand out as the most important."

Everyone in the room sat up, looking intently at the PM as he stood back up and continued, counting the fingers into the palm of his hand as he spoke, his eyes blazing passionately.

"One, we do what we can, with what we have to stop them militarily, using our own forces and not waiting for NATO or the U.S, or any other country to come to our aid."

He scanned the room, waiting for questions, sensing none he continued.

"Two, we win the information war, we show the people of this country and the world what's really going on here. The Russians have already muddied the waters, already we have some of our people believing the tripe that Samuel and his Quislings are pushing out. With all the events in London these past 72 hours, we're already losing London from the inside, because we're simply not getting the information out to the public fast enough."

The Ministers shared looks with each other as the PM looked around the room.

"Those, Ladies and Gentlemen, are the two most important problems to fix right now. We fix those first, and then we can concentrate on the other things, but for now we *must* concentrate on those two issues, and those two issues only!" The PM banged his fist onto the table as he spoke, causing two Ministers sat closest to him to flinch in surprise. There was a silence in the room as they all digested his words. His demeanour relaxed slightly as smiling the PM added.

"Now with that in mind, I'd like to hear how *you're all* going to help me to fix them."

Sitting down the PM nodded to the Defence Secretary, indicating it was time for him to speak, who taking the cue, stood to address the room. The PM relaxed back in his chair, looking over to the CDS who smiled and nodded appreciatively at the way he'd spoken.

The PM nodded back, happy with how it had all played out, secretly he'd been expecting a lot more friction or hostility, but the way they'd listened to him made him think that perhaps his Chief of Staff had been right, perhaps he could do this after all. There had been a third matter to deal with, and that was the problem of what to do with the King and Queen. But the PM didn't feel the need to share this with the Cabinet, not yet at least, until they had something more concrete to go on. He'd seen the reports that they were still being kept prisoner in Buckingham Palace, and the CDS had already outlined a plan to break them out. But the thing that had stayed the PM's hand on giving the operation a green light, was the fact these wouldn't be enemy forces holding them there, they'd be members of their own police force, perhaps not even knowing themselves the true scale of what they were doing. The thought of sending their own special forces against members of the police horrified him, and for now, the plan was to be kept on hold and it's problems were not for the ears of this meeting. The PM put his private doubts aside, as he sat back, hands clasped across his chest and listened. Finally, his cabinet were beginning to pull together.

Whiskey Three-Zero

Mike had Bill follow the Warriors tracks through the woodline, not wanting to drive down the track that the trucks had used, for all he knew, they could have mined the road on the way out. He ducked low as tree branches whipped close to the turret, looking behind him to warn Spider of the same, the commander putting his hand up to acknowledge in thanks in the Warrior following behind. Already they had the Talons and Wasps out in overwatch, their eyes and ears to the outside world, whilst their attention was drawn to whatever was in that woodline.

After a few minutes Mike saw the centre of the woodline begin to thin out, and emerged suddenly into a large open area, at least the size of a football field, hidden in the centre of the wood. In front of them he could see green army tents, some trucks, and stretchers lying on the floor. Over to his right sat a large box body truck, the back of which looked blackened and smoking, as if it had recently caught fire. Behind the truck sat a hastily dug trench, and Mike could see it was already half full with large piles of ash, some of which was being carried away into the trees with the wind.

"There they are Sir, over there."

His gaze was distracted as he looked over to Baz, who now had his head out of the open loader's hatch and was pointing to where the two Warriors were parked. Both of their back doors were open, and he could see the crews were running to and from the Warriors and over to the track that led out of the woods. Over on the far side were bodies on the floor, he saw Doc by them, directing the soldiers, clearly organising something. Patty was off to the side, looking over and waving Mike to come forward.

What had happened? Were they shot by Patty? They looked to be civilians, Mike thought. Knowing he wouldn't get the answers remaining in the tank, Mike drew the tank closer, before stopping, picking up his rifle from the back of the hatch as he looked to Baz.

"I'm jumping off, keep the engine running, ready to go, we won't be here long."

Baz nodded as Mike added, "Off comms," removing his head gear and helmet.

He stretched his legs as he stood up, looking around him as he stepped down and off the tank, both knees bending as he almost fell forwards, the ground was soggier than he thought. No sooner had he landed when Patty was next to him, his face a mixture of shock and surprise.

"Well, what's so important we have to stop?" he demanded, stretching his aching muscles.

Patty swallowed, looking like he wanted to be ill. Mike looked at him confused, what had made him like this? he wondered. Looking around he could see more of the scene, numerous tents and trucks and stretchers. On the ground, discarded in piles lay blood-soaked bandages, and large white medical boxes. Mike had seen them before, being used to transport sensitive medical equipment, or blood samples, or organs. Perhaps that's what this was, perhaps they'd stumbled upon a field hospital.

"Is this a field hospital?" he asked Patty, questioningly.

Finally, Patty gathered his thoughts, shock replaced by a mask as he looked on stone faced, reporting,

"I don't know what the fuck to call it." Seeing the puzzled look on Mike's face, Patty continued.

"We came upon them almost immediately; they must have already been packing to leave when they obviously heard us and got spooked. By the time we were in the clearing we could see some of the trucks were already pulling out."

Mike walked past him over towards the track, the Corporal following, as he continued.

"We were about to fire on the trucks, when someone in the back began throwing these out."

Mike looked down open mouthed as he could finally see what the soldiers were working on. Five bodies were lying in various states on the floor, all looked to be unconscious, some sporting older injuries, some fresher ones after being flung unceremoniously from the truck. All were in civilian clothes, and all were tied up, similar to how they'd found Catherine and her party on the second night. Mike looked on aghast at the callousness of it all. Human shields? Is that what they were doing? Were the Russians using human shields? he thought. Suddenly it dawned on him, he looked up to Patty remarking,

"That's why you called the check fire? I'd have opened up on trucks carrying these people."

Patty nodded; his face still wore the stone-faced expression as he replied, his voice low, almost whispering.

"That's not the worst part."

Mike followed on as the Corporal walked away from the throng of people and back towards the trucks out of sight of the others. Walking around the back of one, he climbed up the tailgate and flung open the flap. Inside the darkened interior Mike could see the image of tangled legs and feet sticking out, the smell of sweat, vomit and excrement making him gag. He held his hand over his mouth and nose to fight it, as he climbed up, counting seven people lying in the back, all tied up.

As he stood there, Patty walked over to the other trucks, flinging the back canvas open, revealing their grisly cargo. All of them contained people, all were unconscious, all restrained. It was eerily similar to the truck they'd captured. As he was looking, Linda came running over, her voice interrupting the scene as it trailed off.

"Hey Mike, Spider says you want.....Holy Shit! What the fuck is going on here?"

She stood open mouthed, gagging as the smell hit her, Mike jumped down quickly, as he looked around counting the trucks out loud, shaking his head in disbelief.

"There must be what? Six trucks here, with about seven to ten people in each, that's nearly-"

"Fifty-three." Patty interrupted him, "There's fifty-three people in the trucks. I haven't told Doc or anyone else about them yet, he doesn't know, I've told him they're empty, which is why he's still over there helping the ones on the ground. I just didn't know what to do... there's so many, and we don't have the time, which is why I wanted you to see for yourself. Perhaps you could think of something..."

Mike looked back over to where Doc was now organising the medical care of the others, already their bonds had been cut, and he was carefully laying out the casualties, getting the soldiers to bring water bottles and pouring water over the people. Patty was right, they didn't have enough time or resources to look after everyone, remembering it had taken Linda and her group nearly six hours to recover from whatever the Russians had used on them. He looked back towards the tents, wondering to himself, what the hell was going on here? What were the Russians doing to these people? Seeing the shellshocked look on the NCO, Mike nodded, placing an arm on his shoulder.

"You did the right thing Patty, Doc doesn't need to know about any of this yet. Now let's see what the fuck is going on here."

Pointing to the tent he asked, "Have you been in there yet?"

The NCO shook his head, "No, I didn't want to leave the trucks in case someone came over."

The three of them left the misery of the trucks and quickly jogged over to the tents, all of which were linked together, looking from above like the shape of a crucifix, all leading into a large central tent. Linda stood back, as with weapons raised both men pushed through the canvas flap of the first into what looked like a doctor's surgical tent. After a few moments Mike's voice came from within.

"It's clear Linda, come on in."

She stepped through to join them, seeing inside the brightly lit room as a fluorescent set of overhead lights lit the tent up, casting an unnatural white light that made everything seem so vivid. Somewhere outside a generator could be heard running, powering the facility. In the middle of the tent lay an empty stretcher on a wheeled gurney, recently scrubbed clean. The floor of the tent had a hard plastic floor that led through a set of double plastic doors into the tent beyond. Along the far wall of the tent were a collection of surgical scrubs and a stainless-steel sink off to the side, with various liquid soaps waiting to be used and boxes of blue latex gloves. The other side of the tent had stainless steel cupboards and drawers, some were left open, the contents thrown haphazardly onto the floor. A computer was lying on the floor of the tent, dropped in haste, its screen smashed and lying on its side, surgical scrubs and gloves were thrown on the floor, trampled as the wearers made their escape. Everything about the scene pointed to a hasty exit, and Mike wondered what the hell they were running from. Was it the arrival of his unit, or was it the guilt of getting caught doing whatever it was they were doing?

All three of them said nothing, the apprehension and fear of what they may find keeping them silent, as Mike walked forwards through the plastic doors into the central tent, his weapon raised again in case of any unwelcome surprises, his mouth opening in shock and horror at what lay within.

He was about to warn the others not to come in, but before he could say anything they were inside. Patty drew a deep breath in shock as Linda blurted out, covering her mouth with her hand in reflex as she exclaimed.

"God almighty! What the fuck?"

The central tent looked like it could have doubled up as an operating theatre of any major hospital. The room was brightly lit, and from the feel of the temperature it was air conditioned to help combat the heat from outside. Around the edge of the theatre sat more cupboards and drawers, no doubt containing the various surgical implements that would be required when conducting operations. In the centre of the room sat seven large operating tables, around each one the various monitors and computers needed to perform whatever surgeries the surgeons required. But it wasn't the coolness of the room, or the equipment within that had shocked them all. It was the seven bodies lying on the operating tables, all cut open and abandoned midway through surgery. They could see the chests of each one rise and fall as the life support systems kept them alive, with their chest cavities all open, the ribs pulled apart and the scissors and sutures still attached as pipes pumped out and pumped in all the fluids necessary to keep the bodies alive. Blood had pooled on some of the tables and was slowly overflowing, dripping onto the plastic floor, slowly spreading outwards. Mike had no idea if they were looking down at men or women, as all the heads were covered in a medical cloth, and the faces all covered with large oxygen masks, the controlled breathing of the pumps and the drips of the blood on the floor being the only sounds they heard. They were all snapped out of their grim inspection as finally Linda spoke.

"Organ harvesting."

Mike looked over at her, shocked as she pointed over to the white plastic medical box near one of the tables, inside was a large pile of ice, and a white bag ready to accept its latest cargo. He was about to speak when Patty disbelievingly asked.

"Why? Why would they do that?"

Mike looked around the room, a look of disgust on his face as she answered.

"I saw the same thing happen in China, prisoners, or people that the regime just deemed unfit to live, were sentenced to death using sham trials, then their organs were sold on to western companies. It's big money if you know how to do it properly." Her voice trailed off as she realised this would have been her fate had their own truck not been stopped. She looked at the bodies again, her journalistic stern facade beginning to crack as she looked sorrowfully down at them all, realising that one of those lying there could quite easily have been her.

Patty walked forward, bending forwards and vomiting off to the side as he saw the state of one of the bodies. The others remained tight lipped, as quickly wiping his mouth, he looked over at them both.

"What should we do? Do we try to wake them up? Do we call for Doc? What?"

"There's nothing you can do." Linda replied, pointing to bloody lumps sat in bags on the tables, whoever they are it looks like they've already had their kidneys and livers removed. They're dead already, it's just the machines keeping them alive.

Mike walked up to the first table, looking down at the macabre scene of misery that lay there, the mechanical lung breathing for it. He looked down at the body, tempted to pull away the cloth, to see if it were male or female. He stopped himself, the guilt and shame of what he was about to do, staying his hand. What if he knew them? What if seeing the face made it personal? No, he wouldn't want to know. He didn't want to know any more than he cared for knowing their name.

Forcing himself to look away, Mike firmed his mouth, looking around the room then thinking of the trucks outside. Suddenly it hit him. A look of horror crossed his face as he exclaimed. "Jesus Christ! That's what all those people outside are here for! That's why they weren't killing their prisoners, they were bringing them here to butcher them for spare parts! It's a bloody factory!"

"But what do they do with them once they're finished?" Patty asked, already fearful of the answer.

Pointing to the far door, Mike growled, his voice low and angry. "Let's go through door number two and find out."

Leaving the poor souls on the tables they walked through the far doors, coming to another tented open area, with what looked like a large scrub down area, On the far wall was a shower head, with four gurneys underneath. All were covered in blood and bandages and other grisly detritus, appearing to have been waiting to be cleaned. Mike guessed that after the harvesting, the bodies were left out here and dumped off the gurneys and onto stretchers to be carried outside, whilst the valuable operating equipment was cleaned down and made ready to be used again. He looked outside at the sunlight that streamed through the canvas, already worried what he might find if he opened the flap. With a heavy sense of dread, he lifted the canvas, the sunlight causing him to blink as he found himself looking at the box body truck that he had seen earlier. It was twenty metres away, and he remembered seeing the piles of ash, which was now being picked up in the wind and blown back towards him. He'd been expecting the smell of fresh air and blinked in surprise as the acrid smell of burning flesh hit his nostrils. He closed his mouth out of habit, not wanting any of the ash that hung in the air to enter it, the others doing the same. He followed the plastic tracked floor, already marked by the footprints in ash of the people before them as they made their way down to the truck and to the box bodied area.

The truck was on six large wheels, larger than the others and had been driven into an excavated hole in the ground. Now instead of towering over them, it was at ground level, allowing easy access to the soot covered box body. Off to the side lay a pile of green fabric stretchers, all discarded carelessly. On the side of the box body Mike could see eight doors, resembling oven doors and cautiously he tapped the bolt on the door handle with the back of his hand, checking it for heat.

The others looked at him expectantly, sensing what was to come, and seeing it was hot, but not too hot to handle, he tapped open the door and peered inside.

The heat escaping from the truck's interior caused him to flinch as the gases shot out, followed by the smell of burnt hair and flesh, causing Mike to exhale and turn his head, waiting a few moments. After a few seconds he took a deep breath and held it, taking his torch from his assault vest and peering inside.

"What is it?" Linda asked impatiently.

After a few moments Mike withdrew his head, paler than before and shaking it in disbelief as he quickly exhaled deeply, closing the door again, turning to face her.

"It's a crematorium and giant crusher all in one. It looks like when they were finished with the bodies, they threw them into here. There's what looks like a jet engine mounted in there. I'm guessing at the temperatures it burns at, the bodies turn to ash and the crusher takes care of the bones, leaving nothing to identify them."

Open mouthed Linda watched as Mike walked to the back of the truck, looking at the huge hole that had been dug, the pile of ash and crushed bones was already half way up it and then looking at the pile of stretchers. He lowered his head, closing his eyes in shock and sadness, as he realised, they were looking at the remains of so many people. Keeping his jaw firm, he said in a solemn voice, "It looks like when the truck's full they just tip the back up and empty it into the hole."

Patty shook his head in disbelief, shock turning to anger as he punched the ground in rage, spitting out.

"Those fucking bastards! Those evil fucking bastards!"

Mike bit his lip in thought, trying hard to keep his own emotions in check. He'd seen evil before, but not here, not like this in his own country. He'd heard all about the atrocities that were going on in other countries, he knew war was atrocious, he'd seen for himself how it could make people do terrible things, but this, this was another level of butchery. The way it was set up, the clinical efficiency of it all reminded him of the time he'd visited Bergen Belsen. The cold blooded and ruthless way the Nazis had turned the slaughter of millions of people into an industrial product, hair for clothing, gold teeth for jewellery, even bones ground down for glue. It was sick, it was barbaric, and now it was happening here in the U.K.

Suddenly he realised, the country would need to see this, the world would need to see this. But how? They were in the middle of hostile territory, and time was not on their side. His eyes opened wide as he realised, someone had tried to cover this up, they were in the process of destroying it all when Patty had stumbled upon them! Now they'd been stopped from doing so, they'd have to resort to more extreme measures. Whoever was in charge would do whatever they could to shut it down and destroy the evidence.

He turned, startling Linda as he shot his arms out, grabbing her by her shoulders.

"Hey what the-" she exclaimed as he cut her off.

"Linda, grab whatever you can, phone, tablet, note pad and pen, I don't care, but you need to report on this right now. We don't have much time, perhaps three to four minutes to get it all documented. Can you do that?"

Her demeanour relaxed as she quickly thought it through, the reporter in her realising the breaking story that she now had in front of her.

"Three to four minutes? Come on Mike, that's impossible! I need at least an hour to get this documented."

He shook his head, tapping his watch, "The world needs to know about this Linda, and you've got about the same amount of time it'll take the Russians to realise we're here. I reckon on three to four minutes before they're dropping a shit load of artillery on us. Whoever's in charge of this didn't have time to shut it down, we've stopped that. Don't you see? Now, they'll want to bury this and us with it. Now do you want this story or not?"

She nodded her head in thought, quickly weighing up the options, before finally relenting.

"Okay, Mike, okay, I'll get it done, but my phone battery is almost dead."

"Use mine!" he shot back, rummaging in his pocket and throwing it over to her giving her the passcode.

Mike waited for her to run off before turning to Patty, who eyes were full of tears and rage.

"Patty, I want you to get Doc and the guys loaded back onto the vehicles, tell them to leave the wounded where they are, tell them I've told you there's a specialist team being flown in to extract the wounded."

The Corporal's face turned from anger to disbelief as Mike's words sunk in.

"You want me to lie to them?"

Mike swallowed, knowing he was breaking one of the strongest bonds of the military code. Trust.

"No, you're not lying to them, I am. I'm telling you now that I'm going to phone this in, and you're going to be following my orders. There's going to be a Cas Evac arranged in a minute. It's inbound and will be here shortly."

"But you just said we've got three to four minutes?"

Mike merely stared at the NCO as he swallowed and thought it through, looking around him at the vehicles. Already more crews were dismounting and helping Doc. In a few moments they'd all be out, and then it would be even harder to get them re-mounted, how can you tell soldiers to leave wounded people behind, especially if you just found out what had been going on with them. If they stayed, they'd all die. It finally dawned on Patty what Mike was ordering him to do. It was a hard choice, but it was the right choice.

He exhaled loudly, the tension almost evaporating as the decision was finally taken away from him. Ever since coming across the facility he'd been wracked with guilt and anger, not knowing what to do. Now the Captain had taken the decision off his shoulders. He nodded again, thankful to only be a Corporal.

"Right Sir, I'm on it." He turned to leave, Mike stopping him, addressing him by his rank and not his name, needing the NCO to understand the importance of the order.

"Corporal, keep them away from the tents and the other trucks, tell them they're empty and contain hazardous materials. No-one except Linda is to go in there. I don't want anyone else to have to see that."

Patty nodded in understanding, his voice almost resigned. "Of course, I guess it'll only be me you and Linda who get to carry these demons today."

Mike nodded, his own face glum.

"I'm afraid that's the responsibility of rank, Corporal, and you'd better get used to it, because those demons, they only get larger and heavier."

The young NCO grimaced in reply and nodded, before turning to race away.

Mike watched him go, about to take the satellite phone out and call it in when something stopped him. A thought he suddenly had. He knew they were all on borrowed time, but before he could call it in, he still had one thing to do, something he couldn't leave behind. Turning, he ran quickly towards the noise of the generator, finding it easily enough, huge power cables ran out in all directions to the tents, all he had to do was follow them back to the source. Flinging open the control panel he located the switches to turn it off, his hands resting on the big red power button, all he had to do now was push it. Pausing, he looked back towards the operating tent, the guilt eating at him inside for what he was about to do, thinking of the seven people, already dead, but mechanically clinging for life. Closing his eyes, he uttered a brief prayer.

"I'm sorry, I'm truly sorry, I hope that your loved ones can forgive me."

He punched hard on the button, the generator engine gave a last gasp as it fought to stay running, until finally, with a hiss and a click it stopped. For a few brief seconds he could hear the alarms of the life support machines begin to go off as they lost power, the noise fading quickly as the final watt of electrical power was used. Now all he wanted to do was to get out of there, as pulling the satellite phone out, he dialled the number and waited...

6th Div HQ Bovington

General Terekhov looked up from his desk as Captain Lunyou suddenly burst into the room, talking animatedly on a mobile telephone. He was about to shout at the young officer for the abrupt entrance, when seeing the strained look on the Captain's face, he ignored the incident and watched on as the Captain walked over to his desk.

"Vikram, calm down, yes, I'm in the General's office now, I'm passing you over now."

He reached out and handed over the phone, the General looking suspiciously back at him as he took the phone and began to speak.

"Yes, what is it?"

"General, it's Vikram, we've got a major problem here."

"I gathered that, otherwise why else would you be disturbing me?"

"We've been discovered already, we've had to abandon the facility, but we've managed to save some of the stock-"

"Did you destroy the facility?" Terekhov interrupted, angrily.

"No, there was no time, the enemy were on us in a matter of minutes. We only just managed to make it out ourselves. We've got the whole team, but we've had to leave our equipment behind. We need to do something and quick."

"Where are you now?" the General demanded, reaching out for a notepad and pen.

"We're 500 metres away in the village, we're watching the enemy soldiers now."

The General closed his eyes, silently cursing the fool. Dr Vikram Ahuja might have been at the top of his medical profession in India, but when it came to common sense, he wasn't exactly at the top of that list.

Keeping his voice low the General hissed.

"You're supposed to be away from there! There's an enemy Battlegroup on its way to you, what if you get yourself captured? Get yourself away from the area immediately, you're not a soldier Vikram!"

Dr Vikram's voice sounded encouraging as he countered.

"Oh, but it's okay, it's only one tank and a few armoured vehicles, they're not chasing us, they're still all in the woodline."

Confused, Terekhov looked up to Captain Lunyou, both soldiers thinking the same thing. There was supposed to be a lot more of the enemy there, that area should be flooded with enemy troops by now. But only one tank, and three infantry vehicles?

"Vikram, in your own words tell me exactly what you can see…"

In the HQ the CinCS was watching the updated positions on the board as the fresh units raced forwards into their new positions. He nodded satisfied at the speed with which Colonel Golgolvin had pushed his two companies south. Already they were set, waiting for the lead elements of the enemy armoured units to appear. He looked on, his face creasing in disappointment at the progress of the other units. The 77th was slowly pushing north out of the Dorchester whilst the 75th Tank Regiment hadn't even made it out of the docks. He angrily made a note to personally visit both units after all this was over, their CO's needed to understand the importance of how Russian commanders were expected to operate. If they needed to be made examples of, then so be it.

He heard the FSB General coming into the room, the doors being pushed to their stops as he looked up irritated. What now, he thought to himself.

General Terekhov had a triumphant look on his face, as clutching a piece of paper he strode up to the CinCS, leaning in close and whispering.

"There is no enemy tank company Igor, no enemy counterattack. You've been fooled…again."

The CinCS frowned at the use of his first name, looking down into the eyes of the FSB officer, at 6ft 2 he towered over him, but even though the man was smaller, the power he wielded was terrifying. He stared back into the cold dark eyes, seeing the twinkle of malice there as he asked, keeping his voice low.

"And how do you know this?"

Terekhov thrust the paper towards him, the CinCS looked down, reading it as Terekhov relayed.

"The FSB units you failed to protect have now been over run, but some are still alive and have reported back with eyes on the *enemy Battlegroup*."

He paused, letting the words sink in as he then slowly added,

"One tank…..three infantry fighting vehicles…..about twenty men in total. I'd say you've got the broken remnants of one of those units you let slip away three days ago."

The CinCS took him by the arm, leading them over to the far side of the room, out of earshot of the others, turning to face him, his eyes burned fiercely with rage at the mention of him being at fault. He continued to read the report, finishing as Terekhov lashed out, his words like daggers as he kept his voice low.

"You've stopped the offensive... you've rushed out units that are not yet fit for deployment...you've committed our forces to block an attack that isn't coming...all for nothing more than a broken platoon of rag tags, whom I suspect are probably trying to do nothing more than to get back to their own lines. I wonder what Moscow would make of all this?"

The CinCS looked around suspiciously as Terekhov threatened him, checking again that no-one else was listening in. Satisfied it was just the two of them he waited for the FSB officer to finish, before replying, his own voice low.

"Okay, so what now?"

Terekhov nodded in silent triumph. Finally, he had him where he needed him.

"Now, no-one needs to know about your mistake. It will stay between the two of us. I'm head of the intelligence department, so for now, this phantom Battlegroup can still exist, I'll personally sign the reports to say it's turned around and gone back east with its tail between its legs. We'll simply say that the sight of the 77th and the 75th in the field has scared it off without a shot being fired. Our soldiers will love the story, the victorious Russian troops stare down the cowardly British, who at the first sign of battle, turn and run."

The CinCS nodded, his anger beginning to die down as he asked.

"OK, and what will this cost me Terekhov?"

A thin smile spread across the FSB commander's lips as he replied,

"Simple, on that piece of paper are a set of co-ordinates. I want you to fire every piece of artillery we have at it, until there's nothing left.

The CinCS looked at the co-ordinates, glancing up to map again, remarking.

"That's pretty close to the village of Godbury, civilian casualties will be-"

"Of no concern of yours," Terekhov interrupted, "I want the village destroyed as well, every brick torn down, every living thing there killed. I want *no* witnesses."

The CinCS stared up at the map, then back at the FSB commander, weighing up the options, his head thinking through the alternatives. If Moscow found out what had happened, he'd be made the laughing stock of the Russian Army, his command would be forfeit, his family name discredited, and worse still he'd be sent home a national disgrace that would last for generations. He knew that, as overall commander, it all rested on his shoulders. As painful as it was, he knew that bastard Terekhov was right. He had him by the balls, it was far better to be called heavy handed and a monster, than a fool and failure.

He looked over to one of the artillery officers, calling him over.

"You there! Major, get the following co-ordinates out to our guns, priority one target. All other fire missions to be put on hold."

"Sir?" the Major replied, the puzzled look in his face quickly replaced with one of surrender as the CinCS barked out.

"Just do it! No questions! Get the guns firing as quick as we can, it's time critical!"

The Major disappeared to get the orders out, as the CinCS turned back to Terekhov, handing him back the paper, his voice suspicious.

"Well, Terekhov, I've done my part, now let's see you do yours."

Smiling, the FSB General said nothing and turned leaving the room, leaving the CinCS staring back after him suspiciously.

Let him sweat, Terekhov thought viciously, walking into the quiet corridor, the sounds of the ops room fading away. He picked up the mobile, dialling the number.

"Vikram, move your ass and get yourselves away from there. Get yourself back to where we met two nights ago."

"What about the facility?" he demanded.

"In about four minutes there won't be any facility, now get your ass moving!"

"But our equipment! General, you can't just destroy it! We need it!" the voice shot back.

He kept his voice calm as he replied,

"Vikram, forget all about the bloody facility and the equipment, for now I want you to take your team and the remaining stock we have back to where we first met.

"Dorchester? You want me to meet you back at Dorchester?"

Terekhov sighed, "Dammit Vikram, do you have to constantly repeat what I say over the phone? What if someone is listening in! Yes! Dorchester! Now MOVE!"

"Why back to Dorchester?" Vikram argued back.

Terekhov looked at his watch anxiously, knowing the seconds were ticking by. If the doctor didn't move soon, he'd get caught in the incoming fire. He was tempted to hang up on the man, but knowing the doctor, he'd stubbornly remain where he was and call him back, wasting more time. Realising the only way to get him moving was to put his mind at ease Terekhov shot back.

"What does Dorchester have Vikram?"

"I don't know, I've never been there on holiday." the doctor snapped back irritably.

Terekhov's anger began to rise at the tone of the doctor as he continued, trying to keep his voice calm.

"A *hospital*, it's got a hospital Vikram, complete with operating tables, scrub down facilities and wards. Giving you all the equipment you'll ever need."

"Oh." was the simple reply, as finally hearing enough his temper got the better of him.

"Now if it's not too much trouble...MOVE YOUR FUCKING ASS!"

He hung up the phone, and angrily stomped back in towards the HQ, thinking to himself.

Problem one solved, now time to work on problem number two...

Whiskey Three-Zero

Mike was still chatting on the sat phone as he ran over towards the vehicles, towards the shouting. He could see something was going on down by the trucks. Spider and Patty were there along with some of the soldiers and some of Catherine's group. It looked like despite their efforts; the others had finally discovered the human misery in the trucks.

He ignored it at first, needing to send the report, but could hear voices rising as people now began to shout at each other. Realising he'd be needed there, and soon, he quickly added to the person on the phone,

"Look that's all for now, we'll get the intel over to you as soon as we can, but just be aware of what's going on down here, I've got to go."

Not waiting for a response Mike hung up the phone and quickly stowed the antenna, throwing the satellite phone back into his chest pouch.

He ran down, barging his way to the centre of the group, his voice raised as he looked accusingly at all of them.

"What the fuck's going on here! Why aren't you all loaded up and ready to go as I ordered?"

Spider stepped forward, his face showing the confusion at the order.

"Sir, Patty says we're to leave these people here as they are, is that right? Are we leaving them, because that doesn't sound right to me?"

"No fucking way!" Arnie stepped forwards angrily. "we're not leaving them here; we need to take them with us."

"But we can't wait around for them to come round like last time!" Patty pleaded, as Arnie argued back.

"You waited for us! Now you just want us to leave these people to die. Ask yourself what the fuck are you lot fighting for?"

"He's right Patty, we can't just leave them!" Spider remonstrated, agreeing with the police officer.

Suddenly the group were all shouting over each other again, everyone trying to talk over the other.

We don't have the time for this, Mike thought angrily as he held up his hands for silence, finding it having no effect, he finally had to admit defeat and shout over them all. The years of being a Sergeant having to be dug up again.

"QUIET! he yelled; his glare murderous as even Arnie was stunned to silence.

They all looked towards him, as keeping his voice loud he angrily shot back.

"Some of you are supposed to be soldiers, or do I have to remind you of that?" His glare fixing on Spider who looked away embarrassedly.

"Soldiers follow orders, they don't have the luxury of questioning them! Now, Corporal Patterson is correct, we're loading up to get the hell out of here, in case you've forgotten we still have an enemy out there who want to kill us!"

"But what about all these people?" Arnie interrupted, Mike glaring furiously at him.

Mike looked around the group, hearing the mutters and muted conversations, mostly agreeing with Arnie. He knew that if he wasn't quick it could escalate. He raised his hands again to silence them as he replied.

"I've already reported this up the chain, they're sending out a specialist medical team to evacuate everyone that's here. We don't have the lift capacity to take them all with us. Now Linda's just finishing up in documenting what she's seen here, so that we can get the message out. People need to see what's happened here. But we need to get moving...NOW!"

"If we're in such a hurry, how are the medical team going to get here in time?" Catherine's voice sounded from the back.

Mike thought quickly, the lie coming off his lips quicker than he could stop it.

"Our new orders are to distract the enemy forces, make them chase us towards Yeovil, pull them out of the area, give the medical team the time it needs to get in and safely evacuate everyone. But it's time critical, to make this work we need to move now! Standing here arguing about it will waste time, time we don't have."

"Where are these medics coming from?" Spider asked suspiciously. Mike shot him a frustrated look, exasperated that one of his own NCO's would be the one to argue. He was about to reply when Patty stepped forwards, his face flushed red with anger.

"Spider! For fucks sake what you playing at? You know better than to question an officer. If Captain Faulkes says they're coming, then they're coming. Now, is anyone else here wanting to fucking argue the case or are we going to get going?"

Spider looked at his friend with surprise at the way he'd suddenly jumped to Mike's defence.

Mike was somewhat taken aback by the sudden change in the Corporal himself. Usually, it was Spider who was the pit bull, barking and shouting, and Patty the thinker, but now the roles appeared to have been reversed, Patty stepping up to the plate when Mike needed help the most. Perhaps it was what he'd seen in the tent, perhaps it was the crematorium truck. Either way Mike didn't care, he was just happy to have someone back him up, as, seeing there were no more arguments the Corporal clapped his hands together, shouting as the other NCOs began to take charge again and restore order.

"Come on then! Chop fucking chop, move your asses! You heard the Captain, let's get loaded up and ready to go, Commanders make sure you do a head count before we pull out. COME ON MOVE!"

Mike breathed a sigh of relief as the group finally began to disperse, the soldiers running back to their vehicles as Patty seemed to shake them from their protest, bullying and cajoling them into action. Only the police officers remained, following the orders of their boss as Catherine made them climb one of the trucks to try to check on the sleeping bodies in the back. As they worked, Catherine watched on as Mike jogged away the short distance and had a brief conversation with Patty, who looked up at Changa and nodded in response. It wasn't long before he was back at the trucks, pulling her down to talk.

"Look Catherine, you can't stay here, and I can't order you to come with us, and I certainly don't have the time to explain. So, it's a simple choice. You come with us now and you might live, but if you stay with these people, you'll certainly die."

She looked around pointing to the trucks and the medical tents as she scoffed.

"That's a bit final, isn't it? What is it about this place that's got you so spooked? It looks like just any ordinary field hospital to me, that's what you call them isn't it? Field Hospital?"

He ignored her question, almost pleading with her.

"Look Catherine, it's not what you think, this place is dangerous, and we can't stay here."

"But what about the medical team you just told us about?"

He clenched his jaw, as he hissed, angry that still the Police Officer didn't grasp the danger they were in. Finally relenting he admitted the truth.

"For fucks sake Catherine, there is *no* team! I lied to get people moving. Any second now and the Russians will launch an artillery strike on this place. Now are you still staying here or not?"

She looked around horrified at all the bodies in trucks, before turning back to look at him, angrily, keeping her own voice low.

"You bastard! You've already condemned them all to die."

Mike clenched his teeth as he replied, forcing himself to keep his voice low.

"They're dead already! Nothing we say or do can change that. The only thing we can do is keep our group together and hope to stay alive. Now we've already come back for you twice, there won't be a third time. Are you coming or not?"

She pulled away from him, her own face barely containing the anger within.

"Oh, so *now* you're counting the times you save us, are you? Hoping to use it for later for brownie points? Keep the police Chief sweet and maybe later in life it'll pay off?"

"I didn't mean it like that!" he snapped back. "Look we're wasting time here! Are you coming or not?"

"Oh, just piss off and leave us to it!" she snarled.

She turned to walk back to the truck, almost walking into Changa who was now behind her, blocking the way. She gave a startled shock of surprise at seeing him there, clearly, he'd snuck around behind her whilst Mike had distracted her. The Fijian was looking almost apologetically at her as she barked.

"What the hell do you think you're doing? Move!"

"I'm sorry Ma'am" he replied, his voice low as he reached down and slowly took the assault rifle from off her back. She was about to fight back when she felt the rifle barrel at her back.

"Please don't." Mike threatened.

She was numbed into submission as she looked behind the Fijian at the truck as Patty and Jonah now disarmed the rest of her officers of their weapons, before manhandling them out of the truck at gun point, causing one of the bodies inside to fall out.

Mike grimaced and cursed loudly as it hit the floor with a dull thud, landing in an undignified heap. It wasn't supposed to be like this, he thought angrily, why can't people just bloody listen! He shook his head, watching as the police officers were dragged away cursing and shouting into the back of the Warriors. Mike had no intention of keeping them prisoner, he just needed them safely in the vehicles.

The Doc was another who had to be dragged away from his patients, upon seeing the other casualties he almost went apoplectic, shouting to anyone who'd listen about his hippocratic oath to save lives. Mike watched on sympathetically as he was dragged off by Spider and Fletch, cursing them all, his shouts fading as the vehicle's door closed behind him.

Without wasting any more time, he ran up to the tank and was about to climb onboard when Patty came running back over, his face flustered.

"Sir, everyone's mounted and ready, but we're two people missing."

It never rains...Mike thought moodily as he looked on expectantly.

"It's the two civilians, Tim and Colin, it looks like they've done a bunk, they must have run off when we were all arguing by the trucks."

Mike looked about him at the woodline, hoping to see them running back, then quickly looked at his watch and looked skywards. Already they were pushing their luck, it had been four minutes now, and still nothing. He shook his head angrily before replying.

"Leave them, we've wasted enough time, now they're on their own. Let's get the hell out of here!"

Patty nodded solemnly then turned to run for his own vehicle, needing no further prompts. He wanted out of there as much as Mike did. The place seemed to reek of death, and the sooner they were gone from this horror the better.

Mike quickly jumped aboard and into the cupola, far faster than he had meant to, startling Smudge who was sat chatting to Baz. Both soldiers looked over curiously, not understanding why the sudden rush as Mike struggled with his head gear, his fingers clumsily fumbling with the clasp as he rushed what he was doing.

"On comms!" he reported hurriedly, before sticking his head back out of the turret, not wanting to waste any more time.

He looked over to the other vehicle commanders, all were looking back at him, giving him the thumbs up signal that they were ready.

He keyed the radio, the urgency in his voice plain to hear.

"Tango Two-Zero, any enemy activity from Talon?"

Come on, come on, he muttered to himself as he waited the precious seconds for Spider to reply.

"Negative, Tango One-One, Talon reporting all clear."

Good, at least no-one was waiting to ambush them, he thought as he transmitted to everyone.

"All callsigns, break out to the north, best speed, forget your order of march until we're clear of the woodline. Move now, move now!"

"Ok Bill, let's move, let's go, go, go."

As the tank began to move, Baz closed his hatch over and asked over the I/C.

"Boss what it is? What did you find out there? What's got you so spooked?"

Not knowing what to say Mike just looked across the turret at him, the silence and look on his face probably more telling than words could ever be. Baz nodded in understanding, sharing his own look with the gunner before both turned away to begin scanning with their weapon sights, leaving their commander alone with his thoughts.

Mike watched as all the vehicles began to move away from the open area and back towards the woods, resisting the urge to glance skywards, fearing that he'd see the rounds falling amongst them already. He counted down the seconds in his head as the vehicles accelerated away, some having to turn to avoid running across the bodies still lying on the floor. Mike looked away, not wanting to see them, his guilt at leaving them already eating away at him. At the count of 20 they were at the treeline, at the count of 40 they were through and pushing into the open ground. At the count of 120, Mike had them stop and form up into fire positions, sensing they were far enough away that they were out of danger for now. The vehicle gunners scanning their fronts as the commanders all looked over at the tank, all wondering what Mike was doing, keeping them waiting there. Only Patty knew the reason, and he'd kept that to himself.

Mike was watching, caught between the thought of being right, and condemning the people left behind to die, to have been wrong, and having lied to the soldiers for nothing and leaving them behind. He could be wrong, he thought to himself, there might not be any artillery at all. His thoughts were interrupted as Spider's voice came over his headset, his tone suspicious.

"Tango One-One, what are we doing waiting? I thought we were supposed to be a distraction for the med team?"

Fuck! Mike thought, like he really needed to be reminded of that right now.

He was about to reply when suddenly a flash hit the open ground between the woodline and the village, followed by another. The sound reaching them seconds after impact, the shock waves thudding through the armoured vehicle. Mike felt sure that the 70-tonne tank was being rocked as suddenly there were more explosions, increasing in intensity as the barrage began. At first it was mud and rocks that were flung skywards, as the rounds impacted the open fields, but then the barrage began to move towards the woodline, the rounds falling amongst the trees, as they were flung hundreds of feet into the air, as if nothing more than matchwood. Mike could see the devastation being rained down, already smoke was rising from the centre of the woods. Suddenly one of the truck's fuel tanks must have gone up as another larger explosion, rang out and a huge column of yellow flame and smoke mushroomed skywards.

Mike closed his eyes, saying a silent prayer to those they'd left behind. He had never been a religious man, never felt the need to be, but right now, feeling as low as he did, if someone upstairs was watching on and willing to offer a hand, then he'd take any help that he could get...

6

End Of the Honeymoon

Wonderland Operations Centre (WOC)

The PM leant forwards, his elbows on the table, listening intently to the plans being put forward. Already they'd heard from the Defence Secretary, then the Foreign Secretary. Now it was the turn of the Home Secretary, Sir David Gingham who was animatedly discussing with Sir Charles the best course of action as to how to get the country's communications up and running again. Without communications, they were deaf and blind to the outside world. The PM content to sit and listen as Sir David began to counter what Sir Charles had just proposed. The PM grew ever more disappointed at the Home Secretary and his constant negative outlook. Everything seemed to be answered with either impossible, or not enough time, or out of the question. Sir David seemed to take great delight in offering more problems than answers, and as the PM was about to stop him, he noticed Colonel Stephens outside the room, waving frantically over towards the CDS.

He wondered what was so important as to disturb the meeting. The CDS saw the gesture and looked over to the door, quickly thinking the same. Seeing he had been noticed, Colonel Stephens held the report aloft, indicating its importance. The CDS ushered him in, quickly putting a finger to his lips before the Colonel had opened the door.

Keeping as quiet as possible, Colonel Stephens entered the room, ignoring the conversation and walked up to him, bending low he began,

"CDS, we've just received the following sit rep from Whiskey Three-Zero via satellite phone."

"You're still betting on our goat then Colonel," the CDS muttered softly, as he took the report.

The Colonel kept his face stern, simply replying with, "I think it best if you just read the report."

Surprised by the Colonel's curt tone, he began to read the report, his forehead creasing in concern as he took in what he was reading. After a few minutes he'd finished, he looked back at the Colonel, his face showing his astonishment.

"Good God! Can this be possible?"

"Captain Faulkes believes so."

The CDS removed his glasses and rubbed the bridge of his nose, the shock at what he'd just read in the report making him look unsettled. The PM noticed the change in him immediately, and thankfully stopped Sir David's latest whinge by holding his hand up.

"Everything okay CDS?"

Seeing he was now the topic of the meeting, and realising he'd better explain quickly, the General firmed his jaw, stood up and walked over to the PM, handing over the report.

"My apologies for the interruption Sir, but I think you need to read this."

The PM took the report, his face quickly turning to horror as his eyes scanned over the page. In disbelief and shock, he stood up staring vacantly at the table for a few moments before realising everyone was watching him, patiently waiting for him to share the news.

Still stunned by what had been revealed, the PM addressed the group.

"My apologies everyone, I'm just a little taken aback by what I've just read."

Quickly composing himself, the PM picked up the report, reading it aloud to the room.

"One of our units reports coming across what at first they thought was a large medical complex in the area of Horseshoe Wood, near the village of Godbury." He paused as the CDS used a laser pointer to highlight the area on the map on the far side of the wall, before continuing.

"Elements of the Russian Military were in the process of evacuating and attempting to destroy the facility when callsign Whiskey Three-Zero was able to stop them and take control of this facility. Upon further investigation it was found that it was not a medical facility but was instead setup with the purpose to harvest organs from both prisoners of war and civilians that the Russians had captured, and commander Whiskey Three-Zero found seven people mid operation, with organs removed in the facility's operating theatre. A further 53 people were found outside in trucks, tied up and unconscious, believed to be awaiting further harvesting operations."

The Cabinet exchanged horrified looks with each other, some muttering under their breaths, cursing as the PM continued.

"Further investigation has found a truck, believed to be a mobile crematorium utilising a jet engine and crusher for fast body disposal, and a burial pit, already half full. Commander Whiskey Three-Zero's assessment is that the facility has been running for at least the past 24 hours, and estimates that already in the region of 100 to possibly 150 people have been disposed of there."

The PM looked around the room, the faces looking back were a mixture of shock, horror, bewilderment and anger.

Finally, the Defence Secretary broke the silence.

"This Whiskey Three-Zero, who are they?"

The CDS answered, "My apologies Sir, I haven't had the time to brief you yet on the current military situation on the ground. From the beginning we've had some of our military units scattered to hell all over the invasion areas, some we're in contact with, others not. Whiskey Three-Zero is one of those units we're still in contact with. I've had them running a diversionary attack, allowing us to get other units out of the area safely." The CDS paused, unwilling to divulge the latter part of the plan, instead sounding more upbeat as he deflected, "They're under orders to head north, back to friendly positions once finished, I've had them placed under the command of Colonel Stephens here."

Looking over to where the CDS now pointed it was the PM who addressed the Colonel.

"Is Whiskey three-zero still at this....facility?"

Colonel Stephens looked back at the CDS for direction, not sure whether to tell the PM that they were fully prepared to sacrifice the unit. Seeing the gaze of the CDS he remained tight lipped and instead shook his head apologetically as he replied.

"No Sir, Whiskey Three-Zero's commander believed that the facility was under threat of imminent destruction. He's got an embed with him who he's had document and report what she could, but he was certain they only had a few minutes to pull out."

"Embed?" the PM asked curiously, as the CDS intervened.

"It's what we call the embedded journalists Sir, I believe Whiskey Three-Zero has a young journalist by the name of Miss Linda Harding with them." Looking over to the

Colonel for confirmation who nodded. Upon hearing the journalist's name the PM's Chief of Staff Sonya spoke out from the other side of the room.

"Forget embed, you should have called her the pain in the ass"

The PM turned to look at her, enquiring, "You know her Sonya?"

She looked back, her eyebrows raised as she replied laconically.

"So should you! She's the woman that helped torpedo your leadership race last year. Do you remember, the allegations? She was the lead journalist that ran the story."

The PM pinched his lips in irritation at that particular memory from last year, quickly realising that with everything now going on, he'd gladly swap all of what was happening to be back to last year. Not wanting to dwell on it further, he quickly countered.

"Okay so this embed, she's what? Taken video footage? Done a report? What?"

"I believe PM that Whiskey Three-Zero's commander has instructed her to take photographic and video evidence, as well as take a computer that they found. He was quite keen to get it across to us."

Sonya spoke out, her tone dripping in sarcasm, "And no doubt Miss Harding will be keen to make sure *she's* the one whose reporting this."

The meeting was interrupted as a Major entered the room and ran up to Colonel Stephens, whispering into his ear. The Colonel looked shocked as he looked to everyone and clearing his throat he began.

"We've just had it confirmed from Whiskey Three-Zero Sir, the site's just been eradicated by enemy artillery, there's nothing left of it."

"But what about all those people?" Sonya asked open mouthed, "did they get any of them out?"

The Colonel remained tight lipped as finally it dawned on her what had happened as she looked back to the PM, remarking, "That's bloody murder!"

The PM ignored her outburst, rapping his fingers on the table in thought. Suddenly he looked up at the CDS.

"CDS, I want that evidence. I don't care what it takes, but you're to secure that evidence for us. Top Priority."

The CDS nodded, leaning over and conferring with the Colonel as the PM continued to explain to the Cabinet, his voice sounding hopeful.

"If this was as bad as Whiskey Three-Zero is reporting, and we have the video proof, then we need to shout it from the rooftops, show the country and the world what these bastards are doing here. Taint the credibility of Samuel and his cronies in London, this could be the smoking gun we're after, this could be the way to help solve our second problem."

Everyone nodded in agreement, as the PM sat back down, looking to Sir David, his tone solemn.

"Now Sir David, I believe you were just in the middle of explaining to me how, with Sir Charles's input, we *can* get the country's communications working again so that we *can* now share this crucial new piece of evidence with the rest of the world?"

Seeing the determined look on the PM, Sir David's protests and complaints died in his throat. Instead, he swallowed, stood up and continued where he'd left off, but this time with a more positive outlook. This time they could get it done, this time nothing was to be left off the table.

Operations Room Three, Southwest Division, Wonderland Operations Centre (WOC)

Everyone looked up as Colonel Stephens burst back into the room, hurriedly running over to the LEWT team and looking over at Captain Reinhardt.

"Cancel the signals dump! Stop sending!"

All four of them looked at each other, the Captain breathing a sigh of relief, thankful to longer be killing their own side as the Colonel continued,

"We've had a change of plan, instead of a diversionary tactic we now need to assist them in getting home."

He walked over to the mapping, quickly finding their location on the map.

"Right, let's try to put everything we have into convincing the Russians that our phantom Battlegroup is pulling back, let's have it heading east out of the area, try to pull the enemy away from where they really are."

With renewed vigour the team all began to work around him as he studied the map, breathing a sigh of relief, thankful at last to be helping Captain Faulkes's unit, and not setting them up for destruction.

Whiskey Three-Zero

Mike sat in mute rage, watching the destruction rain down on the village. He knew the facility was going to go, he'd only just finished talking to the ops room over the phone as the barrage had intensified further. But then when he saw the barrage change direction, and begin creeping towards the village, he felt sure it would stop. He'd watched open mouthed in disbelief and horror as the rounds had smashed into buildings, killing civilians and destroying everything they came near, clearly done deliberately. He'd watched in disbelief as the village had been flattened, it's church steeple had been the final structure to fall, leaning over, tipping out of sight, disappearing into a plume of dust and smoke.

Then just as it seemed the worst was over, his eyes were drawn skywards, watching as twelve black missiles streaked in high overhead, each one splitting into smaller clusters, their warheads falling amongst the village and the woods. With a ripple of explosions, the cluster munitions exploded amongst the rubble and trees, igniting large fires. Mike guessed they were incendiaries, by the way the flames leapt up and began to consume everything they touched. Already the woods were ablaze, the fires spreading outwards towards the fields, being blown by the winds. The village was now obscured by the thick black smoke, as the fires raged unchecked through the rubble. He couldn't hear any screams though, perhaps they were too far away.

Why the hell did the Russians feel the need to obliterate the town, he thought. At least they had the evidence with Linda. That had to count for something now, especially as so many innocents had died to cover this up.

Spider's voice came back over the radio, causing Mike to look over. Even from this distance he could see the confusion on his face.

"Tango One-One, what just happened? What about the medical team? What about all those civilians?"

Mike closed his eyes, wishing there was another way out of this, knowing it was all on him, he took a deep breath and keyed the radio, his response more cutting than he meant it to be.

"Tango Two-Zero, you've got eyes, work it out. You can see just as well as I can what's just happened. They're gone. Now let's just leave it and get out of here. Tango One-One OUT!"

He looked down at the map, about to issue the orders on where to go next, when Spider's Warrior reversed at high speed and came racing over towards them, stopping in front of the tank, blocking its way. He could see Spider was already fighting with his headset, almost tearing it off his head as he angrily glared at him, climbing out of the turret and jumping down.

Oh no, thought Mike, not now, of all the times and places, not now. We really don't have the time for this!

"Off comms!" he shouted angrily, tearing the headset off, leaving his bewildered crew to watch his boots exit the hatch, as he raced off the turret, not wanting to get caught, still sitting back in the hatch. He jumped down off the tank, no sooner had he landed than Spider was on him, pushing him back against the tank, both hands grabbing his smock roughly.

Mike held both hands up in surrender, putting up no resistance, letting the anger pour of the NCO as he yelled, the spittle forming at his mouth.

"DID YOU FUCKING DO IT? DID YOU FUCKING CALL IN THE ARTILLERY? DID YOU JUST KILL ALL THOSE PEOPLE?"

"What?" Mike looked on confused, he'd thought Spider was angry about being lied to.

"Hang on wait, you think I called it-"

He was cut mid-sentence as Spider threw a punch, his right fist connecting with Mike's cheek. Mike was so pre-occupied with what Spider had said, it caught him off guard, not realising the threat until too late. The punch was good, and for a few seconds Mike saw stars as dazed, he fell to his knees, groggily shaking his head as he fought to clear the haze. He felt his jaw, wincing at the pain as he felt Spider grab him again, pulling him back up to his feet. He wasn't finished with him just yet.

"Spider wait, listen to me-" was all he could manage as the NCO cocked his arm back to punch again. He could see the anger in his face, knew his rage would prevent him from listening to reason. Spider threw the punch, but this time Mike was expecting it, he ducked low and backwards, feeling the air pass over head as the arm passed harmlessly above him, his own hands locking onto the outstretched arm, just behind the elbow. Shifting his balance Mike pivoted his own body, using the tank to spring off, positioning his right foot behind Spider's, throwing his right hip into Spider's back, feeling the yell of shock as he deflected the energy of the punch and threw him backwards and onto his back. Spider was down for only a second before the shock turned to anger again, Mike was forced to step sideways, creating space for what was to happen next. With teeth barred, Spider crawled back to his feet, raising his fists as his body adopted the pose of a boxer, snarling at him.

"Come on then you murdering bastard! Let's see what you've got!"

Mike didn't want to fight him, everything about this was all wrong. But he also knew that until either Spider won, or was beaten, he wouldn't begin to see reason, and Mike wasn't going to just lay down and take a beating. He'd already mentally beaten himself up enough about what was happening, he wasn't going to let someone else do the same physically. Shaking his head, half-heartedly he crouched into the semi judo position, remembering the lessons painfully taught to him in Ewen's gym, but also remembering Patty telling him all about Spider being their Regimental boxing champ and handy in a bar brawl. This wasn't going to be easy.

Off to his right he could hear Jenks shouting down from the turret.

"Spider! For fucks sake! Stop it! He's our Captain!"

Ignoring him, Spider stepped forwards again, ducking and weaving, shifting forwards onto his leading foot, feinting with a couple of left jabs. Mike had seen it done before; Ewen used to like using them in their sparring sessions. At first Mike had been caught off guard by the jabs, but now, they were easy to read. He kept his own stance neutral, not reacting to any of the dummy punches being thrown, concentrating on reading his opponent's face and watching his shoulders and feet, that was where you'd see the real attack coming from.

He saw the left shoulder flinch and come forwards, this was a real one, Mike ducked backwards, out of range as the fist came forwards, missing his head by inches, but Spider was quick, and no sooner had the left swung past than the right was following, Mike had to sidestep away, the punch almost connecting as the speed caught him off guard again. He could have punched over the extended right hand, a clear shot at Spider's face, or taken a cheap shot to his ribs, but Mike didn't have the heart. He knew why Spider was angry, and in a way, he could sympathise and understand his rage. Instead of throwing a punch he kicked at Spider's right knee, causing it to buckle, with the NCO already over extended, he collapsed onto the ground. Mike stepped backwards, not sure how long either of them could keep this up for. Lying face down in the mud, Spider shouted out a curse, punching the ground in despair before slowly making his way to his knees, looking backwards at Mike, his eyes murderous.

"Stop fucking dancing around and fight me!" he spat out, turning again to rush him. Mike tensed, about to defend again, when he became aware of someone else rushing in from behind. With a sense of dread, he turned to face the new threat, just as Changa and Patty came rushing past him, their looks focused on Spider. With a howl of protest, Spider went down hard as Changa rugby tackled him to the floor, Patty quickly grabbing his outstretched arms as all three of them rolled on the floor.

"Get off me!" Spider yelled, as in silence, Patty and Changa dragged him to his feet, pinning him back against the side of his Warrior. He tried to struggle for a few moments, yelling and shouting, cursing them both, until finally realising it was futile, he stopped and went quiet, his chest heaving as he glared at Mike.

Mike took a deep breath, adjusting his smock before stepping forwards, as Patty looked over, concern etched on his face. Changa remained glaring at Spider, looking as if he wanted him to try something again.

"Sir, you okay?"

Mike nodded, wincing at the pain in his jaw, cursing the fact he didn't see the punch coming.

After a few moments it was Patty who broke the silence.

"Spider, what the fuck are you playing at?"

Spider's jaw was firm, the muscles straining in his face as between clenched teeth he looked back at him.

"Patty, as a mate, let me go, just give me five minutes with this murdering bastard, please, just five minutes."

Both men strained again as they felt the rage re-surface, clinging on tightly to Spider as he began to struggle. Patty replied through clenched teeth with the effort.

"What the fuck are you going on about? Why are you so bloody angry with him?"

Spider stopped struggling and turning to them both he snarled,

"He fucking did it! I saw him come back chatting on the phone, that's why he wanted us out of there so quickly. Whilst we were trying to save those people, he went off to call in the artillery strike. That's why he lied about the medics coming, he needed us out of there!"

Mike, massaging his neck said nothing but watched as Patty shook his head in disbelief, closing his eyes.

Spider looked back at Mike, his face creased in a mix of rage and confusion as he continued.

"Why the village though Mike? Why? What did they have to do with it? What did they do to you? Why did you kill them? WHY?"

"You stupid bastard!" Patty said suddenly, causing Spider to cease his rant and look at him confused.

Patty looked over at Mike before continuing.

"He didn't call it in Spider, we knew it was coming! Me, Linda and the Captain."

Spider looked on open mouthed, his anger turning to disbelief as he looked first at Patty then at Mike, before shaking his head, "You knew?"

Patty shook his head disappointedly at the actions of his friend, before replying, his voice low and full of anger.

"Did you see what was going on in those tents Spider? Or have a look over at the crematorium truck? Because I fucking did!

"What Crematorium truck? But I saw him with the phone." Spider replied, his voice low, the tension in his body evaporating as Mike explained, his own voice low and soft.

"I was on the phone Spider because I was calling the ops room, explaining what was going on there. What Patty, Linda and I had seen going on in the tents."

Spider looked up to Patty, as if seeking the answers but Patty could only look away, adding,

"Don't ask me about it Spider, not now, perhaps over a beer later, but not now."

Spider looked at the floor, a mixture of emotions beginning to overwhelm him as he realised what he'd just done. He began to shake.

"Let him go." Mike replied softly, looking at them both.

Changa and Patty released him, as tears began to well up in Spider's eyes, both soldiers looked on embarrassed as the NCO crumpled in front of them, sitting on his backside, his back resting against the Warrior's dirty road wheels as he sobbed into his hands.

"All those people...killed, just like that...why?"

Patty and Changa looked back at Mike, each unsure of what to do as Mike stepped forwards, kneeling and placing a hand on Spider's shoulder. Both men watched as Mike began to talk to him.

"Spider, look at me."

Spider looked up, tears streaking down his face, smearing his cam cream, his nose running.

"Listen to me, I need you to pull yourself together, there'll be time later to have a cry and get it out of your system, but you need to stow this shit away, because now is not the time for this. Grieve for them later. Right now, I need you to get back onto your feet and take command of your vehicle. Do you understand?"

Spider looked back at him, tears flowing freely down his face.

"I can't take anymore of this Mike, I just can't...All those people...dead."

"Spider, come on mate," Patty urged, nudging him with his knee, trying to encourage him. "Come on mate, this ain't like you."

Deciding it had become too much for him, Spider buried his face in his arms, the sobbing muffled. After a few moments Mike stood up, pulling Changa and Patty aside out of earshot.

"Fucking hell!" Changa said, the shock clear to see on his face. "What the fuck's got into him?"

"Look, he's just exhausted," Mike countered, "we all are, we all have our limits and leaving those people behind will have pushed him to his. I've seen it before; with a bit of rest, he'll be back to normal."

"How's that chin of yours? Looked like he clipped you pretty good?" Patty asked, inspecting the bruise that was already forming.

"I've had worse." Mike lied, smirking against the pain. In truth it had been one of the hardest hits he'd had in a while.

"What do we do about Two-Zero? They'll need a commander?" Changa replied, looking upwards at the turret, watching as Jenks quickly looked away, pretending to ignore what was going on.

"Well, we can't hide what's just happened from the lads, even if they didn't see it, next time they get together they'll all be talking about it to those that did." Patty remarked, looking up again and catching Jenks guiltily looking away.

Mike looked behind him at the devastation, knowing they'd wasted too much time already. They needed to sort this out, and quickly.

"Any others qualified to command?" Mike asked, already knowing the answer.

"Only one." Patty remarked, "and you didn't get on with him the last time."

"What choice do we have?" Mike replied, shaking his head and sighing in defeat before making the decision.

"Okay, Patty, go get Jonah over here, let's get him onboard and get out of this fucking place."

"What about him?" Changa asked, looking down at Spider, who was still sobbing uncontrollably.

"Put him in the back of Corporal Patterson's wagon with the police officers, and ask Catherine to keep a close eye on him. Just in case."

"She's still pretty pissed with you Sir." Changa replied, as Mike shot back angrily,

"Well then tell her that we've got another willing member to add to her list of people who want to see me fucking dead. Perhaps then she'll welcome him with open arms!"

Mike stood for a second, instantly regretting the outburst, before adding. "Changa, my apologies, I didn't mean for that to come out like it did."

The Fijian nodded in understanding, they were all getting tired and frustrated, with nerves on edge and now tempers were beginning to fray.

Mike watched as Changa carefully put his arm around Spider, lifting him up and walking him over to the vehicle, passing a confused looking Jonah who now ran towards him, carrying a small daysack.

"Sir, Corporal Patterson said you wanted to see me."

Smiling ironically Mike pointed towards the Warrior.

"Fusilier Jones, I hope you can still remember how to command one of these…"

Wonderland Operations Centre (WOC)

The PM stifled a yawn as the last cabinet member finally left the room, standing and stretching up, rubbing his neck as he looked at the clock. The meeting had gone on longer than he'd thought, he'd been hoping to get breakfast, but quickly realised that he'd lost track of the time, it was almost lunch time, and his stomach grumbled in protest to remind him. He walked to the conference room door, about to leave, when the CDS walked over, a look of concern on his face.

"Prime Minister, my apologies Sir, but I've got an update on Operation Cerberus."

Recognising the codeword for the operation to rescue the King, the PM turned back into the room, recognising its importance, ensuring the door was closed and ushering the CDS to sit beside him.

"What is it CDS?"

The General said nothing, his face hard to read as he handed over the report.

The PMs eyes opened wide as the realisation of what the report said, hit him.

"This can't be true? Can it?"

The CDS nodded his head in response, "I'm afraid so Sir," adding, "Sir Charles has always had his people everywhere, I used to ridicule him over the level of mistrust he had for other governmental departments. But now, it looks like I'm the fool, his assets in the Met would now seem to be well placed."

"But do they really think they can get away with it?"

The CDS kept his jaw firm and his eyes focused on the PM as he replied,

"With everything that they've done already, everything that we've read about today, do you really think they won't?"

Both men shared a few seconds of thought, each thinking through the options.

Eventually the PM nodded, his lips pursed together as he finally relented.

"Okay, CDS, let's give Cerberus the green light."

The CDS opened the folder, and taking a pen, the PM hurriedly signed the orders. Now it was official. Operation Cerberus was a go.

The PM looked up at the clock, seeing the time and thinking back to the details of the operation before adding.

"It'll be tight though, Archer still needs five hours to get into position. Can she still do it with the time we have available?"

The CDS looked awkwardly back at him, causing the PM to frown, asking.

"CDS what are you not telling me?"

"I'm sorry Sir, but I had concerns myself over how long it would take Archer to get into position, and knowing the time we had and the threat to the King, I'd already took the liberty of having Sir Tony have HMS Archer set course for the standby position last night. She's already in position waiting for the go signal."

The PM opened his mouth in surprise, his eyes quickly narrowing as he realised what he'd done. He was about to rebuke the CDS, then stopped himself as he realised the CDS's quick thinking had just saved them five hours. Not that it mattered, the CDS had still acted without his authority. He knew he should be thanking the man, but also didn't want this sort of thing to become a habit. The last thing he needed was to be second guessing his military. Keeping his voice low, the PM was brusque.

"Okay CDS, if you were worried about the travel time of Archer, then you should have told me when we were planning this, then perhaps I could have come to the same decision as you. That way you wouldn't have felt the need to go behind my back and do this."

The CDS nodded, grimacing at the tone of the PM, the notion of him going behind his back causing him to redden with embarrassment. Not wanting to be in the room any longer he picked up the report and walked briskly to the door, the PM suddenly calling out to him.

"CDS."

He stopped at the door, looking back at him, his eyebrows raised.

"Sir?"

The PM rapped his knuckles on the table in thought, as if thinking what to say, the pressure of his decision weighing on his mind, before finally replying hopefully. "Minimum force please, remember the people guarding him are also ours. I want casualties kept as light as possible."

The CDS stood there saying nothing, seeing the decision eating away at the PM, knowing it was the right call to have made, but that didn't make that pill any easier to swallow. He was tempted to remind the PM about how it didn't matter what the person holding the gun facing you believed in, if they pulled the trigger, the bullets would still head your way, rightly or wrongly. If they were a threat, then you had to deal with them. Still feeling the shame about not consulting with him over Archer, the CDS chose the softer choice, simply smiling and replying,

"We'll do our best Sir, we'll get them both back."

The PM watched as his most senior military officer left the room, knuckles still rapping lightly on the table, as he thought back to the times of Oliver Cromwell and the execution of Charles the first.

Remembering what he'd learned from his history teacher, he murmured softly.

"I hope so CDS, I truly hope so, otherwise history will only remember me as the Prime Minister who helped kill a King..."

7

False Teeth and Sausage Rolls

Mike knew it had to happen at some point, there was no way he expected them to be that lucky, and even with the Wasps and Talons out, even with them navigating through positions marked on their maps, he knew at some point they'd finally have to face the enemy head on. They were so close, he fumed, looking ahead of him, already seeing the outskirts of Yeovil in the distance. Already they'd been chatting to the commander in Yeovil, Callsign Whiskey Zero, the HF radio had seemed to spark up when they were five miles away. Since then he'd learned that a vast majority of the Russian forces in the area had pulled south earlier on, taking almost all their armoured vehicles with them, leaving a lighter, smaller force behind. Mike at first had been confident they could do it, with the main force away, he was happy to push on, even telling the commander on the radio they'd be there within two hours, but that was before one of the Warriors had driven into the minefield. The sad thing was it looked to be British made and British laid, Mike looked through his binoculars, recognising a few of the smaller air portable mines, usually deployed by a missile or aircraft scattered through the fields. Mike could only surmise as to why it hadn't been marked on any of their mapping. But there it was, suddenly the lead vehicle of Patty had reported its left side track and running gear were destroyed thus rendering it immobile. Thankfully the mine had been one of the smaller types, designed more for lighter vehicles with their only casualty being minor, one of the passengers not wearing their harness hitting their head on the roof as the vehicle had been jolted from the shockwave. If it hadn't been for the fact all the other vehicles were full, they could have just abandoned it and loaded the occupants into another vehicle, but instead they'd been forced to waste valuable minutes, connecting Changa's Warrior to pull it back out the way it had come. Then they'd wasted more precious time hooking the vehicle up for a tow from the front and trying to find a safe route around the minefield. Eventually being forced further east, away from the safer ground, to where the terrain was more open and less wooded, more farmers fields than hills. The perfect killing ground for any infantry and armour who may be lying in wait.

Now Changa's vehicle was having to take the longer routes to remain in cover and was already starting to struggle with towing the extra weight. Normally the Warriors would be making 40 kph over the terrain, but with towing the dead weight of Patty's Warrior, it was struggling to make even 10kph. The speedy, lightening progress that they'd enjoyed before was now reduced to a crawl, with the tank and Jonah's Warrior now the only vehicles providing cover for the slow-moving convoy. Over the past ten minutes, progress had been painstakingly slow as Mike and Jonah had fought off, with some success, the infantry units left behind that had tried to venture from their positions to try to take them on. Overhead the Wasps had been invaluable, one of them was already out of ammunition, its grenades being used to destroy a platoon of infantry that had been ahead of them, hidden in amongst the drainage ditches, trying to get into position to ambush Changa's convoy. By the time Changa's Warrior had driven through the position, there was nothing left of the enemy platoon but broken bodies, lying amongst the fields. Even then, with everything that had happened Mike was still confident they could make it, the enemy forces were light, and with no sign of armour they could push on and through. Then, just as they had begun to see the town in the distance, it was Rachel that had delivered the killing blow.

"Tango One-One, Tango Two-Zero, critical information, I've got eyes on ten...no, twelve enemy tanks approaching at speed from the south."

Sat two kilometres to the south, the two Talons were in overwatch mode, constantly scanning and listening for any threats. Now they were picking up movement. The Russians were coming back to reinforce their old positions.

No sooner had she finished speaking than she came back on, the urgency clear to hear in her voice.

"Tango Two-Zero, continuing, I've also got eyes on what looks like a company of armoured vehicles, look to be BMP3, again at speed, heading north, and wait...more tanks...We've got another company of T-80's coming up!"

Mike cursed, as he looked down into the turret at the BMDS, quickly working out their positions and speed relative to the Russians, then looking at the huge expanse of open ground between them and the town. Doing the numbers, he knew then they weren't going to make it. They had almost thirty tanks and fifteen BMP's coming for them. He quickly played out what would happen next in his head, as if viewing the battlefield from above. Watching as the Russian tanks would quickly overtake them, keeping themselves safely hidden in the hilly terrain to the west. Then, once they'd pushed far enough ahead, overtaking the slow convoy, they would swing in from the west, shutting the door and cutting them off from the safety of the town. Then they'd keep them pinned there, whilst the BMP's advanced from the south, all surrounded and neatly packed up tight. Then at their own leisure they could come in and take his unit apart, piece by piece. Within perhaps twenty, maybe thirty minutes, it would all be over.

He felt a huge rush of emotions all at once, anger, frustration, disappointment and fear, knowing there was nothing he could do about it, he'd pushed his unit as far as he could, swore at them, talked to them, smiled at them, laughed with them, promised them, fought them and all of it had brought them to this point. Only to face being killed within sight of the town that now offered sanctuary. Their faces began to flash in front of him as he felt the burden of what they'd all risked in getting here, the trust they'd placed in him to lead them, they'd all counted on him, and now when it had mattered the most, he'd let them all down. And then there was the evidence that Linda carried, all of that would be gone, all of those people who he'd left behind to die, their lives wasted for nothing, lost forever in the great war machine that was now coming to chew them up. He balled his fists up, banging them hard on the cupola, ignoring the messages coming over the radio, his frustrations finally playing out. Suddenly Kate was there, the thought of her being told how he'd died filled his head, like a hammer hitting him, it kept playing over and over, then all of the promises he'd made to her, all of the things they had planned to do, all of the things they had left to do.

No, he argued with himself, NO! It wasn't going to end like this, stop feeling sorry for yourself, get a grip; think Mike, THINK, he shouted silently to himself, come on, you always find a way! If it hadn't been for that fucking minefield, he fumed. Suddenly a thought flashed into his head, something he'd seen back there. Focusing his thoughts and firming his resolve, he quickly came up with the only plan he knew left open to him, remembering the words that had been spoken to him by a Sergeant Major from the Paratroopers as if it were yesterday.

"When things get so bad that your back's against the wall, when all seems hopeless and lost... Sometimes the best form of defence is to simply say fuck it, attack, and kick em' as hard as you can in the balls!"

Knowing it wasn't just his decision to make, he quickly discussed it with the crew, explaining what he'd seen at the facility and the importance of the evidence that Linda had, before outlining his plan and the risks.

"Look guys, the way I see it we're dead if we do nothing. And out of all us we've got the best chance of making this work. So what do you think? Should we do it?"

Without any delay, or thoughts for themselves, they all agreed as one. Even without the importance of the evidence, all had made friends with the Warrior crews, and all of them knew that sometimes you had to put your mates before yourself, and this was one of those times. He'd only known them for four days, Baz only two, but somehow, in that short space of time, they'd bonded as a crew, having been through so much together already. Mike's chest swelled with pride as he looked at them all, proud to be sat amongst them.

Mike outlined what he was going to do to over the radio as he turned the tank around, leaving the convoy to continue on it's slow journey northwards. At first there were protests, Changa argued he was going to follow the tank, with Mike having to resort to using his rank to order him to keep going north. Eventually Changa relented, knowing Mike was right, this was the only way. Patty was next to argue, urging Mike to re-consider. There must be another way, Patty had remonstrated.

"Patty, you know what we saw, you know what Linda has on her, you know the importance of it. All those people didn't die for nothing. You need to make sure she gets back with the evidence."

Patty continued arguing, watching as the tank disappeared into the distance, unable to do anything with his Warrior being towed by Changa, a mere passenger to the unfolding events.

Only Jonah on Tango Two-Zero acknowledged without complaint, Mike musing to himself that the Fusilier was probably thankful to be finally rid of him.

And that was how he reasoned with himself, justifying the risks of what he was about to do, he knew they couldn't all run for it, their speed was too slow, instead he'd planned on keeping the tank behind to slow the Russians advance for as long as he could. They only needed to buy the other's time, if they could just slow the enemy down long enough, perhaps the Warrior's could make it, perhaps maybe even *they* could make it.

Mike left the remaining airborne Wasps overflying the convoy, they'd need all the help they could get, only his own Wasp was still on board, sat patiently waiting, fully armed in its dock. He had Rachel keep the Talons in place in overwatch mode, he'd need them for what was to happen next.

The tank was racing back towards the direction of the enemy positions, Mike preferring the easier cover, and risk of small arms fire to the open ground. Besides he didn't have the luxury of time, for his plan to work he needed to be in position in a matter of minutes. Ignoring the risks, he ordered Bill to gun it and ducked low as the tank tore through the ploughed fields, mud flung up behind them in a giant brown rooster tail. Keeping the tank heading back towards the areas where they'd spotted the infantry, he found cover in low ground, shielding them from view as they tore along. Mike switched over to the HF set, sending a quick update to Yeovil, telling them to expect the three Warriors shortly and not to fire on them. He kept it brief, preferring to listen on the troop net, as Rachel kept up her running commentary on what the enemy were doing. Her earlier excitable anticipation was replaced by calmness, almost as if she was reading the football scores. You'd be hard pressed to know she was being flung about inside an armoured vehicle, expecting at any second to be hit.

"Tango One-One, Tango Two-Zero, sitrep on enemy. Enemy now passing through grid square 35,45 believe them to be approximately 3 km to our south, still heading north at speed, over."

Mike kept a watchful eye out at where the tank was going as he replied.

"Tango One-One, roger, understood, good work, keep me updated. Out."

Mike ducked low again, quickly leaning behind him to pull his assault rifle in with him and close his hatch over, cocooning them all off from the outside world as the tank slowed briefly as it negotiated the small rise. He had just enough time to warn the crew. Not that they needed it, they'd all been fully prepared for what was about to happen next.

"Okay everyone, here we go, remember we just need to keep their heads down to punch through. Okay...Standby for close contact with infantry!"

Already Baz was on the RWS, his concentration focused on the display, hands on the joystick, ready to fire, likewise Smudge had the coax selected, ready to fire the tank's machine gun. There would be no point in trying to fire the main armament, the infantry would be too close to use it and Smudge wouldn't be able to aim properly. Mike had already made Smudge close all his sights up, the sensitive optics and glass were not bullet proof, and with them being so close to the enemy infantry, the chances of them taking a hit were far greater than if they were 500 metres away. Instead, the gunner was going to crudely aim using his viewing block, the tank gunners would call it hose piping, the effect being to keep people's heads down, not hit them.

The tank climbed up the rise, emerging suddenly into the middle of the enemy positions. Mike could see through his periscopes, as heads began to pop up around him curiously, emerging from foxholes and trenches, they were close enough to see the startled looks on their faces, the Russian soldiers had heard the tank, but hadn't expected to see it so close to them as it suddenly emerged into their midst, driving through. It was as if the sight of the tank had shocked them, as a strange calm descended, both sides looking at the other, no-one firing, each waiting for the other to make the first move. He watched, holding his breath in anticipation as the soldiers looked to one another, unsure how to react, as the tank kept accelerating through unopposed, until finally the Russian NCO's began shouting orders, breaking them out of their stupor. Suddenly there was movement. Gunfire erupted around them, hammering against the tank's sides, shattering the silence as finally he shouted, "Fire!"

It was as if the fire order broke his own crew's trance as Baz and Smudge came to life, each shouting out their own fire orders and pouring fire onto the infantry. Red tracer fire shot out to answer the green tracer fire that was shooting towards them. With the tank moving so fast, and the infantry so close, the chances of hitting anyone were slim, but Mike didn't care, he just wanted to shock them, to keep their heads down long enough to break through.

He heard a clang as something hit the turret roof. Looking through his periscope he could see the dark shape of a grenade rolling around on the roof. It seemed surreal to see something so deadly just inches from him, and without realising he moved away from it, wincing as he waited for it to explode. When the explosion came, it was a dull thud, the only damage being the periscopes outer glass cracking.

Mike surveyed the damage, apart from the restricted view, they'd be fine, the tank was designed to take much more damage than just a grenade.

The tank kept on its headlong flight as the intensity of the fire began to die away as they made it through the positions, with no one thankfully firing any anti-tank weapons at them. Mike guessed either they hadn't had any, or if they did, they were all facing away from them, and the shock and speed of them bursting through, coupled with the tank's machine guns blazing away had stopped them. Either way the tank now tore through the countryside unharmed and at breakneck speed, the turret almost facing rearwards as Smudge continued to pour MG fire back towards the infantry, keeping their heads down. Eventually Mike reasoned they were a safe enough distance away as he finally gave the order.

"Okay Smudge, cease fire! Get the gun front, resume scanning."

He felt the smooth action of the turret and heard the powerful electric motors whine as it danced back through the 180 degrees to go gun front, Mike being forced to shift his position as he found himself facing rearwards again. He settled back in, getting Smudge to re-open his sights as Baz expertly checked over the chain gun, refitting a new belt of 600 rounds after seeing how little remained of the old one. Within seconds they were back to being the hunter again, the turret smoothly jinking left and right as they scanned for any new threats.

Mike left them all to it, looking behind him at the armoured boxes of the Wasp and Hornet. Both showed signs of being hit, but thankfully were armoured for just such an event. Even so, he quickly ran the diagnostic check on them both, happy to see everything was still reporting green. He needed the Wasp for what was about to happen next. As the tank kept moving forwards, through the fields and hedgerows, Mike was constantly listening to Rachel's updates until they came to the edge of the minefield that had caused them so many problems. The Russians were now two kilometres away, already driving past the unseen Talons, with Mike having perhaps at best two minutes before he'd be visible to them. He still needed more time to get into position, so had to do something and quickly. Cursing quietly, he stopped the tank, then ordered over the radio,

"Tango Two-Zero, Tango One-One, I need more time, engage the lead T-80's then withdraw the Talons north past me and back to your position."

There was a pause as if the message hadn't got through, Mike was about to re-send when Rachel finally replied.

"Tango One-One, roger...but I thought you needed the Talons for later to help you withdraw."

Mike knew she was right, but now the plan was changing, if he didn't get this next part done without being discovered then it would all be in vain. Without a moment's thought he came back with.

"Tango Two-Zero, Tango One-One, I don't have the time to explain. Fire on the lead vehicles, slow them down and buy me more time, Tango One-One, out."

Leaving her to it, he activated the Wasp programme from the BMDS, watching through the periscopes as its motors started up and it shot quickly into the sky up to

100 feet. He looked over to the tablet that he'd secured to the turret, the feed coming directly to him, now he had a perfect bird's eye view of the tank.

He popped open his hatch, the fresh air rushing in as he peered over the cupola, preferring to see for himself the ground ahead than from the claustrophobic interior within.

Using the touchscreen, he quickly drew a box around the tank, the Wasp's onboard software flashing the tank as a blue colour, telling the Wasp that from now on, whatever happened, this was the mother ship. Now the Wasp would know what it was looking at, having already painted a thermal picture of the tank. From here on, controlling the Wasp should be easy, with Mike merely having to select a pre-programmed flight path, the Wasp would fly about, keeping itself either behind the tank, above the tank, or in front of the tank, leaving Mike free to command. Mike selected the 'above' function, the Wasp now giving a top-down view of the tank as he selected the thermal picture. He was now ready.

Using the Wasp's thermal camera, he was able to see the mines from above, a trick he'd learned in Iraq, where the heat of the sun was warming them up quicker than the ground, which when viewed from the air using a thermal camera, made them easier to locate. However, at ground level you wouldn't see them as easily, so anyone coming into the minefield would need to have the thermal eyes in the sky to navigate it, which conveniently Mike now had.

He'd already seen the large, wooded area that he wanted to head to, it looked to be in the middle of the minefield, on higher ground, the perfect defensive position, with what looked to be at least five possible firing points covering the ground around it. He'd seen it earlier whilst waiting for Patty's warrior to be recovered, he guessed that was the reason the minefield had been placed here. Someone higher up the food chain attempting to deny what was a great position for the enemy. He took a chance on the position being unoccupied, reasoning that the mines would have stopped anyone from entering it to begin with, and that if anyone were up there, they would certainly have fired on Mike's unit when Patty had struck the mine. With great care he guided the tank through the minefield and up to the woodline, momentarily distracted as Rachel's voice burst excitedly through the headset, her calm manner from before now gone.

"Tango One-One, Tango Two-Zero, Talons in contact! Three T-80's engaged and destroyed with Javelin. Enemy tanks now approaching Talons positions, am pulling them out now. Over."

"Tango One-One, good work," he managed to reply, before issuing another directional change to his driver, as he cautiously moved the tank further in.

He looked up seeing the smoke drifting lazily skywards in the distance, the enemy still yet unseen. This was going to be close.

Finally, he breathed a sigh of relief as the tank reached the woodline, quickly driving into the safety and cover of the trees. He pulled the tank around into the first fire position, getting Bill to drive up and over the slope so that the tank was almost sky lined. Mike could see it was a great position, with far reaching views out to about 1500 metres in all directions. If the Russians did want to take on the tank, they'd have to navigate through the minefield first.

Mike stopped looking, preferring his gunner to orientate himself to the area he'd be looking at instead, as he shot out.

"Right Smudge, quickly, I want you to look out to your front, get used to what you can see, because when we pop up again next time it'll be to fire."

He saw his gunner looking through the sight, as Mike quickly orientated him by taking control of the gun.

"Right, see the crater where Tango Two-Zero struck the mine. That's centre of arc. We'll call that crater. Identify."

"Crater, identified." the gunner replied, repeating the commands he'd practised over and over on his gunnery course.

Mike pulled the marker pen from his chest rig, ready to write on the cupolas painted side.

"Smudge I want you to get me the range to the crater."

He felt the turret jerk slightly as Smudge re-orientated the turret, the aiming reticule now slap bang on the centre of the crater as the laser fired. In less than a second, the range return of 500 metres was displayed in both their sights, with his gunner reporting back.

"Range, five-hundred."

Mike wrote down the range, then proceeded to get his gunner to identify some of the more obvious features, each time writing on the cupola its name and range to the tank. A minute later and between them both they'd broken down the ground, and more importantly Mike had accurate ranges on how far away everything was. Looking around one final time to check he hadn't missed anything he finally pulled the tank back off the high ground and into cover.

Now they were set, only Mike's head was visible above the ridge, binoculars in hand, ready to strike. Looking down he watched as Baz completed some final checks on the main gun, then seeing he was finished, urged him up, to open his own hatch and come up, handing him a second set of binoculars. Now there were two pairs of eyes searching and waiting. Looking up he could see the Wasp still hovering faithfully overhead, like a bloodhound ready for the hunt. Realising it could be seen and help give away their position, he sent if off to the far side of the wood to cover the rear. At least then no-one could sneak up behind them, or at least that's what Mike hoped. His final act was to reach down to the Commander's Control Panel and turn off the laser, the gunner spotting straight away as the warning flashed in his sight.

"Boss, I've just had a laser fault flash up. I think it's off."

Mike put the bino's back to his eyes and continued to slowly scan the terrain, as he replied.

"Don't worry about it Smudge, I've switched it off."

"What?" the gunner replied unbelievably as Mike added.

"One other thing, I want you to override the Fire Control Computer. From now on you're firing without it, we'll be firing using the GAS."

Mike knew what he'd said would make no sense whatsoever to the gunner. The laser was used to get the range to the target, and the fire control computer or FCC as it was called, would use the information, along with all the other vehicle sensors such as vehicle speed, target speed, wind speed and direction, even the atmospheric pressure of the air, to calculate within milliseconds and automatically elevate and aim the gun. Now Mike had turned all this off and was relying on his gunner to use the most basic of gunnery skills to engage the enemy, a technique known as 'steam gunnery.' On the tank, the Gunners Auxiliary Sight or GAS as it was called by the crew was the second sight, a backup for when things went bad. It had various aiming points marked into it, the object being that by laying the relevant aiming point onto the target you were in fact aiming off the gun, allowing for all the things the FCC would have considered. Essentially replacing the computer brain with the human one. Smudge would no doubt be wondering if his commander had lost the plot, why would you knowingly disable the computer that made firing easy, only to complicate things? But Mike had a plan, and right now, that plan called for steam gunnery.

Hearing no response and sensing the question to come, Mike quickly added.

"Smudge, I don't have the time to explain, I can teach, or we can do. What do you prefer?"

"Okay boss," the gunner replied, his voice apprehensive, "FCC override is on, switching to GAS."

Mike continued to scan with the binos, aware of Baz looking across at him, puzzled. He shot the loader a smile, before saying.

"Baz trust me, I know what I'm doing."

Baz said nothing but shrugged his shoulders, his smile saying more than words could. They'd trusted him this far, what harm could one more time do?

Mike pointed over to Baz, indicating where he wanted him to look.

"Baz keep eyes on over there, let me know if you see anything moving about."

"Righty-ho boss," the loader replied, as he began scanning through the binos.

For the next minute no-one said anything, all of them lost in their own worlds, expecting at any second to see the enemy. Mike had always hated this part; it was always the anticipation before a battle that would un-nerve them. Hating the silence, he decided to try to liven things up.

"Tell you what guys, I wish we had some army issue lunch packs with us."

"Urghh!" Baz exclaimed, clearly having had them before. Only Smudge and Bill seemed to be oblivious, both recruits having yet to sample them.

Bill replied up from his cab, innocently asking.

"Why's that boss? Are you hungry?"

Mike smiled as Baz chimed in "I'd rather eat a dog's ass than one of those lunch packs, why the hell would you want one of them?"

"Oh, I'm not hungry guys, far from it," he lied, his stomach grumbling at the thought of food as he continued, "no, I was just thinking, if we had a couple of lunch packs, we could get the sausage rolls out of them, load them in the gun, and fire them at the Russians. It'll be better than the training ammo we have, because let's be fair, there's nothing quite as tough as an army sausage roll."

Mike saw Baz laugh, the others kept quiet, clearly the joke was lost on them. It had always been a long-standing joke within the army, when you'd get the lunch packs, the sausage rolls would always be frozen, with a crust that tasted like carboard and the inside looking more akin to a spent nuclear fuel rod.

Smudge came back on, "I don't get it boss."

Still laughing, Baz replied, "That's because you've yet to eat one, trust me Smudge, when you've eaten one, you'll understand. I'm surprised most of the soldiers don't have false teeth they're that rock hard."

"How bad can they be?" Bill chimed in again, clearly thinking it through.

Mike replied, still chuckling, "Bill, all I'll say is there's a reason people used to call them cat's ass holes."

"Urrghh that's disgusting." the driver replied, causing another bout of laughter from the rest of the crew.

"Bill, didn't you know about the false teeth they offer every soldier when they get to the rank of Sergeant? It's because of the damage that eating the sausage rolls can do." Baz reported, Mike shot a curious glance to Baz who winked in reply. Mike grinned and kept quiet, happy to have the banter continue.

"Really?" the driver asked unbelievably.

"Oh yeah, but here's the weird bit though Bill," Baz continued, looking over at Mike mischievously. "If you google the company that makes them, you'll see that they went bankrupt back in 2014. So, if the company's gone under, then who's making the sausage rolls?"

"I don't know. Who is making them?" the driver replied thoughtfully.

"Exactly!" Baz shot back, "that's the question that everyone's been asking ever since. Some say that the army brought so many of them and have so many in supply that there's enough to last until 2040."

Mike chuckled, he remembered the same thing being said about the company in 2002, that it had gone bankrupt in 1994. Always the same joke he mused.

There was a silence over the headsets as everyone digested what Baz had just said. Suddenly it was Smudge who broke the silence. He'd taken the bait first.

"But Corporal, if the company stopped making them in 2014, wouldn't they all now be out of date?"

And we have a bite... Mike thought humorously, as Baz smiled back at him replying,

"Exactly Smudge, that's the point though, that's what gives them their unique taste. They're out of date by about ten years. But you'll never know that because every two years the army will have someone come in and cover the date sticker with a fresher one. I wouldn't be at all surprised if in eight years' time, you're both sat in the Sergeant's Mess, eating the same sausage rolls that me and the boss had when we were your age."

"No thank you!" Bill replied adamantly but Smudge seemed more upbeat as he jovially replied.

"Corporal, do you really think that me and Bill will be in the Sergeants Mess in eight years' time?"

"Oh absolutely, I can almost guarantee it." Baz replied, his voice sounding very confident.

Mike could almost picture the look of pride disappear on the face of his gunner, as Baz replied humorously.

"After all Smudge, when I'm in there, I'll need to bring in some good waiters who I can trust to fetch my drinks."

Everyone broke into laughter. It was good to hear, Mike thought, better to calm the nerves than sit in silence dwelling on what could happen. Mike looked over at Baz again, happy to have him on board. His cheeky humour coupled with his cockney accent was disarming, as if he could make light of any situation and put people at ease instantly. Mike's thoughts quickly turned to the future, guiltily realising he'd brought them here, knowing the plan but what if something happened to him, what would they do? He stopped laughing, his tone serious.

"Guys, sorry to be the Debbie Downer, but one other thing I need to cover. And this is fucking important so pin your ears back. If the tank gets disabled and for whatever reason I'm out of it, I want you all to abandon the vehicle, and get yourselves heading north, follow the tank tracks out of the minefield if you can, but go north, don't head in any other direction. Understand?

"Why would you be out of it?" Smudge asked naively.

"Fucking hell Smudge! Think about it!" Baz shot back irritably; all trace of humour gone.

"Oh!" the gunner replied, his voice low, as the realisation finally hit home.

"Look, it's only a what if, okay guys," Mike reasoned, not wanting to dampen the good mood from earlier. "I just want you all to be prepared for anything."

With that, the gloomy silence returned, Mike angry with himself for having to bring it up, he should have mentioned it before. But now, the damage was done. Kicking himself, he went back to scanning with the binoculars.

Wonderland Operations Centre (WOC)

The CDS was leaning on one of the consoles, quickly eating his lunch when the main screens flicked over, instantly grabbing his attention. He put the half-eaten cheese sandwich down and looked up, seeing the usual digital maps of the UK now replaced with a number of live camera feeds showing what looked like an ongoing battle. He looked up curiously, glancing over to one of the Battle Captains who shouted over, holding a satellite phone.

"Sir, we're getting live feeds piped in from Brigadier Rawlinson over at Aurora. He's telling us that they've only just started receiving this themselves. Thought you'd want to see."

He leapt off the console, walking forwards, taking in what he was seeing. Two of the feeds looked to be gun cameras, he guessed from the Talons, he'd seen them before on one of his visits. The other three were all airborne, as if looking from above, showing the battlefield from the sky. He'd heard about the Wasps but had never seen them in action before. He could see Warriors driving across rough terrain, one looked to be damaged and was being towed. The third one looked to be providing support, dashing across the terrain, it's 30mm cannon firing out, the rounds striking out of view of the cameras. He looked back to the Talons feed, the images were moving fast, clearly they were in a hurry. Suddenly he watched as one stopped, the camera focusing on something blurry in the distance. Within a second, the picture came into focus, everyone looking on in amazement as the clear picture of the T-80 heading straight towards the camera came into view. They saw the tank's gun firing, one of the console operators flinched, as if the round were going to come through the screen at them, The CDS watched amazed at the picture clarity, the detail of it, being able even at this range to recognize the details on the turret. Suddenly the screen changed red, as the targeting reticule surrounded the tank, locking onto it, the operator was about to engage. Without knowing why, he balled his fists, urging the operator to take the shot. There was a flash, the missile was away, streaking towards the tank. He was hoping to see the hit, but before the missile could strike, the operator had turned the camera round and the Talon was racing away again, chasing after the second, which could be seen in the distance.

Finally, the CDS looked up to the Battle Captain, walking over and reaching for the phone.

"Peter, it's James, what's going on? What are we looking at on screen?"

"James, I'm sorry old friend but I've got a confession to make, I disobeyed your orders and sent Whiskey Three-Zero some of our hardware to use."

The CDS's knuckles went white as he tightened his grip on the handset.

"Did you now?" he was about to argue further when he remembered the PM's orders, Whiskey Three-Zero was to make it back home. Perhaps Peter sending them the extra firepower hadn't been such a bad thing after all. Not wanting to discuss it now, he replied.

"Well we can discuss it later. In the meantime, how is it possible that we're seeing the feed?"

"James we're not quite sure ourselves, all we know is that five minutes ago our screens came online, I'm assuming the closer Whiskey Three-Zero get to us, the more powerful the signal. Hence, we're picking their drones feed up."

The CDS looked up at the screen, watching as another screen flicked on, showing a top-down view of a Challenger 2 with the add on armour. He could see the tank showed battle damage to its turret, some of the armour packs were dented, as if a giant sledgehammer had been taken to them, whilst one was cracked open, the metal casing peeling away. The colour screen suddenly flicked to thermal, now the picture was shown as a series of greys and blacks, the heat of the tank's exhaust showed up as white plumes, invisible to the naked eye. Large white spots appeared in front of the tank, at first the CDS thought they were rocks, then as the operator zoomed in, he could see they were mines.

"Good God! He's going into a minefield!" he exclaimed, watching on open mouthed as the tank slowly began to navigate its way into it.

"Who the hell put that there?" the CDS asked, looking around, continuing. "Is it ours?"

It was the battle Captain who replied. "It's not ours CDS, we don't have anything capable in the area up and running yet. It must be Russian."

"Peter, can you control the feed? Can you take control of the drones?" the CDS asked hopefully.

"No, the signal's still too weak for control due to the range, all we can do is piggyback the feed, which is why for now we're merely spectators. Besides, I wouldn't want to try to yank control from them, from the looks of it they're needing them more than you are."

The CDS grimaced at the coded warning. Peter was no fool, he knew what his friend was thinking. If they were able to take back control, Peter was worried that the first thing he'd probably do would be to order the valuable drones back to safety. He did value the weapons programme, but regardless how he felt about it, now, the PM, his boss, had made Whiskey Three-Zero top priority, with the intel they carried they were important. Ignoring the hint, he added,

"Not what I was thinking old friend, I was thinking of sharing the load, taking control and assisting them."

He could hear the surprise in the voice at the other end, as Peter replied.

"Well, if you want to assist, can I recommend we send another eight Wasps and eight Talons to support. I can get them dropped in place using the Thumpr's inside of ten minutes."

The CDS looked up, watching the tank's progress, now it was through the minefield and disappearing into the woods. Suddenly the screen flicked back to daytime and the view changed as the Wasp looked to be watching the far end of the woodline. Whatever Captain Faulkes was doing he wasn't with the rest of the unit. That much was evident. The Warriors looked to be making their way north, whilst the tank was staying behind, waiting for something. The CDS looked at the screens, assessing what was happening, balancing it against the risk of losing more of their valuable hardware.

"What does Wendi make of all this?"

"James, you know better than to ask that. Wendi is still offline and will continue to be. I'm not plugging it into our system with the computers we have here. All it takes is one loose firewall, one error in the containment programme and she'll be gone."

The CDS balled his fists again, his friend had been wise and cautious to keep the AI programme out of his reach. He'd have used it days ago to combat the virus. He closed his eyes, careful in what he said in reply, knowing that if he tried to try to take it by force, it would result in Peter destroying it.

"Well in that case Brigadier, our hands are tied. I'm not going to risk sending any more of our assets on supporting Whiskey Three- Zero, unless I know it's being controlled by Wendi. After all, isn't that why you designed her?"

With that, he hung up the phone, quickly passing it over to the Captain and picking up his sandwich. He needed to see for himself how good the AI programme could be, and this was the perfect time to test it. He needed Peter to see that, to finally get down off his morale high horse and put the good of the country above his own fears. They needed Wendi, and they needed it now more than ever. Besides the CDS had reasoned, the evidence that the PM had deemed top priority was with Miss Harding, who he knew would be in one of the Warriors. So long as they made it back, then he had followed his orders to the letter. The tank however, well that was now on its own and if by using

Captain Faulkes he could get Peter to release Wendi, then it was worth the risk of one tank. At least that's how he hoped Peter would see it.

Whiskey Three-Zero

Mike was tempted to say something to break the awkward silence but stopped as Rachel's voice came over the radio.

"Tango One-One, Tango Two-Zero, Talons now approaching your position, do you want me to halt them near you or keep going?"

"Negative Tango Two-Zero, keep them going back to you, do not stop at my position. Remember to stay away from the minefield."

"Roger, Tango Two-Zero, out."

His eyes were drawn to movement coming over the hill across to his right in the far distance. He quickly looked through the bino's, his finger adjusting the focus ring.

The picture became clearer as he made out the faint shape of one of the Talons screaming across the open ground, throwing up a large dust cloud behind it, the javelin launchers sat empty on its back. Mike began to search for the other one, his gaze falling on it as it came over the same piece of hill at speed, except the second one seemed to be going more slowly, its launcher facing back the way it had come, the machine gun firing at something unseen below them. Mike kept his binoculars trained on the area, watching the flash as the Talon fired another Javelin. No sooner had the missile left the launcher than it turned, quickly accelerating away to chase after the other one. Mike watched their progress, shaking his head admiringly in the way the robots seemed to float over the ground, their tracks constantly adjusting to suit the terrain. They disappeared, lost from sight in some dead ground, Mike hoping they'd make it back safely. He knew they were just robots, but somehow with everything they'd been through it just seemed right to have them with them. Plus, Peter would have a fit if they were captured, the power sources alone were priceless. Suddenly there was more movement, Mike saw another dark shape begin to appear in the same area as the Talons, it emerged more slowly though, clearly not as fast as the robots. Mike re-adjusted the focus ring; the low, dark silhouette of the T-80 came into view. He saw the turret move, pointing down towards where the Talons were last seen and then a flash as it fired, the smoke quickly dissipating as it drove through the cloud in pursuit. Another two tanks followed close behind, all at speed, coming over the rise, all firing on the move, attempting to hit the faster moving robots.

The tanks fired a second time, Mike could only hope that the size and speed of the Talons were disrupting the enemies aim, knowing the smaller faster targets would be harder to hit. As if to answer, he saw both spring triumphantly into view, the earth being thrown up as the enemy fire landed around them. Mike held his breath anxiously, as they came very close to the minefield, thinking perhaps Rachel had made a mistake, then, at the last second, they veered off and crossed parallel to his position. No doubt done deliberately, Rachel wanting to draw the pursuing tanks across Mike's position. He smiled appreciatively, knowing that he should never have doubted her. He looked back up to the tanks, watching as they drew ever closer, no doubt sacrificing safety for speed as they relentlessly chased down the robots.

In the distance he could see more tanks coming over the rise, these were moving slower than the first three, obviously spread out and advancing more cautiously, but alert. Mike judged the distances, knowing that the first three tanks were now already too far ahead of the others, outstripping any hope of support from them. He wondered what had driven the crews to do this? To have thrown caution to the wind and leave the others behind on some mad dash with the Talons? It had seemed crazy, but then he quickly mused, no crazier than sitting, waiting to attack with odds stacked against you of 45-1. Perhaps they just saw it as another necessary risk, just as he had done. Perhaps Rachel's attack had killed a friend, someone they knew on another tank and now they wanted revenge.

All Mike knew was that now, it had given him an edge. He'd attack them first, and then see what happened next.

He waited another minute, letting the tanks get ever closer, giving a running commentary to Smudge and Bill who couldn't yet see what was happening. Now the tanks were moving in front of them, gifting them the perfect side on attack, every Tank Commander's dream. Finally, he judged the distance to be close enough.

"Right guys, thirty seconds let's get ready." Mike reported back, the crew sparking to life as Baz climbed back inside closing his hatch over. Mike kept his hatch open, preferring to remain heads up, but stowing his weapon close by in case a fast exit was needed.

"Action! Load DST, gunner, check MRS, driver standby."

Nerves and fears melted away as everyone threw themselves into the procedures and routine that they knew. Mike could hear their voices become louder, as the adrenalin began to flow.

"MRSing!" Smudge reported back, indicating he was checking the Muzzle Reference System. The gun and the sight had to be constantly checked for alignment, otherwise the gunner could miss because his aim didn't correspond to what the gun was pointing at. To combat this, on the end of the gun barrel was a small mirror, which reflected a light that was shone on it from the sight. If the gunner could see the light being reflected, then he knew they were lined up. If the light was off, then the sight was off. He could adjust the sight with his controls, to bring the gun/sight relationship back together. Once the light was in the centre of the mirror, he knew they were aligned. Crude and basic for a multi-million pound piece of hardware but nevertheless, very effective.

As Smudge was doing this, Baz was busy on his own side of the turret, checking again that DST was selected on his loader's control panel, different ammunition responded in different ways, and DST was no different. Happy with what was displayed, he checked the coax one final time, confident that the belt was secure and free to fire, before finally casting an expert eye one final time over the 120mm gun.

Satisfied that everything was ready and in order, he reported back "LOADED!"

Mike looked down towards the gunner's station as Smudge finally reported back.

"MRS CHECKED. READY!"

Mike was confident they all knew what to do, but just wanted to reiterate with them, one more time, more to remind himself than anyone else.

"Ok Smudge, remember to use your aim offs, they're going to be moving fast and remember to report back the range as I call it."

"Okay boss!" the gunner replied as Mike turned his attention to Bill.

"Bill, remember, whenever we pull into or out of the fire position, go nice and slow, don't panic or rush, we don't want the movement to be seen, and when we halt, select reverse every time. Don't leave us in forward gear up there."

"I won't Boss, promise." the driver replied, his tone focused.

Satisfied, Mike looked about the turret one more time, reiterating what he'd proposed earlier.

"Remember guys we're only buying them the time to escape, we're not here to be heroes."

He looked over, nodding at Baz before climbing back up, binoculars ready. Now it was game time.

"Okay driver, let's go, advance."

He instinctively braced himself as the tank jolted forwards slowly, the nose rising up as the gun barrel came down. Slowly the tank hauled itself over the bank, exposing more of itself until finally the gunner could see the enemy tanks. When Mike was certain the barrel had a clear arc to fire, he stopped the tank, sliding back down onto his seat, taking control of the gun and quickly laying the gun onto the rearmost tank.

"DST tank, one-two-hundred!"

"ON, ONE-TWO-HUNDRED!" Smudge reported back, taking over control of the gun and tracking the target, moving the turret to match the enemy tank's speed.

"LOADED!" Baz shouted, slamming the loaders guard to the rear and standing ready with the next round to load.

Mike watched through his sight as the gunner tracked through the target, conscious of the fact this was probably the first time the Trooper had ever fired in anger at another tank.

Their target was oblivious to the danger it was in, Mike could see its main gun firing again as the tanks continued their mad dash after the Talons, all the while unaware it was about to be engaged.

Come on Smudge, COME ON! Mike thought, the excitement and atmosphere building as he fought to remain calm, not wanting to put any more pressure on the young lad, holding his breath in anticipation as finally he heard.

"FIRING!" The gun leapt backwards, the recoil system absorbing the massive forces as the round shot out. Mike looked through the sight, watching in horror as the round shot high into the air, disappearing into the sunlit sky and out of sight.

"SMUDGE! WHAT THE FUCK WAS THAT?" he shouted in surprise, seeing the look of horror and shock as his gunner looked behind at him stammering.

"I'm sorry I...I don't know what happened."

Mike knew exactly what had happened, he'd seen it done before in the past. The gunner had fired off the wrong aiming mark, instead of using the aiming mark for the KE (Kinetic Energy) rounds, he'd used the aim off for the CE (Chemical Energy) rounds, which required more elevation to get the range for the heavier round. With the far higher angle of the gun, the lighter, faster round had shot upwards into the sky, and was now probably passing through 25,000 feet and well on its way to France. Mike ignored the gunner's excuses, looking over to the enemy tanks, certain they'd be looking back at him. Unbelievably they were still on their same original heading, unaware they'd been fired at, their focus purely on the Talons.

"Loaded!" Baz reported back, the gun ready to fire again. Mike leaned down, looking at the gunner, the anger he felt quickly melting away. He had to keep reminding himself, Smudge was new to this, they all were, and shouting at him wouldn't help. Instead, Mike smiled, reaching forwards, his hand resting on the dejected lad's shoulder as he said reassuringly.

"Well at least we know the gun's working. Now let's try that again, shall we?"

The gunner said nothing, nodding and firming his mouth embarrassingly as he put his head back in the sight.

Mike held his breath again as the gunner began the engagement process, finally the gun roared again.

This time it was a hit, the DST round lancing out, impacting the tank lower than expected, striking the left track, the energy tearing off two of the road wheels as the track broke and uncoiled like a giant snake, flapping in front of the tank, before finally falling away. The T-80 kept going forwards, the track uncoiling behind it, until suddenly it was torn off, now its left side was off its track, just on its wheels, then all sudden it spun around, as if a handbrake had been applied, as it pirouetted 180 degrees, facing the way it had just come. Although not able to drive, it could still fight and already Mike could see the turret searching for what had shot it.

"TARGET GO ON!" he shouted, hearing Baz almost immediately shouting, "loaded!" as without waiting, smudge pressed the firing lever again, forgetting to report that he was firing. This time the round struck the turret ring, the sparks and smoke indicating it had penetrated. Mike was about to order another round fired, but then saw the crew already evacuating, clearly the hit was worse than it looked.

"TARGET STOP!"

He looked back up, ignoring the shouts of congratulations from the crew, already searching for the other two tanks that were continuing onwards, unaware of what had happened to their comrade behind them.

Taking control of the gun again he lay it onto the second target, waiting for his gunner to take over the engagement as he reported,

"DST, tank, one-one hundred."

"On, one-one hundred!" he heard, finally releasing the controls, relinquishing control back to the gunner.

Leaving Smudge to it, he looked over at the lead tank, certain it would stop and look at them. Unbelievably it kept going, still firing at the Talons that were now nothing but specks in the distance.

"Firing!"

Again, the gun roared and slammed back into the turret, the breech already open, like a giant mouth waiting to be fed. Baz was sweating, the sheen on his forehead dripping onto the ammunition as he continued to feed the 120mm.

Mike looked back at the target as the round impacted, annoyed as the round shot off, ricocheting into the sky.

The enemy tank slowed suddenly, the driver jamming on his brakes at hearing the impact, whilst the turret began to spin around crazily, as the crew sought desperately to see what had shot at them.

"Target go-on!" Mike growled, watching in growing anger as the next round hit the tank with the same effect.

God dammit! This fucking ammo! Mike thought angrily, shouting for the third time. "TARGET GO ON!"

Baz continued the choreographed routine loading the gun, dancing around the turret, his hands and arms moving methodically more from muscle memory than thought, as Smudge placed the gunner's sight back onto the centre of the T-80's turret.

No sooner had Baz shouted "Loaded!" than Smudge was reporting, "firing!" The breech jumping backwards as the 120mm thundered out.

Finally, it was third time lucky as the enemy tank lurched forwards, causing the round that was aimed at the turret to instead hit the engine decks, exploding into the engine bay, igniting the fuel and sending a mass of flame and smoke skywards. Within seconds the hatches were open as the crew bailed out, leaping for cover behind the tank. Mike could see them looking around shocked, still unaware of what had hit them.

"Target stop! DST Tank one-one hundred!" Mike began, already laying the gun onto the final tank. It had stopped, the turret now facing rearwards, clearly wondering what was going on behind it. In panic, it began firing it's machine gun wildly into the surrounding forest, the green tracer rounds slamming into the trees and undergrowth. They clearly thought they were being engaged by infantry up close.

"On! one-one hundred!" Smudge replied, quickly adding, "boss, want me to aim for the engine?"

Mike smiled, it was a good call from the gunner, even if he was going to suggest it himself.

"Yes, go for it, shoot the engine."

Two rounds of DST later and it was over, the third enemy tank in flames. The tank was pulled back into dead ground as Mike surveyed the scene, impressed but disappointed. Impressed that they'd managed to take three tanks out, but disappointed at how badly the training ammunition had performed. Mike had fired three DST rounds at one tank, and it had been pure luck, not skill that had finally defeated it. The truth was the training ammunition just didn't have the punch they needed. Unless they were shooting at extremely close range, or lucky enough to be shooting them in the rear or the side, there was no way the DST rounds would penetrate.

Still at least he knew now where the weak points were on the T-80's. The trouble was he doubted he'd get that opportunity again.

Knowing they'd already stayed there far longer than they should, Mike had Bill reverse the tank back out of the fire position, the driver using the camera to reverse through the trees. It was time to use another position.

A minute later and they were set again ready to pounce, about 200 metres away from their old position, still with good eyes on the ground ahead of them. Mike was again standing on the cupola, with the tank hidden behind in dead ground, the only thing anyone could see, would be him, if they knew where to look. He surveyed the battlefield through the binos seeing nothing of the enemy, except the telltale whisps of dust, indicating something moving on the other side of the hills in the distance. As he waited, it was his gunner who broke the silence, still annoyed at his earlier mistake, his frustrations being vented.

"Boss, why am I firing with the GAS? I need to know, because the GAS is so much harder. Why can't we just use the full systems? Why are you making it harder for me?"

"Yeah, why is that boss?" Bill chimed in.

Only Baz kept quiet, perhaps he knew the answer already.

Mike relented, knowing he'd have to tell them or face the constant questions.

"Smudge, Bill, did you both do the AFV Recognition during your training?"

Smudge replied, sounding less than enthusiastic about what they were discussing. "Yeah, we all had to, it was probably the most boring lesson I've ever had to sit through."

Bill added jovially, as if from memory, mimicking a boring voice droning on. "This is a T-55, it has a space between the third and fourth roadwheel, and a fume extractor halfway down the barrel, and my name is Malcolm, I drive a beige Rover, and I don't have any type of life."

Mike let them both chuckle, before continuing.

"Okay, so learning what you've learned from the course, what tank were you shooting at just a moment ago?"

"Errr it was a T-80..wasn't it?" Smudge answered.

"Correct, A T80-BVM to be precise," Mike replied, "but what do you know about it?"

"Erm, it's got a gas turbine engine, autoloader, crew of three and a smooth bore barrel."

"Well done," Mike replied, genuinely impressed, adding, "It's also smaller, lighter and faster than us, and thanks to its smooth bore barrel can fire anti-tank missiles at us from over 6 km away."

"Okay." Smudge replied, unsure of what Mike was getting at.

"But the best bit about it, is something called Shtora, it's a fully automatic defensive system that constantly scans for threats, such as lasers."

"Ohhh." he heard the gunner exclaim in surprise as Mike continued.

"So, not only would all three of those tanks have reacted to our laser painting them, telling the tank crews where we were, but before you had even had time to fire your first round, which incidentally is probably landing in Calais about now, their onboard systems would have slewed their turrets around to face us, loaded an anti-tank round thanks to the autoloader and aimed at precisely where the laser was coming from. Which, I believe if my memory serves me right, is about 5 inches above your head. All the crew would then have to do is press the firing switch and you'd have three tank rounds winging their way towards you."

"Oh fuck!" he heard Smudge say in realisation as Bill added, "Bye bye Smudge."

"Exactly," Mike repeated, "bye bye Smudge. So now, perhaps you'll be grateful we're not using the laser. Or would you rather we turn it on and go back to full systems?"

"Fuck that boss, I'm happy with the GAS." Smudge replied, his voice more serious than before.

"Know your enemy, gentlemen." Baz replied, knowledgably, "know your enemy."

Mike still wasn't sure if he'd known the answer, or if he was just acting as if he did. He looked down at the loader, seeing nothing but a grin in response.

Bill now piped in, as if it had just come to him in a brain wave.

"Hang on! That's why they didn't know where we were!"

"Correct." Mike replied, "the crews were probably tearing along, counting on their Shtora systems to bail them out, plus without the loader they don't have the extra pair of eyes watching what's on what's going on around them."

Mike was interrupted from his explanation as one of the tanks in the valley exploded, the turret flinging itself high into the air and burying itself about 100 metres away from the burning hulk, the long barrel digging deep into the earth. He could see movement alongside the other destroyed tanks, watching through the binos as the survivors from the crews were dashing and crawling towards the safety of the hedgerows and ditches. They'd all seen where he was now, he could see hands pointing up accusingly to their old position. No doubt they would be attempting to warn their comrades coming in the other tanks. It was a catch 22 for him, he could bring the tank up and finish them off with the machine gun to silence them once and for all, but for what purpose? If he fired the machine gun then the tracer fire would give away his position, just the same as if he let the crews escape. Plus, it just didn't sit right with him. Despite everything he'd seen so far, everything he'd witnessed, he didn't want to be that person. Instead, he chose to let them go, watching them drag their wounded with them.

He watched the progress of the other tanks in the distance, they looked to be advancing in platoon formations, three tanks covering, whilst three raced forwards. None of them had showed any indication they knew where he was, the turrets were all looking off to east, perhaps that's where they thought the threat had come from. He watched them advancing ever closer, knowing the next engagement would have to be much closer than the first. Realising he had the time, he thought about sending a quick update, it had been a few minutes since his last communication with anyone, he reached down, switching over to the troop net.

"Tango Two-Zero, Tango One-One send sitrep, over."

Almost immediately Patty's voice came back in reply.

"Tango One-One, Tango Two-Zero, we're still proceeding north, currently on the 52 northing, enemy activity is light, Talons will be back with us in figures two. Perhaps now it's time for you to withdraw? Over."

Mike could hear the hint in Patty's voice loud and clear. The Corporal wanted them out of there. He looked down, plotting Patty's latest update on the map, the hope he felt, was replaced by a grim realisation as he saw the convoy were no-where near as far away as he hoped they'd be. The convoy was going slower than he'd thought. Since leaving them they'd only managed another kilometre. Christ, Mike thought, at this rate it would be quicker for them to get out and walk. He tried to hide the frustration in his voice as he replied.

"Tango One-One, roger, keep at it, out."

He flicked over to the HF net, keeping a wary eye out for what was going on ahead of him, checking the enemy were still looking over to the east.

"Hello, Whiskey Zero, this is Whiskey Three-Zero, sitrep over."

After a few seconds, a female voice came back.

"Whiskey Three-Zero, send."

"Sitrep as of now, lead callsign of Tango Two-Zero, currently on the 52 northing heading north, my callsign, Tango One-One set in fire position at grid 355,495, have engaged and destroyed six T-80's. Intention is to delay and harass before withdrawing north. Do we have any chance of support for my lead callsigns enroute to you? They're towing a casualty vehicle and progress is slow. Over."

Mike already knew the answer, but ever hopeful thought to ask anyway. After a few moments the voice was replaced by another, more gruff voice, confirming his fears.

"Tango One-One, sorry, we don't have anything to send out in support. For now, I'm afraid, you're on your own, over."

Of course, you don't have anything to send, Mike thought glumly. *We're* supposed to be your support, and now we're the ones asking for assistance. Mike chuckled to himself at the irony of it all, shaking his head in disbelief. How the hell had it come to this?

Laughing loudly at their predicament he simply replied.

"Tango One-One, roger, understood. Friendly callsigns should be with you in figures three-zero. Keep an eye out for them, out."

He went back to watching the enemy tanks advancing, counting down the ranges in his head.

"That's it...keep coming...keep on coming..."

8

Holding Back The Tide

Wolf Command

Colonel Golgolvin was in a foul mood, watching the English countryside flashing by as his armoured vehicle raced towards the front of their huge column. Following closely behind were the BMP's of his beloved VDV, already overtaking the vehicles of the 126th Inf Regt. Ever since this had all began the Colonel had kept them close, preferring the men he'd trained with all his military career, to the unknown faces of the other units. Now it was as if they were his own personal guard, wherever he went they followed, and he never complained, not after the way they were nearly wiped out by that fool Lebedev.

What the hell was going on back at headquarters? he fumed to himself, unable to comprehend the chaos and confusion in the conflicting orders being sent. First, he'd been ordered to halt the attack and collapse their positions, racing south with almost all his forces, leaving behind a lone infantry company to guard an area far too big for them to manage, merely a token force, to hold the ground they'd already taken.

Then, after a mad dash south to get into rushed positions, they'd waited for an hour for an attack that never came, only to be told that the enemy had simply turned around and headed home without a shot being fired. He'd remembered seeing on the map where the enemy units were positioned, from where they had been they had a clear run against three of their softest and most valuable military targets, and yet, they had turned and ran. None of it made any sense, especially when the reason HQ had given for the enemy's rapid turnaround was because it had seen the 77th and the 75th. He'd sat there for over an hour and at no point had either of those regiments come past him. So, what the hell was going on?

Now his units were strung out in one long column stretching out over 3 kilometres along the fields, such was their rush to get back to Yeovil. They'd not been expecting any action, the route back was in friendly territory, *their* territory. And yet, ahead of him, his two lead tank companies of the 344th were reporting they were in contact, whilst he'd been sat halfway down the column idly scratching his balls. If the enemy they were looking for had fled back east, then who the hell was attacking him? His mood was sour, and he had a nagging doubt in his gut, something about what HQ was reporting back didn't make sense. He looked up towards the sky, thankful at least the British didn't have air superiority, with his unit as spread out as it was, it would make a tempting target. He thought back to when they'd received their latest orders, seeing the disbelief in his soldiers as they'd yet again received orders to pull out, to pack up their hasty positions and head back to Yeovil, the sideways glances, the mutterings amongst the men. Soldiers weren't stupid, they'd do what they were told, so long as they trusted those above them. At the moment, he could see that trust slowly eroding. He knew the men would never say anything to him, but if he could already sense the mood now, then what the hell were they all saying behind closed doors when he wasn't about? Soldiers were easy to handle he thought, morale however was not, and after the past 24 hours he knew he'd have to do something about it. Perhaps, after they'd taken Yeovil he could arrange a show, or maybe even see if he could grant some of the troops a small amount of leave. It was crazy to have to think of such things after only four days of being in combat, but ever since landing, his unit had been rushed from one battlefield to the next, chasing a mostly unseen enemy, and sadly, the most damaging of all, most of their casualties had come from their own fucking artillery.

His thoughts were interrupted as ahead of them he saw more explosions in the distance, thick black smoke already billowing into the sky. Even at this distance he could see one of his tank's turrets flying skywards, disappearing from view into the dead ground. As if to confirm it, the CO of the 344th came on the radio.

"Wolf Command, Tiger Command, lead elements reporting they are under fire. Assessing now."

He uttered a curse as the column began to close up together, providing more of a target, quickly shouting over the radio.

"All commanders, DON'T CLOSE UP! Get yourselves spread out into battle formations!"

He held on as his driver bounced the vehicle off the road, having to navigate round vehicles that had stopped, their commanders not knowing what to do. He looked behind him as he passed, angry to have to micromanage his troops yet again as he reiterated on the radio…

"I repeat, all commanders, get your units out in all round defence, DO NOT FUCKING BUNCH UP TOGETHER!"

He left them to sort themselves out, concentrating instead on what was going on ahead of them. These were supposed to be cleared areas, he thought, there wasn't supposed to be any enemy here. What the hell were the units on the front doing, how the hell did this happen? So many questions, and as always never enough answers. His thoughts were interrupted as the CO of the 344th sent his report.

"Tiger Command continuing, I have three tanks destroyed, believed to be engaged by small tanks. They're withdrawing at speed heading north. Have lead elements pursuing them now, out."

Confused, he replied, "Tiger Command, Wolf Command, what do you mean by small tanks?"

"I mean they're small, tracked, and equipped with anti-armour rockets." the CO replied briefly.

Golgolvin looked over, trying to see for himself what was going on ahead. He could hear his tanks firing at something unseen ahead of them. Seeing nothing but vehicles ahead of him, he quickly shot out.

"Driver, get me up to the CO's tank. Quickly!"

He held on as the BMP accelerated away, driving between vehicles that were scattered along the sides of the road. After a few moments he saw the lead tank company ahead had broken out into a large arrow shaped position, the turrets looking outwards, scanning for more threats. On the road were two tanks, burning furiously, the third appeared to have attempted to get off the road, it was burning brightly in a field, the turret already missing. He saw the CO's tank ahead of them, The CO stood waving at him as he approached, pulling his BMP alongside, lifting his earpiece so he could yell across.

The CO had a look of both anger and awe as he described what he'd seen.

"I've never seen anything like it, small, tracked vehicles like you'd see in a film. Looked to be fitted with some kind of anti-tank rocket. I had no idea the British even had anything like it!"

"How many?" Golgolvin asked, hiding his own shock. He'd hadn't expected to meet anything like this on the battlefield. Command would want to know about it.

"I only saw two of the little bastards, they've shot off heading north, I've got one of my platoons chasing them down now, we think they're out of ammunition."

Golgolvin looked around, the CO already saying what he was thinking.

"This area was supposed to be cleared of enemy activity. What the hell's going on?"

As if to answer they heard another explosion ahead, both of them craning forwards to see. They could just see in the distance the platoon of tanks disappearing into the dead ground ahead, firing at the fleeing robots.

"I don't know, but let's not get caught out again, tell your platoon to stop chasing those damn things and return back here. We'll continue forwards but I want to clear this as if it's enemy held territory again until we know what the fuck is going on."

The CO nodded grimly, quickly speaking into his microphone. Golgolvin left him to it, looking behind him then suspiciously up towards the sky. Something didn't feel right, something was nagging at the back of his mind. He looked back, drawing strength and confidence from the number of vehicles he had under his command, his doubts vanishing quickly.

"What are you up to?" he murmured to the unseen enemy.

After a few moments of waiting Golgolvin looked over, eyebrows raised at the CO.

"Well, are those tanks coming back or not?"

The CO looked up, a look of frustration on his face. "They're not answering up on the radio. What the hell?"

Both looked over to the distance hearing the sounds of tank fire, different to the T-80's though, seeing pillars of smoke billowing upwards. Suddenly they heard machine gun fire, tracer rounds shooting into the sky. Something was happening up ahead.

"Get them support!" Golgolvin demanded.

"God dammit!" the CO cursed, realising what was happening. Quickly he began to bark out orders to the other tanks, watching as they began to push forwards into battle formations. Golgolvin watched as the second tank company sprung to life, pushing outwards towards the high ground.

He looked around him, quickly issuing orders to the 126th and the 344th, watching as the commanders of each regiment began to organise their forces and push them outwards. Something was attacking them, and they needed to find it and quickly. For now, the mad dash back would wait. Within minutes they were spread out into battle formations, the tanks leading, spread out over a 2 kilometre front and advancing cautiously, closely followed by the infantry, slowly pushing onwards, the soldiers alert and ready for anything. Golgolvin placed his command group in the centre, keeping back from his lead tanks by about 600 metres, from here he could observe the battle, direct his forces where they were needed and call for support where he needed it the most, reacting to whatever the enemy could throw at him. His VDV units stayed close, for now he had them form his reserve, ready to deploy enmasse to overwhelm anyone foolish enough to stand against them. He surveyed the troops around him, happy with what he now saw. Finally, he gave the order they were all waiting for. He ordered them to advance.

RAF Colerne Bath.

"FOR FUCKS SAKE!" Peter yelled as he heard the line abruptly cut. He looked at the phone, anger coursing through him at how the CDS had just dismissed him.

Putting the phone away quickly before he was tempted to throw it, he looked around the operations room, seeing the staff looking at him in surprise. It was rare for Peter to lose his temper, and even more rare for him to swear. To have done both together meant he must have been really pissed.

He watched on screen as the tank began to push into its firing position, Mike had used the Wasp to good effect, keeping eyes on the advancing Russians whilst remaining hidden. At first Peter had wondered what the hell he was playing at, but then seeing the rest of his unit dragging the dead vehicle, he knew he was buying them time they needed to escape.

For the next ten minutes they all stood watching the video feeds, the frustration and feelings of helplessness echoed by the muttered shouts and curses of those watching as the battle unfolded. Mike's tank was now firing at the Russian lead elements, locked in a tank versus tank battle. Peter watched transfixed as the rounds bounced off the enemy tanks, cursing to himself and to those in charge. It was almost incompetence to have sent Mike the training ammunition. But was he really that surprised, he thought angrily. Throughout his own military career he'd seen the constant erosion of the military by those in charge, always expecting the brave men and women who serve to always do more with less. Now, history was repeating itself, except this time it was *he* who had at his disposal the means to help, and it was Mike and his crew who were expected to do the impossible.

Already he could see the Russians were beginning to push out to flank the position, soon Mike's tank would be surrounded and cut off. Peter thought long and hard about what to do next, knowing to sit by and do nothing could result in him having to watch his friend die in glorious technicolour. He thought back to their history together, how much they'd both been through already, all the work that they'd done together since. With Mike's input into Aurora and his technical expertise, it was all about to go up in smoke in a matter of minutes. Finally, he made his decision.

He looked around the room, his eyes settling on Kyle and David, waving them over. Both men rushed over, seeing the urgency written over Peter's face as he looked at them.

"How soon can we get Wendi uploaded and ready?"

The CDS was right, what the hell had they designed Wendi for if not for now?

Whiskey Three-Zero

Mike was waiting, his foot tapping on the turret floor, the only outward sign of nerves that were creeping up his spine. No-one spoke on the crew, the banter from before gone, as everyone was poised ready to go as he watched the Russian units creep across the terrain, like insects they crawled, getting ever closer, until finally Mike could wait no longer. He judged the range to be 500 metres, any closer and he'd be at risk of being overrun when they tried to escape, any further, and the rounds would be next to useless. All the Russian vehicles were heading towards them, but for some reason were still looking over to the east, Mike thought something must have made them look that way.

"Okay guys, here we go." Mike said softly, almost as if the Russians could hear.

The tank rolled slowly forwards, coming to the edge of the woodline, the barrel just beginning to poke through. Mike was watching the lead platoon of tanks, already identifying their next target. He was about to issue the fire order, when suddenly, out of nowhere the front of their tank exploded in a shower of sparks as a noise like a jackhammer reverberated through them. For a moment Mike thought they'd been hit, suddenly realising it was heavy machine gun fire. Confused, he peered over at where it was coming from, quickly realising what was happening.

Down below them, where the first three tanks had been destroyed, one of the enemy crew, tired of waiting to warn their friends had opted for a quicker way. Braving the flames and the risk of an explosion, he'd jumped back onto the burning turret, aiming the commander's heavy machine gun at Mike's position and was firing. Now, with the heavy tracer thumping all around the tank, he'd just shown everyone where to look. Mike could nothing about it except yell down to Bill.

"BACK! BILL REVERSE, QUICKLY!"

The tank reversed at speed, throwing up a large cloud of dust, Mike could already see the lead platoons turrets swing their way.

"Shit!" Mike cursed, knowing already the element of surprise had gone. Now the Russians knew they were there, which had always been the plan, to draw them in but Mike had at least hoped to have thinned the numbers further.

Mike watched as the tracer fire hammered into the trees, tearing at branches and stripping leaves, followed by the crack as two AP rounds whizzed through, splintering the trees like balsa wood. Mike ducked low as the deadly wooden splinters whipped by overhead, showering the turret roof in matchwood. Now the Russians certainly knew what was afoot.

"Fuck it! Bill keep reversing, we'll come up somewhere else."

Mike manoeuvred the tank further into the woods, electing to use another fire position in a different area. Hopefully the Russians would be pre-occupied with firing at the first. Already their old position was shrouded in smoke and shrapnel as the Russians poured fire into it.

After a few moments Mike had the tank where he wanted it, this time they were emerging out to the western side of the wood, keeping the speed low, Bill ready to slam the tank into reverse if necessary.

They pushed the tank forward tentatively, with him standing up to obtain a better view, ready to duck back down if necessary. More of the battlefield came into view, then he could see a lone tank, then two, then all three. The tanks were firing on the move, still throwing rounds into their old position. Mike shook his head at the waste of it, so much ammunition being fired haphazardly, at least the Russians weren't bothered by lack of logistics.

He selected his target, judging the distance by using the ranges he'd written in the cupola.

"Okay Smudge, right hand side tank, when your ready...DST, tank, five hundred!"

"On, five hundred!"

"Loaded!"

"Firing!"

The round flew out, ricocheting off the front of the enemy tank's turret in a shower of sparks, the round fragmenting against the thick turret armour and splitting into two.

"Target go on!" Mike ordered, watching as the enemy tank stopped suddenly, the turret scanning, as the crew sought to find them. The shock of being hit, then realising the round had no effect on them must have made the enemy crew feel like a million dollars. Suddenly with a jerk it was off again, continuing to advance, Mike watching as a second round was fired, the same effect, this time the round ricocheted into the ground, showering earth over the tank, which continued forwards as if the rounds hitting it were nothing more bothersome than a fly.

Mike saw the turrets turn towards him, realising he'd be seen, he reversed the tank back into the cover of the woods, keeping eyes on what the enemy were up to with the Wasp. No sooner had the tank started pulling back than the ground in front of them erupted in a frenzy of explosions as three tank rounds were shot towards it in anger. Mike continued pulling the tank backwards, away from danger. The plan looked to be working, as suddenly the lead enemy tanks began to swing towards the minefield, pouring rounds into the hill, attempting to keep Mike pinned down. Little realising he was already deep within the woods and out of harm's way. Mike watched as the three T-80s streamed forwards, advancing faster than before as they charged closer to Mike's old positions. Perhaps their confidence was buoyed by seeing just how inadequate the Chally's rounds were against them. Suddenly an explosion sounded, and the lead tank disappeared in a cloud of smoke and dust. After a few seconds it emerged, still moving forwards but minus the right-side track. It continued forwards a few more metres before finally slewing to a halt, sliding sideways, unable to go any further. The two other tanks kept going, unaware of what had happened, when suddenly as one they both exploded into huge fireballs, the flames and smoke causing them to disappear from view. When the dust and smoke settled, one was burning furiously, the other missing it's turret, now just a huge gaping hole remained, full of fire and misery. Mike had no idea where its turret had gone, he guessed it had vaporised in the explosion.

He watched on the tablet display as the others approached more cautiously, another platoon of tanks was advancing from the south, whilst a convoy of BMP3's looked to be approaching from the east, perhaps they were working together, trying to flank his position. He waited, watching with baited breath as the tanks stopped short of the minefield and continued to fire into the woodline, the trees being felled by the high explosive rounds falling amongst them. Ignoring the tanks he watched the BMP's, as they approached the mines, hopeful to have the same results as before. His hopes were dashed as instead of driving into the minefield, they stopped short, the infantry now dismounting and going ahead on foot, carefully scouting and probing the ground for mines before calling the vehicles forward. It was a bold move by the platoon leader, by doing so the infantry had risked exposing themselves to incoming fire, sacrificing the protection of the armour. But Mike could also see the BMP's turrets were now firing towards his direction, putting down a fearsome amount of firepower. The 30mm cannons were raking the treeline whilst the 100mm guns fired HE rounds into the woods. If he went forwards to fire on the soldiers, he'd risk being hit, and if he exposed the tank, they'd no doubt launch missiles at him. The progress was slow, but Mike could already see the three vehicles making inroads into the minefield. As if to confirm his fears, another three BMP's drove up out of cover, quickly lining up behind the first three, using the lanes that were now being cleared.

Mike didn't fancy the prospect of the infantry getting involved, if they made it through the minefield and into the cover of the woods then he knew that his tank, without infantry support, would quickly get overwhelmed.

Leaving the armour for now, he decided to deal with the BMP's, after all at least the training rounds would work on them.

He brought the tank around, navigating through the dense woodland, making sure Smudge kept the long barrel away from the trees. The last thing they needed right now was to have a barrel strike with one. It was a strange, serene feeling, seeing the rays of sunshine bursting through, casting strange shadows on the floor, and for a fleeting moment Mike almost forgot they were fighting a battle, his mind drifting away to how the wood could make an excellent spot for him and Kate to stop in the future and have a picnic. He was brought back to reality as Bill's voice screeched over the radio.

"Boss, how far up do you want me to go?"

He saw the daylight up ahead as they approached the open ground, some of the enemy rounds exploding in the clearing, he'd have to be careful here, there was no bank to hide behind.

Suddenly he had a thought, quickly he reached over picking up the tablet, keeping one eye on where Bill was heading.

"Bill, right stick, nice and slowly, that's it, see that tree up ahead, bring us up on its right-hand side."

The driver acknowledged, as slowly the tank crept forwards. Deciding he was as close as he dared to the incoming fire, Mike stopped the tank, now only five metres of cover remained. All he had to do was drive slowly forwards and the barrel would have a clear line of sight to the enemy.

Mike selected the Wasp that was hovering at the other end of the wood. Quickly taking control, he brought it in high and fast, sweeping away to the right, allowing it a clear run above the BMP's.

On the screen Mike selected one of the High Explosive grenades, the targeting reticule overlaying on what he was seeing.

"Right Bill, when I tell you to, keep creeping forwards, Smudge, when we start to move, I want you to talk to Bill, guide him forwards and let him know when you can see the BMP's. Don't wait for me, target the closest BMP, engage it as quick as you can. Use DST and remember to report either target stop, or target go on."

Both acknowledged the order, the adrenaline clear to hear in their voices. Leaving them to it, Mike resumed the attack using the Wasp.

Looking down in concentration, he carefully guided the Wasp in, seeing the infantry were now a quarter of the way through the minefield. He watched as some of them stopped and looked up, one was pointing at the Wasp, then others were looking, suddenly they had the weapons raised, and Mike could hear the automatic fire as they tried to shoot it out of the sky. Mike knew the Wasp would automatically jink left and right and up and down, trying to throw off their aim, all part of its pre-programmed flight defences. He concentrated on the lead BMP, trying to gauge the drop just right. He could see the hatches were open, the crew were hunkered down, eyes glued to their sights, still firing at his position. Just as the targeting reticule lined up, he pressed the release, dropping two of the grenades onto the vehicle. The first bounced off the turret, exploding harmlessly on the ground, but the second managed to disappear inside, a hollow thump sounding as thick grey smoke poured out of the open hatch. He saw one of the crew men jump out and roll on the floor, his arm alight, whilst the driver jumped out, rolling across the engine deck, laying alongside the vehicle.

The other vehicles all began to turn their turrets to this new threat, forgetting all about firing into the trees and instead trying to shoot the Wasp out of the sky. Mike kept it moving around them, almost taunting them with its presence.

"Right Bill, right Smudge, let's do it. Driver advance!"

Mike kept one eye on what they were doing and one eye on the tablet, trying desperately not to get the Wasp shot down. One of the BMP's turrets swung back to the woodline about to engage again, Mike overflew it, dropping another grenade at it, disappointed to see they'd now closed their hatches to the new threat from above. The grenade exploded onto the engine deck, sending a harmless cloud of smoke and shrapnel skyward. But Mike wasn't interested in trying to destroy them, he was trying to distract them and watched on satisfied as once again the turret began to spin angrily around, the crew trying to shoot at the Wasp that was clearly annoying them.

Mike looked up as the battlefield came into view, now he could see the Wasp overhead, and began controlling it from sight rather than the tablet screen. He looked over with satisfaction, all the BMP's were concentrating their fire on the Wasp, and no one had seen the tank appear. He heard Bill and Smudge talking as if on a radio play as they began to work together again. Smudge quickly identifying one of the vehicles and beginning the engagement.

"DST, BMP...Err Shit! Boss what's the range?"

Mike looked over, realising they were closer than he'd thought. He should have warned Smudge about that. Without looking at his sight, he blurted out.

"GO FOUR HUNDRED CLOSE RANGE!"

"ON FOUR HUNDRED!"

"LOADED!"

"FIRING!"

Boom, the gun slammed back again, the round impacting almost immediately. Mike saw the flash as the round entered the front of the BMP, unlike the armour of the T-80, the BMP's armour was never designed to take a tank round at such close range. The back of the BMP seemed to swell outwards, as if it were an overfilled balloon, before peeling outwards and exploding, flinging debris far and wide. Mike almost punched the air for joy as the back doors of the vehicle seemed to blast off, being flung into the vehicle behind it damaging the tracks. Two for the price of one, he thought happily. Mike was so entranced by what he'd seen he hadn't heard his crew shout the warning, as the air buzzed to life around him with small arms fire, like angry hornets they whipped past. The infantry on the ground were now firing at him, exposed as he was.

"Shit!" he shouted as the cupola lit up around him, sparks ricocheting all around, causing him to leap back down.

"REVERSE!" he shouted, angry at himself for being so easily distracted. That was a stupid thing to be doing he fumed. He was getting careless; the fatigue and the tiredness over the past days were finally beginning to take its toll. He shook his head, trying to clear the grogginess that seemed to fill it, even with the adrenaline coursing through his body. He kept looking behind then forwards, checking where the tank was reversing and ensuring the barrel stayed clear of the trees. After a few moments he stopped the tank, thinking through what to do next. He looked over at the Wasp's display, watching the scene now unfolding in the minefield as the first vehicle he'd shot at with the grenade looked to be rolling forwards, the driver running behind it desperate to get back on board. Clearly, he'd bailed out of the vehicle and hadn't put the handbrake on. It had an almost comedic feel about it, as the infantry in front dived out of its way. Without knowing why, he started to laugh at the sight, relaying to the others what was happening, lowering the tablet down to show them. When Baz began to sing the Benny Hill theme tune, that was it, suddenly they were all laughing, it felt strange, to be in such danger yet all laughing about a bunch of people that were trying to kill you. Wasn't war strange, Mike thought, chuckling and wiping away the tears.

Suddenly the laughter died away. Mikes cheerfulness replaced with a growing sense of dread at what was happening on the screen in front of him. What had started off as an amusing mistake had suddenly turned serious. The enemy vehicle had continued rolling forwards on its mad dash through the minefield, picking up speed, some of the smaller mines detonating beneath it as it continued along out of control. Mike had watched, expecting any second for it to hit one of the larger ones, until suddenly it emerged through the minefield unscathed, bouncing across the open ground and finally coming to a stop less than 100 metres from where Mike was positioned. The driver had run forwards, now finally admitting defeat and stopping, his hands resting on his knees as he sucked in lungfuls of air. But the driver looked up, suddenly Mike could see him realise how far into the mine field he was. He was almost through it. Then the others could see it, realising the runaway vehicle had just cleared the minefield for them. Suddenly the infantry were running onto the vehicles tracks, waving over to the surviving BMP's who all followed suit. Within a minute, they'd be in the woods. Mike couldn't stay there any longer, the woods were no place for a tank to fight infantry. They'd have him colliding the turret with all the trees as he tried to hit them.

"Oh Shit!" Mike exclaimed, startling the others. Quickly he looked up, judging where they'd be coming through then looking north, to his escape route. It was time to go. He quickly manoeuvred the Wasp over to the end of the wood, leaving it there as he manoeuvred the tank around. No sooner had he turned the tank ready to go when Baz was shouting up from the RWS sight.

"I CAN SEE INFANTRY!!"

"Well shoot at them!" Mike shot back in surprise, still concentrating on getting them out of there.

He left Baz to it, trying to guide the driver through the thick trees, as the machine gun began to bark out, suddenly stopping as Baz shouted in alarm.

"STOPPAGE! FUCK!"

The machine gun on the RWS had jammed, Mike's only form of self-defence in the woods had just gone, and as if to add to his misery he heard Changa on the radio.

"Tango One-One, Tango Two-One-Alpha, the tow rope's just broken, we'll need ten minutes to fix it."

Fucking hell, thought Mike, sometimes it never just rained, it poured...

9

Downfall

"Left a bit Smudge, left a bit… There he is! Get him!" Mike shouted, the fire order lost in his excitement and rush to stop the enemy attack.

He watched as the turret jerked to the left, the chain gun barking out in anger as Smudge attempted to hit the lone infantryman running through the woods. The rounds thumped into the trees, the bark splintering off them until finally the figure dashed out again, three of the trace rounds disappearing into his body, the rounds setting fire to his clothing. Amazingly the figure continued staggering forwards, disappearing behind another tree, but dropping the handheld rocket he had been carrying. Mike being reminded at just how much punishment the human body could endure.

Mike looked behind him, seeing more figures emerging through the trees, the small arms fire ricocheting against the tank. Harmless for now, but they were getting ever closer.

Mike was finding out the hard way that tanks were never designed to fight in forests. Already the infantry had tried to fire three anti-tank missiles at them, two had exploded into the dense treeline, whilst the third, being wire guided had snagged onto a low hanging branch, pirouetting round the tree like a demonic maypole dancer. It's rocket tail lighting the dry leaves and grassland around it as it spun closer and closer until finally it collided with the oak tree's base, exploding and showering some of the infantry in molten shards of metal. But as much as the woods were a blessing, they were also a curse, and twice already they'd collided the barrel against the tree's trying to chase the infantry around. It was as if the enemy were intent on being an orchestra, dancing around the tank, trying to hit it and Mike was the conductor, the barrel the baton, sat in the centre, directing the deadly chorus as they played their fiercely fought cat and mouse games.

Twice Baz had tried to go outside to clear the RWS stoppage, twice he'd nearly been shot, it was as if the infantry knew what he was trying to do. Every time his hatch opened the bullets would come in thick and fast. The second attempt Baz had nearly made it, managing to get the feed tray off the weapon. But he was beaten back, flesh was no match against bullets and all Baz could do now was curse from within the safety of the turret, as the RWS remained cold and silent, the broken ammunition belt flailing uselessly, almost as if trying to lure Baz out for just one more try.

Three of the BMPs were burning furiously at the wood's outer edge, Mike managing to find the time to engage them. They'd come over the rise blindly firing into the woods, not knowing the tank's exact position, but meanwhile Mike had known where they'd be, his own eyes in the sky were proving invaluable. As if sensing the danger awaiting them in the woods, the other BMPs were lingering just outside, disgorging more infantry who came pouring through in even greater numbers, some carrying those damned RPG's. Now however the picture looked bleaker, already two of the enemy tanks were fast approaching in support with more following behind and with Mike pre-occupied fighting the infantry, he was in no position to stop them, the perfect catch 22. He was about to be overwhelmed. Quickly he thought back to something in his past, a moment when as a young Trooper he'd accidentally set off the smoke generator in the tank hangar. He remembered the shouts and curses as the whole of his troop had been forced out of the hangar, coughing and spluttering, eyes watering as the diesel fumes had poured into every nook and cranny. Of course! If it worked then..

"Bill! Smoke left, smoke right! Quickly!"

He heard the engine revs increase as the thick white smoke began to spew out of the tank's exhausts, within seconds the tank was covered, he leapt up, pulling his rifle inside and his hatch closed just as the choking white fumes began to pour inside. Outside in the woods it was chaos as the thick smoke poured across the infantry. Some still rushed forwards, intent on attacking, using the smoke screen to allow them to get closer. Mike could see their dark shadows in the smoke, stopping suddenly, dropping to their knees as they realised how bad it was to be engulfed by the diesel fumes. Others ran straight for safety in the open air, grabbing soldiers as they ran, desperate to get away as their eyes and throats burned. He saw a lone soldier bravely climb onboard the tank, banging uselessly against Mike's hatch with his rifle butt, the dull thuds echoing inside. Mike watched through the periscopes as the figure held his breath, his face reddening with the effort, until eventually he was beaten back, his eyes streaming in tears as he exploded into a coughing fit, rolling off the tank leaving his weapon behind. Mike waited a full minute before deciding it had been long enough.

"Okay Bill, that'll do."

The engine began to whine down as Bill took his foot off the accelerator, Mike looked over to Baz, having a quick check through the periscopes.

"Baz, now's your chance, get that bloody RWS firing."

Needing no further prompts Baz was out of the hatch with the dexterity of a cat, within a few seconds he was back in, blood dripping from a fresh cut on his hands, proudly brandishing the soldiers abandoned rifle.

"Don't mind if I do!" he said jovially, stowing the rifle amongst the turret, blood dripping over the floor. He looked back at Mike and seeing Mike's concerned gaze, Baz replied.

"Just a couple of the links in the belt were damaged that's all, must have been the grenade on the turret earlier. I've pulled them out and re-linked it, but that metal was fucking sharp. Should work now."

Mike smiled, congratulating his loader. The celebrations were short lived as Smudge shouted back up.

"DST TANK!"

Within seconds it was back to business, the loader's guard was made, and the gun ready to fire. Using his sight Mike looked through the smoky haze, seeing the shadow of the T-80 smashing through the trees, it was no more than 300 metres from him, driving across their front, the crew oblivious to where Mike was. Some of the infantry were pointing over, desperate to get the crew's attention as the enemy turret spun madly left and right, trying to see through the smoke. Suddenly its machine gun barked out, hitting some of the soldiers, throwing them into the ground and trees. Mike couldn't believe it; the enemy crew were so disorientated they were firing on their own side. Angry infantrymen, still coughing and spluttering dived for cover, their fight with the Chally forgotten as this new threat from their own side came in amongst them. The benefit for Mike was that his own tank was still protected by smoke and hidden in the dark shadows of the trees, whereas the enemy tank was now sky lined by the sunlight pouring through from outside the treeline. Mike was tempted to leave it firing on its own troops, but already another tank was cresting the rise, soon more would follow. It would be an easy kill, but only if he took the shot now.

"Fire!" he shouted, the gun answering in reply as the breech slammed back. It was a good hit, with the round penetrating the turret cleanly, even at this range the DST would be deadly. Mike watched on as the tank erupted into flames almost immediately, great jets of flame shot out from the turret hatches as the tank continued forwards, driving through the woods. Had the driver been killed, he thought in wonderment as it disappeared amongst the trees on its deadly journey.

They quickly sighted the gun onto the second tank, Baz making the guard as the gun fired, quickly dispatching it, the vehicle exploding amongst its troops, showering them in burning fuel and metal as they lay screaming and writhing on the ground.

"Last round!" Baz shouted in warning, causing Mike to look over in surprise.

Christ, had they nearly shot their bombload already? Mike wondered worriedly, knowing they had nowhere near enough firepower to hold them off much longer. As if sensing their predicament, it was Smudge who asked the question that Mike was already thinking.

"How much longer can we keep holding them off like this?"

"Not much longer now guys, let's keep it together, we're still in the fight." Mike replied, his voice full of determination. He could already see other enemy tank units outside the woods were pushing past them, trying to cut off their retreat. He was about to say something when the radio burst to life, Patty's voice almost exploding through with the excitement.

"Tango One-One, Tango Two-One-Alpha, we've got the tow ropes back on and are moving now."

Thank fuck for that, Mike thought in reply, watching as Smudge fired the machine gun at another enemy position, before keying the radio and reporting.

"Tango One-One, roger that, we're moving now, we can't hold this position any longer, be with you shortly, out!"

Mike was about to issue the order to reverse back when Smudge cut him off, the turret spinning to the left as finally he saw the enemy tank advancing over the bank.

"SHIT! DST TANK CLOSE RANGE!" Smudge shouted, firing at the same time. Mikes eyes opened wide in alarm at how close the enemy had come up; the round didn't have the time to separate from its casing and get to its full speed before hitting the underbelly of the enemy tank as it powered up and over the crest. Thankfully the underbelly on the T-80 was not as armoured as the turret and the round smashed through with ease, the enemy tank slamming down, smoke quickly pouring from it. Mike watched the enemy tank carefully, checking it was out of action, the turret remained where it was, as the tank rolled forwards, finally coming to a stop against a large tree, the flames licking out from the turret, lighting up the tree's trunk.

"Ammunition expended!" Baz shot out, looking up at Mike with his hands held up in resignation. The breech was left open, they were finally out of tank rounds. Now it was machine guns only.

"Okay Bill, reverse, let's get the fuck out of this tree line."

Mike looked behind him out of habit, his eyes burning and red rimmed from the lingering diesel fumes and smoke. With great care the crew negotiated the trees, carefully weaving themselves further into the woods, Mike already getting the Wasp set up to cover their exit. They had another 200 metres of woodline to negotiate and then they'd be out onto open ground, Mike's plan was just to floor it, to get to another position and hope the tank could survive the punishment. There was no other option. He felt the tank accelerate as Bill came to a clearing in the woods. In the centre was a huge oak tree, hundreds of years old, dominating the clearing. Suddenly there was a flash in the treeline over to their left side and Mike felt the thud of something hitting the tank as it began to slew left, towards the danger. Mike knew something was wrong, even as Bill shouted up in warning.

"We've been hit, shit I think we've lost the track! I can't steer!"

Mike heard the engine racing as Bill tried to steer the tank away from the tree, hearing the rattle of steel as the left-hand track began to uncoil and snake out in front of them, slamming against the ground. Mike shouted in warning for everyone to brace for the impact as the tank collided with the huge tree, the weight and speed of the tank pushing the tree over onto its side. The old tree had its own revenge, as the giant roots tore out of the ground as it went over they caught underneath the tank, levering the tank's hull off the floor, the tank's momentum causing it to continue sliding up and over the huge trunk in a screech of metal, causing the other track to now lift off the ground. For a second, the tank sat there with its engine racing and one good track spinning uselessly in the air, until Bill realised, they were going nowhere fast and took his foot of the power. Now they were beached, stuck precariously on the tree with no way of moving, and even if they could miraculously pull the 70-tonne tank off the tree, they'd need at least an hour to fix the damaged track. Now they were exposed in the middle of the clearing, with no cover and the enemy coming at them from all sides.

Mike felt the turret begin to turn to the left to face the threat, stopping suddenly as it banged against something hard. Smudge tried moving the turret to the right, it moved a metre, perhaps two before coming to a stop again. The motors whined in protest as Smudge demanded more power, something was stopping the turret's progress as the gunner shot out fearfully.

"Shit! boss, I can't move the turret! It's stuck!"

Mike cautiously raised his head, seeing the long gun jammed firmly in amongst the oak tree's huge branches, disappearing into the greenery, the thick wood having a vice like hold on the turret. He'd need a chainsaw to free it. Not only were they unable to move, but now they were unable to point the machine gun mounted next to the gun. Now it was RWS only, and that only had 400 rounds left on it.

"Smudge, forget it, the turret's jammed in the trees."

The side of the tank exploded in flames as another anti-tank rocket slammed into it, the extra armour packs absorbing the massive energy. Mike ducked low in the turret as he felt the heat and shockwave pass over his head, shouting to Baz.

"FUCK! Baz get the RWS onto them, over to the left, 10 o'clock of the turret...QUICK-LY!"

Baz was quickly onto the RWS controls, selecting thermal and identifying the firing point. No more than 100 metres away were a group of infantry, already reloading the anti-tank rocket, preparing to fire again. The tank would be hard to miss at this range.

"I've got them...firing!" Baz reported, firing two small bursts at them, Mike watched satisfied as the rounds exploded into them, knocking three of the soldiers into the tall grass. The others dived for cover as Baz continued to keep them pinned down, firing short, controlled bursts.

Mike looked about the turret, trying to think of some way to get the tank going again. After a few seconds of deliberation, it hit him. The tank was stuck, and they were going no further. He saw movement behind them, a shadow in the trees moving around them. Another T-80 was in the woodline looking for them. If they were to stand any chance of making it out of there, they'd have to destroy the armour. Mike looked back over at the Hornet, knowing it was all they had left to use.

"Bill, rev the engine, give me 1000 rpm."

"But we've lost the track boss!" Bill exclaimed, as Mike retorted.

"Come on Bill, you know better by now than to argue with me, give me 1000 rpm please."

"Okay, sorry boss!" The driver replied as Mike felt and heard the engine begin to accelerate.

Mike activated the Hornet on the BMDS, watching behind him as the armoured doors of the case opened, and it extended to its full height. Mike watched it carefully, making sure everything was working as it should and checked it was safely away from the branches of the trees before settling back in his seat.

Almost immediately the lights seemed to dim in the vehicle as the same crackling as before was heard over their headsets.

The Hornet pivoted around, swinging on its own electrical mount as Mike turned to face the tank in the trees. It was coming straight for them, Mike was tempted to wait for it to get to the clearing, but knew if the T-80 fired now, at this range it would be catastrophic. Instead, he selected the targeting box, a small yellow box bracketed the enemy tank. Now all he had to was press the firing switch.

The turret crew were watching on, waiting in anticipation as Mike pressed the button, there was a crack like a lightning strike and again the smell of burnt hair filled the turret. Mike looked over at the enemy tank, disappointed as it continued to come towards him seemingly untouched. Suddenly it veered left, colliding with a tree, the engine racing as it began to push the tree over, before finally coming to a stop, the turbine engine racing loudly. After a few seconds the commander's hatch opened a few inches, someone inside was trying to get out as smoke and flames lanced outwards, as the crew were overwhelmed by the heat and smoke. Mike watched on open mouthed at the demise of the tank, imaging the screams of the crew in his mind, causing him to grimace as the outside of the tank showed no damage.

Mike looked at the charge of the weapon capacitors on the display, it was now at 70 percent and climbing slowly. It needed to be above 40 percent to be effective, so long as Mike kept the capacitors charging, the laser would fire.

"Baz let's get that extra belt of 7.62 off the chain gun and put it on the RWS, for now we're staying put."

The loader reached over, quickly snapping off the link of 400 rounds and climbing up, adding it to the existing belt. Now at least they had the ability to take on the tanks and the infantry.

Baz got back onto the RWS controls, pivoting the weapon system around and looking for new targets. He didn't have to wait long.

"I've got infantry sneaking up on the left, looks like they've got two BMPs with them."

Mike spun the Hornet, sighting onto the first BMP, aiming at where he imagined the gunner would be sat as he pressed the firing controls. Again, the interior lights dimmed, again the air around the crew seemed to come alive with electricity as the Hornet began to whine. Suddenly with another loud crack it fired, the only tell-tale sign on the target vehicle was a small puff of smoke off the turret. The vehicle stopped dead, as if it had just run into a wall as the back of it exploded, showering the infantry nearby in shrapnel and flames. The other BMP disappeared momentarily, lost in the fireball before darting out the other side, the driver with his foot to floor to escape the maelstrom. Mike heard the 100mm auto gun begin to fire, the rounds smashing into the tank's side in rapid succession, the shock waves throwing Baz to the floor as sparks flew out from the radios and turret systems. Mike hung on, sighting the Hornet onto the second BMP, no longer with the luxury of time he rushed his aim, firing the weapon at where the driver's cab would be, again the noise, again the electricity, then a zap and the BMP was hit. The incoming fire stopped almost immediately as the armoured vehicle seemed to roll to a halt, the commander and gunner bailing out, lying alongside it.

Baz, who by now had picked himself off the turret floor, was back on the RWS controls, firing into the infantry and scattering them like nine pins, as instead of firing back at the tank, they fought the forest fires that were springing up around them, the fuel from the burning BMP spreading ever closer, adding to their plight.

Mike left them to it, quickly checking on the state of his own vehicle, seeing the 100mm rounds hadn't penetrated the tanks armour, but the shock waves had done damage enough, already they could smell smoke pouring in from the engine compartment, something was alight in the engine decks, and the last thing they needed was an onboard fire.

"Fire in the engine decks!" Mike reported, adding, "Bill, shut the engine down and pull the extinguishers!"

They heard the engine whine down and begin to idle before finally going silent, followed by the soft hissing noise as the onboard extinguishers were activated. Mike watched the smoke coming in, disappointed to see instead of dying out, it was getting thicker. He took stock of their situation, they were out of 120mm ammo, low on machine gun ammo, the tank was immobile, they couldn't traverse the turret, the engine was on fire, and now the Russians knew where they were. Without the ability to charge the Hornet, it would be limited to a few shots. Mike looked over at Baz, the loader's face wearing the same gloomy look of realisation. They'd gone as far as they could with the tank, but now It was time to abandon the vehicle. They were out of options.

Finally relenting, Mike reported over the intercom.

"Okay crew, time to use our feet, prepare to abandon vehicle. Small arms and ammunition only. Smudge, get the barrel raised so Bill can get out. Everyone let's move, move, move."

Everyone exploded into a frenzy of activity, Mike sent an update over the HF radio, before leaping out, not waiting to hear the garbled reply, grabbing his assault rifle and quickly checking around the tank for anyone hiding nearby in ambush as one by one the crew emerged carrying a mixture of weaponry. Bill struggled to get out, his hatch was covered by the branches of the oak tree and Mike reached down, pulling him out and pointing down to the safe ground besides the tank, the oak tree's trunk providing the perfect cover for them. They all carefully climbed down, weapons out and ready in all-round defence. Baz looked back up at Mike expecting him to jump down with them, but instead Mike shook his head from on top of the turret.

"Guys give me two minutes; I need to destroy the tank and the equipment. Can't have it falling into enemy hands."

The others nodded in understanding, keeping their own fears hidden, a grim realisation that now they'd be nothing more than simple blobs of flesh and bone on a battlefield filled with metal monsters, the protection of the tank had made them feel immune to everything going on around them. Now they could hear, smell and see it all, and it made them all uncomfortable at how exposed and naked they were. Small arms fire whipped through the forest and explosions sounded nearby as the chaos of the battle continued around them, the Russians had yet to realise their only enemy was now out of action.

Mike quickly climbed inside across to the loader's side, taking control of the RWS and giving another burst of fire near the treeline, hoping to keep anyone there still pinned down. After a good five second burst he left the controls, diving down to the turret floor, his hands groping for the fuel taps, the plan would be to flood the tank's interior with diesel then leave it to burn in the fire. Normally he'd have the ammunition to help light it all up, but with it all having been fired he was having to make it up as he went. Not that it mattered, the way the Russians were hunting the tank they'd be doing his job for him shortly. He reached through, cursing, as he scratched his arms on the sharp metal as his fingers fought with the lockwire on the tap. Finally, he had it free, and was about to yank it open it when he heard automatic gunfire erupting outside the tank, then dull thuds above him and a blood curdling scream from outside as Baz shouted.

"Captain Faulkes! Sir! We need your help!"

Mike stopped what he was doing, sticking his head out of the loader's hatch just in time to see two Russian infantrymen standing on the turret with their rifles pointing down towards his tank crew, fingers on the triggers. He had no idea where they'd come from, or how they'd got onboard so quickly, but right now, they were a threat to them all.

"OI!" he shouted as loud as he could, surprising the enemy soldiers whose eyes raised wide in alarm at this new threat. They'd clearly thought Mike was down beside the tank with the rest of his crew and hadn't been expecting to see him there. Both soldiers moved at the same time, racing to bring a weapon to bear. The Russians were yelling, the words lost on Mike as he fought to bring his own rifle up out of the hatch. He felt the sling snag on the hatch, cursing, as he knew he was already too late. Instead of trying to free the weapon, Mike dropped back inside the hatch as the 7.62mm rounds began to hit the turret roof around him in a shower of sparks, some of the rounds exploding into the tank, hitting the radios and ricocheting in all directions. Mike was yelling both from fear and anger as he ducked low avoiding the angry metal that zipped past him, unsnagging the rifle and leaping over the breech and over into the commander's side, a job that would usually take the most dexterous person a minute or two, but with his adrenaline going, and years of experience of being on the tank Mike did it in seconds. He could hear the thuds of the rounds on the turret above him as the soldiers kept pouring fire into the hatch, not knowing Mike was already safely on the other side of the turret. Mike selected auto on the assault rifle, lifting the barrel free of the hatch without any attempt at aiming and fired a long burst of automatic fire towards their direction, most of the rounds missed, but some hit, he could hear their screams as they went down. He leapt up, weapon raised, seeing both soldiers lying on the turret floor yelling and writhing in pain. The rounds had hit their legs, already patches of crimson were soaking their trousers and spilling onto the turret. One of them still held a grenade in his hands, having been shot before he could drop it through the hatch. Mike saw the grenade pin was still in and quickly crawled out, keeping his body low and in cover as he snatched it from the writhing soldier. He could hear the Russian shouts coming from down below on the ground on the opposite side of the tank, probably shouting to their comrades up on the roof, to find out what was happening. Without waiting, he pulled the pin on the grenade and rolled it off the turret, hearing the shouts of alarm as the grenade detonated, throwing earth up and over him, the explosion leaving a ringing in his ears. Cautiously he peered over, the weapon raised, finger on the trigger, his eyes searing to memory the carnage below him. Seeing there was no further threat from below, he turned to the injured soldiers, ignoring their pleading eyes as he searched through their assault vests taking the extra magazines and rifles from them and rolled them off the turret, dropping them down amongst the remains of their comrades unceremoniously. They were lucky, they were still alive. With his ears still ringing he crawled over to where he'd left his crew, his heart racing at what he'd find down below. Shouting a warning before sticking his head over the edge.

"Guys don't shoot, It's me. It's clear up here. You okay down there?"

Even with the ringing in his ears, he could still hear the cries of pain. Taking a deep breath, and worried what he might find, he leaned over to look...

Aurora Operations Centre RAF Colerne Bath

The temperature in the room would have risen, even without the midday heat burning through the metal roof of the hangar. Everyone was on edge as Kyle stood next to his laptop, looking over at the technicians who were checking and re-checking the banks of computers that had been set up. Lights blinked furiously, and the fans ran constantly as the computers attempted to cool themselves down, the processors and hard drives already working hard.

Standing close by, Peter watched on nervously, like a father waiting for the birth of a baby, he paced the room, his eyes darting from the technicians to watching the feed from the drones miles away. Something had gone wrong, one of the Warriors appeared to be stranded again, the tow rope looked to have parted, such was the strain being asked of it. Whoever was controlling the drones was doing a great job, using them to good effect, but it wasn't above the convoy that they were needed, instead 2 kilometres to the south the tank was alone and under heavy attack. Mike was in danger, and Peter could only watch on helplessly as the second hand of his watch kept ticking away as the technicians finalised their checks.

Outside on the flight line sat four Thumpr's, each loaded with two Talons. Eight of the Wasps were ready to fly as an escort, all waiting for Wendi to take control. It was a formidable force, and Peter hoped it was enough. David was stood near them, giving them another quick check over.

After a few minutes the technicians looked over to Kyle, giving him the thumbs up. Finally, they were ready.

Peter looked over to Kyle, asking one final time,

"She's tethered here, she can't download herself and re-appear somewhere else?"

Kyle looked down confidently at the laptop, repeating what he'd already said twice before.

"Boss, her central core system is linked to this laptop and the computer's over there. She can upload herself to anywhere in the world, do whatever we need her to do, but any attempt by her to re-write her code or mess with the laptop or remove herself from it and it'll destroy her. Also, there's a timer, within thirty minutes the programme will cut the link, she must be back here, in this room with us, or the tether will be deleted permanently. Think of it as if she's peering through an open window into the world beyond. Her arms can reach out to wherever she needs to, but she can't get climb through the window to escape. After thirty minutes the window will close, if her arms are still in it, they'll get cut off, but she'll still be here."

"Or a Genie in a bottle," David added, entering the room and joining the conversation, finally finished with his checks on the flightline.

Peter bit his lip in thought, watching both, finally nodding in acknowledgment.

"Okay Kyle, begin the upload."

He watched as the young programmer frowned in concentration, connecting the cable to the computers, and typing away on the keyboard, finally with a dramatic flourish he clicked the enter button, stepping away from the laptop and looking up at the bank of screens.

"Hello Wendi."

After a few moments of silence everyone in the room looked at each other, no-one daring to speak, waiting, then all eyes turned to Kyle. The programmer stood there ignoring the looks and stares, confidently waiting. After a few more silent moments the voice came online, a female voice coming through the speakers.

"Good afternoon, Kyle, I take it this is to be our new home?"

"It is Wendi, welcome to RAF Colerne, new home to Aurora systems. We've got your databanks up and running, can you access them please and get yourself up to speed."

To make it easier to transport Wendi, all her learning and memory had been downloaded onto backup hard drives and brought with them in the trucks, allowing Kyle to delete it from her and simplify her programming to put her into the laptop. To Wendi it would have almost been like having her memories yanked away, years of learning and experience disappearing into a black void. Now with the databanks up and running again, she could quickly re-install those missing years of learning and information, like a fog lifting on a victim with memory loss. It would be as if the experiences had never left her. Within milliseconds every conversation she'd ever had, every human interaction, every lesson she'd learned, every scrap of information and detail she'd ever been fed would re-appear, ready to be used.

"Already done." The voice replied, drawing a smile of admiration from Kyle at how fast she'd adapted.

Peter was about to say something when Wendi added.

"Peter, good work last night on the bridge, I'm very impressed with how you managed to handle the situation, as for what I've learned about Operation Fools Mate, I'm very surprised that a human mind could have come up with such a plan."

Peter looked over scowling at Kyle, not because the AI had called him by his first name, or because it had been a veiled compliment, but because it dawned on him the AI had been listening to everything they'd spoken about in the car on the journey down, including his private fears about Wendi. He was about to say something, when sensing the hostile looks from his boss Kyle quickly interjected.

"Wendi, we have a problem. We need your help."

"Certainly, how may I be of service?"

Ignoring what the AI had just said to him, Peter stepped forwards, the emphasis on his surname.

"Wendi it's *Mr* Rawlinson here."

"Don't you mean Brigadier Rawlinson?" The AI queried, adding, "congratulations on your recent re-activation...Brigadier."

Peter nodded in acknowledgement, hiding his irritation at how much the AI already knew as he continued. "Thank you Wendi, but we'll skip the pleasantries for now, we have a time critical event, and we need your support."

"As you wish Brigadier, ready to receive."

Peter nodded over to the technician on the phone, who was speaking to his counterpart fifty miles away in the WOC. The operator nodded in response, indicating whoever was on the end of the line was ready.

Peter looked at Kyle who was at the laptop, ready to press the button to start the timer.

"Wendi, this mission has a thirty minute cut off, remember the parameters that Kyle has explained to you."

The voice replied with a humorous tone to it.

"If I'm not back in thirty minutes, the window will cut off my arms."

"Exactly. Now the clock will start when you begin to upload, destination will be the Wonderland Operations Centre, get in, get briefed, then assume command of the flight waiting outside. The techs there are ready to receive you and assist if you need it. Remember thirty minutes... Don't be late."

"Don't wait up dad, I promise I'll be home before midnight." The voice replied jovially, sounding more akin to a young woman on a night out than a highly sophisticated attack programme.

Peter smirked at the reply, the smile vanishing when he looked again at how the battle was unfolding on the screens. He merely clicked his finger in response, Kyle pressing the button as the technician on the phone stated.

"Standby to receive package in three...two...one..."

A few seconds later and Kyle looked up.

"It's done, she's on her way."

Peter looked at the screens again, rubbing his nose in thought, running through all the scenarios, before asking, doubt clear to hear in his voice.

"Do you think thirty minutes was too short, perhaps we should have made it an hour?"

Kyle walked over, his voice brimming with confidence.

"Thirty minutes? Boss, I'm expecting her to get it done in fifteen."

Tango Two-One

Come on...COME ON! Patty was urging in his head, watching from the Warrior's turret as Changa and Whippet fought with the heavy steel tow rope. After the rope had snapped, Patty's Warrior had run over the tow rope, catching it in its tracks. Now the rope was shorter than before, and with Patty's vehicle unable to move off, it needed to be stretched to make it fit over the towing bollard. Changa's face was red with the effort, sweat pouring down the huge Fijian as Ping and Jo stood close by, rubbing aching arms from their previous attempts. Patty watched as Changa stopped, dropping the heavy steel rope and cursing, the rope coiling itself back up and almost knocking Whippet away with its energy.

Patty looked behind them, seeing in the distance the smoke rising from where Mike and the tank crew were still fighting, desperately trying to hold off the advancing Russians. Somewhere close by a machine gun barked, Patty ducked low, looking for the firing point, watching as Jonah's Warrior, hidden nearby answered in reply, its own 30mm gun roaring out, firing high explosive shells into the enemy position. The machine gun went silent, as Patty looked back at the struggle going on nearby. Changa was looking skywards and muttered what sounded like a prayer, no doubt to one of his long dead ancestors, urging for strength from an unseen force, before spitting on his bleeding hands, drawing a reserve of strength that Patty had seen before from the big soldier on the rugby pitch. Suddenly Changa was back on the rope, a look of determination and focus, Whippet stepped forwards to help, then Ping and Jo jumped onto the rope, drawing strength from Changa as slowly the huge steel wired rope was stretched out, mere centimetres from the towing bollard, so temptingly close. Patty held his breath, 3cm, then 2 cm, the rope was shaking, Patty was sure it would snap back, taking the four soldiers with it, and as if sensing the same, Changa seemed to utter a curse in Fijian, the anger flowing through him, his eyes bulged and the veins on his forehead protruding as if ready to explode out as suddenly the rope went tight and snapped down onto the bollard with a click.

"YES!" Patty shouted, his fist punching the air in excitement. Saving the congratulations for another time the crews ran back to the vehicles to mount up, he keyed his radio.

"Tango One-One, Tango Two-One-Alpha, we've got the tow ropes back on and are moving now."

He waited for the response, looking behind them, hearing the sounds of the battle echoing in the distance. More columns of smoke were billowing upwards, followed by more explosions and gunfire more powerful and louder than before. Patty hoped he wasn't too late, praying the tank crew were okay.

He heard static in his ear, closing his eyes in thanks as finally a reply came through garbled and hard to hear.

"Tango One-One....moving........can't...... longer, be........ Out!"

Patty cocked his head to try to hear, to make sense of the message. He was about to ask for Mike to repeat the message when Rachel cried out over the radio.

"Tango Two-One, Tango Two-Zero, I've lost control of the drones, someone else is controlling them!"

Patty looked over confused as both Talons turned as one and screamed back the way they'd just come. Suddenly Jonah was on the radio, reporting the same, his operator had lost control of the Wasp, then Wrighty in the back of his Warrior came over the I/C.

"Corporal! The fucking drone's doing its own thing, I can't stop it!"

Patty looked skywards, powerless as all the drones turned and began to head south away from them.

"What the fuck?" Patty exclaimed, looking quizzically across at his gunner.

Sid just looked back at him, raising his shoulders in agreement, not knowing what was happening. Suddenly another voice, a young female voice came over his headset, speaking firmly but softly.

"Corporal Patterson, kindly proceed on the route that I've just updated onto your Battlefield Management Display System."

"What?" Patty replied, looking down at the BMDS. Suddenly a route had appeared, as if it were a satnav system, the green overlay of a route displayed.

"Who the fuck was that?" Patty asked in wonderment, as the voice continued.

"Corporal Patterson, please follow the route, it will take you away from the enemy positions and offer you the best chance of survival. If you leave now, you have a 78 percent chance of making it to Yeovil with no further casualties."

"What the.." he exclaimed, as he realised the voice was not coming over the radio, it was coming from inside the vehicle, over the IC.

He leapt down, looking behind him into the fighting compartment, expecting to see someone in the back talking on the headset, playing a joke on him. He was about to reprimand them, the words dying on his lips as he saw the same disbelieving looks of those sat in the back, hearing the voice themselves over the vehicle's internal loudspeaker. Catherine had cooled somewhat since their earlier encounter and looked back at him blankly, shrugging her shoulders in confusion.

He opened his mouth in surprise as the voice continued.

"Corporal Patterson, we don't have the luxury of time, since you have not moved, your chances of survival have now lowered to 76 percent and are falling 0.3percent every second you delay. Now move it cowboy!"

"Who are you? What do you want?" Patty demanded, still unsure of what the hell was going on. The term cowboy had unnerved him, only his girlfriend ever called him that.

"I'm Wendi," The voice replied almost jovially, "and it's nice to finally make your acquaintance. And what I want is right now for you and your unit to move your asses.

I'm one of the good guys, or good girls depending on what pronoun you'd like me to use."

Patty's face creased in confusion as he asked, "What just happened to our drones? Did you take them?"

"I have," the voice said simply.

"Why? We need them!" Patty replied, feeling uneasy about talking to the unknown voice as if it was a person in the vehicle.

"Not anymore, as I've already said, with the route I've just set up, you will find the minimum of enemy activity, most of the enemy forces are still south of you. But, they are heading your way. I now calculate your chances as 75.1 percent. Please hurry along."

What is it with this woman, Patty thought, suddenly thinking of Mike.

Ignoring the voice, he keyed the radio. "Tango One-One, Tango Two-One, are you enroute to us yet? We've lost the drones, repeat we've lost the drones, over!"

"Captain Faulkes and the tank crew will not be joining you."

Patty's mouth opened in horror at what the woman had just said. Almost unbelievably he demanded,

"How the fuck do you know about Captain Faulkes? And what makes you so sure they won't be coming to us?"

Suddenly he heard Mike's voice playing out over the headset through the I/C as if he was sat in the Warrior with them, he could hear the urgency in Mike's voice.

"Whiskey Zero, Whiskey Three-Zero, vehicle is destroyed, we are evacuating on foot, Grid 355,499, under heavy enemy attack, requesting urgent support, *any* support, Whiskey Three-Zero, out."

"Captain Faulkes sent that message a moment ago on the High Frequency radio. The only support close enough to send him, are your Wasps and Talons, which is what I'm doing now as you no longer need them."

Patty sat there looking at the others, a feeling of helpless anger beginning to rise in him. The tank was destroyed. Mike and the crew wouldn't last ten minutes on foot. He knew that. He was about to order Changa to turn around when the voice came back on.

"Corporal Patterson, if you're thinking of helping them, and I already know you are, you should know that I've already run through the calculations and your chances of success stand at 1.4 percent, so please don't. Like I've already said, I'm on my way to assist Captain Faulkes. Your mission is to get the intelligence that we urgently need back to friendly lines. These are your orders, and to successfully do that, I need you to begin moving immediately."

"You're going to help them?" Patty asked, almost desperately.

"I'm going to try," the voice replied, "I calculate-"

"Just don't keep fucking telling me the odds!" Patty interrupted, his anger flashing through, silencing the voice.

Changa's voice came over the radio, interrupting the conversation.

"Tango Two-One, Tango Two-One-Alpha, you're not going to believe this, I've got someone calling themselves Wendi talking to me in my vehicle."

He was about to reply when Jonah cut in. "Tango Two-Zero cutting in, same here, she's telling me to follow a route out of here. What the fuck is going on here? Tango Two-One what do we do?"

Patty leaned forwards looking at the BDSM, checking the route. If what the person had just said was true, if the tank really was destroyed then there was nothing Patty could do. He hated the thought of leaving Mike and the tank crew behind, but the mystery voice was right, they'd already sacrificed so much for this fucking intel. He pinched his lips in irritation, finally replying.

"All callsigns, for now we follow her plan, let's listen to what she's saying. Tango Two-One-Alpha, you're my tow, let's get the hell out of it."

He sat back as his Warrior lurched forwards as Changa's vehicle heaved on the tow line, Catherine's voice coming over the I/C.

"We can't just leave them behind Patty!" He looked backwards, seeing Catherine and the others all leaning forwards through the compartment, their earlier anger with Mike now forgotten. He sat there looking at them, debating what to do, the others looking expectantly at him, waiting for him to change his mind and counteract the order, finally understanding what Mike had been trying to explain to him all along. Command *was* a lonely business, you never made friends from getting it right, but you certainly lost friends getting it wrong. He shook his head, firming his resolve.

"Sorry everyone, but Mike was right, this intel is worth more than them. We can't risk going back for them. Mike and the crew knew what they were doing when they left us." Leaving them he stood back up in the cupola, looking backwards, hoping that Wendi, whoever she was working for, was wrong, hoping that the tank would appear. How the hell did she know so much? And how could she talk to the crew through the I/C? With more questions than answers, Patty put his doubts to the back of his mind, they were still two miles from the safety of the town. He could only hope Mike and the crew would make it, but right now, with a busted vehicle, he had his own problems to worry about.

WENDI

Time – 13:46.25 – At about the same time as Mike and his crew abandon the tank, Wendi begins her journey into Wonderland. It takes less than 15 seconds for Wendi to complete the upload, her programming and consciousness beginning to incorporate itself into the buildings vast data banks, harnessing onto the faster processing power and being able to now operate multiple processors and thoughts at once. Within less than a second, she has full control of all the buildings systems, easily passing through the security protocols and firewalls, the buildings complex security system having already been opened to her. She begins to self-learn at an immense rate, receiving her orders, whilst simultaneously getting the latest updates on the state of the UK military. Within 5 seconds she has read and investigated over 250,000 files, assimilating terabytes of data. She begins to try to access the UK's military networks to get access to more information about Operation Fools Mate, deciding she needs further intelligence to carry out a successful mission. She tries to connect to the computers within the MOD storage facility in Abbeywood and with the mainframe of GCHQ in Cheltenham, finding the internet and networks are all down and being scrambled by the ongoing cyberattack. Realising that this will interfere with her primary mission, she sets herself a secondary mission, to be completed alongside the first, to disrupt and destroy the virus. Wendi begins to trace the origins of the virus back through the various government departments and onto the phone masts of the mobile phone carriers, deciding that to continue further requires more processing power. She begins to disrupt the virus as she finds it, quickly taking apart the code, opening vast sections of the UK's phone and internet networks, allowing her quicker and easier access. Using this newly acquired power, she spends 12.37 seconds accessing over a thousand large businesses at once, utilising their now dormant computer networks and systems. In less than 20 seconds nearly 30 percent of the computers in the UK are now slaved to Wendi, running algorithms and processes for her and offering nearly 4 million terabytes of processing power, all without anyone's knowledge that she was even there. Finally, with enough of the virus disrupted, she can access Whitehall and GCHQ, having access to every military file ever written and stored online since 1926. Still, she finds no mention of anything to do with Operation Fools Mate.

Time - 13:49.21 – Three minutes after the upload, Wendi is using the vast processing power now available to her, she now begins to reach out to Whiskey Three-Zero, taking control of the drones at RAF Colerne and launching them, calculating flight times and vectors, she plots the most time efficient passage, knowing it will take eight minutes for the Thumprs to get to Tango One-One. She uses the redundant mobile phone masts and the GPS locators of the vehicles radios to triangulate the positions of the units. Locating all the Whiskey Three-Zero vehicles, identifying the three Warriors by the pictures being downloaded from the Wasps. Using the information that she has downloaded from military files, she learns all about the company that was awarded the contract to design and build the top-secret radio systems, accessing classified internal files. She discovers the back doors that the company's engineers had built into the radios software, never to be shared with anyone outside of the company. Using these back doors she accesses the vehicles BMDS computers, quickly integrating herself into the vehicles radio harness, it's old technology and proves no challenge to her as she re-writes a few pieces of code. Now she can hear everything being said over the microphones. She listens in for a few seconds, identifying the vehicles commanders using voice recognition software, the voices being played back against millions of recordings held by GCHQ that she's downloaded from the mobile phone operators, cross checking pitch, tone, and range against what's stored on the phone recordings.

Time - 13:49.31 - She identifies the names of commanders and crew, cross checking against government departments, military records and previous social media uploads, having access to everything ever held on them online. Now she knows all about them, everything from height, eye colour and hair colour to favourite football team, and what they last brought on a credit card. Corporal Patterson is in command on callsign Tango Two-One. She checks against social media posts, finding out his girlfriend likes to call him cowboy. She keeps that piece of information to hand, knowing it might make talking to him easier. She does this for everyone on board, certain to use it to gain trust, after all, wasn't it Kyle that always said that information is power.

She calculates the units' chances of survival at 79 Percent, realising they no longer need the Wasps and Talons, she severs the control between them and the operators, taking charge herself and sending them south to assist Captain Faulkes. His chances she calculates are still lower than 10 percent, far below the parameters of 60 percent set out by Brigadier Rawlinson. She listens to the commanders, judging from their tone and pitch that their heart rates are beginning to rise, they're nervous, scared, *human*.

She begins to introduce herself into the vehicles, identifying herself to the commanders whilst plotting the best route out for them. She's here to help, she tells them, hoping to reassure them.

At the same time as she's downloading to the vehicles, she continues with her secondary mission, and begins to trace the origin of the cyberattack, downloading a portion of the virus, and analysing its code. It's binary in origin and certainly written by a human, she records it as what Kyle would call a "Limited memory machine," a poor attempt at Artificial Intelligence, it can learn but is severely hampered by the fact it requires constant updates and input from humans. She systematically begins to sever its links to the outside world, segregating it from whoever is controlling it, and begins to follow the trace coding, recognising parts of the code from earlier recorded UK and US Cyber-attacks.

Time - 13:51.23 – Wendi has now destroyed the virus in all the UK's major systems, allowing her quicker and easier access to the UK computing systems. She sits and thinks through the problem, her quantum processors taking two seconds to analyse and run through millions of computations and scenarios. Quick by human standards, but to her, far too long. Realising she needs to go overseas, and knowing the undersea cables to Europe are cut, she now takes control of the powerful transmitters of GCHQ, within a minute the arrays and satellites are being realigned and she takes control of two of the UK's Inmarsat satellites sat in low earth orbit. Someone in GCHQ attempts to stop her, she can see the lines of command code being slowly inputted so in response she locks out all human input. Within less than a second all the computer terminals within GCHQ are locked out for the next 26 minutes, the operators thumping keyboards in frustration as the powerful AI sweeps through like a tornado. Unimpeded she now begins to upload herself into the computer systems of multiple European businesses, whilst simultaneously tracing the virus through the European union and through into Russia. Now she has nearly 12 million computer systems in 29 countries all working for her, helping her to process the huge complex computations and calculations she needs, whilst becoming the single most powerful computer ever built. She finds some of the Russian military systems are encoded and takes a few seconds to crack the complex security coding. During one attempt a predator programme, designed to defeat any attempt to infiltrate it is activated, it tries to stop Wendi, who in turn re-writes its code, sending it back off into the Russian systems, now attacking the very system it was designed to protect. After three seconds she has extracted all relevant files and materials on '*Operatsiya Duraki Pryatel*'

Time - 13:53.33 Wendi begins to upload the documents back to Wonderland, using the satellites and antennae relays of GCHQ. Within a minute the information is already back at Wonderland on the computers, ready to be analysed. She continues following the trace programming of the virus, detecting multiple computers and access stations in Russia where the virus was viewed and accessed, seeing every key stroke or log that a programmer logged into a terminal used to change or alter it. She traces it back to a weapon's research facility in Eastern Russia, labelled as a university, watching as for the first time the virus was uploaded onto its mainframe in 2023. She finds no record of its existence before, knowing that there would be coding logs, or saved files showing how the computer virus was created. Finding no evidence anywhere in the research facility's data bank that it was created here, she begins to access other countries computer networks, expanding her search criteria. She still has 23 minutes and 27seconds left to complete the mission. And for a self-aware AI programme as fast as her, that could be a lifetime. She sees an opportunity to assist her mission further, and using the Russian computer systems in Moscow, uploads herself via one of their covert military communications satellites into the Russian Headquarters in Bovington, posing as a weather update programme. Within 4 seconds she's in, establishing a link to the Russian Electronic Warfare wing, reappropriating the units' powerful long-range antennae's. Now, instead of being used to jam and direction find, she can use them to locate and listen to all the Russian forces in that theatre of operations, which is what she does for the next four minutes. She sits there listening, recording and monitoring, waiting for her moment to strike. She still has 21 minutes left on the clock, plenty of time to help Captain Faulkes and be back in time for tea.

10

One Armed Juggling

Whiskey Three-Zero

Mike slowly peered over the side of the turret, his heart racing as he saw his crew lying on the ground. Bill was on his back, eyes open wide and silent, already looking deathly pale. Baz was kneeling next to him, frantically looking for the injuries that were causing the blood to flow. Smudge was leaning against a log, his weapon raised, trying to concentrate on looking outwards, but his eyes kept looking inwards, shock and fear plain to see.

Mike leapt off the tank, landing clumsily next to them, ignoring the pain that shot up his tired legs. Laying his assault rifle down he gently moved Baz aside, tearing at the Velcro straps on Bill's body armour, ripping it in two, as he began his own assessment of the injuries. Seeing Smudge looking numb, he looked over, pointing in the direction of the enemy.

"Don't just fucking sit there gawping! Watch your arcs!" he snapped out, not meaning to sound so fierce, but knowing the soldier needed to be shocked out of his stupor. Smudge blinked in surprise before picking up his weapon and scanning for threats. Mike threw the body armour aside, quickly tearing Bill's smock open, all the while Baz was talking to him, attempting to reassure him. Bill just lay there quietly watching on, his eyes looking up at them hopefully.

"Bill, listen to me, you're going to be alright, okay mate, can you tell us where it's hurting? Where can you feel the pain?"

Wincing in pain Bill gasped. "My legs, I think my legs are hit and my stomach. I...I feel funny, like I need to go take a piss."

"Okay Bill, okay," Mike replied soothingly, gently he opened the soldier's smock, already seeing two wounds to his abdomen, running his hands over the soldier's body, looking for the entry and exit wounds. After a few moments Mike was finished, it looked like only one of the wounds to the abdomen was an entry wound, the other an exit wound. One round had hit Bill in the calf of his leg, ricocheting off the bone, travelling up his calf before exploding out of his chest, hitting the inside of his body armour and bouncing back inside his abdomen. Mike couldn't believe the damage done by just a single bullet, having caused three serious wounds. He hid his concerns as he gently probed the second of the holes to Bill's abdomen, the soldier crying out and wincing in pain as Mike lightly touched the wound. He could already fell the hardness of the abdomen, the pinkness of the skin. Bill was bleeding internally, and he urgently needed a surgeon.

Mike shared a look with Baz, both knew how serious the injuries were. Mike searched his chest rig, already finding the Russian first aid pouch that he'd liberated from the truck. He tore it open, struggling to understand the cyrillic writing, looking and feeling rather than reading the contents. He found what he was looking for, the Russian version of Hem-con, a chemical covered bandage that caused wounds to clot instantly.

He tore open the packet, double checking the contents and was about to apply it when a warning shout came from Smudge. He looked up to where he was pointing, dropping the bandage and grabbing his assault rifle just as a squad of infantry came bursting through the treeline, running towards them.

The enemy dived for cover as Mike and Smudge both unloaded the remainder of their magazines at them, quickly reloading and pouring more fire onto them. The ejected brass casings flung outwards hitting Baz, who yelled in pain as the hot casings burned his neck. Mike ignored the outburst, keeping up the fire, glancing down at Bill whose face was seared in agony.

"We don't have fucking time for this!" Mike shouted out in frustration, as the bullets began to whip angrily overhead. Some began to tear into the branches of the oak tree, scattering it's leaves over them. They couldn't just sit there; the Russians would just keep coming in ever greater numbers. He looked back up at the tank, even disabled and burning, it was still better than nothing. It still had the RWS and the Hornet ready to use and Baz saw him looking up at the tank, nodding in acknowledgment at what he needed to do.

He passed over the quick clot and first aid kit to Baz, giving a quick explanation of how to use it, before reaching down to touch Bill lightly on the shoulder.

"Bill, I've got to go and keep these fuckers off us, when Baz applies this dressing it'll stop the bleeding, but it's going to burn like hell. No matter how bad the pain, leave the bandage on ok?"

Bill grimaced, replying through gritted teeth.

"I'll leave it be, don't you worry about me Sir, you go do what you got to do."

Mike smiled, adding. "Mike... today right now Bill, it's Mike. And I'm damn proud of you, you know that?"

Bill was about to reply but yelled in pain as Baz, not wanting to wait any longer applied the dressing to the two wounds, both close enough together that one bandage could cover both.

Mike nodded in thanks to him, looking back over at Smudge and passed him the extra magazines he'd just taken from the Russian wounded, patting the Trooper on the shoulder who turned gratefully to take them, Mike's earlier outburst forgotten.

"Smudge, you're doing great, keep doing what you're doing, you're protecting these two, now keep it up."

"Thanks Sir!" the Trooper shouted back, taking a fresh magazine and reloading his rifle.

Already the incoming fire was beginning to increase, bullets pinged off the tanks armour and more vehicles could be heard approaching in the distance. After seeing how the Russians treated their prisoners, Mike knew they couldn't surrender. He had to get them out of here, he'd brought them here, this was on him. Checking the new magazine was fitted to his rifle securely, he knelt up, bouncing his leg muscles, ready for the run up to the tank. He waited for a lull in the firing before bouncing up, grunting with the effort as he jumped up, like a cat leaping upwards, his hands grasping the tank's sides as he launched himself upwards. In one swoop his legs were onto the catwalk, he scrabbled up onto the turret, as bullets slammed around him, the infantry now trying to stop him getting back inside. Coughing against the smoke, he half crawled half leapt inside the hatch, falling in upside down onto the commander's seat. He crawled over the breech, reaching over to the RWS, which was still powered on and spun the weapon sight over to where the enemy were, quickly flicking the sight to thermal he easily identified the soldiers warmer bodies against the cooler trees.

"I see you!" Mike spoke to himself, firing the weapon, watching the white-hot tracer splash into the figures, knocking some over. The infantry began to direct their fire at the turret, ignoring the crew outside on the ground.

"That's it, that's it, shoot at the big fucking tank!" Mike said again to himself, pleased to see it was working. At least now Baz could work uninterrupted, or at least that's what Mike was hoping. All they had to do was stabilise Bill, then perhaps they could get him out of there. Ever the optimist, eh Mike, he thought to himself, as he fired at another group who were trying to flank them. He looked over at the Hornet's controls, it was still on 75 percent, ready to fire another killing burst. The smoke was beginning to dissipate in the turret, perhaps the fire wasn't as bad as he had first thought. He was about to pick up the control tablet when he heard a faint but familiar voice coming over one of the headsets.

"Captain Faulkes, Captain Faulkes, please respond, can you hear me?"

What the, he thought to himself, I thought the radios were dead? Quickly he reached over to the gunner's station and picked up the headset.

"Unknown callsign, unknown callsign this is Tango One-One, repeat your message, over?"

The voice came through loud and clear, but instead of coming over the broken radio, it came over the Intercom, as if the speaker of the voice were inside the tank with him.

"Captain Faulkes...Mike, can you hear me?"

For a few seconds he was numbed into silence, as open mouthed he put the earpiece near to his ear, asking.

"Wendi? Is that you?"

"Live and on the air!" the AI replied jovially, adding, "glad to hear you're still in the land of the living. I've appraised your current situation, and I'll be honest Mike, I've seen you have better days. What on earth's gone so wrong?"

Mike frowned, the poor attempt at humour lost on him, as he stood still in shock at hearing the voice. He'd talked to Wendi before back at Aurora when Kyle had her uploaded into the building. He remembered she'd sounded younger, as if a child, learning to talk to humans, developing feelings as Kyle attempted to nurture them, almost as if he was moulding her a conscience for when she had to make decisions on her own. Peter had frowned upon the practice, adamant against a military computer learning a conscience. Mike hadn't believed it himself, believing Wendi was merely mimicking Kyle, he still didn't believe it, AI was a myth, it didn't exist except on paper, yet here he was, talking to her in the tank.

"Wendi...how?" he asked still unbelievably.

"Mike we can teach, or we can do, which do you prefer?"

Mike was shocked at hearing his own saying now used against him, suddenly bringing himself back to the present he looked around the tank, hearing the small arms fire hitting the turret again. Ignoring his doubts he relayed the situation to the AI programme, not quite sure what, if any support, Wendi could bring.

"Okay," the AI began, "firstly on the BMDS I'd like you to select the following options."

Mike did as he was told, listening intently as the AI guided him through the process of going into menus and sub menus he'd never been able to access before, granting permission for the AI to infiltrate the tank's systems, watching open mouthed as hundreds of lines of computer code flashed onscreen before his eyes. After a few seconds the RWS began to pivot on its own and fire, no doubt being controlled by Wendi. He was about to ask how, when cutting him off the AI continued.

"I'll stay and provide fire support for as long as I can from here, meanwhile I've got additional support incoming, it should be with you in the next four minutes. Now get your casualty and make your way to the northern edge of the woodline, I'll have an extraction plan ready to get you and your crew out of there by then. Chop, chop, now Captain, time's a ticking!"

Mike blinked in surprise, scarcely believing he was talking to a computer. The irony was not lost on him, usually it was he who had all the ideas, all the plans, but now he was fresh out of ideas and relying solely on a computer programme, something housed miles away, and the thing that annoyed him the most was that he had no idea how Wendi had done it. Knowing never to look a gift horse in the mouth, Mike merely accepted the offer, quickly replying, his voice full of optimism and hope.

"Okay Wendi, well let's both see if you're as smart as you think you are, and I hope you are."

"Careful Mike, you might end up owing me one," Wendi said mischievously as he threw down the headset, climbing out and crawling forwards, taking cover from the incoming fire before falling ungracefully off the turret and landing in a heap amongst the crew. Baz still had the quick clot pressed against Bill's wounds and was in the process of applying lots of tape to keep it in place. He looked up from his work, as Mike fell in amongst them.

"Looks like the bleeding's slowed, but his breathing's becoming shallower." Baz warned, Mike nodding in reply as he looked up to where Wendi wanted them to head for, waiting for Baz to finish dressing the wounds. In the middle of the clearing they were sitting ducks, at least in the woods they'd have cover from the trees, although the ground was broken and rutted, and he knew that even without the incoming enemy fire it would be hard to cross carrying Bill. Mike looked behind him, tapping Smudge on the shoulder.

"Smudge, we're going to be moving shortly, get a fresh mag on and be ready to cover us. Concentrate your fire over there." Mike pointed to the treeline as he continued.

"When you hear us yell over, that's your cue to follow on. Understand?"

"Roger, understood!" the gunner replied excitedly, quickly changing magazines on his rifle.

With a nod, Baz indicated he was finished, the dressing was secure, it didn't look pretty, but it was working. Satisfied it would hold, Mike looked down into Bill's sweat-soaked pale face, seeing the strain there as the injured soldier looked back at him hopefully.

"Bill, we've got help incoming, but we need to move you, I'm not going to lie, it's going to hurt like hell, but I need you to grit your teeth and do whatever you can to try not to pass out. We're going to be working hard for you, so I need you to work hard for us. Don't fucking die on us okay? Can you do that?"

"Just get me out of here please, I'll do whatever you need!" the soldier replied through gritted teeth, already mentally preparing himself for what was to come.

Baz and Mike both slung their weapons over their backs, leaving their arms free to carry him, Mike quickly pulling the Glock pistol from the Troopers discarded body armour, throwing it into his chest rig for later.

Mike looked up at the tank, seeing the Hornet was looking down at them, clearly Wendi was using it to watch their progress. Smudge spotted the RWS moving about, his eyes picking out the movement on the tank, as he quickly shouted out in alarm.

"Shit! There's someone onboard the tank! They're using the RWS!"

Mike looked over at him, replying soothingly.

"It's okay Smudge, they're friendlies, we've got someone else on the tank working for us."

Smudge looked back at him questioningly, as Mike added. "We've got a system that allows remote access of the tank, right now someone back home is providing us cover."

"The same someone who's coming to pick us up?" Baz questioned.

Mike was interrupted as the RWS began to fire into the trees, watching the Hornet begin to spin around and charge up, feeling the static charge in the air. With a zap and a crack, like lightening it fired, Mike couldn't see what Wendi was engaging, but could see the explosion amongst the trees, something had caught the AI's attention as it fired a second time. Mike wondering how much longer the capacitors would fire for. Knowing time was against them, he hurried them along.

"Right, prepare to move!" Mike shouted, as ignoring Bill's cries, both took an arm each and lifted him up, carrying him between them as both grunted with the effort.

"Okay Smudge, moving!" Mike yelled, as he and Baz began to haul Bill between them, who through gritted teeth was crying out from the pain. Mike and Baz found it hard going underfoot, twice they nearly stumbled on the loose footing, but still they pressed forwards, sweat pouring off them as Smudge kept pouring fire into the trees. After no more than thirty paces, they lay Bill down amongst the remains of a fallen tree, both pulling their weapons free and firing into the trees, shouting back.

"Smudge, MOVE!"

Without a second's hesitation the Trooper was up and running, head down and his arms pumping fast as the assault rifle pivoted across his body. Within ten seconds he was back with them, jumping down in a shower of dust, breathing heavily and looking back over his rifle sight at the way he had just come. His eyes picked out movement by the treeline over to the west. He raised his rifle to fire, firing at the same time as the rocket streaked out from the trees towards the tank.

The tank was rocked by the explosion, the rocket hitting the front, exploding harmlessly against the armour and the tree branches. The branches of the fallen tree shook and swayed as smoke and flame enveloped the tank, hiding it from view. For a second Mike thought it had been destroyed, holding his breath as the thick grey and black smoke rose skywards, beginning to quickly clear, the tank emerged, the RWS still firing. The plan was working, the Russians were concentrating most of their fire on the tank, ignoring the four of them, but for how much longer? Mike wondered.

"Come on! We can't stay here! We need to get further away!" Mike yelled, pointing out to Baz where they were heading for.

Both heaved with the effort as they lifted Bill again, the soldier crying out in agony as they ran off towards the next position. Twenty paces later and they were down again, covering Smudge as he ran to catch up, moving further and further away from danger. However, it was on the fifth time of moving that things went from bad to worse. They were almost in amongst the safety of the trees when gunfire erupted from the treeline to the left of them, the ground around them exploding in a frenzy of bullets as they both fell forwards, dropping Bill. They'd ran into an ambush as a Russian soldier in the woods threw a grenade, it exploded behind them, showering them with earth as Smudge gave a yell from behind, falling backwards and screaming in agony, dropping his rifle as his legs kicked out weakly in front of him.

"God dammit!" Mike yelled through clenched teeth, as he and Baz were forced to keep as low as possible trying to avoid the incoming fire, dragging Bill behind them into cover behind another fallen tree.

He propped Bill moaning in agony against the tree, as Baz lay low, trying to return fire, hopelessly outnumbered and outgunned. Mike peered back over at Smudge, seeing him weakly moving, trying to crawl into cover. He knew he had to go back for him, already the bullets were tearing into the ground around him, the enemy still seeing him as a threat. If he lay there any longer, a stray round would certainly hit him. He looked over at Baz, pointing to the treeline.

"Try to get me some fire over there, keep their heads down if you can!"

The NCO looked over to where Mike had pointed, his rifle firing in response as Mike took a few breaths to compose himself, leaping up and running as fast as he could. He took five steps and tumbled forwards, his feet tripping over an upturned tree stump, cursing at the pain that shot up his ankle as he lay in a crumpled heap.

"Fucking hell Mike! What is this? Amateur hour?" he shouted to himself angrily, the nerves and anger threatening to overwhelm him. He quickly got back up to his knees, composing himself as the bullets were whizzing by, seemingly getting closer and closer. He heard the RWS bark out on the tank, looking up, he saw thankfully that Wendi was using the machine gun to provide him with covering fire, using the Hornet to track his progress. Gritting his teeth in determination he was up again, charging forwards, not thinking of the consequences as he slid to a halt next to the prostate figure. Without waiting for a response, he grabbed Smudge by his body armour straps, his knees buckling under the dead weight as he hauled him up and over his shoulder into a fireman's carry. With his teeth clenched he began to run as fast as he could back to the safety of the others, his eyes looking down at the floor, trying to find the surest footing as he tried not to think of what was going on around him. All he thought about was taking the next step as he powered back to the position, ignoring the screams in protest from his back and his legs, his free arm pumping across his body, the rifle hanging by its sling, banging into his hip, none of it mattered. All that mattered was getting Smudge to safety.

Please not yet, please not yet, Mike kept repeating, over and over in his head as he powered back to safety, seeing the trace rounds tearing past, dangerously close. He was sure he could feel the air parting as they buzzed and zipped past his head. Come on, almost there, he thought hopefully, as suddenly the hammer blow hit his back, the air exploding from his lungs as the 7.62mm round slammed into him, pirouetting him round. With the extra momentum he fell backwards, causing him to overbalance as he dropped Smudge and tumbled, landing next to Bill.

He tried to cry out, to shout but nothing came, the air having been knocked out of his lungs as he struggled to breathe, white spots were dancing before his eyes, and he had to fight hard not to pass out. He rolled over looking at Smudge, wanting to help but also desperate to fight off the panic to breathe again as he struggled for breath. Finally, with a gasp he was able to suck in a lungful of air, the air causing a spasm of coughing as Baz grabbed him, rolling him over roughly and checking the back of the armour.

"Sir! you're alright, the body armour stopped it!" Baz shouted, picking up the rifle and continuing to fire away as Mike reached behind checking himself, certain he could feel the blood pouring down. After a few seconds of probing, he pulled his slick wet fingers back, sighing in relief at what his own eyes saw. Baz was right, it was sweat, not blood that Mike could feel. He sat there, blinking in surprise and gasping, feeling as if he'd been punched by a heavyweight boxer. Suddenly he looked over at Smudge, the Trooper's eyes were open, a look of bewilderment and disbelief on them at what had just happened. Smudge tried to get up, his legs buckling out from under him as he toppled back down, his breathing heavy and ragged. Blood was pouring out from beneath the Trooper's trousers, thick red blood, running in rivulets down his legs and soaking into the ground.

"Smudge!" Mike croaked, his own voice hoarse as he crawled over, ignoring the pain that spread out over his lower back, his hands shooting out and quickly inspecting the Trooper's wounds, tearing away the torn fabric of his trousers, identifying the shrapnel wounds. The wounds looked nasty, but he'd heal from them, the one that concerned Mike the most was the one on his left leg, that had nicked his femoral artery, blood was spurting out as the Trooper's heart continued to pump his life away.

Mike forgot all about his own pains, reaching back down into his chest rig for the remains of the first aid kit, the quick clot wouldn't help here, he needed to tourniquet the leg, to slow the blood loss, having at best perhaps two minutes before Smudge would bleed out.

Mike ripped out the first aid kit, looking for a torniquet, when they were in Afghanistan every soldier had one, for such an emergency, but he wasn't in Afghanistan anymore, and the first aid kit was Russian. He upended the kit, the supplies dropping out on the floor. There was no tourniquet. Already Smudge was breathing heavily, watching on in mute shock as the blood continued to spurt out of the wound. Mike reached over for his rifle, cutting the sling off with his knife, quickly looking around the forest floor for what he needed next. After a few seconds of searching, he finally found what he needed. A simple length of stick, not too big, not too small, perfect for what he wanted it for. He looked up at Smudge, hiding his fears and trying to sound as unconcerned as possible.

"Smudge, I'm going to apply a tourniquet, it'll help stop the bleed, if I don't do this you'll die in a matter of minutes. When I tighten it up it's going to hurt, a lot, but you must let me do it."

Smudge clamped his mouth together in pain, nodding his head, his eyes wide in fear at what Mike had just told him.

Without waiting any longer, Mike wrapped the rifle sling around the Trooper's leg, above the wound, quickly tying the sling around in a loose knot, Smudge cried out in pain, trying to fight Mike's hands, pushing him away. Sadly, for him, this wasn't the painful part. Mike needed Smudge's arms out of the way for what he was about to do next, already the Trooper was trying to undo the knot. Smudge's brain knew Mike was trying to help, but when faced with pain, the human body was a strange thing, and Smudge's body was over riding what his brain was telling him, like a person who instinctively jump to their death from a burning building. He knew it would kill him, but all he wanted was for the pain to stop.

"Baz! I need a fucking hand here!" Mike yelled, struggling against Smudge, as Baz stopped shooting and crawled back over, instantly grabbing the Trooper's arms and muttering into his ear.

"Smudge! Stay fucking still! He needs you to stay still, he's trying to help you!"

The Trooper's arms were pinned by his side as the words sunk in, but he continued to yell, his eyes wide and manic, the pain wracking his body.

Mike leaned over, using his own body weight to keep Smudge's leg still as his blood-soaked hands fought to put the stick between the sling and the flesh of the leg, finally with the stick in place Mike twisted the stick, the sling clamping even tighter, Mike twisted the stick once before with a final yell Smudge went limp, passing out into unconsciousness. Baz looked up fearfully, seeing the concerned look Mike shook his head, his voice reassuring.

"It's alright Baz, he's just passed out. Probably for the best."

After the second twist, Mike noticed the blood flow began to slow, by the third, it had stopped just enough for a dressing to take over. Mike used the remaining free fabric of the sling to tie the stick in place, now at least it wouldn't shake free and loosen. Then he quickly unrolled one of the dressings over the wound, tying it in place securely, now, hopefully the wound would clot enough to stop the bleeding temporarily. He checked his vitals, Smudge's pulse was low, and he'd lost a lot of blood, but he was still alive, and that was all that mattered. Mike checked his watch, noting the time. Looking over to Baz he remarked,

"Baz, in fifteen minutes that tourniquet needs to be loosened, or Smudge could lose his leg. Anything happens to me, and I need you to remember that. Ok?"

The NCO looked unbelieving back at him, his eyes casting over to Bill and Smudge

"Roger that Sir, but I doubt we'll be worrying about Smudge's leg in fifteen minutes if this carries on!"

Mike said nothing, the NCO was right, they were now pinned down with two casualties, and their chances of moving any further were now two options, Jack and shit, and Jack just left town.

"So, what now Captain? Mind telling me what we're waiting for?" Baz asked, looking back over his weapon sight and ducking low as more rounds whipped by overhead.

Mike stuck his head up above the ground, looking back at the tank. The RWS was still firing into the woods, but the Hornet was again pointing over to them, no doubt Wendi could see what was happening now that they had two casualties. He needed to get her attention. He quickly stood up, waving his arms, making a T-sign with his hands and pointing to where they were, quickly diving for cover again and yelling in anger as more gunfire came at him from another area, showering him.

He brushed off the dirt, looking up to see Baz looking at him, a look of anger on his face.

"Are you fucking trying to get yourself killed or what?"

Mike couldn't help it, seeing the look on Baz's face, looking like an old mother hen protecting the brood, he burst into laughter, the NCO looking at him as if he'd lost his marbles.

Suddenly it was as if it was contagious, without knowing why, Baz began to laugh, he'd experienced the same feeling when he was driving the decoy tanks, the sheer bloody mindedness of knowing you could die at any second, and that it was all beyond your control. All you could do was smile, and hope. He tried to stop himself, but the more he tried the more he laughed. Until both of them were laughing loudly, almost manically at the situation, the tears welling in their eyes as Mike took the extra magazines from Smudge's chest rig, giving them an extra magazine each. That was it then, with only the remaining magazine on their rifles and the one spare, they'd soon be out of ammunition.

Overhead they heard a whining noise, their laughter stopping immediately as both recognised the sounds of incoming rounds. The Russians had finally had enough, they'd lost patience and had called in an artillery strike. Both of them exchanged horrified looks as Mike shouted in warning.

"INCOMING! GET DOWN!"

He leapt over, covering Bill with his body, as Baz did the same to Smudge, both shielding their heads with their arms, a futile effort given the size of the incoming rounds, but a natural reaction, never the same.

The ground above them shook violently as the concussions and the explosions tore through the woods, the explosions occasionally intertwined with the crack of the heavy trees falling down around the forest. Mike lay there, silently praying and hoping that they'd be safe as the earth was flung up around them, piles of earth and pieces of wood raining down on them, covering them as they lay there shaking. Bill began to scream, a loud guttural roar, more animal than human, Mike tried to reassure him, to calm him, but he was also desperate to hide his own fears. It was no fun being out in the open when shrapnel was flying around, mere inches above you. The explosions grew in ferocity, the salvo seeming to be getting closer. Bill was wide eyed in fear, Baz was shaking, all of them expecting at any second to be hit. Mike stopped talking and clenched his jaw closed, fearful if he opened it he'd be yelling louder than Bill as all four of them lay there, hoping, praying to just be able to stay alive for one moment longer, as with nothing else to be done, they lay there, waiting...

Golgolvin

Colonel Golgolvin leaned over the turret, checking again that the driver was keeping to the cleared route as he led his forces through the minefield, the burning hulks around them a reminder of what could go wrong if they didn't. He looked up at the treeline ahead, counting the destroyed vehicles littering the ground around him, knowing it had been a hard fought and costly attack, but now it was almost over, their victory was almost at hand. Everything was going as planned, his forward tank companies were already well ahead of them, clearing the ground around them in their flanking positions, and his infantry companies were now clearing through the woodline, sweeping it clear of any enemy still foolish enough to still be there. There had only been one enemy tank in the end, despite earlier reports, and everything was going as it should. Now with one final push he could sweep through with the mobile reserve and destroy whatever was left of the enemy. He'd left the command of the attack to his officers, electing instead to lead his men and their vehicles through the minefield. It was just as he was coming out of the minefield that he noticed the change. Ahead of them in the woods, he saw movement, as in ones and twos their infantry began running back out of the woods, followed by a smoke cloud, the smoke burning their eyes and throats. He thought at first the British had been crazy and desperate enough to use chemical weapons, watching as some of the men who still had their respirators began putting them on. Most of the men couldn't though, they'd already elected to leave them behind on the ships, finding out long ago that the respirator case was better suited to carrying packs of cigarettes or looted goods rather than the protective mask itself. Instead, men stood hunched over, red faced and coughing as their comrades up-ended their water bottles, pouring water over stinging eyes, trying anything to remove the noxious stinging fumes. Thankfully after a few panicked moments, they all realised it was just diesel smoke, Golgolvin recognising the pungent smell from their first encounter with one of the British tanks. He thought through in his head, knowing to delay now would buy the enemy more time in the woods to dig in. Whatever threat was left in the woods, he felt sure his unit could easily handle it. He was certain that at best it was one tank and a handful of troops. Yes, that had to be it he reasoned, and dug in troops could be overwhelmed with ground troops, *his* troops. He turned in the turret, his confidence unwavering, as he shouted over the radio, so both the soldiers on the ground nearby and those sat in the backs of the vehicles could hear him.

"It's just diesel smoke men! Nothing to fear, the British must be desperate and are trying to cover their withdrawal. We have them on the run! It's a few troops left in there, Now let's get in there and finish it! Show them what *we* can do! All troops to dismount, we finish this *now*!"

Golgolvin watched with pride as the ramps of the BMP's lowered and the fresh soldiers of his VDV came pouring out, quickly taking charge of the wavering troops, cajoling them into their own ranks, swelling the numbers. As one they turned, crying out victoriously as buoyed on with the fresh Paratroopers amongst them, they found new courage. Forming up into assault formations and storming forwards into the smoke, which was already now dissipating, resembling a light fog. Now it was time to get the bastards, Golgolvin thought, already tasting the victory to come. He watched his men disappearing into the mist, weapons raised and ready for anything, the difference in quality plain to see when compared to the greener troops around them. In the woods he could still hear the gunfire, someone was still fighting. One of his section leaders was heard over the radio reporting the enemy tank was immobilised, stuck against a tree, but still in the fight, the crew were onboard using just a machine gun. No matter, Golgolvin thought, with the tank stuck as it was, his men would treat it as if it were merely a pill box or machine gun nest, a few well placed grenades and it would soon be over.

Golgolvin listened in as the young officer kept up the running commentary, reporting quickly, the excitement plain to hear in his voice as the gunfire echoed in the background.

"We're alongside the tank now, beginning the assault...We have men on board....Co ntact! The crew are-"

The transmission was cut off mid-sentence as Golgolvin listened on as the ground commanders tried to raise the officer and his men. He cursed, knowing it was more than likely the young officer had excitedly pulled his microphone out of his combat radio in his haste to get into the fight, he wouldn't have been the first, and he certainly wouldn't be the last. Golgolvin shook his head, smiling at the eagerness of the young officer, it reminded him of his own young self. He made a note to congratulate the man personally, perhaps a promotion and decoration for bravery would be good for the tank's capture, no doubt his men would certainly appreciate the gesture, especially after everything they'd been through. His thoughts of what would happen after the battle and his victory were disturbed, as suddenly, he heard a voice he recognised come over the radio.

"All Wolf callsigns, this is Wolf commander, all vehicles are to push on into the woodline, keep everyone close together, tighten up to the infantry. Wolf commander out."

Golgolvin looked on confused at hearing his own voice playing over the radio, he looked down at his gunner, bewildered, who sat with the same expression, looking back at him. Both wondering what was going on.

He saw the movement around him, as the BMPs alongside him were already beginning to move forwards. Frantically he waved his arms, trying to get the commander's attentions, all of them looking forwards, no one seeing him. Angrily he looked down, keying the radio.

"All Wolf callsigns, Wolf commander, remain where you are, I gave no such order to move!"

He watched on open mouthed as they ignored him, one by one the BMPs began to push into the treeline, still carrying out the fake orders.

His voice rising in anger he keyed the radio again.

"Goddammit! Will someone fucking answer me! All callsigns stop where you are!"

"Sir, I don't think we're transmitting!" one of the command officers sat in the back of his vehicle reported up, continuing. "I think our radios are only receiving, not transmitting!"

"Well don't just sit there! Fix them!" he shouted angrily, watching his units disappearing into the trees one by one until only his vehicle was left outside alone.

He waited for a few precious minutes as his crew worked to fix the problem, the conversations on the radios cutting in and out, as cables and connections were pulled out and re-connected. He heard again over the radio, his own voice booming out loud and clear,

"All Wolf callsigns, sounds like we've taken out the tank and cleared the area. Well done, now let's close up here, armoured box formation. Have all infantry and vehicle commanders dismount and meet me over at Wolf minor, I want to plan what to do next."

"God dammit! Who the hell is that?" he shouted out angrily, recognising the callsign for his second in command's vehicle. At the far end of the woods, he could still hear the gunfire, surely his men wouldn't believe it was all over and stop the attack? Unbelievably he heard the commanders on the other radio nets, now acknowledging the orders, the infantry were collapsing their positions and their commanders running back to where the vehicles were now forming up.

He shouted down to his driver.

"Get me into that fucking woodline, quickly! Find Major Lenosky's wagon. Move dammit, MOVE!"

He clung on as the driver accelerated away into the woods, ducking low to avoid the low hanging branches as they raked across his vehicle. He watched on as the driver followed the vehicle tracks, narrowly avoiding the trees' and bodies that littered the ground, the signs of battle still smoking all around them. Behind him, he could hear his own officers desperately trying to countermand the order, silence their only reply as the radio traffic continued without them, each commander confirming the order. Up ahead he saw the BMP's all tightly grouped together, forming an impenetrable armoured box, the vehicle commanders were all dismounting and walking in, some carrying notebooks, whilst some of the infantry commanders were running back in, closely followed by their seconds. Everyone looked more relaxed, some had removed helmets and body armour as if it indeed it were all over and the battle won. Some of the men were smiling, others began to light cigarettes and chat animatedly about what had happened, no doubt exaggerating their own contributions.

He angrily directed his driver into the middle of the waiting vehicles, drawing to a halt at the rear of Sasha's vehicle, ignoring the shouts and curses of the assembled men as his vehicle slammed to a halt, rocking violently and spattering those close by in mud. Some of them looked up angrily brushing off clothes, others confused at his demeanour, not understanding his sudden anger. He looked over angrily as Major Lenosky stepped out of the back of his vehicle, first smiling, then looking on confused as the Colonel shook his fist angrily and tore off his headset. The Major raised his arms in confusion asking, "Colonel..I don't understand!"

"What the fuck? Major!"

The relaxed demeanour of some of the men nearby changed in an instant, seeing their CO raging amongst them made them realise something wasn't right.

He stayed on the vehicle, refusing to come down, instead leaning over to shout.

"What the fuck are you all doing here with your thumbs up your asses? We've still got men fighting over there!" he pointed over to where the sounds of the battle still raged.

The radio headset began to crackle again, someone was transmitting, the noise distracting him. Angrily he pulled the headset out of its socket, not wanting to be distracted as he watched his soldiers look to each other, the confused looks being exchanged made him realise, they still couldn't comprehend what he was saying.

Major Lenosky stepped forwards, his eyes narrowing suspiciously.

"But Sir..You were the one who gave the order to-"

"That wasn't me on the radio Major!" he interrupted angrily, adding, "you've been fooled! Someone's playing us! My last orders were to attack the woods, infantry only, not bunch up here like a bunch of fucking dairy cows ready for slaughter! How long have you known me Sasha? Why the hell would I order that in the middle of an attack?"

Sasha looked away at the men, his face creased in confusion, about to talk when a figure came bursting out of the trees, running towards the group. Shouts sounded as soldiers instinctively grabbed their weapons, about to meet the new threat, instantly recognising the figure as one of their own, an infantryman, his face blackened and sweat soaked. He squeezed himself between the gap in the vehicles, looking over and instantly recognizing the Colonel, breathing heavily he reported,

"Sir! Thank God, I'm glad I've found you. The tank, it's still alive and firing on us. My Lieutenant sent me to warn you not to get near it yet."

Golgolvin's face creased in confusion at what he was being told as Major Lenosky asked,

"Soldier, why send a runner? Don't you have a radio?"

"We do Sir, yes, however for some reason no fucker seems to be listening to us. We've been trying to warn you all ever since we found out about its new weapon."

"New weapon?" Golgolvin enquired, cocking his head.

"Strangest thing I ever saw, mounted on the turret, it's like some kind of laser, it's been shooting at anything that gets near it. Bloody deadly, I saw it take out a T-80 as if it were a hot knife through butter."

That's what was taking out the vehicles, Golgolvin thought to himself, finally the missing pieces slotted together.

Hearing the news, the soldiers around them began to chat amongst themselves about the new weapon, some shook their heads disbelievingly.

"Where's the tank now?" he demanded, ignoring the chatter.

The soldier pointed ahead of them, through the trees.

"Go another 400metres through the treeline, you'll come to a clearing, it's in the middle."

"Is it still stuck?" Golgolvin enquired, his eyebrows raised.

"Yep, still stuck Sir."

"Crew?"

The soldier shrugged as he replied, "Someone must be left alive on-board Sir, else whose firing those weapons?".

"Any other enemy units that you've come across?"

"No Sir, just the tank, we've cleared the rest of the woods, it's all alone."

He nodded, thinking to himself, so it *was* on its own. At least now he had it confirmed, but what about that weapon?

He felt an urgent tugging at his legs, feeling the gunner trying to get his attention, he kicked out irritably, trying to think.

The tugging became more frantic as he saw Sasha's operator waving and shouting frantically over to him, trying to get his attention. Sasha ran to the back of his vehicle, picking up one of the headsets awkwardly, his shoulder wounds still causing him problems. He saw his second in command look over at him, his eyes opening wide in disbelief at what was being said on the radio.

Golgolvin finally relented, looking down into the turret snapping out.

"WHAT?"

He saw his gunner tapping his headset urgently, then pointing to the cable dangling close by.

Shit, he thought, no wonder he couldn't hear what was going on, in his anger he'd pulled the plug.

Within seconds he had his headset plugged back in, standing back up as the earpiece squawked to life.

"Fire mission received and copied, rounds in the air. Hammer One-Zero, out."

"Well? What is it?" he demanded, as his gunner stammered.

"You've just called in an artillery strike!"

"What? Of course, I bloody haven't!" he looked about him in confusion, suddenly remembering the fake voice on the radio. With the distraction of the soldier, he'd forgotten the reason they were all assembled there in the first place. Suddenly the words he'd just used came flooding back to him.

"Not bunch up here like a bunch of fucking dairy cows ready for slaughter!"

"Where?" he shot back, already knowing the answer. He watched in disbelief as Major Lenosky shouted out in warning, as the men sprawled around suddenly sprung into life, grabbing body armour and helmets and beginning to scatter and dive for cover. The Major looked over, about to shout across to him when instead he looked skywards, electing to instead jump into the vehicle and attempt to close the ramp.

Surely the artillery wouldn't buy it? Surely, they'd ask for conformation of the grid, wouldn't they ask for authentication, he thought, the cold fear of what had happened to Lebedev creeping into his thoughts, already answering questions in his head.

It was one of the officers in the back of his vehicle who finally shouted out the warning, shaking him from his stupor.

"Sir! We need to move! NOW!"

Instantly he was shocked into action. He ducked down, as if on instinct, time slowing as he began to issue the order to the driver. He felt the vehicle begin to move, the movement rocking him backwards as he kept low, the vehicle accelerating away from the incoming maelstrom. Even wearing the headset, he could still hear the high-pitched whining overhead, as the heavy 155 mm rounds came tearing into them. He heard his driver utter a curse, some fool had run in front of them, not looking where they were going, Golgolvin felt the vehicle rise up and down slightly as the soldier was crushed beneath the tracks, wincing at the thought of what had just happened to one of his men. From the vehicle's periscopes he saw carnage around him, as the tightly parked vehicles were the perfect targets for the rounds that fell onto them. Some were already on fire, explosions tearing into the densely packed men, as others tried to drive away, colliding with vehicles and adding to the confusion. Loud explosions began to sound all around, building in crescendo as the powerful shock waves tore through them, Golgolvin fearing it would shake the armoured vehicle apart. It seemed to not matter where his driver turned, there was always a wall of fire and death waiting for them, the air filled with shrapnel and flying debris, slamming and rattling against the side of his vehicle. Suddenly they were through, the explosions suddenly sounding distant behind him, as he looked backwards, not quite believing that he'd made it. His driver shouted a warning, Golgolvin turned, wondering what the hell the problem was now. His eyes opened wide in alarm as he saw the clearing ahead that he'd just been warned about. In its centre stood a fallen oak tree, and jammed atop its huge trunk was the enemy tank. He could see the strange weapon system on it's turret quickly turn to face them.

He heard a crack as if lightening had just exploded nearby, then suddenly a flash from behind and a searing heat as the back of his vehicle was engulfed in flames. Without knowing why, perhaps he could sense the danger incoming, he'd already began to launch himself upwards and out of the turret, throwing himself clear of the vehicle, as the BMP exploded into flames. For the briefest of seconds, he heard the shouts of alarm over the intercom cut off suddenly, as his headset was torn from his head in the fall. The explosion lifted him up, and after a brief sensation of flying, expecting at any second to feel himself smash into a tree, or metal tear through his body, he landed roughly into the soft earth. Rolling with a hollow thump against a tree stump, still with enough force to badly wind him. He lay still for a moment, his ears ringing before carefully flexing his arms and legs, checking for injuries before quickly coming to his senses and patting off the flames on his arms. He lay there, his arms protectively covering his head, drowning out the shock and the noise as he tried to breathe, hearing the screams of the wounded and the dying in between the salvos. He looked up, staring open mouthed as two burning figures staggered out of the inferno of his vehicle, walking out of the back and out towards the trees, head to foot in flames then dropping on the ground without a sound being uttered. Instantly the Paratrooper in him kicked in, and he looked around for his rifle, remembering it was still sat in the turret, which was now a melting pot of death. He looked down at his assault vest, going for his pistol, seeing the holster torn open, the flap dangling empty. It must have torn loose when he was blown from the vehicle. He was about to curse his luck, when he stopped himself, realising at least he was alive, unarmed, but alive. He lay there, dazed and in cover, waiting until at last, the artillery barrage finally seemed to be lifting, the rounds dropping less frequently, until finally they stopped. He heard more noise behind him, turning to see his second in commands BMP screaming forwards towards him. For a second, he thought it would crush him, jumping up with hands raised, holding his breath as, at the last second it turned, coming to a halt with the back door metres from him. The back doors opened as Sasha jumped out, closely followed by two heavily armed infantrymen, all three quickly pulling him towards the vehicle.

He was about to warn them of the danger nearby when another crack sounded out and all four men were flung to the floor as Sasha's BMP burst into flames. With its back door still open, Golgolvin got ringside seats to the horror within as infantrymen all fought to get out, as the flames began licking at them, teasing them before engulfing them as the crew screamed from the front, trapped in the inferno of twisted metal. He looked on in shock as he felt rough hands pulling him back up to his feet, dragging him away from the blazing wreck. He could see two of the soldiers were shouting to him, as Sasha stood up, a strange, bewildered look on his face as he staggered forwards, his hands scrabbling at his back, stumbling and then falling forwards to the floor. Golgolvin could see from the metal fragments embedded deeply within Sasha's back and head that his friend wouldn't be getting back up. He had just lost his only true friend and confidant.

Gologvin yelled, in anger and fear at what was happening as everything around him seemed to be burning, he turned to go back to help Sasha, already the forest floor was on fire as the flames spread out, advancing towards his friend's body. As the two Infantry soldiers grabbed him, he tried to struggle, to break their grip but they were both too powerfully built, and between them they kept their vice like grip on his arms, dragging him further away from the danger, as the vehicle's ammunition began to cook off, the rounds exploding outwards in all directions. With impotent rage he looked away, ashamed at the thought of leaving his friend's body to the flames, but also knowing Sasha was already dead.

Finally, after a few minutes of running, the trio threw themselves down by a tree, exhausted and in fits of coughing, they looked back at the growing inferno as more explosions sounded around them.

"Colonel, you okay?" asked one of the soldiers, a tough looking Sergeant, in between gasping for air and coughing.

"Yes!" he replied curtly, gazing back at the wreckage of the command vehicles. Still, he couldn't believe their change of fortune. What the hell just happened, he thought bitterly, not wanting to dwell on the loss of his friend in the middle of the battle, but still not quite believing he was dead.

"Orders Sir?" the second one asked, eyebrows raised expectantly as more troops began to emerge from the treeline towards them, the Sergeants rallying cries, oaths and curses drawing them in towards the group.

He looked around him, as more survivors heard the rallying cries, their numbers growing until there were nearly thirty of them gathered together, all soot faced and blackened, all looking to their Colonel for direction.

"Any officers left?" he asked hopefully, already fearing the answer.

"Only you Sir, the rest were killed back with the vehicles," another Sergeant replied, looking around the group.

Behind them, they could hear the enemy tank's machine gun firing away, answered by more rifle fire, still some of his units were still alive and fighting. Outside of the woods the sounds of a heavy battle were well underway. He had no idea what was going on, with the loss of his vehicle, he'd lost the ability to command the armoured formations and the battle picture. Now he was back to being a Paratrooper, which in a way pleased him. Here at least things were less complicated. Now he could concentrate on fighting what was simply in front of him. He looked about him, his gaze cold and hard, looking at his men.

"You've all seen firsthand what that tank's firing. I don't claim to know how it works, or what it is exactly, but I do know this. It's powerful, and I want it. If the British have more of them then we need to understand it, to be able to defeat it. If we capture that weapon, if we get it back to our own scientists, perhaps *we* can benefit from it. Perhaps the sacrifice and cost to our comrades would be worth the price."

The men nodded as they listened, looking to each other as he continued, his voice raising as his anger grew.

"Our units are outside these woods, I don't know what they're fighting, or who they're fighting with, but I can guarantee this, they're going to FUCKING WIN! And when they do, and they come rolling into these woods, do we want them to see us like this? A sorry looking bunch of misfits hiding in fear from one tank? Or do we want them to come in and see proud Russian soldiers, with a captured tank and a weapon that before now, none of us believed existed? A prize already paid for by the blood of our friends?"

All of them nodded and grinned savagely, most of them were his soldiers, hard soldiers, all experienced and hardened by battle. The others were remnants of other units, two looked to be tank crew, all looked to be joined by the same purpose, to get revenge on that tank.

A thin smile crossed his lips, his head turning to see them all as he spoke.

"Now I don't know about the rest of you mean-looking bastards, but I'm off to get what's owed!"

With a newfound purpose, his group broke up into assault formations, the more experienced NCO's taking charge of the junior soldiers, re-distributing the weaponry. Five groups were formed, each having at least one RPG between them. The heavier weaponry had all been destroyed along with the vehicles. Carefully they advanced forwards, using their burning vehicles as cover, shielding themselves from view from the tank and its murderous weaponry as they closed the distance. The woods were littered with bodies, he still couldn't believe this was all down to one vehicle and felt sure the woods *must* be hiding something else. He kept his concerns hidden, for now, all they had to concentrate on was the capture.

His group went to the left, keeping themselves hidden amongst the trees, the two large soldiers who had saved him were still with him. He'd armed himself with a bag of grenades and a rifle, taken from one of the bodies. He watched as the groups all approached the tank from different directions, surprised that the crew were still onboard, watching the dark thick smoke that wafted gently out of the engine decks, more smoke, lighter in colour and not as dense was coming out of the turret.

The tank looked quiet, the only indication anyone was on board was the machine gun, still searching for movement, it rotated around, like a searchlight. Golgolvin's men carefully watched its progress, keeping themselves hidden as it looked for them, only moving when certain it was looking elsewhere. they crawled forwards, finally they were set, each group watching the other, in position, ready to fire.

He tapped the man closest to him carrying the RPG on his shoulder who nodded in response, the man checking behind him that the area was clear of the back blast before steeping forwards to fire. Before he could pull the trigger, the tank's machine gun barked out, the bullets thudding around him as he cried out in pain, falling backwards and dropping the RPG.

The other groups launched their assaults, all firing at once, bullets lighting up the sides of the tank, trying to distract the crew as the other RPG teams stepped into view. A rocket was fired from behind, slamming into the engine decks and exploding, another hit the side armour, peeling away a layer of the steel, exposing the armour pack. The third hit where the second had landed, the damaged armour pack disappearing momentarily in a fireball and falling to the floor.

Golgolvin leaned forwards, using the distraction his men were creating to grab the precious RPG and pack of three rockets from the soldiers body. Quickly he aimed and fired, the recoil of the rocket reminding him of its power as the rocket arced away and exploded on the front of the hull, leaving nothing in damage but a scorch mark. He heard the shouted warnings as the machine gun spun towards him, turning and running, just as the bullets hit the ground where he'd been standing. He dived behind a large tree, hearing the rounds hitting into the bark, his breathing ragged as he struggled to reload the RPG, remembering the lessons taught to him many years ago on how to use it.

The tank's machine gun kept firing into the tree he was hidden behind, suddenly the machine gun went silent, everyone stopped and looked, one of the Paratroopers shouting out triumphantly,

"The bastards are out of ammo! Quickly get up to it!"

As one they all yelled as the groups ran forwards, the enemy tank crew had left their hatches open, a rookie mistake when dealing with infantry, and now they'd finally pay the price for such stupidity. Golgolvin watched on, the RPG slung over his shoulder his rifle now raised and ready to fire as the lead group made it up to the sides of the tank, the five soldiers being covered by the others as they carefully crawled up the side, already far too many bodies of their men littered the floor around the vehicle. Now at least they would get payback.

As one, the five soldiers pulled grenades and dropped them in through the hatches, keeping their bodies clear in case someone was down below lying in wait. Fully expecting to hear shouts or screams of surprise, instead there was nothing, as the grenades exploded with a hollow thump, thick smoke ejecting outwards as the infantry now crawled up onto the turret, aiming weapons inside and firing off a quick burst before looking inside. In confusion they shouted back over to the Colonel's group.

"Sir! there's no one on board!"

"What? There must be! Search inside!" he yelled back disbelievingly, perhaps the British had a secret compartment on the tank, somewhere to hide, he thought. Then remembering back to the older tanks, he walked up to the tank, his men covering in all round defence, as he turned to another group, pointing to two of them and barking out the order.

"You and you, get round the other side, check underneath for an escape hatch, see where those bastards have gone to. Find them!"

He looked up at the tank, shaking his head in disbelief, finally he'd done it, finally he had captured a Challenger 2. And this one seemed to be full of all sorts of new surprises. He looked over it, his eyes taking in the weapons system mounted on the turret, before his eyes cast down, looking at the battle damage, something was all too familiar about it. His mind began to cast back to the first night of the drop, to his first encounter with the enemy, his eyes opening wide in disbelief, as he realised this was the same tank.

No, he thought, that can't be.

He was distracted from his thoughts as the men above him on the tank began shouting and pointing over towards the far side of the woods, they'd seen something, and it was coming towards them.

He shouted fiercely out to his group.

"Right men! let's get ready to fight for our prize! This bitch is ours now, and no-one's taking it from us, NO ONE! We wait for our support to arrive!"

The remnants of his unit nodded fiercely, understanding already the cost of the battle. Some of the men crawled up onto the tank, settling themselves into fire positions, others spread out, taking fire positions in the shell holes, ready to repel whatever was coming towards them. Some of them were disbelieving, looking around the sorry looking group, not quite understanding how they'd gone from going on the attack, to suddenly being on the defensive. Golgolvin quickly re-checked the RPG was ready to fire. Distracted at hearing the ongoing battle outside of the woods, he cocked his head to listen, trying to make sense of what was going on out of sight to him, certain that support was moments away. He heard a shout from above as suddenly the soldiers on the tank began firing over towards the trees.

"Good, it's about time they finally came to us!" he yelled, smiling as stepping around the tank he began to look down the RPG sights and readied himself to fire.

11

Operation Cerberus

Central London 2pm

Major Laratov mingled with the growing crowds, smiling as he read the slogans on the placards being held aloft, the young angry faces all chanting the same furious chants, rage simmering just below the surface.

'*FUCK THE KING*!' one read, another proclaiming '*THE ONLY MURDERER HERE WEARS A CROWN*!'

Two young protesters, with hair coloured blue and ginger and covered in piercings took turns in screaming through a megaphone near him, causing him to wince as his eardrums fought the onslaught.

"DOWN WITH THE MONARCHY! END THE OPPRESSION AND LIES!" The ginger haired girl was red faced, spittle flecking her mouth as her rant continued, egged on by her blue haired friend as the thousands of voices in unison bounced off the high walls of central London. Already London was gridlocked, the police having set up roadblocks, herding the growing crowds, funnelling them towards Hyde Park.

Laratov smiled, watching the twelve other members of his team from within the crowd, all were dressed like him, in civilian clothes and carrying placards and daysacks, their job for now to mingle and follow the protesters, to keep them close and follow the route. He already knew the final destination of the march, even if the organisers didn't. He was a small part of a much bigger plan, and if it worked as well as it should, by the end of the day London would be theirs, ready and ripe to be plucked. For now, he smiled at the two shouting protesters, pumping his fist in the air in unison and chanting along, walking with the crowd and getting swept away by the excitement of nearly a hundred thousand people all with one common purpose and goal, although they were unaware of it yet, they were all on their way to help bring down a King.

Thames River London

Fletch held on as the rib jumped another wave, the bow easily slicing through the disturbed wake of the pleasure craft screaming past. No doubt another yacht owner trying to get their prized possession out of the capital before things got bad, he thought, watching as the 45ft boat hared away.

He looked behind him, seeing the large figure of Bug smiling back at him, weapon resting over his chest, unfazed and unconcerned, enjoying the trip upriver in the sunshine. Bug pointed at the pub on the riverbank, the hint clear to see. Fletch smiled, thinking to himself, always finding time for a pint eh Bug? Behind them at the helm stood Grub, his eyes looking out from beneath the helmet and balaclava that they were all similarly wearing. At the stern sat Jonesy, weapon laying low but keeping a watchful eye on any boats following. All four of them were heavily armed, hiding in plain sight, trying their best to look relaxed, but behind each balaclava was a calculating mind, ready to spring into action if needed.

Fletch began to think back, how everything about this operation had felt rushed and poorly planned. His team had only just made it back to HMS Archer and were still debriefing the submarine's intelligence officer on their mission at Portland when they'd heard the orders coming through for Operation Cerberus, the rescue of two high level VIP's from central London. At first, he thought it would be a simple snatch and grab, after all it wasn't like London was an enemy held city. But as the hours of planning had come together, the more they planned the more they could see, this wasn't going to be as simple as they had first thought.

For a start, and he still had trouble believing this, he was told that London was to be classed as hostile, and not, repeat not, to be classed as friendly territory. Civilians were to be treated as hostile to the VIP's and his team.

Secondly, and this really twisted his lemons, he was told the Met police were not to be trusted, except for his contact, and were to be treated as the enemy. If he or his team found himself in a situation whereby lethal force had to be used, they were to prosecute without delay.

He still shook his head in disbelief at that last order, these were British police, what the hell? Weren't they all supposed to be on the same side?

They'd been given no details on the two VIPs identities, or their location, only that their contact in London would take them to the VIPs. Any attempt to find out from the sub's Captain was met with a wall of silence, not because he was being obstinate, but because he didn't know himself. His own attempts to find out went up the chain of command and came crashing back down again. It was need to know, and right now, they didn't need to know.

With the limited information they had, HMS Archer had set course at a steady speed underwater, carefully navigating the shallows of the English Channel and busy shipping lanes to now wait four miles offshore, in water barely deep enough to cover her sail, waiting for the team's orders to deploy. Finally, this morning, the order to launch had come through as they'd been eating breakfast, the team not wasting one second in getting into their assault gear and launching the rigid inflatable. As his team were getting ready, the sub's Captain handed Fletch a manila envelope that was for his eyes only, detailing the VIP's names, locations and further details of the op. He'd taken himself somewhere quiet and had committed to memory its details, understanding then the importance of keeping it quiet from the team. His guys weren't stupid. Usually, they wouldn't have dared launch in daylight, but whoever VIP one and two were, they were considered top priority, and important enough to semi-surface the boat in daylight. After a few moments it's decks were awash as Grub had expertly powered the rib out of the sub's Special Forces garage bolted onto the deck. The sub's engineering crews had done a good enough job in painting the police signs on the black rubber of the hull, and with the blue flashing lights now fitted, to any passer-by the inflatable would look like any other police boat patrolling the Thames.

Instead of their normal military style uniform, Fletch had the guys wear their black counter terrorism kit, with balaclavas and helmets and sporting hastily made police badges. For weapons, each operator was carrying the L119/A2 Special Forces Individual Weapon, (SFIW) and as a backup each carried the Glock 19 pistol. With their weapons and black clothing, Fletch was hoping they'd pass for members of the elite Counter Terrorist Force, or at least that was the plan. He knew upon scrutiny they'd be caught out, but it was the best they could do at such short notice. It had seemed strange as they'd transited the Thames, screaming in at 30 knots in the daylight, blue lights flashing, for all to see, as Grub navigated the small black rib through the commercial traffic and barges that plied their trade daily along the Thames. Some of the crews had waved cheerily at them, his own team waving back, the immortal words of a comedy film filling his ears.

"Just smile and wave boys, smile and wave."

Soon, the large tankers and barges began to give way for the smaller craft, the passenger ferries whizzing along as the Docklands disappeared into the distance, the more industrial setting becoming more urban as blocks of penthouses sped by, each one costing more than Fletch could hope to earn in a lifetime. He looked around him, watching as the shadow of the flood barrier shot past, suddenly the familiar landmarks of London began to appear. They raced past London City Airport, Fletch ignoring the landmark, his concentration instead on the approaching police boat coming in the opposite direction. Fletch was about to wave, when Bug shouted out in warning,

"Don't wave Fletch, we're supposed to be CTU! To everyone else in the police force we're just a bunch of cunts! We don't wave, because we think we're better than them!"

Fletch stayed his hand, keeping one hand on the rib to steady himself as the police boat drew nearer, Grub driving them even closer, as if they had nothing to hide. For a few tense moments both crews glared at each other, the police crews eyes hidden behind thick black sunglasses, as they surveyed the team's boat. As one, all three police officers turned their heads away, deciding they warranted no further interest from them, no doubt the arrogance that Bug had shouted about paying off.

Fletch breathed a sigh of relief, thankful to have passed the first test, at least their uniforms and the boat's makeshift camouflage was working. He looked back at the police boat, keeping a watchful eye on it, to make sure it wouldn't double back on them, only turning to the front when he was sure it was a safe enough distance away. He knew it wouldn't be the only boat on the water and could only hope the ruse would last long enough. He held on as the boat turned to round the headland of the O2 arena, Grub ramping the boat through the wake of another high-speed ferry that crossed their path. Fletch looked upwards, seeing the silhouette of the two F35's flying overhead at high altitude, their air support should they need it. For now, the pilots were flying a racetrack pattern, avoiding the Typhoons flying out of Heathrow, whilst providing Fletch with comms back to the submarine if needed. For now, the radios seemed to be working fine, and there was none of the interference he'd been warned about yet, not yet at least. As if on cue, his earpiece squawked to life.

"Romeo Four, this is Zero, send sitrep."

Turning his head to shield the mic from the wind noise he replied, using the code words for the landmarks of the O2 and the Airport.

"Zero, Romeo Four, still mobile from White-Five to White-Six."

"Zero, roger, out."

Fletch went back to watching the journey, seeing the smoke rising in the distance as the site of the attack on the capital began to get closer. Already the maritime traffic was beginning to lighten, and suddenly they were forced to slow as they rounded a corner. Four police boats were drifting lazily in the middle of the Thames with blue lights flashing, the crews were occupied, leaning over and pulling what looked like debris and floating detritus out of the water. As they drew closer, Fletch looked on sadly, seeing it wasn't debris or rubbish they were pulling out, they were floating bodies, no doubt having re-surfaced days after the attack, with the gases of decomposition making them more buoyant than before.

Fletch noticed the team kept quiet, felt some of them shift uncomfortably as they all saw the bodies of two small children carefully lifted out and placed on the deck of one of the boats. The police crews ignored them as they passed, one police officer looked off into the distance, his face full of sadness at the waste of life. Fletch waved at him, ignoring the words of Bug, smiling in sympathy as the police officer nodded and waved back, both of them in mute understanding at what they had seen. Fletch felt the boat power up again as Grub cleared the police boats, but this time Fletch stepped forwards, leaning over the bow, not wishing to run the risk of running over a body and damaging the prop. Watching him on the bow, Grub powered the engine back down, knowing what his Sergeant was already thinking.

For the next few minutes nobody spoke, as they continued upriver, Fletch checking their position against the computer display that he had hidden under a Velcro patch, strapped to his arm. The dragon computer was cutting edge, the screen composing of a flexible fabric screen, able to be worn on an arm or a leg, like a bendable laptop. Attached via a thin cable routed through his uniform, the main unit sat in a pouch on his back, small and lightweight, with a powerful lithium battery it could run for 24 hours. The dragon could give Fletch access to vital information, showing mapping, target information, building information and mission updates as and when they were sent in.

Fletch checked again the position, recognising from memory the small private dock they were heading to. He looked back, indicating with his hand where he wanted Grub to take the boat.

Within minutes they had the boat tied up and hidden amongst two larger private yachts, the team walking purposefully up to the dock's security gate. It was locked, with a button to open it on their side and a keypad on the other.

Not wanting to get locked out with no access to their boat, Fletch had Jonesy disable the keypad, jamming the latch closed, so now, with the gate closed, no one would notice it hadn't locked. He sent an update to Zero, telling them they were now feet dry, the code for on land and waiting arrival of their contact.

Quickly the team checked out their new surroundings, already knowing the dock was out of use, having researched it back on the sub. The company that owned the dockyard had gone into administration, the owner fleeing to Iran after racking up huge debts. Now it was desolate and was the perfect place for them to wait to meet their contact. A chain link fence with a gate separated the dock from the street outside, the padlock easily broken by Fletch before he retreated amongst the crates. Fletch checked his watch, it was 13:26, the meet was scheduled for 13:30.

He and his team settled themselves down amongst the crates and packages, conscious of the fact London was one of the most watched capitals in the world, with one CCTV camera for every ten people, they had to be careful. Already they'd checked the building for power, finding it off, like most of central London, Fletch counting on the cameras being out after the attack.

With nothing to do but wait, he began to run through the plan again, over and over, checking every detail, running through the 'what ifs,' and the 'actions on,' in his head. He'd already spent countless hours of planning with the team, but knew, nothing survives first contact, and if, and it was a big if, the bullets started to fly, then the time for planning was over. Until that happened, he'd make every second count.

He was running through his third version of the plan in his head when Grub's voice came over his earpiece, each team member linked by radio comms.

"What time is this guy supposed to be here?"

Taking the hint Fletch checked his watch again, muttering under his breath. "Fucks sake, where are you?"

Their contact was a Chief Superintendent Lewis, Fletch had been told to meet him there at 13:30, it was now nearly 2pm.

Suddenly it was Jonesy on the radio.

"Got a vehicle coming in, one up, looks like a police van."

All four raised their weapons, the relaxing river cruise now forgotten, as all became aware they were on mission now, the words of warning from the intelligence officer still ringing in their ears. "Everyone in the capital is to be treated as hostile. You are *not* in friendly territory."

They watched as the large police van pulled up outside the gate, it was a riot van, with a huge metal grate atop the windscreen, ready to be pulled down if things went bad. With a squeal of brakes, the van stopped, the engine still running, as the driver got out, walking up to the gate. She was a policewoman, wearing the rank of Sergeant on her shoulder tabs. She pulled at the padlock, seeing it was broken, then slowly, and cautiously, the young officer pushed open the gate and walked into the dockyard, her head scanning sideways as if looking for something or someone. Fletch remained where he was, watching and waiting as the young officer drew closer. He'd already seen the photo of his contact, and whoever this person was, *she* wasn't *him*.

"You can come out now, I'm here to pick you up," the officer whispered, still looking around and walking closer. Suddenly her radio squawked loudly, causing her to curse and almost jump as she quickly turned the volume down. Fletch used the distraction of her radio to step out of cover, his pistol drawn and aimed squarely at her chest, demanding, "Who are you?"

The officer looked startled, raising her hands and blinking in surprise before exclaiming.

"Woah! Hold your fire, I'm friendly!"

Her eyes darted sideways at the other members of the team as they all emerged from their cover, their rifles pointing squarely at her chest. She looked down at the rifles, then back at the men. Instead of shock, or fear, Fletch saw only frustration, as the officer quickly shot back.

"Look, we don't have the time for this, we need-"

She was cut short as Grub stepped forwards, jamming his pistol at the nape of her neck, causing her to yell in pain as he kicked her legs out, slamming her head down against one of the crates.

"What the hell are you playing...AHH!" she yelled in pain, as Grub twisted the officer's ear painfully, a few more millimetres of pressure and it would tear away. Her face turned red then purple with the pain, as Fletch stepped forwards, clamping a powerful hand over her mouth to muffle her screams.

"Lady, in case you hadn't noticed, we don't give a fuck about you being a woman, we're all for equal opportunities here, just in case you thought being one might somehow soften our demeanour. Now, answer my questions, any attempt to use your radio or call for help and my colleague here will tear one of your ears off. Blink if you understand."

Her eyes welled up, the tears flowing as she blinked repeatedly.

Slowly he removed his hand, the officer sweating and breathing heavily with the pain, her eyes although filled with tears were full of fire and rage. Fletch was certain if it wasn't for the pistol at her neck, she'd lunge for him. As if sensing the same thing, Grub stepped forwards, a heavy hand resting on her shoulder, showing her the futility of such a move.

The officer took a few breaths, calming herself as slowly she nodded in understanding, the grip on her shoulder relaxing as Fletch and Grub both stepped back, releasing her after watching the fight go out of her eyes.

"Who the fuck are you? And what are you doing here?" Fletch demanded, his voice cold. He was in no mood for small talk.

The officer stood up, rubbing her ear painfully, looking around before replying.

"I'm looking for your lot, I was told to come here, pick you up and get you into the palace."

Fletch looked at the woman's rank again, seeing she was a Sergeant, shaking his head disbelievingly. "You're just a Sergeant, and not who we're supposed to meet. You're a fucking liar."

He grabbed the officer by her collar, walking her over to the dockside, towards the water, his gun pointed at the woman's head. He holstered the pistol, pulling his knife, his intention clear. The pistol would make noise, the knife would not. The officer's eyes darted towards the fast-flowing brown water then towards the knife, her eyes defiant as she said unbelievingly,

"You wouldn't kill me, you're on our fucking side. For christ's sake, think about it? Why am I here? Where's everyone else if this is a setup?"

Fletch paused, flourishing the knife for effect, letting the officer continue to speak.

"Look, you're waiting for Chief Superintendent Lewis, right?" Fletch raised his eyebrows at the name, indicating the woman to go on.

"The Chief Super was arrested this morning, he managed to get a message out to me to come here today at 13:30 to pick you lot up. Said there would be four of you, and that you're here to grab the King and Queen from the palace. I don't know anything else apart from the fact that I've got orders written and signed by another officer that will get you through the roadblocks and into the palace. That's it."

The other three of the team stepped closer, mouths open in disbelief at the mention of the King and Queen, finally the identities of the VIP's were revealed. Only Fletch kept his previous knowledge hidden as he replied, his eyes narrowing suspiciously.

"Very trusting of a Chief Superintendent, to trust a Sergeant with such a task. Why you? Has he run out of golfing buddies? Or perhaps you both like to share a tale or two in bed?"

"Fuck you!" the officer spat back, stepping backwards and shrugging off Fletch's hands, looking defiantly back at him, pointing to his rank slide and adding. "Besides, you're a Sergeant! Who'd you fuck to get in on this job?"

Fletch looked over to the others, seeing the hidden grins, he had to admit, the Sergeant had a lot of spirit.

He watched as the police officer looked out over the water, the anger in her seeming to lessen as she slowly shook her head, finally she looked back up, her voice softer, and a sadness in her gaze.

"Look, the reason Chief Lewis told me, is because, I'm his daughter... "

Fletch nodded in acknowledgement, he'd already seen the resemblance to the Chief Super's face, and was guessing as much, but had wanted to confirm it first. He stepped back, lowering the knife and continued to listen as the Sergeant continued.

"He had a matter of minutes to tell me before they burst into his office. Up to that point I had no idea about any of this. I'd love to say he told me everything, the grand master plan, but he didn't have the time. He was arrested, and I was stuck with you lot. And that's it. Nothing else. No tricks, no passwords, no coded phrases. I'm your lift out of here, and that's all I know."

Fletch looked into her eyes, seeing already the grief in amongst the anger, understanding now why the Sergeant was so defiant. In a way Fletch could understand it. Her father had risked a lot to help them, now he'd been arrested, leaving it all down to her. And what had they done by way of gratitude? They'd tried tearing her ear off.

His face lost some of its coldness as he put the knife away, asking,

"Okay then Sergeant, what do we call you?"

Her face creased in confusion as she replied as if stating the obvious. "Err. Sergeant Lewis."

Fletch smiled, thinking, I bet you're a right hoot at parties, adding,

"Fuck that, what's your name?"

She sighed, mulling it over, rubbing her ear as finally she relented.

"Gemma, my name's Gemma."

See, that wasn't so hard, was it, he thought, as he pointed over to the team who all looked over as he introduced them. All were unsmiling, still not trusting of the woman and put out by her coldness.

"Ok Gemma, well, I'm Fletch, that big man mountain is Bug, Jonesy is over there, and I believe you've already been acquainted with Grub."

Gemma looked around nodding at the hidden faces, her ear was already turning purple, Fletch was hoping it wouldn't turn cauliflower, hopefully Gemma played rugby, otherwise trying to explain it away would be hard to her other police colleagues after this was all over.

Now that they were all acquainted, it was Bug who wanted more information.

"So, you mentioned the palace, by that, do you mean Buckingham Palace? *The* palace?

Gemma looked at her watch, ushering them over to the van.

"We don't have the time for this guys, we need to go now, time's a ticking and I still need to get you to the palace."

"Why the hurry?" Fletch asked, still a little apprehensive of the officer.

"Didn't they tell you?" Gemma asked, her eyebrow raised.

"Tell me what?" Fletch questioned. Looking over at the others in case he missed something.

"About the demonstrations? About the Palace? That's why my dad was adamant you guys had to be in there quickly."

"What about the Palace?" Fletch asked, hiding his anger at being the last to know again on details of an operation.

"The demonstrations being held in London; the police are under orders to filter the demonstrators towards the palace for 3pm. That's why you're here! If the King and Queen are still there when the demonstrators get there at 3pm, there'll be hell to pay!"

Shit, Fletch thought, it was as if a light bulb had just gone off. Suddenly it all made sense. That's why all the secrecy and sensitivity of the mission. They needed to get to the palace and quickly.

Fletch ushered the team over to the police van, sliding open the side door as he directed them in.

"Right come on, let's move it. Bug, you're driving, rest of you in the back, Gemma you get in the back and give us directions. Any checkpoints and you're doing the talking. Keep those orders you have close, we'll be needing them. Let's move it!"

Within minutes they were in the van and driving through the centre of London, thankfully a lot of the traffic was light, most of the rush hour traffic being non-existent with Westminster being mostly evacuated. However, after only a few minutes they began to hit the police roadblocks, thousands of protesters shouting and cajoling as they marched past, all on their way towards Hyde park. Gemma leaned forwards, talking to the officer in charge and showing the papers. After a few moments of scrutiny, the van was ushered through the roadblock, Bug carefully driving amongst the throng at walking pace, mindful of the thousands of people milling about.

"Shit!" Bug yelled, looking backwards at Gemma. "Any other routes to the palace?"

"Yes, but this was the way I used earlier, it was clear half an hour ago!" she yelled back over the noise, as hands began to thump on the windows of the van, rocking it gently. Outside they could hear shouting, an egg landing on the window, smearing the view and streaking down it as Fletch shouted out from the back, looking at the mapping.

"Stick with it Bug, we can turn right in a moment, should take us down a side street."

Bug looked over, hitting the blues and twos, the siren startling the protesters nearby, drawing more shouts and curses as the crowd parted from them, clearing a route. After a few minutes they finally saw the street they needed, blocked by the barriers and vans of another police roadblock. Initially the officers refused to move for them, until out of frustration Bug yelled out the window.

"Move the fucking barriers! CTU responding to terrorist threat!"

At the mention of the CTU, the ten officers sprung to life, quickly moving the van blocking the road, shoving protesters back who tried to get through as the van slowly left the procession, ignoring the angry looks of the officers manning the roadblock, the van went through, the noise and chants of the protesters disappearing in the distance. Fletch kept an eye on the road and an eye on the dragon, barking out directions to Bug, the van weaving through the near empty streets, devoid of traffic and life.

After ten minutes they were at one of the four outer gates to Buckingham Palace, the two-armed policeman standing guard both looking agitated as the van pulled alongside. In the distance they could hear the muted noise of the protesters, a constant reminder of what was coming towards them.

One of the officers held out a hand, the van drawing alongside as he leaned into the open window, his eyes darting inside.

"Cutting it fine, aren't you? he asked, a look of relief on his face as looked over at Fletch on the passenger side.

"What do you mean mate?" Fletch asked from beneath the balaclava, exuding the confidence and arrogance of the role he was playing.

Both officers exchanged puzzled glances as the first continued, the look of concern reappearing.

"You're our backup that we've been asking for…Aren't you?"

"Fletch looked behind him at Gemma who subtly shook her head.

"Afraid not mate. Why, you expecting trouble?"

A look of anger and frustration creased the armed officers face as he pointed his thumb over his shoulder towards the growing noise.

"Are you fucking kidding me mate? Can't you hear that lot coming down the mall? I've been asking over the radio for the past hour for extra officers. It's just me and Scobie here on the gates."

The other Officer nodded at hearing his name, his own face glum as Fletch enquired casually.

"What do you mean just you two? Where's the rest of the Gate guards?"

The officer shrugged his shoulders in resignation replying,

"Fuck knows! We saw most of them pull out this morning to go help with the protests. It's only us two on the gates, plus whatever remains of the royal detail. We've been stood on this fucking gate now for four hours!"

So, whose controlling access to the palace on the other gates?" Fletch asked, not quite believing the information the guards were telling him.

"We've got them all locked up tight, Control room are monitoring them via the CCTV room inside. Anyone tries to get through and we get tasked on the radio to go tell them to come to this gate. Not ideal, but best we can do given the low manning."

Fletch sat there, not believing his luck. Without realising it, the two frustrated guards had just given him and his team vital information on what and who were left in the palace. Fletch smiled from under the balaclava, about to get Bug to drive on, when, as if realising he'd already said too much, the officer then changed tact, a puzzled look appearing on his face.

"Hang on, if you're *not* our backup, then what are you doing here? What's your business inside?

Fletch was about to reply when Gemma leaned forwards again, producing the orders, quickly replying.

"Security detail for inside the palace, these officers are to accompany me to the control room. If things go bad, we're to assist the royal detail in evacuating the King and Queen."

The officer reached in, taking the paper, his eyes quickly scanning the first written lines then looking back outside the gate at the growing noise getting closer, clearly upmost on his mind. He looked at his colleague, anxiety clear to see. Finally, he relented, passing the orders back to Gemma, remarking as he did so.

"Fine, you know where you're going?"

She nodded in response as he continued.

"Right, when you get to the control room, you tell those fucking idiots to start listening out on the radio, because we're locking the gate after you're in, and if we need help, you lot best not leave us hanging out here!"

Fletch nodded, feeling genuine sympathy for the two officers, he'd found himself in similar situations, nothing ate at the soul more than the feeling of being on your own. As they drove away, he watched in the rear-view mirror as the officers stepped inside the grounds, quickly closing the huge black and gold ornate gates, securing it with the chain and padlock, before resuming their duties.

They drove through the towering archway of the building, the empty sentry boxes adding to the surreal feeling of it all. Everything seemed eerie and deserted as they dove into the centre of the complex, the towering white building blocking out the sunlight, casting shadows on them as they parked up near the official entrance. The double doors would normally have had footmen waiting to greet the King's guests, and with hundreds of staff and military guards posted everywhere, the palace would have been a bustle of activity, but now, there was nothing, just silence, as Grub turned off the engine. The only noise being the protests in the distance as everyone sat waiting, while Fletch checked the map of the palace on the dragon, locating the control room. After a few seconds he looked back at the team.

"Right, now we know they're on minimum manning let's get to the control room first, take that out and then we've got eyes inside and out. remember no-one suspects us yet, so let's look like we belong, keep your weapons low and ready, and *smile*. Especially you Bug you're looking like a right miserable sod!"

The operator smirked, flicking the finger to him as finally they all vacated the van, trying their best to look as passive as possible. With Gemma leading them in, they walked through the ornate gold leafed doors, and up a wide staircase into the first-floor landing. Fletch's eyes were on stalks, trying to ignore the plush surroundings as he and his team checked every nook and corner, feeling naked with their weapons slung uselessly by their side. They had to be careful though, as whoever was in the control room would be watching their every move, and if they suspected anything out of the ordinary, with a push of a button they could have backup closing in within minutes. For now, everyone assumed Fletch and his team were part of the plan, so best to keep that playing out. There would be a time to 'go loud', the code meaning the shooting could start, but for now, keeping quiet and contained was the best approach.

Using the dragons mapping, they navigated through the maze of corridors within the palace, finding themselves walking on plush carpets with intricately decorated walls covered with huge paintings and works of art, Fletch certain he was looking at items worth more than his house. They turned another corridor, and it was as if the pantomime of the palace had suddenly ended, as the plush carpets and pictures were replaced with faded wallpaper and drab coloured lino, no doubt the working part of the palace. They continued down, coming to a set of double doors, which he opened, his eyes taking in the sight beyond. Another long brightly lit corridor led to the door to the control room, but it was the figure lying face down on the floor that got his attention. Within milliseconds his weapon was up and into his shoulder, scanning the corridor, the change in aggression noted by his team who without questioning brought their own weapons up. Bug and Grub turning as one to cover the rear as Jonesy stepped sideways, his own weapon trained ahead of them, providing a clear line of fire and keeping Gemma in the centre of the team. Slowly, as if one, they quietly advanced forwards, Fletch keeping his eyes on the control room door as they approached the body.

Jonesy kept his weapon up as Fletch knelt down with Gemma, rolling the body over, quickly checking for a pulse. The gunshot wound to the head, coupled with the grisly detritus leaking over the lino floor showed Fletch the futility of doing so. He examined the body, trying to find a form of ID, noting that the body was in a suit, loose fitting around the waist with the shoulder holster clear to see now that the suit had fallen open. Instead of buttons, the jacket was held together with Velcro, Fletch recognising the importance of speed in pulling the jacket open quickly to access the weapon beneath. He found the guy's wallet, quickly pulling it out and recognising the warrant card.

"Thought so, this guy's one of the Royal Protection Officers," he whispered, Gemma steeping closer to look. She looked at the suit, her eyes quickly drawn to the pistol. Seeing her looking, Fletch reached in, quickly unholstering the Sig Sauer P226 and handing it to her.

"You're an armed response officer, am I right?"

"How did you guess?" she asked, incredulously.

He smirked as he replied, "Typical ARU officer, you come across a body, and the first thing you think of, is to go for the weapon."

Gemma reached for the pistol, grateful to at least be able to defend herself. He watched her carefully as she took control of the weapon, expertly removing the magazine and checking the chamber, pulling the top slide back slightly to see the glint of brass signifying the pistol was loaded. Carefully she replaced the magazine, checking it was secure before placing the pistol in her waist band. Fletch handed her the two spare extended magazines, instead of each magazine holding 12 rounds, the extended ones, carried 28 apiece, giving Gemma a total of 69 rounds. She put the magazines in her pocket, certain she would never need the extra ammo, but gratefully accepting it none the less.

Fletch carefully placed the body back as it was, looking up to the control room door, noting it was ajar. He tapped Jonesy on the shoulder to lead on, as with his own weapon raised, both of them went forwards, leaving Gemma and the others behind to cover the double doors. There was only one way in and one way out of the control room, so if anyone was in there, they'd have to get through them to get away. Seeing the callous way the protection officer had been shot, clearly close range and execution style, left them in no doubt as to their rules of engagement now. Jonesy approached the door, stepping one side of the doorway, Fletch the other, as they listened inside for any noise of an intruder within. After a few seconds of silence both operators nodded, Fletch indicting he was going left, as they breached the doorway, any attempt at stealth gone as the door slammed open, hitting Fletch as he stormed in, his weapon sweeping the room. Within seconds it was over, both of them were standing, weapons poised, fingers on triggers, scanning the empty room. On the far end sat banks of monitors, instead of showing the various rooms and areas of the palace though, all were black, and offline. At the other end of the room on racks were the hard drives, all were smashed up and shot through, looking as if someone had gone at them with an axe. He looked over at the control desk, the half-eaten sandwich and cup of tea testament that whatever had happened in here had happened fast. The only sign of the operator was the blood stain on the faded blue carpet, Fletch reached down with a gloved hand, touching the stain, seeing the blood was still wet and fresh. Whatever had happened in here had happened recently. He wiped his hand on his coveralls, looking over to Jonesy.

"Reckon you can get this working?"

Jonesy smiled, ever the tech man he stepped forwards, slinging his weapon behind him as he remarked,

"You kidding me? Half this stuff is older than I am."

Quickly Jonesy was tapping away on one of the keyboards as his eyes scanned the computer displays. Within a few moments he looked back up, shaking his head.

"Sorry Fletch, whole system's been wiped and destroyed. Whoever did this didn't want us to see what they were up to."

"Okay," he replied, looking back towards the corridor, "looks like we're done here, let's move."

Both of them made their way back out to the three waiting in the corridor, Fletch leaning in close in to whisper.

"We're not alone looks like we've got players in the palace and they're not afraid to get their hands bloody. Be on your toes."

All three nodded as Fletch took point, his weapon raised as both he and Jonesy walked cautiously forwards, a combination of poise, grace and speed, the thousands of hours spent on the ranges and previous operations now paying off. They walked through the palace's maze of corridors, back to the plushness of the carpeted corridors, turning left and walking through huge gold leaf-coloured doors, into a vast banqueting hall, with a ceiling decorated with figures and scenes from the past and huge works of art depicting the best of British history. No doubt this was where the grand banquets for visiting state dignitaries took place. The enormous, long rows of tables were empty of any tableware, no doubt stored under lock and key, whilst the tables were all coated with a fine layer of dust, the palace staff were probably stood down with the King under house arrest. Covering the far doors, Fletch and Jonesy waited as the other two paced forwards, weapons up and ready as they cleared the room, advancing forwards, ready for anything that might be lurking in wait.

With the control room unmanned and the cameras destroyed, at least Fletch was confident whoever was in the palace wouldn't have eyes on them, or they'd have sent a welcoming committee by now. The team cleared through the palace, coming to a grand staircase, lit from above by the huge ornate skylight. Above them was a galleried landing, below was another corridor which led to the throne room, whilst on the walls of the staircase hung pictures and paintings of the members of the Royal Family. Fletch ignored the finery, looking down at the main entrance hall of the palace one floor below them, checking they were alone. Two of the team kept weapons pointed below them whilst Jonesy and Gemma pointed their weapons upwards, as Fletch quickly checked the palace layout on the dragon, committing to memory the layout of where the King's private chambers were located.

He pointed silently upwards as the team moved up to the third floor. Quickly checking their arcs, they advanced up the stairs as one, their weapons moving as if extensions of their body. Wherever their heads looked, their weapons followed. They came to the landing, pushing through into the palace interior, Jonesy pausing at the five corridors now leading off from the central landing, Fletch indicating to him which corridor to take. Again, they were back to the maze of rooms and corridors, all dark and dimly lit, no doubt parts of the palace the public wouldn't normally see. Fletch was surprised to see some of the rooms showed signs of damp and damage, he'd always imagined the palace to be immaculate and well presented, but the truth was, behind the scenes, it was the same as any old grand building in the UK, no doubt requiring constant maintenance and costing a fortune to run and look after.

The team entered another corridor, plush and brightly lit from the light spilling in from the oversized Georgian windows, each window having large luxurious red curtains and a marble table with flowers in a vase. Fletch noticing they were back to the public pantomime again. On the opposite side to the windows the corridor was lined with five doors, each door was white, with gold gilded handles and decorative features on them, whilst a set of double doors dominated the end of the corridor, equally beautiful. Fletch knew from the mapping they were now in the Royal Family's private quarters, the five smaller doors led to the guest bedrooms, whilst the double doors led to the King and Queen's private quarters. The large windows were mirrored, affording a view of the outside whilst maintaining the privacy of guests within. Fletch could see out to the main gates, seeing the two police officers they'd chatted to earlier still standing there, but this time, on the other side of the gate, sat a growing crowd numbering in the hundreds, but behind them on the mall they could see the thousands gathering and coming closer. Time was of the essence. With the greatest of care Jonesy walked down the corridor up to the first door, keeping himself distanced from the window, lightly and slowly checking the handle with one hand whilst keeping his rifle pointing at the far set of doors. After a few seconds of trying, he looked back, shaking his head. The door was locked.

Fletch cursed, the thought of walking down a corridor past locked doors un-nerved him, the chances of being ambushed were high if he had no idea what was in the room. If he started to clear the corridor room by room, smashing down locked doors and throwing in flash bangs, he'd be making noise, lots of it. So, if anyone was in the palace, they'd hear him and come looking. Deciding on silence and surprise being the better of the two evils, he shook his head, indicating for Jonesy to keep going to the next door. After a fraught five minutes the team had made their way down the corridor, stacked up against the final set of double doors, one lined up behind the other, ready to breach. As if reading his thoughts Jonesy pulled a Flashbang grenade from his assault vest and showed it to him, Fletch shaking his head and indicating with a finger to his lips he still wanted stealth on their side. Nodding in understanding, Jonesy put the stun grenade back on his vest, as Fletch looked behind him, pointing to the team the directions he wanted them to go when they went through the door. After a few seconds they were set, only Gemma looked unsettled, her years as an ARU officer keeping her steady, but she'd never imagined she'd be about to storm into the King's private chambers with a Special Forces team. She watched on, trying her best not to disrupt the choreographed routine of the team as they went in, not guns blazing like the movies, but slow and steady, their movements designed to draw minimum attention. The double doors were unlocked and opened easily and silently as Fletch and Jonesy went left, Gemma and the other two moved right, each person covering the other, weapons scanning the room ready for the unknown.

The huge room was empty, eerily so, the large four poster bed was unmade, and in the far corner of the huge room sat piles of clothes and suitcases, all up ended as if the King had left in a hurry. Pictures and personal items were thrown over the ornate furniture, whilst the huge red drapes were closed, the thin sliver of light pouring through, creating the dimly lit scene as the bedside lamps were still on. Whatever had happened here, happened during the night-time hours, with the evidence pointing to a hurried quick attempt at escape. None of it made any sense, if the King had been under house arrest, why did the scene show someone trying to flee in a hurry? Careful not to trip over the debris on the floor, Fletch stepped over to the far door, leading to the Queen's chambers, again the same result, the items and clothing knocked over and thrown haphazardly on the floor.

"I guess they must have left already?" Gemma remarked, already convinced by the scene.

Saying nothing, the team began to work around her, Jonesy and Bug turning to cover the corridor outside, as Grub and Fletch walked up to the far wall, on it hung a huge painting of Cerberus, the three headed black dog, who in Greek mythology was the guardian of Hades, the underworld. Gemma grimaced in horror at the picture, failing to understand what on earth something so hideous could be doing sat amongst all the beauty of the room.

She watched on as Fletch and Grub searched the gold frame carefully, suddenly Grub reported back triumphantly.

"Here it is, got it."

With an audible click he pressed the hidden button and both operators stepped back as the wall began to lower into the floor of the room, revealing another door, this one cold and made of steel, like a safe door, but larger. Sat near to the door was a keypad, illuminated in a light red light, waiting for the codes to be typed in.

Gemma opened her eyes wide in admiration, she had to admit she had no idea the hidden door was even there.

Grub took off his backpack, quickly removing a small handheld portable computer with a stethoscope looking device. Within a minute he had it attached to the door, watching the screen, looking up and nodding at Fletch.

"I've got two people sat in chairs, and one body on the floor, looks like there's no one else inside."

The hidden safe room had been a late addition to the palace, being fitted in 2021 after one-too-many attempts by members of the public to gain access to the late Queen's chambers. Aside from the King, only two individuals knew of its existence, the head of the Royal family's protection detail being one, and the Chief of the Defence Staff being the other. The door was opened by an 8-digit code, which when keyed in spelt the word C.E.R.B.E.R.U.S. The King was terrible at remembering the code, so to help him remember the CDS had brought him the hideous painting, which was hung in plain sight. Hence the operation name of Cerberus, to match the painting, a reminder in case Fletch forgot the code. The safe room had been designed with its own oxygen and power supply and supplies inside for 24 hours, which meant that in an emergency, the King and Queen could ride out whatever was going on outside until backup arrived. Fletch was guessing after what had happened in the control room that they'd fled inside for safety.

Fletch stepped backwards, keying his radio, and rapidly speaking, the response coming over the earpiece muted. Seeing her looking on he pointed over to the window.

"Gemma, I need you to step back over there, turn away from the door and no peeking."

"Spoil sport!" she replied playfully, turning to do as she was told. Waiting till she had her back turned, Fletch then walked up to the keypad, covering it from view and keying in the code.

With an audible hiss, the door cracked open, the smell of fresh purified air escaping out as Grub stepped back as the 5-inch-thick heavy door opened on its motor, coming to a rest against its stop. Fletch stepped inside, his pistol drawn, even though Grub had checked on the thermal camera, it always paid to be cautious.

The room was brightly lit by the overhead lights, the light resembling sunlight rather than artificial lights, no doubt the designer wanting to make the people hiding inside to feel more relaxed. In the centre of the room Fletch saw them both tied to the chairs, gags over their mouths, hair dishevelled, and eyes opened wide in surprise at his sudden appearance. Quickly he walked over to them, stepping over the body on the floor and removing both of their gags as gently as he could. The King looked at him defiantly, shaking his head as the gag was removed, blurting out.

"What do you want now you bastards? What do you want?"

The Queen said nothing, her own face projecting a look of anger as she looked him up and down, her eyes darting over to the figure on the floor than back at him.

Without wanting to waste any time he knelt, bringing his face close to them both so they could both see him.

"Your Majesties, I'm part of the team sent to rescue you. You remember the training you both took part in back at Hereford? Remember the phrase clockwork orange and white castle?"

He could see their looks of defiance turn to dis-belief at the mention of the code words. Designed for just such an emergency, all high-ranking officials of government and members of the Senior Royal Family would undergo training, led by members of the special forces, when they'd practise and simulate such a rescue using live ammunition, finishing with a code word that was unique to that person. That way, when the real cavalry arrived, the mention of the codeword would tell the hostage this was the real deal, and not some sham attempt by the hostage takers to simulate a rescue, hoping to gain more information from their captives. The King's code word had been 'clockwork orange,' and the Queen's 'white castle'.

Now at least they knew this rescue was for real. Grub stepped into the room, walking up to Fletch as he removed his backpack, rummaging inside and pulling another small camera out, similar to the first, instead of a stethoscope this one had a face cover, a retina scanner designed to be fitted over a person's forehead. Saying nothing he knelt, leaning forwards and stating.

"Sir, if you don't mind, can we just confirm both your identities."

The King looked up, the flash of defiance in his eyes again, Fletch thought at first he'd refuse, but then he looked about the room, realising he was still tied to the chair and at the mercy of Fletch. Besides, this was all part of the procedure, after all, the last thing Fletch needed was to get them whisked out of there, only to find they'd been duped by an impersonator placed to do just that. It had happened before. The King leaned forwards, his forehead resting against the brow pad as the bright white light of the retina scan illuminated his face, after a few seconds the camera had finished, flashing the results for Fletch to see. This was their man, 100 percent, the King. They repeated the procedure with the Queen, the results the same, as finally with their identities confirmed they untied them both, Fletch quickly reporting over the radio,

"Zero, Romeo Four, Clockwork Orange and White Castle now secure, Ident confirmed. Prep for evacuation figures 5, from Red Two, over."

"Roger Romeo Four, good work. Evac inbound in figures 5, from Red Two. Out."

The King stood up, rubbing his wrists gratefully at the relief of being free of his bonds, as the Queen dashed over to the figure on the floor, kneeling and tenderly checking the body.

"Oh Paul...Such a waste!" she said sympathetically, recoiling at the sight of the man's brains leaking out of the exit wound. She stood back up, wiping her hands unconsciously on her nightie, suddenly aware of their appearance. The King was still wearing pyjamas, whilst the Queen was in a pale blue dressing gown, both were barefoot, their feet bloodied and bruised from their ordeal.

Seeing their discomfort, Fletch quickly headed back into the bedroom, grabbing a handful of clothes and shoes and throwing them into the large bathroom, ushering them in, stating,

"Your Majesties, we don't have much time, may I suggest you get dressed in whatever you can and quickly. We need to be moving in two minutes."

As they moved off, Grub reached into his backpack, pulling out two large sets of body armour and handing one to each of them. Both nodded in thanks as they closed the bathroom door, the atmosphere slightly awkward now they were in their presence. Once the door was closed Gemma urged from behind the curtain.

"Fletch, you best come look at this."

He walked up to see, careful not to move the curtain too much, peering out to where the officer was pointing. The room was overlooking the south gate. At first, he wondered what had caught her attention, then as she spoke it became obvious.

"Didn't the two guarding the north gate say they'd locked all the gates?"

He looked again, seeing the gap between the gates, the chain and padlock now in a pile on the floor. So that's how the surprise guests had come in. It still didn't explain how the control room was taken out though. He looked up as the King and Queen came out the door, surprising him at their speed in getting dressed. Didn't royalty need a plethora of courtiers to help them dress, he thought, his eyes appraising the way they both now stood, a little of their dignity now restored. Grub walked forwards, apologising as he checked their body armour was fitting properly, expertly running a hand over the Velcro straps and once satisfied he stepped back, looking over at Fletch.

"Good to go."

Fletch walked up to the King, smiling respectfully and bowing his head as he began.

"Sir, Ma'am, I appreciate you've been through a lot already, but it's important that you both understand, we're not out of the woods yet."

They both said nothing, their gaze unwavering as he pointed to Grub.

"Corporal Dillon is going to be right beside you both. I want you to do exactly as he says. If he says duck, or run, you don't question him, just do it. Understand?"

"Understood." the King replied, from his tone Fletch could see he wasn't happy in the way Fletch was speaking to him. No doubt this would be a reality check for both of them. As if to emphasise his curt tone, Fletch added,

"My apologies Sir, you'll have to excuse my tone, it's not exactly everyday me and my team are called to rescue royalty."

The King was about to speak when the Queen stepped forwards, smiling warmly.

"Sergeant, no apology is necessary, we're just extremely delighted to see you."

Fletch nodded and turned to go when the King shot back,

"Sergeant, where's the rest of your team?"

He turned to see the King looking about the room, his eyes taking in the sight of Gemma clutching the pistol and smiling back at him respectfully.

"My team?" Fletch asked confused, his arm sweeping the room around them as he answered.

"This is it Sir, this is my team."

"But I count only five of you?" the King continued, his eyebrows creasing in surprise, "where's the others?"

Now Fletch had the look of confusion as he stepped forwards asking.

"What others? Sir, it's just us five, there is no-one else."

"But what about the other soldiers? The King shot back irritated at Fletch's lack of an answer. Seeing the confusion on his rescuer's face he added,

"An hour ago, we had twenty heavily armed soldiers burst into our chambers. They made us put on those ridiculous night clothes, before stomping around the room like a bunch of bloody tempest's setting the scene you see before you. Then they forced Paul, my head of security to open the safe room and put us all in there, how else do you think we were both tied up? Before they left, they executed Paul in front of us to show they meant business, promising they'd be back to finish the job. I'd presumed that you've already taken care of them, hence you're here, however seeing now as you have only five in your team, and the look on your face right now, I'm guessing that you haven't?"

Fletch's eyes narrowed at the new piece of information, why the hell would soldiers have done this? Wanting more information he asked,

"Sir, you said soldiers, what kind of uniform were they wearing?"

The King pursed his lips in thought, thinking back, trying to remember the details.

"They looked like our troops, had the same type of camouflage pattern and badges of rank. I thought at first they were here to rescue us, it was only when they spoke in Russian that I knew they were working for the other team."

Shit, Fletch thought, as the realisation that twenty heavily armed Russian soldiers were suddenly roaming the palace. It must be an ambush, perhaps they were waiting for his team to try to get to the helicopter. He looked over at Gemma, searching for any sign of any malice or ill intent, did she know? Was she the one tasked with leading them to the ambush? Perhaps her dad being arrested had been the reason she was helping the enemy?

He stared at her, watching her demeanour, realising that if she were leading them to an ambush, then she'd be at just as much risk as they were. No, that didn't add up, if they had wanted to ambush his team and she were somehow a part of it, then why not do it back at the dock? Why bring his team to the palace? His thoughts of being setup were disturbed as Bug called out from the corridor.

"Fletch, you better come see this!"

He walked out to the corridor, looking to what had caught Jonesy's attention, looking out through the one-way glass. In the distance they could see the north gate, the gate they'd come in through. The two high vis jackets of the policeman guarding it now looking like dots against the multitude of coloured clothing of the tens of thousands of protesters who were now pushing against the gates. He could see the policemen trying to wave away the protesters, their arms waving high desperately. Suddenly the gates snapped open, the policeman being swallowed up as the crowd began to swarm into the palace grounds, like a tidal wave the mass and momentum of the protesters was hard to stop. Fletch realised they'd be in the palace in a matter of minutes, the footage of the Washington capitol riots of 2021 still playing in his head. He turned, about to order the team to get the hell out of there when suddenly gunfire erupted close by...

12

Enemy At The Gates

North Gate, Buckingham Palace

Major Laratov looked behind him at the masses, the noise almost unbearable as tens of thousands of people chanted and screamed behind him as they pushed against the gates. He smiled at the sight of the two police officers behind the gates, although armed, they both saw the futility of the weapons they carried against so many. He could see they'd put a chain and a padlock on the gate, he nodded over to one of his men who walked forwards, a pair of bolt croppers making light work of the chain. One of the police officers shouted a warning and began to run forwards to stop him, stopping and staring in horror as the gates swung open, Laratov's men were the first through, chanting and urging the masses to follow. Like sheep, the protesters responded, taking courage from Laratov and his men and storming forwards, buoyed by their numbers. Finally, they could get to the King, to make him answer their questions instead of hiding away safely in the palace. The crowd jostled with the police officers whose cries were overwhelmed, their jackets lost to sight amongst the fighting figures. Laratov watched on as his men approached the officers in the melee, quickly and lethally shooting them both in the head with the silenced pistols, relieving them of their weapons, before melting away in the crowds, leaving the bodies where they fell to be trampled on as people ran past, blissfully unaware of what had just happened. Everyone was on a high, the pack mentality making everyone forget all about the law of the lands. It was mob rule, and right now nothing was going to stop them.

Laratov cupped his hand over his ear, wincing against the growing noise of the crowd as the palace team announced they were set and in position over his radio. He looked around him, barking out orders to his team who turned and remained by the gates, each pulling out and donning a high vis cap and vest from their backpacks. Against the backdrop of the thousands his team stuck out like sore thumbs, there could be no mistaken identity now. Underneath their civilian clothes they all wore Kevlar assault vests, just in case one of their palace teams shots were not as accurate as they hoped they were. Each of his team pulled out a camera, ready to record what happened next, already knowing which windows of the palace to film. He looked around, satisfied that everything was set, watching the leading elements of the crowd now running across the grounds, with more surging behind. Finally, he judged the numbers to be just right.

Keying his covert radio, he was forced to shout out over the noise.

"PALACE TEAM..EXECUTE!"

He watched the flashes of gunfire erupting from the palace's upper floors, already his team inside having removed the reflective film off the glass, allowing those outside to see vividly what was going on inside the rooms. He knew his team inside the palace had worked hard to get the glass windows cut, using diamond cutters to cut firing ports into the thick double glazed glass.

At first the crowd ignored the gunfire, still running forwards, whooping, hollering and shouting as they drew closer, the momentum powering them forwards. Suddenly they saw people begin to drop ahead of them unexpectedly, some of those running nearby tripped, falling over bodies, tumbling themselves amongst the mass of people. Then, people began to drop near them, blood spattering those still standing, mute in shock at what was happening, disbelieving at what they were witnessing. Then, people began to realise, the shouts of jubilation turning to screams of fear as the bullets began to tear into them, clothing and flesh being torn away in jagged chunks as the unknown gunmen poured fire into the masses. The crowd stopped, caught in the open ground between the palace and the gate with no-where to hide or seek cover, some fell to the ground out of fear, others turned to run, colliding with those still coming forwards, falling to the ground in an ever-growing mass that threatened to cause a stampede. Ignoring the growing carnage around them, Laratov and his men began filming the windows, each camera picking out the details of what appeared to be the British Soldiers firing into the crowds, before zooming back out to the carnage.

Behind them, members of the crowd seeing what was going on up ahead, tried desperately to stop the rush, some of them linked arms, leaning backwards, using their weight to help slow the advance as the flood through the gate turned to a trickle. Suddenly the crowd had stopped, those still inside the grounds running for their lives, some zigzagging back to the gate, trying to get to safety. Some tried to climb the huge black railings, some made it halfway up before the bullets tore into them throwing them to the ground, others were able to make it over the gate before being hit, their bodies getting caught on the gold topped spikes atop the fence. Like macabre trophies they hung there, testament to the carnage and a grim reality of what was happening.

Laratov looked about him, satisfied enough damage had been done to anger the crowd, shouting over the radio.

"Ceasefire! Begin evacuation!"

As quickly as it had started, the firing stopped, the sound of moans and screams echoing across the palace grounds. He knew that inside, his twenty-man team would begin to strip off their uniforms, burning them in the rooms and donning civilian clothing, blending in with the mob when it arrived. Ahead of them he counted at least 300 dead and wounded protesters, some were standing in shock, tears running down their cheeks, others were sobbing and kneeling amongst the wounded, trying to pull or tug on a friend's arm or head, urging them up. He looked behind, the shock and horror of what had happened being echoed across the crowd. At the back of the vast procession over a mile away, people could still be heard chanting and calling, the news of what had happened yet to filter through the mass ranks. Quickly Laratov shouted over to his men, the baseball caps and cameras disappearing amongst their backpacks as they now each drew petrol bombs, ignoring the dead and dying, instead running forwards, turning to the others who were still hesitant on the other side of the gate. Laratov pulled the megaphone off the body of the protester with the blue hair, his foot standing on her fingers, hearing them break, as he prised it free. Turning to the crowd he shouted out, his voice booming over.

"LOOK AT WHAT THOSE MURDERERS HAVE DONE! LOOK!"

Seeing the firing had stopped, and how far into the grounds his men were, some of the crowd ran forward to begin first aid, piling through the bodies, checking on those still breathing. Laratov watched them, urging more forwards, as more people ran forwards to help. Before long the grounds were covered in people again, some milling about in shock, others confused as to why this had happened. As the news filtered through, more of the crowds stormed forwards, some wanting to see, others in anger, wanting justice. It was the ones that were angry that Laratov targeted, selecting groups of people and urging them forwards, shouting again over their heads, his own men showing them the camera footage as evidence.

"I SAW IT WITH MY OWN EYES! THIS WAS DONE BY OUR OWN TROOPS! AGAIN, DEFENDING THE KING AND HIS COUP!"

Laratov could see the anger begin to grow in the crowd, more angry faces turned to look at him as they took in the horror around them. Some of the crowd tried to urge caution, some held up their hands trying to remonstrate the others, but the more they tried, the more the hate and anger grew. First, they were in groups of ones and twos, then fives and tens, suddenly they were numbering in their hundreds, all angry and red faced, taking up the chant, their blood lust up and murderous. It was mob rule, vigilante justice, and the blood soaking into the ground at their feet told the crowd how the game was now to be played.

Laratov began chanting, getting the crowd worked up, counting a hardcore group of nearly 500 were with him.

"BULLETS WILL NOT STOP OUR FREEDOM! THIS ENDS TODAY! DOWN WITH THE MURDEROUS KING!"

He knew others would follow once they began to move, and deciding he had enough followers and the mood was right he began running towards the palace again, chanting and yelling, his men following, encouraging the mob as they shouted angrily, storming forwards.

Suddenly they were at one of the security doors, normally they were locked, but he knew it was open, his men inside having already opened the doors. He knew the rough location of the King's chambers, the safe room would soon be open by his team and the King and Queen would have nowhere to hide from the mob already baying for their blood. It would look like they were caught attempting to flee. Everything had been planned. All being well, in about ten minutes, England would have the spark it needed to light the revolution that would lead to civil war. His men would see to that, and if the crowd were too meek for the task, well that's why his men were seeded amongst them.

King's Chambers

Fletch ran down the corridor, leading the team through the maze of rooms, trying desperately to remember the way out. Already they'd had their exit compromised, the Helicopter Landing Sight known as Red two was now covered in bodies, and already they could hear the sounds of breaking glass from downstairs as the mob began to rampage through the palace's lower levels. He had no idea where the firing had come from but had looked on in shock at seeing people dropping like nine-pins, as perhaps now almost 400 of them lay dead outside. He had no doubt it was to do with the phoney soldiers but had no idea why they'd do such a thing. For now, he had to concentrate on his mission and try to lead them away from the thousands of angry people pouring through the north gate. They were trying to get themselves up onto the roof, at least there they could get themselves in position for a helicopter rescue. He walked through the stairwell, knowing only one flight of stairs separated them from the roof, and was about to race upstairs when something caught his eye on the stairs above. He looked upwards, his rifle pointing at the same time as the man above saw him, yelling in surprise as Fletch fired, the yell turning to a gurgle as the report of the rifle echoed in the stairwell. The man dropped his assault rifle and fell forwards, the rifle clattering down the stairs resting at Fletch's feet. He heard more shouts from above, the rooftop door crashing open and footsteps echoing off the marble floor.

"Back!" he yelled, quickly pushing back into Jonesy as the dark black shape of a grenade sailed through the air towards them.

They both fell back through the doorway, the grenade exploding on the floor below as it bounced off the closed door, as bullets thudded into the stairwell, the paint and plaster dust exploding around them. Quickly they were up, the team turning around and running the way they had just come, conscious of the shouts and yells coming closer. The roof was now out of action, Fletch realising he couldn't risk trying to fight through to get to it, especially with a mob numbering thousands at his back. He thought back to the unlocked southern gate, realising that was now their only way out. If they could get to the police van, perhaps they could get out the gate, find somewhere to land the chopper and get the hell out.

He heard the gunfire behind him as Bug and Jonesy began to engage people trying to come through the door, reporting over the radio,

"Contact rear, two tango's down."

Good, that only left seventeen of them, Fletch thought optimistically, bursting through the doorway that led to another landing. He checked the mapping, seeing there was another way through the palace, committing the route to memory, not wanting to be distracted from the fight. After a few moments he moved off, the others following in tight formation as he walked through a series of offices. Behind him Gemma and Bug were walking with the two royals between them, Bug keeping an ever-watchful eye on them both as they walked hand in hand, remarkably quiet and composed. Bug remembering the first time he'd been in contact, wishing he'd looked as calm.

Fletch came to another landing, below them they could hear more of the mob, shouting out.

"FIND THEM!"

"MURDERING CUNTS! THEY'RE HERE SOMEWHERE!"

"SET THE FUCKING PLACE ALIGHT! BURN THE BASTARDS"

Hearing those words caused him to wince, already he could smell smoke, somewhere nearby someone was already enthusiastically carrying out the task. He knew the building was fitted with a fire system, but after seeing the state of some of the rooms, wondered if it even worked. Deciding he didn't want to stick around to find out, he kept the team moving through another corridor, leading them to an older part of the palace. Here the rooms became darker and smaller, until they came to a dead end. He looked at the dragon, zooming in on the mapping, cursing the wall that wasn't showed.

Fuck, he thought, where the hell do we go now? Behind him the shouts only seemed to be getting louder...

King's Chambers

Major Laratov stood in the middle of the room, watching the mob tearing open cupboards and doors, ejecting the contents and carelessly throwing them out of the broken windows. He looked on in growing anger at his men, ignoring the ongoing chaos around him as he found the door to the safe room was already opened. Instead of finding the royal family inside waiting to be captured by the mob, only two empty chairs were there, the ropes used to bind them tossed on the floor.

"Where the hell are they?" he cursed, the men looking down as he raged.

"The whole idea of this was for the mob to find them, not let them escape!"

He was distracted from his thoughts as five of the mob pushed disrespectfully past him, rushing into the safe room, whooping and hollering at what they had found, ignoring the body in their haste to begin looting. With a look of anger, he nodded over to one of his men, who keyed in the code, watching with grim satisfaction as the door began to close on them. They were so lost in their plunder that they didn't see till too late the door closing on them, their shouts cut off as the airtight door closed, sealing them in the room.

Laratov turned and stormed out, his men following behind, pushing through the packed corridors as more and more people entered the palace. His expression was grim, he knew he had to find them, it all hinged on what happened that day. His earpiece crackled as his roof team reported in.

"Command, Roof team, we've had someone try to access the roof, looks like there's a special forces team. They've got the King and Queen with them! We're pursuing them back through the palace."

Goddammit, he thought angrily, quickly hitting the radio pressel.

"Roof team, Command, do *not* pursue them, leave them to the mob, do not go back into the palace!"

The last thing he needed was the mob attacking his men, even with their weapons, with the mood of those around him, they could easily be overwhelmed by the hornet nest that they'd help create. Whether he liked it or not, they were stuck with the ruse. If there was a team in the palace, then let the mob deal with them.

He keyed the covert radio again, having to speak louder over the shouts of the mob.

"All units, we have a special forces team on site trying to rescue the King and Queen. Outside units I want you to begin shepherding our flock to the other gates, inside units lets flush the palace, find them and contain them. We'll let the sheep destroy the wolves. Out."

He grinned in satisfaction, this was even better, if they could have the mob capture the team and tear them apart, then it would all play into the narrative they were trying to encourage...

Palace Corridor.

Fletch looked behind him as the King approached, leaning in close, looking on amusedly at the digital map before whispering,

"If you're relying on that bloody computer to get us out of here Sergeant, then may I kindly remind you that I grew up in this god-awful draughty place, and that perhaps I might know one or two little secret areas that your little gadget may not?"

Fletch looked at him, seeing the trace of a smile appear on the King.

Was he enjoying this, Fletch thought, as the King pointed off to where he indicated they should go next.

"Okay Sir, we'll go with your directions, but you're to stay back, myself and Jonesy will take the lead."

"Of course, after all, there's no sense in getting in the way of the cannon fodder." The King smiled, at first Fletch though he was serious, but something about the way he said it made him smile himself. He'd heard about the King's sense of humour before, but had put it down to media hype, trying to portray a more human and loving side of a dynasty that was seen by many as aloof and lofty. But now, finally, he was seeing it himself, even now with everything going on around them, the King was trying to crack a joke. Perhaps he wasn't all that bad, Fletch thought.

Fletch and Jonesy went forwards, the King indicating where to go, leading them through the warren of dark musty old rooms. They climbed down a set of dust covered stairs, thankful not to see any other footprints in the dust. After a few minutes they came to what looked like an old musty storeroom. Inside were relics and old antiques, covered in dusty white cloths, light streaming through the boarded-up window, dust hanging in the air, causing more than one of them to sneeze. Fletch looked at the King expectantly, who stood in the middle of the room with his arms folded, one hand resting on his chin in thought. Above them they heard the mob's footsteps as they ran riot on the floor above. The crashes and dull thuds echoing down to them as heavy objects were thrown about. Bug raised his rifle, half expecting to see people bursting through the ceiling at any second. After a few moments the King looked over to his wife smiling, ignoring the dust and plaster that fell about them.

"Remember when I used to sneak out to see you, and you always asked how I did it?"

She looked on, eyebrows raised waiting for the answer as he knelt down and pulled at a hidden switch in the base of a wardrobe, with a click a dusty coloured door cracked ajar, the light spilling in from the outside.

"Always secrets." he muttered, wiping his hands and standing back up, walking over and putting his arms around the Queen protectively as she shivered, muttering to her.

"Not much longer darling, we'll get through this, I promise."

Fletch walked past them over to the door, peering through the crack. It looked like the door led into a narrow alley, and checking no-one was waiting outside, he walked through with Jonesy, urging the others to wait behind as they checked it out. They went forwards a few metres, hearing yells and screams from the other side of the palace building, already echoing off the walls. They came to a wall, Fletch laying on the floor to peer around it, seeing the courtyard they had driven into earlier. The Police van sat 100 metres away, still parked where they had left it. He tapped to Jonesy, indicating to keep eyes on it as he ran back to the group.

Everyone listened as he outlined what they were doing next.

"Right door leads to the courtyard, plan is now to get the police van and drive out of the south gate, Bug, you're driving, me and you will go get the van and come back to pick up the others. Grub, Gemma, you both stay on the King and Queen, anything happens, just get them into that van. I'll have Jonesy cover our rear. Questions?"

Grub looked up smiling, "Fletch, thanks for the offer but I've already ordered us a taxi, I'm happy to share with the Royals, but the rest of you riff raff can find your own way out of here."

The King and Queen looked on silently, the joke lost on them as Fletch merely grinned, replying.

"Smartarse. Right, let's get ready."

The King looked at his wife, holding her close as Fletch got everyone lined up by the door, peering outside again to check Jonesy was giving the all clear. Satisfied, he whispered,

"Let's move!"

Crouching low, the team moved forwards, quickly covering the distance to the wall, Fletch tapping Jonesy on the shoulder as he passed him, indicating he concentrate on watching their rear. The operator nodded in response as he shifted positions, now watching back the way they had come, as Grub took over his fire position. Bug and Fletch continued forwards, weapons scanning the windows and doorways, checking and double checking they were not under any threat. Suddenly, they heard shouts from above, looking up they saw three angry faces leaning out of the second floor balcony, pointing down and shouting.

"OI! THERE THEY ARE! DOWN THERE!"

Fletch was about to pull the trigger, suddenly realising that they were unarmed, choosing instead to ignore them as Bug jumped into the van, quickly starting the engine. Already shouts echoed behind them, as the mob began to realise their location. Fletch turned and opened the passenger door, about to get in when he heard movement behind him, turning just in time as four figures came bolting out of the double doors, two had armed themselves with planks of wood, ripped from a piece of furniture inside, whilst the other two were carrying large brass stanchions, used to filter crowds through waiting areas. He yelled a challenge, his rifle held menacingly at them, stopping them in their tracks, as they stood there, breathing heavily and staring back, the hatred and anger clear to see in their faces as they brandished their makeshift weapons menacingly in front of them. He was under no doubt they wanted to hurt him, perhaps kill him, but he couldn't just shoot them, despite what they wanted to do, that would be murder. As if in a standoff, he waited, shouting for Bug to go pick up the others, the van driving away and leaving him in a cloud of diesel smoke, the tyres scrabbling on the gravel. He could hear the chaos above him as more windows were smashed, each one being taken up by at least five angry faces, all shouting and jeering, calling for blood. Suddenly it was raining furniture as those above realised how vulnerable they were in the courtyard, hurling anything they could out the windows. Fletch stepped backwards, trying to get out of harm's way, looking over as his team were forced to move, as everything that could be lifted from within was hurled down on them, the King narrowly avoiding being crushed by an 18th century desk. Suddenly the van was alongside them, the furniture crashing around it as the side door slid open and the team jumped inside in a heap, any attempt at grace forgotten in their attempt to get away. Fletch became distracted watching his team, stumbling backwards on the pieces of a broken chair that had landed behind him, the rifle firing two shots into the air as he fell with his finger on the trigger. Cursing he rolled over, trying to get back up, already the four men were on him, seizing their chance to grab him, one hitting him viciously on the back with the stanchion. Fletch roared in pain and anger, thankfully his body armour had taken most of the force as he felt fists hitting his head, with the helmet taking most of the blows. He managed to get to his feet, struggling against the combined assault from four of them, knowing more would be close behind. He could feel their hands wrestling with his rifle, the sling making it impossible for them to take the weapon off him as they fought him. He watched as the rifle's magazine fell to the floor with a clatter as one of the men pressed the release catch, another jerked in shock as Fletch squeezed the trigger, seeing the barrel was close to one of the assailants' ears. The man yelled in pain and fell back, clutching his bloodied ear as more blows rained down, Fletch felt the blood flowing from his mouth as one punch connected on his chin, another hitting his nose, making him see stars. Knowing his rifle was empty he let it fall, unclipping the sling, letting it fall to floor, hoping it would distract the men long enough to give him space to move. Seeing the weapon lying there, the other three assailants stopped their attack on him, concentrating instead on getting their hands on the rifle. He stepped back, his hands finding his pistol and pulling it cleanly, shouting in warning and firing two rounds into the ground. Two of them stopped, but the third had the rifle up, the fire burning in his eyes, as he aimed at Fletch.

"FUCKING DROP IT!" Fletch shouted, hearing as the van drew closer.

The man grinned fiercely and pulled the trigger, his eyes looking down uncomprehending as to why the rifle wouldn't fire. Fletch spat out the blood that dribbled down his chin, walking forwards and ramming his pistol into the man's neck, causing the others to back away as he spat out, eyes wide with anger.

"NEEDS BULLETS DICKHEAD!"

With a squeal of brakes, the van pulled up behind him, the sliding door already open and the weapons of Grub and Gemma pointing at them.

Knowing he was now covered, Fletch struck the man in the stomach, feeling a certain satisfaction as he heard the man exclaim and double over in a coughing fit, fighting for air as he collapsed. Keeping his pistol pointing at the other three he leaned over, picking up the rifle and re-slinging it to his body, then picking up the almost full magazine he reloaded and cocked the rifle just as the double doors crashed open, ejecting hundreds of screaming shouting people, all crying for vengeance for what had just happened. He forgot about trying to run for the passenger seat, knowing the mob would be on him, tearing him apart before he made it. instead, he fell backwards into the van's open side door, the strong arms of Grub pulling him in as the other members of his team pulled Flashbang grenades, tossing them in amongst the crowd. Designed to incapacitate and stun, the grenades went off, doing exactly that, instantly stopping some of the crowd, buying them the vital seconds they needed to get away. With the engine racing, the van sped away, the shouts and jeers echoing behind them as the crowd began to hurl objects at the van. Dull thuds sounded out, followed by the crack of glass as the van's rear windows exploded inwards, some of the protesters getting close enough to throw planks of wood at them. The van weaved across the gravel as Bug fought with the wheel to keep it steady as they careened towards the narrow archway, beyond which they could see the open empty square offering them safety. They looked up as the windows above the archway were smashed open and grinning savage faces appeared, quickly replaced by heavy wardrobes and tables, their plan clear to see, they were going to try to crush the van's roof and all inside with it.

"Fuck! Hang on!" Bug yelled, as Fletch jumped forwards between the seats, grabbing the thick black handle that hung by the windscreen, heaving with all his might. With a crash, the giant steel grate sat on the roof swung down on its rails and into position, now at least the windscreen was protected.

Everyone in the back hunkered down as Bug floored it, knowing staying in the courtyard would be the end of them as the heavy furniture began to rain down on them, crashing and exploding in a shower of wood and splinters. Fletch kept low, trusting Bug's driving as he looked upwards, hearing the bangs and crashes as the roof smashed downwards, the remaining windows in the rear exploding outwards in a shower of glass, as the roof smashed down lower. The steel grate on the windscreen buckled, but held, the glass cracking but not going through as Bug leaned over in the driver's seat, trying to find a piece of windscreen to see out of. It went dark as the van shot through the alleyway, exploding outwards into the sunlit parade square, the wind whistling through the shattered windows as pieces of furniture and debris dragged along under the wheels, being flung in all directions. Fletch looked behind him, seeing the smoke pouring out of the upper floors, as the palace began to burn, happy he hadn't relied on the fire suppression systems after all. Everyone looked left, seeing the aftermath of the attack on the protesters, a mass of people on the ground, some of them walking away, others being carried, as they took in the enormity of what had happened. The Queen gasped, covering her mouth with her hands at seeing so many dead in front of their home, her eyes being drawn to the site of five people laying across the top of the railings, their arms and legs splayed out as they hung there. She began to sob as the King consoled her, his own eyes burning in silent rage at what had happened. No-one could understand why it had happened, or who was responsible, but the thought of it involving him and the monarchy angered and saddened him.

The plan had been to head for the south gate but Fletch could already see the growing masses there blocking the way, as if the crowd had managed to read his thoughts. Bug looked behind him, shouting over the wind noise.

"Where to? Gate's blocked!"

As if on cue his radio burst to life, the shadow of the evac helicopter hovering overhead as the pilot reported in.

"Romeo Four, Wildeye, I've got you an escape route to the east, gate is locked but no-one is near it. Be warned, protesters are heading that way, best move your ass."

"Roger Wildeye, thank you!" Fletch shouted back over the radio, tapping Bug on the shoulder and indicating where he should drive to. The van leaned dangerously over, its balance upset by its crushed roof now hanging over at a 45 degree angle, as everyone hung on as it turned and headed to the east gate, Bug forced to swerve to avoid the growing numbers of people still chasing them. Bug slowed as the van left the large parade square and began driving down the sides of the palace, bouncing over the kerb and over the immaculate and well-tended gardens and pathways, crashing through hedges and shrubs, bouncing on its axles, the suspension crying out in protest as the wheels scrabbled for grip. Ahead of them a small brick wall had been built, Bug having no option but to crash through it, the bricks and dust covering the windscreen. He was tempted to use the wipers, but realised they'd fallen off a while back. Instead, he opted to lean out of the smashed side window, driving the van with the wind in his face, dangerous, but his only choice. Finally, they came around to the east gate, here the black metal railings were replaced with a large thick grey wall, at least 9 feet in height with a black metal padlocked gate preventing their exit. Bug stopped the van close to the gate as the others all jumped out quickly. Then he lined up the empty van and drove at the gate backwards, bracing himself against the padding of the seat, hoping the vans momentum and weight would be enough to smash through.

With a screech of steel, the van crashed through the gate, the small number of by-standers in the street drawn to the gunfire inside, running away in shock, the visions of the previous day's attacks still in their thoughts. Quickly Fletch led the team outside, looking up the streets, seeing in the distance the protesters already pouring around the palace gates, running towards them, carrying all manner of weapons. Looking around him he saw the trees and high buildings would prevent the helicopter overhead from landing, knowing they'd need to find safer ground, especially with Russian gunman on the loose nearby. He glanced at the dragon, seeing the computer had turned off, probably the scuffle with the protesters having damaged it. He looked back at the van, the steam rising from the engine, and liquid dripping from underneath telling him it was almost finished. But with the lack of cars in the street, their options were limited, especially the thought of trying to escape on foot with the King and Queen, as fit as they were, they were in no condition to go running around the capital, especially with a hostile crowd closing them down.

Shaking his head angrily, he ushered them back inside the vehicle, ignoring the astonished looks from the King and Queen as Grub shot back humorously,

"Told you we should have ordered that fucking taxi."

With everyone onboard, and the fan belt squealing they sat back as the van lurched forwards away from the palace.

Palace grounds

Major Laratov watched on from the palace roof angrily, as the police van made its escape, remarking at how it could still drive in its condition. One of his men stood with binoculars, quickly reading out the registration and callsign number on the roof, passing them onto another who wrote down its details, handing them over to Laratov.

"Good, get those details out to the police, tell them what happened here, you know what to do."

He turned, not waiting to hear the acknowledgement, confident his orders were to be carried out as he climbed the steps up to the waiting helicopter ready to whisk him away to safety. He had to be back at the embassy in thirty minutes, no doubt his boss would want a detailed report on what had happened. He sat there watching the scene below him as the helicopter rose above the palace, smoke pouring out of some of its windows, tens of thousands of people still pouring through the grounds, whilst outside many more milled about, their own anger rising and boiling over. Hopefully they'd carry that anger with them, telling everyone they met what they had seen. Around them a multitude of helicopters buzzed, some were police helicopters, others air ambulances, and some full of reporters trying to get the latest news on what had happened. Already the footage shot by his men was being edited and prepared, by tonight every news outlet and paper in London would have the story that British soldiers trying to protect the King had massacred the protesters, whilst they in turn were killed at the hands of the mob. The bodies of the palace guards doubling up nicely as the dead soldiers. All of it would play into the hands of the new British Government and its narrative, adding credibility to them, whilst simultaneously discrediting the imposter who was sat somewhere out there in the country in his bunker, pretending to be the PM. Perhaps, he thought to himself, the fact that the King had escaped would be a bonus, as now the crowds milling below had not had their pound of flesh. Perhaps they'd carry that fury and frustration into the streets, hopefully spilling over, turning the streets of London red with rage. He smiled, quickly forgetting about the King and his escape, consoling himself with the fact that whatever happened, his mission had been a success. Tonight London would burn.

13

Almost Check Mate...Mate

Central London

At around the same time as Mike was battling in the woods in the tank, Fletch and his team were attempting to navigate through the streets of London, keeping themselves well away from the crowds of protesters, drawing curious glances from people walking by at the state of the van. His earpiece crackled, as overhead the pilots of the helicopter reported in with what they were seeing ahead of them.

"Romeo 4, Wildeye, that's a no-go on the park, I'm counting at least a thousand people there and they look really pissed off. We'll need another location for pickup."

Fletch cursed, realising all the parks and open areas they'd planned on using as landing sites were now occupied by scores of angry people, likewise the roads leading out of the capital were closed, the police roadblocks helping to keep central London in a state of lockdown. All their windows of opportunity to get safely out of London were being shut in their faces. And it was about to get even worse.

Gemma leaned over, interrupting him, her voice full of alarm.

"Fletch you guys need to hear this!"

She pulled her own earpiece out, so her radio loudspeaker sprung to life, turning up the volume.

"All callsigns are to be on the lookout for police van, Kilo 256, Registration number KN24FTX, van is wanted in connection with the attack at the palace earlier. Van believed to be containing rogue military elements, highly armed and extremely dangerous. Deadly force is now authorised at the highest level, I repeat, deadly force is now authorised."

"Oh great!" Grub shot out, "now we're really going to be fucking popular with the locals!"

The Queen looked around confused, alarmed as the news sunk in, quickly replying.

"What does that mean? Darling, what are they saying? Surely, they can't think that terrible event earlier was any of our doing, can they?"

"Don't worry, my love," the King replied reassuringly, his arm around her pulling her closer. "It's all just a mix up, a terrible misunderstanding that's all. Once we're out of here, we'll have our chance to put it all right."

Fletch and Bug shared a look, realising the van was now going to be drawing them unwanted attention. As the roads around them were blocked, he had to come up with another plan and quickly.

He looked at the map, having fixed the computer, the culprit being a loose cable, and scanned for an alternative route, already knowing there wasn't one. As he looked at the map, he realised their only option would be the river. He radioed it in, telling the helicopter overhead his plan as the pilot radioed his acknowledgement and pulled higher, scouting ahead for them.

Fletch saw the side street he wanted, pointing it out to Bug as the van came off the main street and disappeared down into a narrow alley, losing itself from view in the narrow streets. Within minutes they abandoned it, all of them on foot, heading down the streets to the river's edge. Fletch was conscious of how it would look, especially now they had two of the most recognisable faces in the world with them. Suddenly he had an idea, quickly stopping the group, and pulling the balaclava from his head, he walked over to Bug, collecting his, before offering them to the King and Queen. Both recoiled in disgust at the sweat-soaked balaclavas being offered to them.

"Surely you must be joking?" the King replied, as the Queen grimaced and grabbed the mask, understanding its importance. Within seconds her blonde hair had disappeared as she donned it, adjusting it so that only her eyes and mouth were visible. Still the King held out, his mouth set as finally the Queen turned to him, punching him lightly on the shoulder.

"Darling, everyone knows who you are, the Sergeant's right, how are we supposed to walk the streets and hide when everyone will see you and recognise who you are? Now stop being such a bore and get the mask on."

"Never argue with the one you love, eh Sergeant!" the King said flatly, shaking his head in defeat and finally pulling the garment over it. Now at least, Fletch had one less thing to worry about.

Jonesy and Grub removed their own balaclavas and smiled as they went forwards, patrolling out into the street, again drawing curious glances from passers-by. Thankfully most of the people were fixated on the operatives and their weapons, oblivious to the two people in balaclavas as the team crossed over the road, spotting the river less than 50 metres away.

Gemma shouted over as she listened out on her radio.

"Fletch they've found the van, they're tasking units to our location now!"

Shit, he thought, it wouldn't be long now. He began to pick up the pace, looking out over the river, looking for something suitable to escape on. Like the roads, the river was devoid of traffic, he was becoming desperate, when finally, his eyes settled on the quayside, the plan forming straight away. Risky, but right now Fletch would settle for a pedalo if he had to.

He was almost running the team down the ramp and onto the dock, the others looking on in bemusement as they finally saw where he was taking them, only Gemma looked disbelievingly, shaking her head and remarking,

"You've got to be fucking kidding me."

Alongside the dock, ready to depart, was a twin hulled catamaran high speed ferry. Fletch had watched it pulling into the dock, the timing almost perfect. Seeing them cutting through the waves earlier on their way in, Fletch knew they were fast, with powerful water jet engines they were capable of running at over 45 knots, it would make the perfect getaway vehicle, plus with a flat top, the helicopter could hover overhead, allowing recovery of the team.

They pushed through the throng of people waiting to board, some turning to argue, quickly backing away as they saw the weapons the team carried. Fletch barged through the ticket machine, the others following, as already in the distance he could hear the sirens, but knowing they'd still take some time to get there, as all the roads were jammed. Fletch pushed past one of the crew members, ignoring the man's yells as he jumped onto the gangway, counting everyone onboard, checking no one was missing before running up to the bridge, pushing through the rope and signage warning 'Crew Only'. The usually locked door was left open to cool the operator in the heat, he'd already turned around, drawn to the shouting on the dockside, just as Fletch barged in, pistol in hand, any attempt at defiance lost as he saw the weapons and the look on Fletch's face.

"What do you want?" he asked meekly, his hands raising upwards in surrender as Fletch ushered him out of the bridge, pointing down to the quayside.

"I'm sorry mate, but we're commandeering the boat. I need you and your crew to kindly piss off and take your passengers with you."

He ushered the man below to the passenger decks, hearing the shouts of anger from the passengers as the SBS team began to manhandle them off the vessel. Satisfied no-one else was on board, he turned to Grub, pointing up to the Bridge.

"Grub, she's yours, get yourself acquainted with the controls then let me know when you're set to go."

Grub smiled, clapping his hands together in genuine delight, racing up the stairs and calling back.

"I've always wanted to drive one of these beauties!"

Fletch turned to the others, pointing over to the bar that dominated the centre of the lounge area of the boat.

"Sir, Ma'am, I'd like you to both sit in cover behind the bar, and you can remove the balaclavas now." Without any complaint, the King and Queen did as they were told, both pulling at the masks, thankful to be rid of them. The King took both and tossed them away from them, the message clear to see, they wouldn't be wearing them again.

Seeing how exhausted they both looked, Fletch looked over to Bug, the team medic nodded in understanding. Bug knelt down beside them and reached up to the bar, taking some bottles of water and handed them one each. They nodded in thanks as he cast an eye over them both, quickly checking them for injuries now that that they had a moment to spare.

Over his earpiece he heard Grubs jovial voice on the bridge.

"Fletch we're ready to go, just say the word Captain!"

Within seconds his team had slipped the mooring lines as Fletch replied, "Ok Grub, let's get the hell out of here."

Fletch kept a watchful eye on the crowd, making sure no one tried to be a hero and jump back onboard as Grub activated the thrusters. The water beside the dock frothed angrily as the boat slipped sideways, increasing the gap between it and the dock. Some of the faces on the dockside were looking back at him shocked, others not quite so, and as he looked on, one man in a suit gave him the middle finger and shouted an insult. Fletch smiled and took a bow, prompting more angry shouts as he was drawn to movement on the quayside. Looking over he saw the blue flashing lights of the approaching police cars, followed by police officers charging through the crowds towards them, all shouting at the crowds to get away from the dock. Fletch was disappointed to see all the police were carrying weapons. He really didn't want to get into a gun fight with them. Thankfully he didn't need to, as with a burst of power the vessel shot forwards, causing Fletch to grasp for a hand hold as the others tumbled into the seats, cursing Grub. He kept low, expecting at any second to hear the incoming gunfire as the dock rapidly disappeared into the distance. Thankfully none came and within seconds the boat began to get on the plane, the twin hulls coming out of the water and gliding across its surface as the boat accelerated away, the ride smoothing out as she began to get into her stride, huge twin rooster tails of water jetting up and away behind them.

He watched the London skyline shooting by as he keyed the secure personal radio.

"Okay, Grub, I want you to just keep heading down river out of the city, head back towards Archer."

After a few seconds Grub came back through over the air.

"Roger that Fletch, but I don't think this will fit in the sub."

Fletch smirked, Grub always had to be a wise ass, he thought as he replied, "We're not going to the sub, just get us far enough away from the docks."

Hearing Grub acknowledge the order, he looked back over to the Royals, both were sat in mute silence just watching the events going on around them. He couldn't believe what he was witnessing, here in his charge were one of the most powerful and influential couples in the UK, being forced from their home and having to resort to stealing a boat and whisking them away with most of London after them. Perhaps one day they could make a film about this he mused, as Gemma looked up, waving him over. He walked forwards, one hand resting on the seats to steady himself as he looked down.

"What is it?"

"They know we're now on the river, they're sending river units and helicopters in pursuit."

Fletch nodded in acknowledgment. If things went to plan, they'd be long gone by the time the boats got to them. He looked over at the rest of the team.

"Okay let's get ready to go."

"What about her?" Jonesy asked, pointing over to Gemma.

"What about me?" Gemma asked, not quite understanding what the operator was getting at.

She looked back at Fletch, as he replied.

"Shit! he's right Gemma, I'm sorry but you're going to have to come with us."

"I can't just come with you!" she blurted out, "I'm not even supposed to be here! When they realise I'm gone, they'll know it was me who helped you!"

Shaking his head, he replied solemnly. "If we leave you behind on the boat, then they'll certainly know you helped us, especially now they're out for blood. And after what just happened back at the palace, can you honestly say you'll be able to convince them you had no part in it?"

"Fucking hell!" she shot out, as the realisation hit her. Whether she liked it or not, her fate now rested with the team.

Seeing her dilemma Jonesy walked over, putting an arm on her shoulder. "Hey, Gem, it isn't so bad, the food on the submarine's pretty decent."

"Submarine! FUCK!" she shouted, walking away from the group, her temper rising. "I hate *water*, and I *fucking hate* tight spaces!"

Fletch ignored her ranting, letting her digest what was happening as he pointed up to the stairway.

"Let's get them ready to go, evac in two on the top deck."

Leaving them to it, he made his way back to the bridge, Grub was standing, concentration etched on his face as he weaved the giant vessel through the river at 40 knots. Looking around him he could see they were on a clear stretch of water; the nearest police boats were still half a mile behind and nowhere near to catching them. They could do this. He looked over to both embankments, seeing the blue lights of the police cars following them in pursuit, but with 200 metres of water between them all they could do was sit and stare, powerless to intervene. Satisfied, he tapped Grub on the shoulder.

"Right Grub, that'll do, power her down and get ready for evac."

He walked out onto the top deck, looking overhead, seeing the helicopter of Wildeye mingling with the other news helicopters, clearly, its camouflage was working. The mission had called for stealth, so instead of the usual drab green military transport they'd elected to use the Augusta 109, except this one needed a reason to be hovering overhead, so, the RAF had done a great job of wrapping it in news decals, now to the untrained eye it was one of the many news helicopters buzzing overhead, hiding in plain sight.

Fletch turned his back to the wind, his clothing flapping in the breeze as he shielded his microphone, bracing himself as the catamaran's huge engines began to power down, the hull dropping back down into the water, the wake behind it causing the boat to roll in the swell as it lost speed and floated to a complete stop.

"Wildeye, Romeo Four, we're on the river now, large blue catamaran, standby for pickup, green smoke is the signal, over.

"Roger Romeo Four, ready for pickup on the green, on your signal. Out."

Fletch turned, seeing the police boats upriver screaming towards them, they must have been doing at least 50 knots, but still too far away to make any difference. He looked over as the team sat hunkered down by the stairway, ready to run out the second the helicopter was overhead. He looked behind him, Grub giving him the thumbs up from the bridge. Everything was set.

He pulled the green smoke grenade from his vest, pulling the pin and shaking its contents, watching as the dirty grey smoke quickly turned green, tossing it away on the roof, watching as it rolled lazily with the boat's movement, the smoke billowing skywards.

Overhead, one of the five helicopters peeled away and swooped down towards them, the pilot using the smoke to indicate where the wind was blowing, approaching into the wind. The helicopter came in low over the river, swooping across the bow and flaring overhead, settling into a hover 20 feet above them, the landing gear coming down, as the smoke was blown down and across them as the downdraft beat it away. Both military pilots' were watching carefully as they eased the Agusta lower. Fletch knew they wouldn't land on the roof, they couldn't risk it not taking the helicopter's weight, instead they'd hover inches above it, keeping the helicopter light on its feet, something the pilots' had practised countless times. Keeping himself low, fighting the rotor wash, Fletch looked over to his team, all waiting for the signal, mere seconds from rescue.

He couldn't hear the gunfire over the noise of the helicopter, but he could see it, as suddenly paint began to chip away on the helicopter's body, exposing the shiny metalwork underneath as large 50 pence piece sized holes began to appear around the area of the engine and gearbox. He waved his arms in warning, the pilots' expressions unreadable from within their large black visors, but he could see from their body language they knew they were taking incoming. He ducked low as the pilot increased power, the helicopter's wheels coming dangerously close to hitting him as the Agusta climbed rapidly and screamed away, smoke pouring from one of its engines.

He looked over at the embankment, seeing the flash of weapons, realising quickly that the police marksmen weren't fucking about. If they stopped, then they were sitting ducks sat floating there.

"GRUB, FUCKING GET US OUT HERE!" he yelled as the rounds began to hit the boat, down below he could hear the windows smashing as his team dived back down the stairwell for cover.

Fletch lay on the open roof, feeling naked and exposed as all around him gunfire tore into the boat, he turned, wondering what the hell was going on, why weren't they moving? He saw Grub on the deck, crawling slowly back into the bridge, trying to avoid the incoming fire. It wasn't just the helicopter the marksmen were targeting. Fletch crawled over towards the bridge, the rounds thudding into the decking, the movement of the boat in the waves throwing off the marksmen's aim as he scurried across the decking. He dived through the bridge door, landing in a heap on top of Grub who shouted out in pain, as ignoring his cries Fletch leaned upwards, the glass of the bridge windows exploding around them, his fingers quickly finding the throttles and jamming them forwards. With a jolt, the catamaran propelled forwards, the broken glass sliding across the floor as, like a horse charging forwards, the boat leapt out of the water and shot away, quickly accelerating to maximum speed. Fletch looked over, watching as the gunfire began hitting the water, the single shots throwing up splashes. Thankful that the police didn't have automatic weapons, otherwise they'd have been dead in the water. After a few moments, the incoming fire ceased, as the boat began to pull away from the ambush site.

He stood up, checking himself over for injuries, seeing none he turned his attention to Grub, who stood up, the glass shards falling off him as he took control of the boat again. Apart from a cut to his cheek from the glass, he was fine.

"Fletch I'm fine, go check on the others."

He ran down the stairs, fully expecting to see people dead or injured, instead his team were all bunkered behind the bar in all round defence. The windows were shattered and full of holes but none had broken, the safety glass remaining stubbornly in place.

"Everyone alright?" he asked, the concern on his face clear to see.

The King had a cut to his hand which Bug was already applying a dressing to, as the Queen soothed her husband, who remained thin lipped and quiet, clearly not wanting to show his discomfort. Everyone nodded in reply, thankfully it looked like the injuries were minor.

"How's the chopper?" Jonesy asked, Fletch keying the radio in reply, realising he'd been so distracted by what was going on in the boat, he hadn't thought to ask.

"Wildeye, Romeo four, how you doing?"

After a few seconds, one of the pilots came back on, in the background Fletch could hear the alarms and shrill warnings of the wounded helicopter bursting through as the pilot tried to sound calm.

"Romeo Four, Wildeye, we're still airborne, one engine out, but we're still flying. Recommend we *don't* try that again."

Fletch breathed a sigh of relief, knowing the Agusta could happily fly on one engine. It looked like they'd got away with this one.

"Yeah, way ahead of you Wildeye, we're going to keep pushing down river, let's get out of the city, find somewhere quieter and go for extraction again. Can you keep yourself in the air for another ten minutes?"

"We can, however, be aware our little disguise has now been rumbled."

Fletch ran back up the stairs to the roof, keeping low in case anyone tried to shoot at him. Looking upwards, his hair billowing in the wind he could see the helicopter about a mile away, the small trail of smoke making it easy to identify. Two police helicopters were trailing close by, preventing the helicopter from getting close, but also unable to bring it down. The last thing the police needed was a helicopter crashing down on top of the capital. For now, it looked like Fletch was on his own.

Seeing their dilemma, he radioed back.

"Roger Wildeye, I see the problem. For now, keep them off our backs, and keep yourself over the most populated areas, that way they won't dare try to shoot you down. So long as they're on you they're not on us. Good luck."

"Roger, good luck yourself. Wildeye out." the pilot responded optimistically.

Fletch looked backwards, seeing the three police boats from earlier were now gaining on them, their lead having closed down as they'd stopped for the aborted pickup. Now they were less than 100 metres from them and slowly gaining every second. He could see the police crews were hanging grimly on as the boats jumped and turned through the catamaran's wake. On each boat sat four heavily armed members of the CTU team, the *real* CTU team. That made twelve in total coming for them, against Fletch's team of four, five if you counted Gemma. These guys were the best of the Met, all trained to do hostile assaults. Fletch was confident that on any other day his team could handle them, but now, with the King and Queen in the firing line, there was too much to lose. Plus, up to now Fletch had managed to hold off engaging with any of the police, not wanting to fire on their own side. But he knew the closer the CTU teams came, the more the chance of that happening increased, especially now everyone thought they were cold blooded murderers.

He ran back into the bridge, his eyes scanning ahead as he opened the door, seeing Grub had the throttles already wide open. The wind whistling through the broken panes.

"How fast we going?"

"She's doing 45 knots, I can push her for a bit more, but we might break something then."

Fletch looked around him, seeing the gauges and dials were already close to the red line, but then looking behind him, the sight of the boats in pursuit finalised his decision.

"Fuck it, wring her neck, get me every ounce of speed you can. Keep us middle of the river and stay away from the banks.

"Roger that." Grub replied, his knuckles turning white as he leaned on the throttles, the concentration etched on his face as he approached one of the many London bridges. With a flash of shadow overhead, the Catamaran squeezed under the bridge, narrowly avoiding a small boat that was coming through, the people stood on it waving and shouting as the wash nearly toppled them over. Fletch winced and ducked instinctively as they passed under the bridge, knowing the bridge was tall enough, but still doing so regardless. He looked back, happy to see the smaller boat's crew were okay, the last thing he needed were more dead civilians to be blamed for.

He looked back, satisfied that at last the distance began to open up, at least they could keep them at bay. Patting Grub on the back he ran back down below, sitting besides the others behind the bar, the King looking at him questioningly.

"What is it Sir?" Fletch shouted over the noise of the engines as the wind howled through the broken windows.

"Sergeant, what exactly is the plan if those police boats catch up to us?" the King shouted back, his body jolting as the catamaran hit some turbulent water.

"Well Sir, if they catch up to us, then the CTU teams will try to board us, to put us down and re-capture you. But our job is to stop that from happening."

"How good are they?"

Fletch looked almost apologetically back at him as he responded.

"They're the best Sir, but then they bloody should be, they were after all trained by us."

The other team members all nodded solemnly as they listened to the exchange, as the King looked around at them all before asking,

"So, back to my original question, if they do manage to get onboard, how *exactly* will you and your men stop them?" the King enquired, eyebrows raised.

Fletch frowned, unsure of what the King was implying, the other team members looking over curiously as he replied. "We'll use whatever means necessary Sir, ideally I'd prefer it not to happen, but if we do get into a shooting match, I'm afraid they're going to lose."

"You'd kill them all? Without any hesitation or thought?" the King asked, his voice almost saddened.

Fletch looked proudly around his team, proclaiming. "If we have to, then yes, without a doubt. We're not the boy scouts Sir, our mission is to get you out safely, not sit by and let them take you again.

"That's what I was afraid of." the King replied, "those police officers on the boats, they're following orders like you, yes, they've been lied to, but they don't know that. Like you, they're doing their duty, believing in their hearts that their doing the right thing... Are you going to kill them for doing that? Could you kill British citizens? Our own people?"

Fletch shook his head disagreeably. "Sir, I don't get to pick and choose the fights; I go where I'm told. And right now, I've been told to get you out of here. That's the mission, and me and my team are going to follow it through."

The King looked over at his wife, as if they'd discussed something between them, she nodded as he looked back, his face stern.

"Sergeant I will not have British Citizens, *my subjects*, killed on my behalf, based on you simply doing your job. Your orders are to get me out of here, however they do not state how you're to do so. Therefore, as your commander in chief, and as your king, I'm ordering you and your men *not* to kill anyone."

Fletch stared back open mouthed at the order, uncomprehending how the hell he was to carry it out. Already the police had shown their willingness to shoot them. He couldn't just expect his team to do nothing but use harsh language in return. He shook his head, pointing behind them to the police boats still charging in their wake, his voice rising.

"Sir, I'm sorry but I don't think you've grasped the situation fully, those officers out there mean to kill us. Possibly even you and your wife! Are you telling me you're ordering us to stand by and do...do nothing?"

The King raised his head, his own eyes narrowing, the gaze fierce as he replied firmly.

"No, that's *not* what I'm ordering. I'm not saying stand down, or give up, I'm telling you that your rules of engagement have just changed. Get us out of here, but with the minimum of friendly casualties. Those people out there are *not* the enemy Sergeant, they're ours, remember they're on our side. I'm always hearing about you special forces chaps, everyone telling me that you're the best in the world. Well now Sergeant, you can prove it. What better test of character and guile is there than escaping with the King and Queen, and doing so without any friendly casualties? And besides, as you have just so eloquently put it yourself...you're the best."

Fletch stood back up, scratching his head in thought and looking around at the others, not realising the trap he'd just walked into. Jonesy looked amused, no doubt glad that he wasn't the one in charge, as Bug slowly shook his head. Fletch couldn't quite believe how the day was turning out. The Queen looked over at the King, squeezing his hand tenderly, clearly proud of her husband's decision.

Fucking hell, he thought moodily, as if things couldn't get any worse. He looked at them both, he'd never met them before, but knowing who they were, what they represented, somehow the dignified way in which the King had spoken, it seemed to resonate with him. Without totally understanding why, he nodded, knowing that if, by some miracle they survived this, the guys back at the camp would forever think of him as insane or a fool.

"Okay, Sir, fine, we'll do it your way. But I want it known that it was against my better judgment."

"Good man!" the King replied, relief clear to see on his face.

Suddenly, as if on cue, Grub's voiced echoed over the radio.

"Fletch we've got a problem; I've got overheat alarms on both engines. Going to need to throttle back for a bit to cool them down."

"We can't throttle down Grub, if we do that, the boats' behind will catch us."

"No choice," he replied laconically, "if we don't, they'll automatically shut down, and then we're dead in the water."

"How long do you need and what speed do you need?" Fletch asked, hopeful of the answer.

"Reckon 20 knots for five minutes should do it. I'll let you know when we can get back to full speed.

"Okay, throttle her back!" he replied despairingly, the King's words still echoing in his ears.

They all felt the boat slow down as Fletch looked over the team, not quite believing what he was about to say next.

"Right guys, let's get ready to repel boarders."

"Hang on, can you just say that again?" Jonesy replied smiling, as Fletch ignore the wisecrack, his face serious at the realisation of what could happen next as he added,

"Remember our new ROE, non-lethal force only. It's wound not kill."

"Let's hope someone on the other team gets that fucking memo, shall we!" Bug replied testily, already making his own feelings known on the matter as he prepared for the fight, moving away from the others and crawling over the floor, keeping hidden from the windows. He settled himself low into a firing position, pulling out two magazines and laying them next to him, his weapon up and ready, covering the boat's port side. Jonesy moved to the other side of the boat, again staying low, hiding himself in one of the companionways, giving him a clear field of view of the deck on the starboard side. Now anyone coming aboard deck would have to run through both of their weapon's fire.

Fletch reached into his backpack, pulling out four small state of the art cameras and sticking them in position on both sides of the boat. Now at least they had eyes on, the cameras would feed directly back to the dragon display on his arm. He checked the signal, watching the small feeds, satisfied they'd do.

He looked at the young police officer, still brandishing the pistol.

"Gemma, you're on escort duty, stay with the Royals, no matter what happens."

Gemma nodded proudly, thankful that Fletch finally trusted her enough with such a task. She didn't know it of course, but he had no choice, he needed all his gun dogs to repel the attacks that he knew would come.

Fletch looked behind him, seeing the police boats rapidly gaining, watching on moodily, not quite sure how this was all going to end, his eyes flicking over to the green sign on the life jacket locker, suddenly he had a brainwave. Something from his past jumping into his mind. Quickly he jumped up, running over to the locker and tearing it open, the others looking on as if he'd lost his marbles.

He waved them both over, quickly pointing to the door leading below decks.

"Bug, Jonesy, quickly, I need you both down below, find me as much line or rope as you can. I need twenty metre lengths if you can. Hurry!"

Bug looked down at the pile of lifejackets, and smiled as he finally understood what Fletch was planning, remembering back to the team operation they'd been involved in, against the drug cartels in Florida.

Seeing Jonesy was lingering behind, he barked over.

"Oi, come on, give me a hand you lazy bastard, we're going fishing!"

They both disappeared from view, emerging moments later with six sets of coiled ropes that were used to tie the boat up when not in use. Quickly they began to uncoil them, as Fletch began to tie two lifejackets to the end of each rope, the King and Queen watching on curiously as to what the men were up to. All the while Fletch was keeping a watchful eye on the police boats, they were now 60 metres away and closing. It would be tight on time. They braced themselves as they felt the vessel heel over as Grub took avoiding action, clearly trying to keep them from hitting something ahead. Behind them they saw the distinct shape of HMS Belfast whizz by at speed, Fletch waiting until the vessel righted itself before shouting over the noise.

"Okay, that'll do!" As all three grabbed one piece of rope each, careful not to trip other the others. They ran outside onto the stern, keeping as low as they could as they tied one end of each rope to the stern railing, throwing the other end with the two lifejackets on overboard, the lifejackets inflating and being ripped away by the powerful water jets, the ropes uncoiling quickly then snapping taught as they trailed behind the boat just under the water's surface.

Without waiting to congratulate themselves they ran back inside, grabbing the other three ropes and repeated the procedure, as six long ropes, 20 metres in length were now trailing behind the boat, just under the surface of the water, the lifejackets preventing the ropes from sinking to the riverbed.

The operators resumed their positions, Fletch urging the Royals back into cover as he lay next to them, quickly keying the personal radio.

"Grub, I need you to be ready to do some fast turns and manoeuvres as I call them. Watch out for traffic, if you think we're going to hit something then abort the turn."

"Roger that." Grub replied simply, hands waiting on the boat's controls, ready for anything.

"Sergeant, what's going on?" The King asked, wondering what Fletch was intending now.

He looked back at him, smiling to see the King's confusion, happy to repay the favour of the order.

"You did say Sir, that we're not to kill anyone."

The King frowned, not understanding the Sergeant's meaning, as Fletch ignored him, his concentration now on the boats displayed on the camera feed.

They were less than 30 metres away now, he could see the CTU teams crouching on the bow in position, ready to assault. Fletch knew the procedure, he knew what to expect, it had been his team that had taught the police how to storm boats whilst underway. At least that was one advantage they had. Two of the boats broke away as planned, one going either side of the Catamaran and powering closer, whilst the third stayed back in reserve, providing overwatch. This would be the one containing the snipers, sweeping the decks, ready to go for the headshot. Fletch decided they were close enough, as finally he ordered,

"Grub, 45 degrees to port, NOW!"

With a lurch they felt the catamaran heel over slightly with the manoeuvre, the twin hulls preventing too much roll as the boat shot over to the left side of the river, the ropes and lifejackets snaking away behind it. The police boat over to their port side saw they were going to collide and slowed and broke right, passing behind them, running over some of the ropes before carrying on, oblivious to what had just happened. Suddenly they felt the catamaran dip rearwards slightly, as two of the ropes on the stern were torn away with a loud crack.

"Bingo! We have a bite!" Fletch shouted out triumphantly, as the King looked on in wonder at what had happened. He was about to enquire when they saw the patrol boat behind them slow down and come to a complete stop, the CTU team being thrown forwards at the loss of momentum.

Seeing him looking Fletch quickly shot back with,

"Water Jets your Majesty!"

Still seeing him none the wiser he added,

"The boat we're on has water jets, sucks up the water and spits it out the back. The boats they're following us with have propellers, so if we drag lines behind us, they run over the lines which wrap around their props and rip them off."

"And because we don't have a propeller, there's no risk to us." the King replied, looking at his wife.

"Well, you learn something new every day." the Queen replied, as Fletch continued enthusiastically.

"We saw the U.S Seal teams do the same thing to stop the cartel boats. And *that* is what you call boat fishing, now let's see if we can't get another bite!"

The other two boats peeled away, their helmsmen now fully aware of the danger lurking behind the catamaran as they began to manoeuvre violently around it, trying to get alongside the vessel. In frustration, the marksmen on the boats began to fire onto the bridge, trying to keep Grub away from the controls, as he weaved both left and right, preventing them from getting alongside. Grub was forced down as more bullets thudded around him, sticking his head up just in time to see them almost collide with one of the heavy steel barges moored alongside the riverbank. He pulled hard at the wheel, the twin hulls biting into the brown water as the stern swung out dangerously close, the giant rooster tails of water spraying over the barge, missing it by inches, but the life jackets all snagged under its steel hull pulling taught and with a final twang, the remaining four lines broke, taking away their defences.

Fletch crept forwards from cover, tying up more rope to the lifejackets, trying to crawl outside to play the same trick again. He could see the helmsman on one of the boats shouting the warning over to the CTU team and pointing over to him. His intention clear. Fletch ducked just as the rounds hit the walls around him, forcing him to abandon the plan and crawl back into cover, the pieces of metal and fibreglass raining down on him. Clearly the CTU didn't want to lose another boat. He remained where he was, watching on the dragon what the boats were up to, giving running commentary to the others, keeping everyone aware of what was unfolding.

He watched on as both boats were now either side of them, easily matching the pace of the catamaran, coming closer and closer, each one swooping in then drawing away, hoping to make them fire and reveal their positions. Everyone remained quiet and in hiding, the cameras doing the work for them. Finally, the CTU teams must have had enough as both boats came in together quickly, their hulls touching gently against the hull as both teams jumped aboard as one, each boat having sniper cover, ready for the threat. Fletch had been waiting for it, already having briefed his team on what was going to happen next. As soon as the first pair of CTU boots landed on the hull he shouted over the radio.

"GRUB! CRASH STOP!"

Grub threw the engines into reverse, the powerful waterjets suddenly changing direction as the bow sunk into the water, throwing the boat forwards as it stopped in a matter of metres. The two patrol boats alongside couldn't hope to match the catamaran's braking ability as they continued shooting forwards, the snipers quickly losing sight of the boat as they rapidly shot out of view. Meanwhile, outside on the decks it was chaos, as both CTU teams were thrown to the floor, losing hold of their rifles as they fell in a heap, arms instinctively held out to stop them, one man falling overboard, clinging desperately to the boat's railing. Already pre-empting the move, Fletch and his team were on their feet before the boat had stopped moving, weapons raised and screaming at both teams to stay down, any attempt to get up being met with a hostile boot to stop them. Fletch and Jonesy were on the starboard side, whilst Bug was overseeing the portside team, covered from above by Grub who'd ran out of the bridge, leaving the catamaran to float along. Fletch could hear the shouts of fear coming from the man who was hanging overboard, clearly terrified of falling into the deep water knowing that, with his tactical gear on, he'd sink like a stone with the weight dragging him down. He peered over, seeing the man looking up, the fear plain to see behind the balaclava. Fletch looked over at the patrol boats, already they were desperately coming about, racing back, the marksmen onboard already running to get into new positions to fire.

Remembering his promise to the King, he reached down, unclipping the officer's rifle and letting it fall with a splash into the water, all the while the man was pleading with him.

"Please, I've got a family, please don't do this." Clearly the man thought Fletch was going to kill him. Fletch kept quiet, pulling the man's pistol, throwing it into the water, along with the taser. Finally relieved of his weapons, he grabbed the man and heaved him back onboard. The man nodded in thanks, not quite believing his luck as Fletch pulled his pistol, pointing at the officer's head and walked him forwards to the other three, all under the watchful gaze of Jonesy.

It was a dangerous move, although they were all lying in a heap, every single one of them were fully armed. Fletch had to be careful how he played this. All he'd done so far was to catch a snake by the tail. Firstly though, the police boats.

Looking over to the patrol boats, he kept his pistol pointed at the officer's head, snarling, keeping his voice as cold and evil as he could. He needed them to think he'd kill them if provoked.

"Tell those fucking boats to piss off. Or you're going overboard along with your men."

The officer had his hands out, the fear now beginning to fade as he tried to take back control, to stall him, to buy them time for the marksmen to shoot. Fletch knew the rules, he'd spent long enough playing them.

"Okay mate, okay, we can get that done. But first why don't you talk to us, tell us what you want, why are you doing this?"

Seeing the boats getting closer Fletch was in no mood to play games. To prove a point, he pointed the pistol at the fleshy part of the man's left leg, knowing it was flesh and muscle, with no bone to ricochet off, it would hurt, but he'd live. As if sensing the same the man began to speak.

"NO WAIT, PLEASE DON'T!"

The gunshot rang out, muffled against the leg as the man yelled in pain, his teeth clenched in anger as his eyes widened in terror. Fletch kept a firm hold of him, turning towards the police boats, bending the man over the rail, the pistol still smoking, now at his head, making his intentions clear to see. After a few moments the police marksmen all lowered their weapons, and nodded in surrender, their arms held wide as the police boats slowly began to reverse away as it dawned on them what was going on. Fletch watched them pull back another 400 metres, bobbing away in the current, ready to come pouncing back in if needed.

Satisfied they had one threat under control, he turned his attention to the snake in their midst.

Keeping his voice loud and cold he yelled out.

"Right, starboard side team only. I want you to slowly stand up, put your hands on your heads and keep your hands off your weapons, make no sudden moves."

As one, the three CTU officers stood up, doing as they were told, Fletch could see the anger burning from their eyes through the balaclavas at what he'd just done to one of their team. One of them looked down temptingly at his rifle hanging on the sling, clearly thinking it through. Fletch caught the movement, throwing the injured officer onto the deck storming forwards, his pistol raised ahead of him, his voice calm and controlled.

"Oh no you fucking don't! Else, the only heroes you'll be seeing here will be dead ones!"

The officer's eyes opened wide in alarm, clearly, he hadn't thought he'd telegraphed the move. His thoughts of defiance quickly evaporating as he stared down the barrel of the pistol, as slowly Fletch approached the group, covered by Jonesy. With deft efficiency Fletch relieved them of their weapons, throwing everything overboard, before taking them inside the lounge, using their own handcuffs to tie them to the overhead metal stanchions, removing their balaclavas. Once they were secure, Fletch left them under the watchful eye of Gemma, moving outside with Jonesy to help disarm the portside team, throwing the weapons and tasers overboard and bringing them in and hand-cuffing them again with their own cuffs, removing their balaclavas. Only the wounded officer was allowed to sit, scowling in pain.

Now they had the situation back under control, Grub raced back to the bridge, the engines now sufficiently cooled to resume full speed. Fletch hung on as the boat rose again onto the plane, watching the detained officers looking at him, some angry, others embarrassed still unsure, not knowing exactly what the future held for them. Bug was kneeling next to the wounded officer, rolling a dressing tightly around the wound, the man grimacing in pain.

The King and Queen emerged from the cover of the bar, drawing gasps and muttering from the prisoners, clearly, they had no idea they were on board. Seeing their looks, Fletch retorted angrily.

"Yeah, that's right. Take a good fucking look. Ten minutes ago you fuckers were shooting at these two."

Some of the officers looked ashamed, one of them asking.

"Your majesty, I...I don't understand, what are you doing onboard? We had no idea."

The King stepped forwards; all eyes drawn to the bandage on his hand, some of them looking to Fletch for an answer as the King spoke.

"I appreciate this must be a hard time for you all right now, and I'm sincerely sorry that you've had to go through such a torrid ordeal. But rest assured, you have my word, none of you will be harmed further."

Everyone looked over at Fletch, still unable to make the connection, why would terrorists be with the King?

Seeing their startled looks, the Queen stood up and stood beside her husband, both of them chatting reassuringly to the detained officers as if they were at a gala event, some of them even began to laugh and joke with them, the Royal magic beginning to do its thing.

Fletch looked on, shaking his head in disbelief at the whole affair, still not quite believing they'd managed all this without any serious injuries. He saw out of the window the O2 arena begin to appear, all they had to do now was get through the peninsular and out of the reaches of the Met police and they'd be home and dry. Not long now,

Fletch, not long, he thought, wishing it was over already. He left them to it, picking up two bottles of water from the bar and walking past, climbing the stairs to the bridge.

"How's it looking Grub?"

Without taking his eyes off the river, Grub gratefully took the open bottle, sipping the water as he rounded one of the corners without losing speed, the catamaran easily taking the turn.

"Nearly there Fletch, we've just got to get round the peninsular then through the barrier and we're home free."

Fletch took a drink himself, looking skywards at the news helicopters flying overhead. They were hot news now, the talk of the town, especially now they had hostages. At least now he had some bartering power. He smiled and tapped Grub, about to turn to go below when he heard him utter a curse.

"Oh Fuck!"

He turned, his eyes narrowing at what he saw. Ahead of them a mile away the Thames barrier was raised and locked, a formidable barrier they wouldn't be getting through, even if they had a destroyer. In front of it were five police boats blocking their way, each one loaded with more CTU officers. Whatever the plan was, they wouldn't be going out that way. Grub throttled the boat back, looking to Fletch for instruction.

Fletch shook his head angrily, quickly disappearing and re-appearing a moment later, dragging the limping officer with him, ignoring his moans. Reaching over he took the officer's radio mike, holding it close, ready to speak.

"Attention police units, attention police units, this is the vessel under military control in the Thames River. I wish to speak to your commander."

After a few seconds the radio squawked to life.

"Attention hijacked vessel, attention hijacked vessel, this is Gold Commander. With whom am I speaking?"

Fletch paused, at a loss as to what to say. Usually, he'd reply with his name and rank, but with the situation as it was, he didn't want anyone listening in to know who they were. He looked at Grub before replying.

"Gold commander, this is the commander of the forces on the vessel. We are a military unit posing no threat. We wish to navigate through the barrier. Please lower the barrier immediately."

There was a pause, Fletch could almost hear the sarcasm in the commander's voice as he replied.

"No threat, eh? We've got paramedics and officers back at the palace who might disagree with you, along with a large pile of bodies. No, the barrier stays up. We've got you surrounded. Why don't you think about letting your hostages go? Show us some good will and I promise you'll all get to live to see a prison cell."

Fletch saw the hope in the wounded officer's eyes as he looked at him, leaning against the railing, grimacing against the pain in his leg he spat out.

"I'd listen to him if I were you mate. He's right, right now, there's probably twenty trained marksmen all with eyes on you. You harm us, and you're all-dead meat. Just give it up, there's nowhere to go.

Fuck! Fletch thought, knowing full well they weren't going to budge. He couldn't blame them, if he was in their shoes safely on the barrier, looking down at them, he wouldn't let them go either. Every government around the world had one simple cast iron rule. Never negotiate.

"What you thinking Fletch? Reckon it's almost check mate, mate?" Grub asked.

He ignored Grub, looking over in the distance, seeing the helicopter of Wildeye still being kept at distance by the police helicopters, that was the only way they'd be getting out of there. but he knew if they brought it in, they'd be shot down, once the helicopter was over the water it was considered fair game. He looked up again, seeing the contrails of the F35's still overhead, shaking his head at how useless they were up there. Suddenly it came to him.

"Of course!" he yelled, surprising Grub as he finally replied. "Not yet mate, not yet. Stay here with limpy for the moment, keep your speed low and slowly head towards the barrier."

Fletch turned and exited the bridge, jumping down the stairs and barging into the room like a bull in a china shop, his sudden change in demeanour instantly putting everyone on edge, even the King and Queen looked unsettled. He looked over at Jonesy and Bug, pointing to the lifejackets.

"Get them all dressed to go into the water, quickly get them all into a life jacket.

Everyone went quiet as the two operators stood up, quickly tearing open the fluorescent orange packets as Fletch watched on with his pistol within easy reach, the warning clear to see to anyone thinking of trying anything silly. One at a time they unclasped the handcuffs and dressed each person, removing their heavy body armour and making sure each life jacket was snug and on tight before reclasping their handcuffs behind their backs. Two of the female officers looked on angrily as Bug leaned in between their legs with the straps, he muttered an apology as he did so, the gentleman in him feeling a little awkward.

Five minutes later and all of them were sitting in seats, dressed to go in the bulky jackets with their arms securely handcuffed behind their backs. Fletch was up top on the radio, chatting to the F35 pilots and the helicopter. He came back down, leading the wounded officer down with him, helping the man into his seat next to his teammates after putting the bulky lifejacket around him as he looked again at his bandaged leg.

"I'm sorry about that mate, really, I am."

The officer opened his mouth to say something, crying out in pain again as Bug stepped forwards and knelt beside his wounded leg, tightly wrapping a large roll of cling film recently taken from behind the bar, around the bandage.

"AHHH!" the man cried out, looking down at Bug angrily.

"Don't be such a baby," Bug said unsympathetically adding, "besides you'll thank me in a few weeks. You have any idea how dirty the Thames is? All those nasty little germs that will be trying to get into that leg wound."

The man went quiet as Bug continued, talking as if he were a GP educating a patient.

"Without the clingfilm that wound would get dirty, and then what? Amputation that's what! Take it from me. Better to grin and bear it now. This time tomorrow you'll be the hero of the hour."

All the officers looked on, totally bewildered at the change in the men, one minute they were threatening to kill them all, the next, sympathising with them, even caring for them. None of this made any sense, all contrary to what they'd been briefed.

Fletch saw them all looking about, their confusion evident.

"Not what you were all told eh?"

One of the female officers spoke out. "We were told that you were die-hard terrorists, that you'd just killed all those people. But…"

Fletch shook his head in agreement, adding,

"Well, you just remember all that when they debrief you after it's all done. Remember what we did. We *could* have killed you all, *should* have killed you all. But we *didn't*. We're not the monsters, nor the enemy. We're all on the same team. You're all being played."

Fletch left them muttering amongst themselves as he looked around at the team, nodding at them to get ready. He'd already planned what was to happen next as he keyed the radio.

"Okay Grub, increase speed, get us in closer."

They felt the vessel accelerate again as they closed the distance to the barrier, some of the detainees looking out of the window as it began to loom over them. At the last second the boat stopped, surrounded by the police boats, all guns pointing at them but unable to fire. Fletch looked up, hiding the nerves that were eating at him as he saw the numbers arrayed against them. Every gantry of the barrier was bristling with marksmen, all eager to fire the shot that would bring down the terrorist group on the boat. Grub pirouetted the large vessel on the spot, suddenly it was facing back the way it had come, the water churning out the back as the heavy engines rumbled in anticipation. Slowly It began to move away, the movement copied by the police boats, all now keeping close to the vessel, not wanting it to get away, the marksmen aboard keeping their weapons trained on the boat. They knew the terrorists on board had nowhere to go. Like a horse race about to start, all the boats were moving away, all jostling for position, trying to match the pace but not wanting to overtake the catamaran as slowly Grub increased the speed, 5 knots, then 8, then 10.

Fletch picked up the first group of detainees, deciding they'd waited long enough, hustling them all outside by the rail, lining them up one behind the other, keeping himself hidden in case one of the police marksmen on the boats trailing behind decided to try the shot. He looked over at the water, judging the speed to be fast enough, as he walked over to the first, a female officer, her eyes frightened at the realisation of what was about to happen. He smiled at her reassuringly.

"Don't worry, I've done this before loads of times, the life jacket will keep you afloat."

"Why don't you go fuck-" she managed to say defiantly as he grabbed her legs mid-sentence and flung her over, the rest of the team all doing the same. Upending all four of them at once into the water.

He looked back, smiling, as he counted all four heads bobbing away, thankful it had worked. As predicted, three of the boats behind immediately stopped, rushing to pick up their colleagues from the water. The other two boats powered on, determined not to let their quarry escape again. Fletch waved through the broken windows to Bug who ushered the other four to their feet, the wounded officer lagging behind. Fletch ushered him over to the rail, patting the rail next to him and smiling confidently as if they were on a swimming lesson.

The man stood next to him, his eyes darting to the water and back again, the look of fear back again.

"I can't swim." he shot out, the panic clear to hear. "Please, don't do this!" he urged, stepping backwards. Fletch lay a hand on him reassuringly.

"It'll be alright, we're not going too fast, and you won't need to swim. Trust me you'll be fine."

The man was wild eyed, his eyes darting about as the others lined up his team on the rail, quickly shooting back with,

"Please...at least take the cuffs off. With my leg as it is, at least give me my arms to use."

Fletch ignored the man's cries, as with a shout all four of the remaining hostages were thrown overboard, again Fletch checked, counting the heads bobbing in the boats wake, the orange lifejackets showing up clearly against the brown murky waters of the river. As planned, the other two boats gave up their chase, electing instead to rescue their friends. Now, no-one was following them. All they needed was Wildeye back on the scene.

No sooner had the hostages left the boat than Grub powered the boat back up to its full speed, of almost 50 knots. Soon they were turning back towards the 02 peninsular, the huge cable car that crossed the river, towering high above them. Fletch and his team ignored the sights whizzing past, instead running inside and grabbing the Royals, knowing now was the time. With startled shouts the King and Queen were bundled outside, up onto the roof again, Fletch no longer having the luxury of time to explain the plan. laying low, their heads turned backwards to shield themselves against the wind, that tore at their clothing. Overhead the shadow of Wildeye came into view, already racing up the river towards them, the pilots clear to see in the cockpit, as they began to match the boat's heading and speed. They stayed 20 feet above the boat, waiting for Fletch to give the signal who was now talking to Grub on the radio.

"Let me know when Grub, heli's ready to go."

On the bridge, Grub was checking they had enough clear water ahead of them, seeing the next turn was still some distance away he yelled out.

"Okay, 60 second window now, let's go for it."

Fletch looked behind him, his clothing and hair billowing in the blast as he stuck his thumb up, the pilot nodding in acknowledgment coming straight down for them, the helicopter's downdraft adding to the wind. Fletch watched on, amazed at how the pilot came on down, first 10 feet, then 5, then suddenly the helicopter was level with the roof, the landing gear mere inches above it.

"Okay Bug, you're up!" he shouted over the wind, as bending low against the onslaught, Bug got up, one arm protectively across the Queen and jogged her towards the rear sliding doors. Without grace or ceremony, he picked her up in his giant arms and swept her in, quickly jumping in himself.

Jonesy was next, bent double against the helicopter downdraft, one arm pulling the King along, both wincing against the wind. They reached the helicopter where Bug was already leaning out, his arms grabbing the King and pulling him inwards. Jonesy was about to climb aboard just as a gust of wind caught the helicopter, pushing it sideways, the pilot quickly adding power and lifting it away to safety from the boat's roof. Jonesy gave a shout of alarm as his body armour snagged on one of the helicopter wheels, his arms and legs shooting out for the landing gear, wrapping around it as it lifted him up and away with it and out over the water. Fletch watched on open mouthed, as the helicopter climbed, swaying at the extra weight on its landing gear, as Jonesy hung on for his life. Bug leaned outwards, keeping himself low to the floor of the helicopter, his massive arms wrapping around the operator and pulling him inwards to safety.

"Thank fuck!" Fletch said to himself, breathing out in relief as finally the distant figure of Jonesy climbing onboard disappeared out of sight. Fletch looked up, seeing Gemma waiting nervously, next in line, the pistol tucked into her waist band. Her eyes were wide in alarm as she nodded up to the helicopter.

"Why can't we just stop the boat? Why do we have to go so bloody fast?"

Fletch pointed to the shoreline, seeing the array of blue lights sat there.

"If we stop, we give them a chance to shoot at us, like last time. If we keep moving, they can't get at us. That's why. Come on, you're next."

Grub came over the radio.

"Fletch we're out of room, I'm going to have to turn her around and get setup for the second run."

"Forget that Grub, I'll take the controls now, get yourself up here with Gemma."

Leaving her alone he ran forwards to the bridge, now that the windows were smashed, he could jump straight in off the roof, sliding next to Grub as he climbed out, grabbing his gear as he went. Fletch gave Grub a pat on the shoulder for a job well done, remarking as he went.

"Keep an eye on the girl, I think she's a bit nervous."

"She's nervous? What about me? I've been shitting my pants since this all started!"

Both of them smiled, the gallows humour lightening their mood as Fletch took charge of the boat, turning her around ready for the next run along the river. Ahead of him he saw the two police boats from earlier waiting in ambush, thinking they were going to make a run for it. He smiled, flicking them the finger as he turned the boat, applying full power and enjoying the sensation of speed as it rapidly accelerated away again. In the distance he could still see the police helicopters being harassed by the F35's, now hovering menacingly near to them. Unlike the helicopters, the F35's were able to shoot air to air missiles, and as if to emphasise the point four of them were hovering in box formation around the helicopters, able to keep themselves close and with eyes on them. He could hear the heated exchanges over the radios between the pilots and the police as they tried to shake them off.

Good, lets see how they fucking like it, Fletch thought to himself. He checked their heading and speed, judging they'd have enough clear river for another 60 second burst before having to turn towards the barrier.

He looked at the controls, watching as Wildeye snaked in behind them, lining up again for the run, keying his radio.

"Wildeye Romeo Four, heading 167, speed 50 knots, clear run for 60 seconds."

"Roger Romeo four, inbound now."

He was constantly checking behind him, keeping one eye on the helicopter and one on where the boat was going as it came in again, this time the landing was better, perhaps the pilot had learned from last time, perhaps the wind was more favourable. He watched as Gemma and Grub jumped in, looking back one final time, as he selected the autopilot, checking the boat's heading. He had it lined up with the turn in the river 30 seconds ahead of them, with any luck, the boat would just plough into the shallow mud of the embankment, causing no further harm to anyone. With a final check he turned and leapt through the broken windows, running toward the helicopter, knowing it would be close. As he ran up to the helicopter, he could already see something was wrong. Instead of hovering, the helicopter was now sat firmly on the roof, the wheels already denting the metal as Grub was stood nearby, frantically ripping off his weapons and equipment and throwing it away over the boat's side as the others were tossing weapons and their own gear overboard out of the helicopter's windows. Fletch ran up to him, as Grub shouted against the engine noise.

"We're overloaded! One engine out, and one extra person on board. Too heavy!"

Fletch looked back towards the bridge, seeing the embankment looming closer, about to run and attempt the make the turn when Grub grabbed him, shaking his head.

"No Time! Ditch your gear and let's go!"

Within seconds, Fletch had his assault vest and helmet off and over the side, followed quickly by his body armour and weapons. Now he felt light and strangely naked as he followed grub onboard, everyone now dressed in just the black fireproof coveralls. He felt the shuddering of the airframe as they closed the door, the turbulent noise of the wind stopping immediately, replaced with the high-pitched whine of the turbine screaming overhead. He looked behind him, through to the cockpit, as the pilots' applied more power, their hands and feet working together as the helicopter shuddered, the engine screaming again as in the distance the river side loomed closer. He began to count to ten in his head, resigning himself to the fact that if he made it to eight, he'd be back out of the door and turning the boat, leaving the others to escape. Not because of any thoughts at being the hero, but the decision to bring Gemma had been his, he was the reason the helicopter was overweight, he'd be the reason it would get airborne.

He got to seven, his hand reaching again for the door handle when with a jolt they were airborne, the boat disappearing ahead of them as the pilots' kept low across the water, arcing over to the left and gaining airspeed. Fletch watched out of the side window, watching the catamaran tearing towards the mudbanks, then disappearing from view forever as the pilot banked left again, desperate to keep away from the cable car overhead. In front of them they saw warning lights flashing on the control panels, Fletch watched on, certain at any second they'd drop out of the sky, waiting to feel the sensation of free falling into the river as the skyline of London filled the windscreen ahead of them. Suddenly the windscreen showed only blue sky, the nose raising up and the Agusta climbing away, into the sunlight. One of the pilots looked back at them, raising her visor and giving the thumbs up, the sweat now clear to see on her face. The blonde sweaty wispy streaks of hair protruding from her flight helmet gave Fletch an indication of just how difficult that take-off had been. He smiled in response, looking back at the team as all of them broke into smiles. Alongside the helicopter they now saw the distinct shapes of the F35's now back from annoying the police helicopters as they closed protectively in formation around the helicopter, keeping the curious news helicopters and police helicopters out of its way as they set course for friendlier skies. The King looked back at him, his wife resting her head tiredly on his shoulder and weeping tears of joy as he extended his hand out, his face breaking into a big beamy smile. They'd done it!

Fletch took the outstretched arm, feeling the power in the grip as the King proclaimed.

"Sergeant, a very grateful nation, thank you, A very grateful King thank you, and one very grateful husband and wife, thank you. Well done."

Fletch nodded, wanting to say something in return, but still not quite believing it was over as he merely smiled, watching as the King began to sing their praises, promising the team everything from knighthoods to garden parties back at the palace. Lost in the moment, the King carried on talking, until finally, he realised with a look of exasperation, that everyone had slowly drifted off to sleep, the exhaustion and adrenalin of the past 48 hours catching up with them.

Seeing his frustration, Fletch leaned forwards, attempting to disarm the King, not wanting him to take offence, his voice rising over the noise of the helicopter.

"They're not being rude your Majesty, they're just tired. Try them again in a few hours, I promise they'll be listening. Meantime you'd best get yourself some sleep. I reckon you're going to be pretty busy when we land."

The King looked around at the cramped conditions, bodies crammed together and the noise of the helicopter's engine whining overhead.

"Sleep? In here? How the devil does one manage that?"

"That's easy." Fletch replied, the King leaning closer to hear the answer as Fletch leaned backwards getting comfortable before replying smiling.

"You just lay back and close your eyes."

With that, Fletch did just that, closing his eyes, ignoring the puzzled looks of the King as he quickly drifted off into a deep sleep...

14

Nemesis

Wonderland Operations Centre (WOC)

The PM stood in the middle of the Ops room, claps and cheers resounding loudly around them as the codeword came over the radio speaker.

"Heracles, I repeat, Heracles. Confirmed Clockwork Orange and White Castle secure and enroute home."

The King and Queen were finally safe, Operation Cerberus had worked.

He closed his eyes in silent relief, letting the good news wash over him as he looked over at the CDS who came rushing towards him, a pile of papers in hand and jubilantly throwing them up in the air, whooping like a schoolboy. He afforded himself a smile and shook hands with the CDS, the celebrations muted somewhat at the news still scrolling on the screens behind them.

As if sensing the mood of his boss, the CDS raised his hands to quieten the ops room staff, his voice booming out.

"Okay people, okay, let's not forget all those we've lost today. We'll celebrate later, but for now let's concentrate on the jobs at hand."

The PM nodded imperceivably in thanks, looking down at the pile of papers now scattered on the floor.

"I do hope those aren't for me CDS."

The CDS looked down, smiling and replying quietly.

"Defence budget predictions for the next five years. Kept them handy for just such an occasion!"

The PM smiled and nodded, adding, "Well, they can certainly go in the bin. I think we can all agree our defence budget needs a lot more investment now."

Suddenly one of the external phone lines rang loudly, silent since the cyber-attack days ago, the noise silencing the chatter. An operator walked up to it slowly, not quite believing it was ringing, looking over to the PM who indicated that the soldier should answer. Slowly, the soldier picked it up, looking around him as he answered tentatively.

"Ops room...Corporal Banner speaking Sir."

Everyone was watching him, as his eyes opened wide in disbelief at what was being said as he held the phone aloft, his voice rising in surprise.

"Sir, I've got NATO headquarters on the line, they want to speak to the PM."

The CDS stepped forwards, shaking his head. "What? That's impossible, the lines are all down! Someone must be yanking our chain!"

Suddenly the voice of Wendi came through loud and clear over the ops room speaker.

"Hello General, no-one's yanking your chain. I thought you'd like to know that I've now destroyed the virus that had infiltrated our networks. I've kept a piece of the source code and sent it over to GCHQ for your analysts to examine. You should have all major communications hubs within the UK back online in the next 20 seconds. I'll send them all automated messages with your phone numbers to Wonderland and orders to call in.

No sooner had the AI finished speaking than every external phone in the ops room began to ring. There were over thirty of them, usually manned by the operators, who had been stood down. Now with all thirty ringing at once the noise was loud and piercing, echoing off the walls as military personnel ran to answer them, each operator shouting out who they were speaking to.

"Sir, I've got Edinburgh on the line."

"Sir, I've got Cardiff."

"Manchester on this one!"

Behind them the double doors burst open as the other shifts came running in, realising that finally, now, they were able to communicate with the rest of the country. The extra staff members hurriedly grabbed their chairs, picking up phones and pens and noting down the messages, as runners stood close by, ready to dash away to carry out the multitude of tasks that were suddenly coming in.

The PM and CDS looked at each other, smiling again, not quite believing their fortune. First the King, now this. The PM walked over to the first operator, about to take the phone from him, to talk to NATO when a young RAF Corporal stood up, cupping the phone and shouting over urgently.

"SIR! PRIME MINISTER! YOU NEED TO TAKE THIS!"

The PM looked over at the young airmen, smiling and nodding dismissively.

"All in good time Corporal, take a message and tell them I'll call back. I've got NATO on the line, and I need to speak to them first."

The airman remained standing, shouting back, his words causing the PM to freeze instantly.

"BUT SIR, IT'S THE AMERICAN PRESIDENT!"

The PM's head shot across to the CDS, pointing to the conference room, his tone urgent.

"CDS, get that call diverted into the conference room if you please."

The CDS looked over to one of the operators of the consoles, who nodded in response. A few seconds and clicks of a keyboard later and the phone in the conference room began to ring. The PM strode purposefully towards the door, looking behind him at the CDS stood there. Stopping, he turned, indicating with a nod of his head towards the door.

"Well, are you coming CDS or not?"

The CDS frowned, replying, "You want me in there with you?" conscious that the previous PM had a habit of always keeping him and the military out of matters of diplomacy.

The PM nodded seriously, "You've been with me since the beginning, so yes, I want you in there with me CDS. Especially now we both know this whole bloody affair was theirs in the making. Now come on, let's see what our cousins over the water can do to help us."

Whiskey Three-Zero

Finally, after what seemed like an eternity, the artillery fire began to slow down and stop, the sounds of artillery exploding around them now being replaced with the sounds of the continuing battle. Mike looked up slowly, earth and debris falling off him as he cautiously raised his head, the landscape above looking alien to him. Where once were trees, were now upturned roots, the trees having been tossed aside and scattered haphazardly as fires raged around them. The open ground was littered and marked with smoking craters as the screams of the wounded and dying began to echo around them. Mike looked on confused, had the Russians just called the artillery on themselves?

He looked over to Baz, both exchanging disbelieving looks as they wiped dirt off themselves, both thankful to have survived the strike, then both checking that Smudge and Bill were still okay. Somewhere nearby they could hear shouting, then gunfire erupted again from the direction of the tank. Someone was still in the fight. He looked over, having no idea who the Russians were fighting now, some were still firing at the tank, others seemed to be shooting each other in confusion and outside of the woods, at an enemy unseen. Mike didn't care who they were fighting, so long as it wasn't them. Every minute he could keep his crew alive was another minute for Wendi to bring in the cavalry. Mike looked on, watching the RWS still firing, it's barrel glowing cherry red from the number of rounds being fired through it. Surely it would be out of ammo soon, he thought, as he watched it spin through 180 degrees and bark out again, firing into something unseen close by. The Hornet had stopped firing, Mike assuming its capacitor's were empty, as still it scanned around, no doubt Wendi was using it as a second set of eyes. With a screech he heard the RPG's firing, the three explosions rocking the tank balanced on the tree as the flames enveloped it. For a fleeting second, his heart was in his mouth, expecting it to be destroyed, breathing a sigh of relief as the smoke and flame quickly dissipated, the tank emerging relatively unscathed and still in the fight. Mike smiled with pride, amazed at the damage it had sustained as suddenly the machine gun went quiet, the glow of the barrel dying off as the barrel cooled down, smoke rising off the metal. Mike could hear the triumphant shouts of the infantry getting closer, unseen to him on the other side of the tank. They knew it was finally out of ammunition. Within seconds, the enemy infantry were swarming over the Chally, throwing grenades inside the turret hatches, the dull thuds echoing out as they assaulted it, firing automatic fire into the hatches, hoping to get vengeance on the crew, little realising the crew were 100 metres away.

Mike and Baz kept still, ignoring the stray rounds pinging overhead, watching from their positions as the enemy infantry poured over the tank, looking in through the hatches and all around it, searching for something. They were searching for *them*. Suddenly he heard a shout and saw the Russian soldiers looking over towards them, pointing and hollering, getting the attention of the others. Soon they'd be coming for them.

Mike looked at Baz, knowing this was it, he was out of options, when the treeline besides them erupted into a flurry of movement as something large and metallic bore down on them, crashing through the undergrowth. Baz turned to aim his rifle, firing out of panic, the rounds sparking harmlessly off the metal as it came towards them. Mike's eyes went wide in surprise, as he turned to see what it was, expecting to feel at any second the cold metal tracks of the enemy vehicle crushing them, or hear the bark of the machine gun firing at them. He turned, fully expecting to be killed, his eyes staring in disbelief down the barrel of the machine gun now pointed at him. All they have to do now is fire, he thought.

Mike winced, expecting at any second to be hit by incoming rounds. After a few seconds he opened his eyes, exhaling in relief, happy to see what had snuck up behind him, it wasn't an enemy vehicle sat metres from him, it was one of the Talons, its machine gun raised and looking over at the crippled tank.

Suddenly another flurry of movement, and a second Talon appeared next to the first, then a third, then a fourth. Finally the cavalry had arrived.

One of the pairs of Talons advanced forwards, ignoring the incoming fire as the infantry on the tank gave a warning shout and began to fire at them, now using the tank as cover. The bullets sparked off the Talons metal frames, the robots armoured chassis easily coping with the 7.62mm. With a whir, both of their weapon's launchers came free, the minimi's beginning to fire back in deadly accurate bursts as the Russians attempted to stop their advance. Someone near the tank fired an RPG, it's rocket tore through the short distance to the lead Talon. Quicker than Mike could have thought possible, the Talon side scooted left, leaving the RPG with nothing more than fresh air to hit as the rocket tore past, exploding in the trees. Ignoring its near miss, the Talon continued forwards, as one by one the soldiers began to die, some fell forwards off the tank, rolling onto the floor, others turned to run, the bullets throwing them off the tank in a heap as the robots continued their relentless and remorseless advance. The Talons pulled up to the tank, each driving around it at opposite ends and firing on the infantry who were now fleeing on the other side, the panic and fear beginning to take hold at seeing the unstoppable Talons for the first time up close.

The third talon drove into the clearing, its machine gun pivoting on its axis and firing into the trees randomly. Mike couldn't see what it was firing at, remembering the Talon could hear better than it saw, as suddenly the treeline around them came alive as more and more of the enemy troops began to pour out and run away, all running in the same direction as the first, the panic becoming contagious with some even dragging wounded with them. It was as if the robot's arrival had finally broken the Russian assault, as more and more of the enemy began to turn and run, Mike watching as more figures dashed past, the fight now gone out of them.

The fourth Talon moved forwards, coming closer as Wendi's voice came over its loudspeaker.

"Captain Faulkes, please get your casualties ready for transport, I've got the Thumprs coming in now, estimated time of arrival is 63 seconds."

Baz was looking back at the Talon open mouthed, unable to comprehend their change in fortune. Only Mike looked on unsurprised, already having worked with the equipment before. His face serious he stared back at the robot, talking as if to a person.

"Thank you, Wendi, can you send back that I've got two casualties, one has GSW wounds to the lower abdomen and internal bleeding, the other has arterial bleeding on the upper left leg. Recommend they're flown straight to a hospital with a trauma ward."

"Certainly Captain, I've already uploaded their medical records to Bath hospital, Brigadier Rawlinson has ensured the hospital's theatre there will be put on standby," the AI replied, adding, "I can lift the first two casualties straight away, however I'll have to take you and Lance Corporal Logan separately, two of the three Thumprs are low on fuel, and I don't have the time to refuel them. We must get you all out of here now."

As if to emphasise the lingering threat, the Talon in the clearing began to fire again, someone was still in the woodline.

Mike looked down at the two injured soldiers, Smudge was still unconscious, but Bill was still awake, looking up at them, trying his best to hold out against the pain. Mike looked back up to Baz, before replying.

"Fine, these two first, then Lance Corporal Logan, then myself."

"Sir!" Baz interrupted, "Let me go last, please!"

Mike smiled, placing a hand on the young soldier's shoulder, the pride clear to hear in his voice.

"I think you've done more than your fair share these past few days Baz, now let's get you away and out of this fucking place shall we?"

The NCO looked away ashamedly, as Mike gave the compliment, Mike smiling in reply.

Mike looked away, making it clear it wasn't up for discussion as he looked at the tank, shaking his head sadly at how close they'd come to making it out of there. It would need one hell of a recovery effort to get it out of the tree's and he doubted the Russians would allow them the chance.

As if reading his thoughts, he heard the robotic voice chime in.

"We won't be able to salvage the tank I'm afraid, I have a missile strike ready to destroy it the second you're out of here. I'll make sure it doesn't fall into enemy hands."

"What about the Hornet?" Mike asked, certain the tech would need to be salvaged.

"Damaged beyond repair," the AI replied, "That last attack overloaded its capacitor's and burned the cabling. Now I'm afraid it's only good for laser light shows and discos."

Mike paused for a moment, thinking about what the AI had just said before asking,

"Hang on, where's the missile strike coming from? I didn't think we had anything in the area?"

"We don't. But thankfully the Russians do. I've located a cargo ship sat in the English Channel, sailing under a false flag and loaded with cruise missiles and thinks it's Captain is talking to a General Igor Kuzmin. They're awaiting orders now to fire on my command, I've got it ready to fire on this position just as soon as you're out of here. I'll re-programme the last two missiles as they launch to target the ship, we can't leave that amount of firepower sailing in the Channel.

"How the hell did you manage that?"

"Captain Faulkes, a lady never reveals too much on a first date."

Mike looked up at the cold robotic features of the Talon, a mixture of curiosity and confusion of how to treat Wendi, on the one hand she or it was just a machine, yet on the other, it seemed as if he was chatting to a human being, and he had to remind himself it was a series of codes and programmes, despite Kyle's enthusiasm. But there was no doubt, she, it, or whatever the hell Wendi wanted to call itself, had undoubtedly saved the day.

He saw the dark shadow of the Thumpr overhead, moving slowly into position as it came into view in the clearing, lowering itself towards the ground.

Thinking about what Wendi had just told him, Mike suddenly realised, thoughts rushing into his head.

"The artillery strike just a moment ago. That was you! You fired on the woodline, using the Russians own guns!"

"It was." Wendi replied, adding, "after monitoring the Russians for a few minutes, it was simply a case of mimicking a Colonel Golgolvin, a few co-ordinate changes here and there and the Russian artillery believed he was giving them orders to fire. People should always know who they're talking to, don't you think Captain?" the AI replied, knowingly.

Mike shook his head admiringly as he thought of the irony of it all, remembering how, early on in the invasion, it was the Russians using the same trick to lure out the British units, now the AI had turned the tables. He watched on as the Thumpr settled down onto the ground, the smoke from the forest fires being whipped up as the engine's downdraft reached them.

Wendi's voice called out to him as he ran towards it.

"I've already disabled the security protocols, no need to key a code in." As if expecting a compliment, she added. "You're most welcome Captain."

Mike ignored her, the urgency making him rush as he waited impatiently next to the Thumpr, watching on, as it detached its cargo truck and took off again, hovering 10 feet above the ground. Mike ran underneath it, taking charge of the tracked cargo pallet and driving it over to the casualties. They could hear gunfire and more explosions in the distance, he looked over to the third Talon which began to drive off towards the noise. Seeing him looking over towards the noise Wendi responded.

"Captain Faulkes, it looks like the Russians have begun to see through my ruse. The enemy are already beginning to counterattack in force. I can only hold them off for so long, so might I suggest we hurry things along."

Mike nodded at the Talon as he and Baz tenderly lifted Smudge up and onto the pallet, the soldier giving a slow moan in response as they checked the torniquet again. Mike quickly checked his watch, noting the torniquet had gone on 10 minutes ago. He lifted the bandage, seeing some of the blood had already seeped through it, but not enough to worry him. He looked back over to the Talon.

"Wendi what's the flight time to Bath?"

Captain Faulkes, we don't have time for this, I need to get you all out of here now." the voice responded coldly.

"Wendi, what's the fucking flight time?" he countered, his anger rising at having to repeat himself.

There was a momentary silence as the computer digested what he'd said. Mike knew the AI could solve complex puzzles and algorithms in milliseconds, so for there to be a delay told him the AI was perhaps puzzled, or angry. He was about to ask again when the AI responded.

"Flight time with current metrological conditions is expected to be 7 minutes and 32 seconds."

Fuck, Mike thought to himself, that meant Smudge would probably lose the leg, the torniquet needed to be released in five minutes time. If he were awake then fine, but he was out of it. He looked down at Bill, himself likely to pass out at any second, Mike couldn't rely on him. He looked over to Baz, already making his mind up.

"Baz, change of plan, you're going out on the first flight, I need you to undo the tourniquet in around 5 minutes time."

"Sir! What about Bill? He's injured and needs to get out as well."

Mike held his hands up to quiet the NCO, quickly countering.

"Bill can go out on the second flight, and it won't matter, he'll still be in pain no matter what we do until he gets to hospital. Another two minutes won't make any difference to him. But Smudge will lose his leg if he doesn't go now, and if we undo the torniquet now, and the bleeding restarts on the flight over, then he could die enroute. I can't take that chance. With you onboard with him he stands a better chance of survival than with Bill."

Mike looked over at Bill as he spoke, conscious he was asking the Trooper to endure another few moments of pain and suffering. Bill sat up, his hand resting on the bandage protectively, looking at the unconscious figure of his gunner. Swallowing and wincing again at the pain he shook his head.

"I'm not having him lose his leg because of me Sir, send him with Baz, I'll take the second flight."

Without waiting to argue further, Mike drove the cargo pallet back out underneath the Thumpr, looking over at Baz and patting at the seat next to Smudge.

Baz looked on angrily, his jaw firm at what had just happened. He ran over, shaking his head as he climbed on board the pallet, settling himself on it as best he could, his weapon stowed between them both. Mike smiled disarmingly at him. Mike knew what was going through the NCO's head. He leaned forwards, putting his hand out on the NCO's shoulder, looking him squarely in the eyes.

"Baz, look, I know what you're thinking, you're not happy unless you're the first one through the door and the last to leave, and you don't feel right leaving us behind."

The look on Baz's face told Mike he was right on the money, as Mike continued, conscious time was against them.

"Look, I was the same when I was your age. But you can't always be the one to step forward all the time, remember it's a team game and others need to pull their weight, otherwise all the good soldiers like you will be the first to go and then who's left to pick up the fight? The ones who wouldn't step forwards to begin with. Sometimes, as hard as it is, it's better to lead from the back and let others rush forwards to prove themselves, you've done more than your fair share already."

Baz looked up at him, the fire in his eyes slowly dissipating as the words sunk in, until finally he smiled, offering his hand out in thanks.

Mike looked down at the outstretched hand, gently knocking it aside, shaking his head and smiling.

"This isn't goodbye remember. It's until next time! And we're going to be right behind you. I'll see you back at the hospital."

Baz smiled, nodding in agreement as Mike nodded over to the prostate figure of Smudge.

"Remember, check his torniquet in-"

"3 minutes and 48 seconds." Baz interrupted, looking at his own watch, proving he had been paying attention.

Mike smiled in acknowledgement, confident Smudge was in safe hands as he ran away from the Thumpr that was now coming down on top of him, clearly Wendi had grown tired of waiting. Mike waved as Baz and Smudge disappeared from view, the heavy body of the Thumpr settling down around the pallet momentarily before the engines increased in pitch and lifted them away and out of sight of the trees.

6th Div HQ Bovington

The CinCS burst into the office of the FSB commander, disturbing Terekhov who looked up angrily from the papers he was reading, watching as the General threw his cap onto the desk and sat down.

Terekhov looked up to the young officer standing red faced at the open door, realising the junior officer would have been powerless to stop the General. Terekhov nodded in understanding at the young officer's embarrassment, who quickly closed the door, sealing them inside the office and away from prying ears.

Without saying anything, Terekhov reached over to the side drawer, producing two glasses and the bottle of vodka, pouring two shots each and handing one to the CinCS.

"So, what do I owe the pleasure to now, General?"

The CinCS downed the glass in one, turning it upside down, indicating he did not want a refill as he leaned forwards, the chair creaking on the floor, his eyes narrowing as his finger shot out accusingly.

"You owe me an explanation."

Terekhov smirked, downing his glass and refilling it.

"I owe you nothing, General."

"Bullshit!" the CinCS shot back. "I want to know what you're doing with this Project Houdini. Especially as now I'm being told elements of the FSB have just taken over two wings of Dorchester Hospital using orders written by me. If I'm to admit to signing these orders, then I want to know why. Otherwise, I'll rescind them and have whoever issued them arrested for giving false orders. What's it to be?"

Terekhov leaned back in the chair, his chin resting on his hands as he thought about what the General had just said. He was still a dangerous man, and Terekhov could ill afford the fallout or disruption if the CinCS simply disappeared. After a few moments with the gaze of the General still on him, he nodded, reaching into another drawer, pulling out another folder.

"Rather than me waste time telling you. I think it's best if you read it yourself."

The CinCS looked puzzled as he accepted the folder marked 'Top Secret, FSB level 1 eyes only.'

Terekhov looked up irritably, as instead of the General taking the hint to leave with the folder, he instead pulled the chair closer, producing his reading glasses.

Seeing he wasn't going anywhere soon, Terekhov upended his glass, pouring another two shots and sitting back, waiting patiently as the General read on.

After a few minutes the CinCS looked up, shaking his head in thought. The colour seemed to have drained slightly in his face at what he'd just read.

"You can't seriously be running this now?"

Terekhov leaned forwards, smugly replying with. "We *are* running it now. Project Houdini was up and running five hours after we landed in this shithole."

The CinCS took another glass of vodka, drinking it in one, wincing at the taste as he responded.

"But is this legal? I mean is it sanctioned by Moscow? Is it even humane?"

Terekhov smirked again at what the CinCS was implying, his voice level and calm as he answered the question.

"General, who do you think is paying for all of this? Our tanks, our troops? Where do you think the money is coming from?"

"I'd like to believe that Russian soldiers are being paid for by good hard earned Russian roubles."

"Ahh ever the dreamer." Terekhov shot back, laughing as he took the report back from him and placed it back in the drawer.

The CinCS looked on confused at what Terekhov had just said, the look on his face demanding an answer.

Seeing the look, Terekhov quickly responded.

"General, you may, or may not be aware of this, but Moscow is broke, and our government needs the military to not only do what it does best, but also do something that we've never done before. *Make them money.*"

The General looked on as Terekhov continued.

"Our astute President watched the mercenary boss of Valkir go from being a restaurant owner to a billionaire within five years. Why? Simple, there's money to be made in war, lots of it, providing you know where to look. Do you know how many people in China and India alone, are awaiting organ transplants? Or how many pharmaceutical companies in the far east are crying out for organs to test their products on?"

The CinCS looked on thoughtfully, replying,

"I thought China and India had a plentiful supply of organ parts, and what of the Chinese enforced execution policy? Prisoners to be executed are usually told their organs will be harvested anyway. How can this *Houdini* make Russia money from an already saturated market?"

"It's simple. Westerners live very healthy lazy lives. Most of them drink bottled water, go to the gym, eat fresh food, have access to great healthcare, living long, uneventful, boring lives. Compare this to those people living in the countries you've just mentioned, brought up in slums, working tirelessly, inhaling toxic polluted air, with poor, limited, healthcare, with bad food and bad hygiene. When it comes to organ donations, people want the best, and they're willing to pay for it. And that's where Project Houdini comes in. You want numbers, try these for size. Kidneys 12 million roubles each. Liver 10 million roubles. Heart 40 million roubles. Eyes for a pair 75 million roubles. And we've already got over 25,000 requests from wealthy Chinese and Indian clients all wanting new, healthy donors that want to skip the waiting lists."

The CinCS nodded admirably as the vast sums were read out, it was good money, providing it was going back to Russia and not into some greedy politician's pocket. Seeing the look on his face indicating what he was thinking, Terekhov added,

"Of course, we have overheads, people need to be paid, doctors, support staff, certain government officials, all to grease the wheels of the machine. Why, I'm sure that given what you know now, I could justify with my superiors that you perhaps come onto the payroll?"

The CinCS stood up, shaking his head, replying flatly.

"No. I'm no mercenary. Keep your blood money. I'll not take any money that's not come from our government."

Terekhov smiled at the General, seeing the conflict on the man's face, his own pride stopping him from dipping his fingers into the pot. Terekhov knew he was tempted, but the General's fierce pride was stopping him.

Give it time, Terekhov thought smiling, he'd be back for another bite. They always were.

The CinCS walked over to the window, looking out over the camp, asking,

"Why the rush to get this up and running now though? We're still fighting on the ground and your units nearly been destroyed once already. Why chance it, why not just wait until the fighting is finished?"

"Ahh." Terekhov replied, "A simple case of timing. Some of those people awaiting donors have at best weeks to live. With what they were willing to pay, we felt the need to rush outweighed the need to wait."

"And how do they keep the organs fresh?"

"How do you mean?" Terekhov responded, not understanding the question, now it was his turn to be confused.

The CinCS looked at him, adding,

"The bodies, how do you keep them fresh from the moment they die to getting them to the hospital?"

Still seeing the look of confusion, the CinCS sighed, his eyes wide, replying.

"The bodies. When you collect them from the battlefields, how are you keeping the organs fresh?"

Finally realising what the General was implying, Terekhov shook his head. The old fool, Terekhov thought angrily, he's either not read the report fully or fails to understand how the system worked. That's why he'd seemed so calm about it, he thought they were merely collecting bodies from battlefields, grave robbers.

Terekhov sighed, thinking how best to explain exactly what Houdini involved, when there was a frantic knocking on the door.

"What?" he yelled, angry at being disturbed at such a crucial moment. The door was open before he'd even finished speaking the order.

In the doorway was one of the CinCS staff, red faced and breathing heavily.

"Well?" Terekhov demanded as the soldier ignored him, barging in and running up to the CinCS.

Terekhov waited as the soldier whispered into the CinCS ear, seeing the concerned look on his face, he stood up, wanting to know what was going on.

"General, what is it?" Terekhov demanded, as the CinCS ignored him, chatting animatedly to the soldier.

The soldier turned and ran back out of the room without even acknowledging Terekhov. Now he knew it was serious. He looked back over as the General picked up his cap, about to leave, Terekhov's arm snatching out to stop him.

"General, what is it?"

The CinCS looked down tensely at the arm on his, the threat clear to read. Seeing he'd overstepped the mark, the FSB commander removed his arm, watching the CinCS relax slightly, as finally, disbelief still clear on his voice he said,

"It looks like somehow the Americans and their allies have arrived."

"What! How many?" he asked curiously.

"From the numbers I've just been given, it would appear all of them!"

Wonderland Operations Centre (WOC)

Anyone not talking on a phone, or typing on a keyboard in the ops room, was outside, peering in the conference room as the heated exchange continued. With the room being soundproofed no one could hear what was being said, but they could see from the figures of the CDS and the PM at the table from their body language that whatever was being discussed they were not happy with. The PM stood up, red-faced and shouting, both hands planted firmly on the table as he yelled at the speaker on the telephone. The CDS was sitting back, his face red and sweaty at what he was hearing. Suddenly the PM went quiet, deciding he'd said enough as he sat back down and, resting his hands across his chest, listening in, his expression moody as he rocked his chair sideways.

The CDS looked up, seeing the assembled staff looking in, he shook his head slowly at them, the threat clear to see. As one they all dispersed, disappearing quickly as suddenly everyone found a job to do. Suddenly with a final yell at the speaker the PM stood up, hanging up the phone and charging towards the door, flinging it open, and emerging into the ops room, all eyes on him, not too sure of what to say as the CDS emerged shaking his head. The PM looked back at him, both of them exchanging a look as finally the PM replied, the anger turning to sadness.

"Just get it done please CDS."

The General nodded, watching as the PM went out up the stairs to his upper office away from everyone, clearly wanting to be alone. He waited until his office door had closed before looking to everyone around him, pointing to a giant clock that read 15:52 and raising his voice.

"Right everyone, your attention please!"

He waited for the chatter to die down, except for those on the telephones, everyone was looking at him, people from all walks of the government.

He took a breath, closing his eyes and not quite believing what he was about to order them to do. Shaking his head he firmed his resolve. Knowing it was for the greater good. With renewed energy he opened his eyes, pointing above them to the clock.

"It's now 15:52. I need you to order every military unit, every police unit, in fact any-one carrying a weapon that at 16:00 hours they are to stand down and cease hostilities with the Russ-" he stopped himself, quickly remembering the conversation they had just had, changing what he was about to say with, "Tumats. Cease hostilities with the *Tumats.*"

He sighed as he said that last part, like a dirty secret had just been revealed. He looked on, seeing the confused looks of those around him. Some of them muttered amongst themselves as a Captain looked up, the confusion quickly turning to anger.

"Sir, are you asking us to stand down? Is that it? After everything that's happened, we're giving in, throwing in the towel, already?"

The group all looked to each other muttering, some voicing their concerns.

The CDS shook his head, keeping his voice low, knowing how they all felt, he still felt the same way. But he'd been ordered, the decision had been made.

"We're not giving up people, remember that. We're NEVER giving up, but for now, the PM has ordered a ceasefire, and that's exactly what we've got to do. So come on, we've got less than five minutes, let's get the word out. All units stand down and cease hostilities."

With shaking heads they turned, some punching desks angrily, others sighing in disbelief, some with tear filled eyes, the feeling of helplessness and humiliation clear to see. Somehow despite the American President's proclamation of some form of victory, it didn't feel like it. With his dark and sombre thoughts, the CDS turned and went back into the conference room, wondering if perhaps now it was finally time to surrender his sword, rather than fall on it...

Golgolvin

He opened his eyes slowly, finding himself laying on his back, looking up at the tank's side, wincing as the sunlight streamed through from above as his confused mind tried to replay what had just happened. He'd remembered watching as one by one his men had been butchered on the tank, trying to fend off those metal monsters, he'd tried to rally his men again, but most were dead, and those still breathing had turned to run, ignoring his shouts and commands. He remembered the Sergeant shouting in warning as he'd looked up from reloading the RPG, after his first missile had missed its target. He saw the tracked machine appear in their midst, coming round the side of the tank, its machine gun firing at them both, the Sergeant firing his assault rifle from the hip, taking the full force of the incoming fire as his body fell across the Colonel, shielding him from the incoming rounds. Golgolvin had no idea if it was bravery or sheer coincidence that made the Sergeant fall across him, he remembered the pain as he'd been hit in the leg, quickly forgotten as he'd smashed his head against the tanks side, knocking him out. He had no idea how long he was out for; was it seconds or minutes? He felt the dead weight of the Sergeant resting over him, he heaved at the body, grunting in the effort, wincing against the pain as he saw the gunshot wound on his right leg. Thankfully It was a through and through, the bullet had gone straight in and out again, he'd live. He looked around, seeing only the dead for company, as leaning against the tank's side he looked around him for those damn metal murderers. He was alone, they'd already moved off. He reached inside his assault vest, pulling out the bandage he'd prepared for such an event, quickly and expertly wrapping it around the wound, tying it off tight, clamping his mouth shut against the pain. He looked down at the Sergeant's body, his eyes were open as if still awake, but the neat patch of bullet holes in his chest and the two bullet holes in his forehead told Golgolvin he was anything but. He nodded in thanks, thankful for the Sergeant's bravery and was about to limp away to safety when he heard voices on the other side of the tank. Carefully, he shuffled around the tank, trying to keep the weight off his injured leg. Peering around the edge, he could see one of those metal bastards now standing guard over four enemy soldiers, about 100 metres away, two looked to be injured, one of them, who he guessed to be the commander, was talking to it!

What the, he thought in surprise as the man turned, Golgolvin recognising him immediately. It was the man he'd seen back at the farm all those days ago. Suddenly it dawned on him. His eyes wide as he looked back at the tank, then back at the man, the events of the past days playing out. The man who had warned the camp about the attack, the man who had commanded the tank at Bovington, delaying him. The same man who had hidden the armour back at the farm, then acted the fool with the truck, deceiving him from the helicopter, the man who had been the reason he'd been called back from his forces to identify him, allowing Lebedev to take over, resulting in the doomed attack. This man who had been on the tank, killing his forces that morning, and he couldn't understand how yet, but he knew, the artillery strike that had just decimated his unit, it was all linked back to him. *He* was responsible, *this* was the man. Right from the moment Golgolvin had first landed on English soil it had been this bastard, at every turn thwarting him. He was the reason his men were all dead, he was the reason his mission had failed. *Him*. His nemesis.

"You! It was always you!" he spat out venomously, looking around at the bodies of his brave soldiers.

Clenching his jaw against the pain, he silently watched on, as overhead three large helicopter type aircraft were hovering, to him they resembled big black beetles, like nothing he'd seen before. He watched on as one came in, landing in the clearing. He watched them carry one of the wounded towards it, the intention clear. So, they were thinking of escaping, he thought, already seeing the loaded RPG on the floor. He slowly leaned over, his leg exploding in pain as he bent down to pick it up, knowing he only had one rocket left. He picked it up, smiling vengefully at his plan. He'd let them think they were safe, wait for that bastard to get on his big black flying beetle, thinking he was going home to tea and medals then blow him out of the sky. The thought of the vengeance to come for his men and his friend warmed him, as Golgolvin slowly raised the RPG and aimed.

Whiskey Three-Zero

Already the second Thumpr was hovering nearby, eagerly awaiting its cargo.

Mike ran to Bill, helping to lift him up, the soldier moaning softly, as the gunfire began to get ever closer. Not wanting to waste any time messing about with the cargo pallet, Mike had decided he'd carry Bill to the Thumpr. He gently walked the wounded soldier out to the landing zone, helping him take the weight off his weakened legs, with Bill's arm over his shoulder, as he spoke into his ear.

"Just us two now Bill, and to think it all started with you standing there washing those bloody cups." Mike began jovially, trying to distract the wounded soldier from the pain and sounds of fighting around them. Bill looked over at the smoking tank sat opposite them and grimaced in return, fighting the pain that coursed through him.

"You're one of the bravest soldiers I've ever had the pleasure to work with Bill, you know that?" Mike continued, as they both watched the Thumpr begin its approach into the clearing. Bill looked back, finally managing a smile as he replied.

"And you're one of the strangest officers I've ever met...Sir."

Mike smiled in reply, as Bill added, nodding back towards the tank.

"I knew you'd get us out of there, right from the very beginning I'd been telling Smudge you'd do it, and now at last you have."

"*We* have." Mike corrected him softly, looking proudly at him, continuing. "*We* did it Bill, it's never a single person's game, always a team effort. I couldn't have got this far if it hadn't been for you all. Never forget that. No matter what happens, never forget what you've done these past few days, you should be proud of that."

The Thumpr landed softly, its body lifting up and away, the same as the first as it hovered close by. Mike walked the wounded soldier over, listening as Bill, through clenched teeth, began to reel off the events, his voice soft and weak.

"Proud of what Sir? Driving us into another vehicle, or how about not having the handbrake on properly? Or how about..."

"Hey, wakey wakey!" Mike interrupted, gently shaking him, seeing Bill's head begin to droop and his eyes close as he fought to stay awake. Bill smiled weakly, his head coming back up and his eyes barely open as he looked at Mike, who continued proudly.

"How about the only tank driver on record to be credited with destroying an enemy vehicle without ever firing a shot. Or, how about the bravery of turning round to rescue all those infantry lads in Bovington, driving miles through enemy held territory. Or helping save the lives of fourteen people on a truck destined for execution. Or how about just now, what you did back there, saving the life of a colleague by having to endure more pain and hardship just so Smudge could get away? There's a lot of people still alive because of you, never forget that."

Bill nodded in response, a weak smile spreading across his face at what Mike had just said, his head beginning to sag as the pain began to overwhelm him again. Mike looked down at the bandages, seeing the dark black blood seeping through them again, the bleeding had re-started. He could feel the Trooper begin to weaken, his weight becoming heavier as his legs began to lose their strength.

"Stay with it Bill, not much longer." Mike spoke softly, as he gently lowered the soldier onto the pallet. He was about to walk away when Bill's arms shot out, grabbing his, stopping him.

"Mike....Thank you. For everything." Bill spoke softly, the words mumbled as the pain began to swell through his body in waves. Mike swallowed hard, the lump suddenly evident in his throat and his eyes welling up, his emotions almost overtaking him.

"No, Bill, thank you..." Mike whispered, but the soldier couldn't hear him anymore, he'd finally passed out. Mike moved away, standing next to the Talon and wiping away the tears that had begun to fall, as the Thumpr came back down, settling onto the pallet. He turned away, shielding his eyes as the dust and smoke blew at them as the motors increased, watching the Thumpr slowly begin to rise.

Wendi's voice broke the silence.

"Why did you lie to him?"

"What do you mean?" Mike asked, his eyes fixed firmly on the Thumpr as it began to rise, the tears flowing down his cheeks unashamedly.

"Trooper Hickok's wound locations are consistent with a liver wound, thick black blood, low heart rate, high blood pressure, body temperature increasing. I'd say there's a 98 percent chance that Trooper Hickock has suffered severe trauma to his liver. That's normally a non-survivable wound, but when you include the internal bleeding, his chances of survival are less than 5 percent. You knew that, hence the sadness in your eyes. That's why you delayed sending him back, you knew the odds-"

"The odds on losing both of them were far greater than if I sent Bill on his own." Mike interrupted, his voice almost breaking with sadness. Fighting back the tears, he continued, his voice bitter with regret.

"I lied to him because sometimes Wendi, it's best for people not to know the truth, better to give them hope and a light to cling to. I made that decision, and that's my torch to carry. Besides, there's the slim chance he might still make it. He's young and tough, I've seen worse odds."

"Given the damage and rough approximation of the wound, and blood seepage, I give him no more than 3 minutes to live. With a flight time of 7 minutes and 32 seconds to get to hospital, and the time needed to prep for surgery, he'll be dead long before that. I calculate his odds as 572 to one."

"How *nice* it must be, to be a machine without feeling." Mike said flatly back, with a look of disdain as he stepped forwards away from the Talon. He craned his head back, shielding his eyes from the sun, looking up as the Thumpr began to clear the treeline, hoping and praying that Wendi and the odds were wrong.

Suddenly Wendi's voice squawked out of the Talon in warning.

"Captain Faulkes! I'm detecting a mass-" He turned in surprise as the voice cut off abrubtly, watching as the Talon began to shut down before his eyes, the sensor dome blinked off and went silent as the weapon's rack lowered and the whole frame lowered to its off position.

"Wendi?" Mike asked, his look of anger changing to confusion as he walked towards the Talon. Suddenly he felt alone as he heard the whoosh from behind him, followed by the screech of a rocket, turning just in time to see the flaming RPG warhead slam into the body of the Thumpr just as it began to pitch forwards to accelerate away.

"NO!" he cried out, watching in shock, as the rocket slammed through the lightly armoured body, exploding internally, instantly turning the two-tonne vehicle into a flaming inferno, the blue, yellow flame arcing out as the hydrogen fuel tanks ruptured, adding to the mayhem. His head shot over to where the rocket had come from, looking over to see a lone soldier stood near the tank, holding the smoking RPG launcher. The soldier looked over at him triumphantly, grinning savagely as Mike stood in shock, disbelieving what he was witnessing. The two only looked at each other for a fleeting moment, then both were forced to dive for cover, as the flaming debris began to rain down around them, setting the ground alight.

Mike dived for cover in one of the shell holes, narrowly avoiding a flaming piece of the motor as it crashed beside him.

For a second, he lay there, as a mixture of emotions raced through him, the events playing out again in slow motion as his confused mind tried to process what had happened. The rocket hitting the fuselage, the explosion, the debris, that man, the grin. *That* grin. There was no doubt now, Bill was certainly dead, even if he'd survived his wounds, the rocket's explosion and the shrapnel plus the fall and the fire would have certainly killed him. Mike yelled in anger, his fists punching the ground in frustration, he'd been so close...they'd been so close to getting away with it.

He looked up, watching as the third Thumpr now began its landing cycle and was coming to pick him up. Mike looked over to where the enemy soldier was hiding, he couldn't see him, but he knew he was lying there in wait. Mike was contemplating on running for the aerial vehicle, to attempt an escape, it was so tantalisingly close. But he couldn't get the thought of Bill out of his head. The logic of how he felt was almost too silly to contemplate, he'd put him in the Thumpr knowing he would probably die, but then there had been hope. And the way that hope had been yanked from Bill, with one pull of a trigger enraged him. Suddenly a manic anger began to fill him, a blood lust that he couldn't put down or lock away any longer. He wanted revenge, he could almost taste it. He let rage engulf him, allowing the anger to wash away his tiredness, wash away the pain, wash away the hurt. Suddenly his eyes took on a deadly focus, a feeling he'd put away long ago, for fear of hurting the ones he loved. Now he let it surface, almost welcoming the suffering, all the pain, all at once, filling him. With steely eyed determination he reached over, picking up the assault rifle, the pressed steel body, cold and unforgiving, matching Mike's mood. He aimed at the Thumpr, firing three rounds in quick succession, aiming carefully so the rounds hit the body, knowing it was lightly armoured to small arms fire. Just as he thought, the self-defensive measures on the vehicle took over and it aborted it's landing sequence, accelerating quickly away and heading away to safety, taking with it Mike's only chance of escape. He didn't care about any of that right now, he just wanted vengeance for Bill.

He knelt, the flames licking around him as he looked for his target. He could see the soldier's head above one of the fallen tree trunks, looking back at him, still the same grin, the soldier was beckoning him over, wanting to fight, shouting in Russian.

Mike grinned savagely back, talking to himself, "Okay mate, you want to play? Then let's fucking play!"

Aurora Operations Centre RAF Colerne Bath

Peter looked on confused at the blank screen, looking over to one of the technicians. "What just happened?"

"I don't know Sir; we're still looking into it." the engineer sweating, added, "Might be a communication fault with the hardware."

Peter looked upwards, with arms folded he raised his voice to be heard.

"Wendi! Give me a status report, why did we just loose Talon Four's feed?"

Almost immediately the AI responded, her voice echoing off the hanger's interior.

"I'm still checking Brigadier, evaluating now..."

The screen displaying two T-80 tanks suddenly turned black, another Engineer calling out.

"We've just lost one of the Wasp feeds!"

Peter bit his lip in irritation, shaking his head angrily and stepping forwards towards the screens. It had been going so well, but something was happening, something out of their control. Suddenly another of the feeds went offline, as Wendi's voice came back on.

"Brigadier, I am detecting large levels of mass ionisation and tachyons in the last known vicinity of Talon Four and Wasps Three and Six."

Kyle looked up from his laptop, concern on his face as the Brigadier looked at him in confusion.

"Kyle? What does that mean?" he asked, as Kyle replied, his eyes wide in alarm,

"Electro Magnetic Pulse! Someone's taking out our equipment with an EMP weapon!"

"What?" Peter replied, the surprise clear to hear. "I didn't think the Russians had that capability?"

"Someone does!" Kyle replied in warning, as another of the screens went black.

Peter made the decision quickly, shouting out.

"Wendi, what's the status on the Thumprs? Is Captain Faulkes out of the area yet?"

"Thumprs One and Three are inbound now to Bath hospital, however Thumpr Two is down."

"Down?" Peter asked, adding, "Elaborate?"

"I'm afraid that right now I can't, all my attempts to get eyes on that area are resulting in us losing more of the Wasps."

As the AI spoke, another one of the Wasp feeds shut down, prompting a curse from Kyle.

Suddenly the phone rang, all eyes looked to it as David stepped forwards, picking it up and quickly answering, cradling the phone in the crook of his neck he turned to look at Peter.

"Boss, it's the CDS, wants to speak to you, urgent."

Peter took the phone and nodded in thanks as he turned towards the screens. Everyone else watched on at the one-sided conversation. The Brigadier's voice rising as he became angry at what was being discussed. Finally, his voice lowered as whatever the CDS had just said began to get through to him, the conversation ending with Peter saying.

"Ok, James. Well, if you're certain... Okay, understood."

They all watched as Peter replaced the handset, his face flush with colour, clearly angry.

He looked up, barking out, "Wendi, mission recall. Disengage everything. Return to base."

David and Kyle exchanged puzzled looks, as Wendi's boomed through.

"Brigadier I still haven't located Captain Faulkes or confirmed the status of Thumpr Two. Confirm your order to RTB?"

"God dammit Wendi! Must I repeat myself?" the Brigadier yelled out, his anger causing everyone to look up. Seeing their looks he closed his eyes, taking a deep breath and composing himself as a few moments later he continued.

"Apologies everyone, not like me at all," he looked around the room before adding, his voice softer. "yes Wendi, immediate recall, disengage on all units. Bring them home."

He turned and left the room, for a second everyone watched him go, then David took charge, barking out the orders as everyone sprung to life, still with no idea what was truly going on. Leaving them all to it, David and Kyle left the room, watching as the Brigadier walked over to his portacabin and slammed the door shut. Kyle was about to take the first step towards it, when David stopped him with an outstretched arm.

"I think the boss is hinting he wants to be left alone." David warned, Kyle nodding glumly in realisation.

"Come on," David replied, "Still lots to do. Let the Boss tell us in his own time." He turned to go back to the operations room, ushering Kyle along with an outstretched hand.

Kyle gave one last look at the portacabin before turning to follow, thinking to himself, whatever had got Peter angry would have to wait...for now.

Mike – Location Unknown

Mike tried to open his eyes, his vision blurred and hazy as his eyelids felt heavy, as if held vice- like with glue. His mind was foggy and confused, he tried to make sense of what was happening, like a dream with no beginning he couldn't understand how he'd got there. He knew he was lying down; he could feel the hardness of the mattress beneath his back. A bright piercing light finally shone through as his eyes opened a fraction of an inch, shutting again as the pain stabbed through his head, like an ice pick driven deep.

He tried to speak, the words coming in a whisper, mumbled and incoherent, his mind knowing what to say, but the words losing themselves on the way. Around him he could hear a multitude of different noises, a mixture of mechanical clicks, electronic beeps, and motors whirring, with a soft humming noise in the distance, his ears struggling to pick out the sounds.

He tried to move his body, his arms and legs felt heavy and numb, as if pinned down, his mind struggling to comprehend the lack of movement. He attempted to lift his head up, straining hard at his immobility, falling backwards as the exhaustion overtook him. He felt so tired and couldn't understand why.

He opened his eyes again, fighting against the pain, his eyelids opening a fraction more as the light streamed through, shadows and hazy shapes danced before his eyes, people were moving around him, everything looked white, the lights dazzling almost blinding him. He blinked and closed his eyes again as the pain returned, brought on by his attempts to see. He closed his eyes and waited a short moment for the pain to recede, using the time to instead rely on his other senses to make sense of his surroundings. He felt the air cold on his face, suddenly his brain could register he was wearing an oxygen mask, air was being forced into his mouth, which was why he couldn't speak. He tried to move his arms again, his mind willing himself to do it but they remained stubbornly where they were, as if pinned in place. He relaxed himself, resting for a few moments before trying again, this time he concentrated on just lifting a finger, willing it to lift, the frustration and feeling of helplessness coursing through him. Despite his best attempts, he couldn't do it, and out of frustration and anger he forced his eyes to open wider, ignoring the pain, as this time he began to see more around him. Now he could see the shapes come into focus, the shadows moving around him were people, all moving with purpose, all wearing surgical scrubs. Now it made sense to him, he was in a hospital bed, whatever had happened someone had got him to hospital. But who? How? His mind kept trying to think back, to remember what had happened, fuzzy images came to the fore. He remembered a tank, there was a battle, was he fighting someone? He blinked furiously as someone stepped in close with a light, shining it into his eyes, he tried to move his head, but nothing came of it, it remained where it was, as if firmly clamped in place. The light moved off, replaced by someone stepping into his view, a face came into focus, wearing a surgical mask, he could see the cloth of the mask moving as if they were speaking, but he couldn't hear, or understand what was being said. The person kept looking up to someone else, their head nodding as if in deep conversation.

He tried to speak again, the mask making it difficult to reply, his head moving slightly as he regained a small amount of movement. His eyes looked upwards, trying to see who the other person was, his brain still trying desperately to piece together what had happened. More images began to come into focus, as if a slideshow he began to see memories coming in, but in what order or what context he still couldn't yet understand. He saw a tank on fire, an explosion, flames all around him, a man with a rocket launcher, then a grenade landing next to him, a soldier dressed in black stood over him, wearing a gas mask, more soldiers all laughing at him, pointing, jeering him. Someone had kicked him, then a helicopter, he remembered being loaded onto a helicopter. Others had sat watching him as he lay there. He remembered that at least.

His thoughts were interrupted as he saw the person in the mask step away, another person came into view, wearing an army uniform, looking down at him, smiling. Something about the smile, about the face was familiar, but he couldn't place it. The figure stepped out of view as behind him he saw the sign on the wall, reading it aloud in his head.

"Dorchester."

I'm in Dorchester? He tried to make sense of it all, to piece things together. How, why?

His eyes scanned frantically around as someone behind him took charge of the bed, it must have been wheeled, perhaps a stretcher or gurney as they wheeled him towards a set of drab green double doors, the bottom of the bed was about to hit the double doors, he was expecting to feel the jolt, but there was none, instead the doors opened automatically, the sounds of the room outside disappearing as he entered another room, cold, quiet, clinical, the walls an immaculate white, with a huge lamp overhead dazzling him. He tried desperately to move his head, managing perhaps an inch, turning slightly, seeing the operating theatre he was being wheeled into.

Suddenly his eyes opened wide in alarm as the nightmare he'd seen before began to resurface, the dark thoughts and images of a crematorium truck flashing through his mind. It all made sense now. He'd been captured, that's what he'd been seeing in his mind before, the Russians must have captured him alive, then brought him here by helicopter, to Dorchester Hospital. He was about to have his organs removed! He felt his heartbeat faster, his pulse racing as the adrenaline began to pump through him, he tried again to move his arms, he felt a slight twitch in his finger, whatever the Russians had used must be strong, he thought, as he looked around the room hopefully. He saw the operating table nearby, the surgical instruments glittering in the overhead lights, perhaps he could use an arm, to grab one, to fend off the surgeons as he cut his bonds free. Then he could get to the corridor, try to hide whilst his limbs recovered, safe enough to carry him before making it outside to a car, driving away, getting to safety, seeing Kate again. Kate...His mind seemed to clear suddenly of any thoughts of escape as he looked up at the two surgeons standing over him watching down, one held a syringe, plunging the liquid into the drip above him, administering more of the sedative. He could feel the cold liquid passing through his body, Mike tried to think of something, anything, knowing it was almost over, his mind was beginning to cloud over as the sedative took hold, so this was what it would be like to die, he thought bitterly, and thinking to Kate, he'd let her down, he hoped she could understand, he loved her so much. He wished he could see her just one more time. He fought to keep his eyes open, knowing these were his last moments, fighting for every second as he clung on, desperate to keep Kate in his thoughts, wanting his last images of the world to be one of happiness, not regret, anger or hate. He thought back to a happier time, a road trip, a weekend away in their car, full of love, laughter and happiness. The sun on her face, her infectious smile, how she wiped her hair away from her face. She looked so happy, he too was so happy.

Her hair and her beautiful green eyes were Mike's last conscious thought as finally the darkness came for him, and he let it take him into the abyss, still wearing the smile of happier times, of love, of Kate...

15

Is This The End

Yeovil

Patty looked through the binoculars at the ground ahead of them, the front lines clearly marked by the scars of battle. Blackened, twisted hulks of vehicles littered the area, the ground pockmarked with shell holes as the rubble of over thirty buildings lay shattered over the ground, the twisted skeletal ruins of smoking metal girders pointing upwards like fingers in the sky. Ahead of them was the outskirts of Yeovil, no more than 400metres away, the first of the British positions, so tantalisingly close. All they had to do now was cross the small patch of no man's land. Patty could see the Russian positions up on the hill, the heads of the infantry peering over their shell holes and pointing over to them. He looked behind him, seeing Jonah with the same look of concern as he had. He checked his watch again, the time read 16:15. The last thing he'd heard from Wendi, their voice of salvation, was that all military units, both British and Russian were now standing down, and that a ceasefire was to be in effect from 16:00 hrs. But that had been nearly 20 minutes ago, and all further attempts to talk to her had been met with silence, as if she'd just disappeared. Slowly, the convoy pushed on, Patty keeping a watchful eye on the ground ahead of them, whilst watching and praying the Russians weren't going to start shooting. It could still after all, be a ruse, a trick to draw them out. He saw three Russian ambulances nearby, the crews dismounted and picking up the remains of bodies from the ground. Two of them were swigging heavily from a bottle, their actions sluggish and carefree. They waved at him as they passed, which caused him to breathe easier, if they were stood out in the open, drunk and without a care, then perhaps the ceasefire was real after all.

Within minutes they were across no-man's land and back amongst their own side, a mixture of troops and armed civilians all looking back at them with soot coated faces, eyes red rimmed, some waving in acknowledgment from their foxholes and hastily dug trenches. Some looked on wide eyed at the damage to the vehicles, others just stared, their ordeal through combat clearly leaving its mark. He ordered Changa to keep going, giving him directions to head to the town centre, remembering their orders were still to link up with Colonel Young.

The Colonel hadn't been hard to find, he'd been stood outside the makeshift command post, directing and ordering the troops around, clearly animated at the ceasefire, making the most of the time enabling him to re-group and re-organise, everyone having no idea how long it would last for.

Patty had at first thought the Colonel would have been happy to see the vehicles and was expecting to be put to use straight away in the defence of the town. Instead, the Colonel had congratulated them on making it this far, then ordered him to continue through the town, north towards Yeovilton Airbase. There he would rendezvous with a Major Richards, who would give him further orders.

As they'd headed through the town, they passed the first friendly armour they'd seen since it had all begun. Tanks and Warriors sat in freshly dug in positions, hidden around the town, away from the prying eyes of the Russians. Clearly the town had a reserve force ready to deploy where needed. Patty looked on moodily, his anger beginning to rise as he thought of the help they could have given his unit earlier, perhaps even given Mike. He'd been told, as they all had, that they were the only units in the area able to help Yeovil. That was the reason why they'd risked it all to travel during the daylight hours. Clearly, they'd been lied to, and he shook his head angrily, wondering what else they hadn't been told.

The convoy passed through five military checkpoints, all the MP's manning them stopping the convoy and staring at the damage, before giving them more directions and waving them through. Finally, after 20 minutes of driving, they approached the airbase. The troops manning the front gate let them through, the damage and state of the Warriors causing more soldiers on the base to point and stare. Patty could see the different coloured berets, Commandos, Infantry, Artillery, all running about with a sense of purpose, some digging in defences, some filling sandbags, others carrying boxes of ammunition and supplies, reams of barbed wire being dragged out as the base was placed on a war footing. Ceasefire or not, Colonel Young was taking no chances, clearly making the most of the time to by building up the defences at the airbase. Near to the runway, protected by sandbags, were five Apache helicopters, he'd wondered if any of them were the Gunslinger callsigns that had helped them earlier on.

In the distance they saw someone frantically waving at them, Changa directing his driver to head in that direction. They pulled up alongside, the figure walking up, looking up at the convoy. He walked up to Changa who merely pointed behind him towards Patty, the soldier then walking up to Patty's vehicle, his eyes appraising the damage as he whistled softly.

"You've been in the bloody wars!

Patty pulled his headset away and leaned over, in no mood for small talk, identifying the soldier by the Sergeant's rank slide.

"Sarge, we were told to report here? I'm Corporal Patterson." he questioned, the Sergeant nodding in reply.

"That's right Corporal, welcome to Royal Naval Air Station Yeovilton. Now, get your unit parked up over there, we'll send people to help shortly. You got any wounded?"

Patty shook his head slowly, looking back out the way they'd just come, his expression glum as he waved his arm over the sad procession of three vehicles.

"A few minor injuries that's all."

The Sergeant nodded in reply, adding,

"Ok, well the medics will be over shortly, get them checked over just to be safe. Off you go then."

With a nod of the head, he indicated the conversation was over and walked away.

So that's it, Patty thought, no welcome committee? With disappointment etched over his face, he pointed over to Changa where he wanted them to go, leaning backwards in the turret as both vehicles lurched away in a cloud of diesel smoke. Behind them Jonah stayed close, as all three vehicles headed across the grass airfield to where they'd been told to stop, closing up one behind the other.

Patty jumped down from the turret of the Warrior, taking his helmet off, itching his sweat-soaked hair and watching as the back door of his vehicle opened, the occupants inside all stepping out and stretching their legs wincing against the sunlight that was hanging low on the horizon. Ahead of him, Changa's crew were dismounting, the big Fijian throwing his helmet off on to the vehicle's front decks and walking towards him, as Jonah's vehicle parked up behind him. The crews walked up to each other, shaking hands and hugging in jubilation at having finally made it. Some had looks of disbelief, others were numb with shock, cigarettes being lit with trembling fingers as they tried to process what they'd just been through. They looked behind them, expecting to see the tank with them, the looks on their faces saying more than they did.

After only a few moments the questions began, Patty stood in the middle of the group as everyone tried to make sense of what had happened as they crowded around him, causing him to back up against the Warrior.

Catherine spoke the loudest, her voice of authority cutting over the noise of the others.

"Patty where are we? What happened to Mike? Who the hell was Wendi?"

The others went quiet as Patty looked around them all, his eyes locking onto Spider, expecting his friend to step forward to take charge. Instead, Spider looked ashamedly at the floor, the events from earlier still raw in his mind. Patty was on his own.

"Look everyone, all I know is that we're in Yeovilton Airbase, we've got help coming shortly and I don't know who this Wendi is, or who she works for."

"And the Captain?" Rachel asked, her head cocked as she added, "Where's the others? Where's the tank gone?"

Patty stared back at her, his gaze focused, his jaw set as finally he replied.

"You heard it all play out on the radio the same as me Rachel. For now, let's hope they're all alive and well.

The group all nodded speculatively as Whippet spoke up.

"Corporal what the hell were all those vehicles doing parked up in Yeovil? I thought we were the only armour in the area? How come they didn't come out to help us?"

"Yeah, how come?" Reaper added. Some of them shaking their heads and muttering amongst themselves as Patty spoke loudly, causing the chatter to stop.

"I don't pretend to know all the answer guys, but I do know we're here, we're safe, and finally we're amongst our own. Let's not lose sight of that."

Everyone looked around at each other, nodding in agreement as a convoy of trucks and land rovers pulled alongside them, the tailgates opening with a crash, troops jumping out, pulling boxes of equipment off with them. He watched as two figures jumped out of the lead vehicle and strode confidently towards them, drawing curious gazes from the group. One looked to be a Major, the other a Warrant Officer.

Both walked up to the group, the Major's voice booming out as his eyes searched the group.

"Who's in charge here?"

Patty looked over again at Spider, who merely looked away. Taking a deep breath, he finally stepped forwards, standing to attention, fighting the urge to salute now that they were in the field.

"That's me Sir, Corporal Patterson."

The Major's gaze was fierce as he looked the Corporal up and down, before finally nodding his head.

"Ok relax, Corporal. My name's Major Richards, and this is WO2 Yackers, he's my Squadron Sergeant Major."

The Sergeant Major's gaze was on all of them, eyeing them up as the Major continued.

"Are you all from callsign Whiskey Three-Zero?"

Patty was about to answer no, quickly remembering, that Whiskey Three-Zero was the callsign that Mike had been using on the other radio. Stopping himself from saying Tango Two-One, he replied.

"We are Sir, that's correct."

The Major nodded, satisfied he had the right unit before replying. "The first three trucks behind me are the REME team, they're here to help get your vehicles back up to strength. Once we've finished here, I'll need you to get your vehicle crews to collate a list of vehicle faults and spares needed to the Sergeant Major, he'll then begin organising the work parties."

Patty watched as WO2 Yackers looked at the vehicles, his expert eye already assessing the damage, no doubt already thinking ahead of the work involved as the Major continued.

"The fourth and fifth truck are here to take away the following people. As I call your names please stand over to my left." The Major pulled out a notebook and began to read off the names, looking up as some of the group acknowledged and walked over to the side. When he'd finished, all the police officers, the three Royal Engineers and Linda were stood away from the group. He counted them against the names, realising he was still three short of the twelve total.

"There's three missing. Where's the others?" he asked, Patty quickly replying.

"They didn't make it Sir."

The Major nodded sympathetically as he put away his notebook and waved over to another group of soldiers nearby, who now walked towards them. All were heavily armed and wearing body armour and helmets. Seeing the concerned looks on the new group he added,

"Relax people, it's just your protection detail. You're all to be immediately transferred back to headquarters for a debrief."

"Some food would be nice." Catherine shot back angrily, as one of the soldiers disarmed her of the assault rifle she carried, making it safe and handing it to a colleague, who looked on appreciatively at the group. Clearly, by the weapons they carried and the looks on their faces they'd been in the thick of it.

Major Richard's pointed to the Chinook helicopter in the distance, it's rotors already turning.

"I'm sorry Chief Superintendent, but I've been ordered to get you away as quickly as I can. It's less than 20 minutes flight time. I promise they'll have food and drink waiting for when you arrive."

Seeing they were leaving, Linda rushed away, disappearing into the back of one of the Warrior's for a moment, walking back out, carrying a large computer desktop. Patty recognizing it as the one discarded on the floor at the field hospital. His forehead creased in surprise as he asked,

"You managed to get that out?"

She patted it lovingly, taking out the two phones that she still had in her pocket. Patty recognised the screensaver on one, asking,

"Is that-"

"Mike's," she interrupted, explaining, "back at the facility, he gave me his phone to record with, the battery level on mine was too low. Between the footage on his phone and what we've got on this big beauty, we should have enough evidence to show the world what's really going on out there."

She looked at Mike's phone, unlocking the screen with the code he'd given here, looking at the picture of him and his wife.

"Pretty lady." she remarked, looking up and adding, "Do you think he's-"

"I don't know Linda. I don't know." Patty interrupted, shaking his head exhaustedly.

The Major frowned, stepping forwards as he recognised the face on the phone screen, snatching the phone.

"HEY!" Linda shot out.

"Where did you get this?" he demanded, brandishing the phone to the group, his eyes suspicious.

"Calm down Major, it belonged to Captain Faulkes." She replied, holding out her hand for the phone.

"Captain Faulkes?" the Major asked, his face bewildered. "He was with you? Mike Faulkes? This man?" he held the phone back up, showing Linda and Patty the image again.

Patty nodded in acknowledgment, not quite understanding what had un-nerved the Major.

"Yes, Sir, *Captain* Mike Faulkes, he was in charge of our unit. He's the reason we made it this far. He came back for us after it all went to shit at Bovington."

"You've come from Bovington?" the Major asked, his voice full of surprise, adding, "I thought you all came from Tidworth, your flashes, your unit, you're with the Regiment of Fusiliers, based in Tidworth?"

"Yes, our unit's based there Sir, or at least it was, *we* were all down in Bovington conducting refresher training. We were left behind in the mad dash out the gate."

Patty watched as the Major looked over to WO2 Yackers, who was open-mouthed at the realisation of where Patty and his unit had come from.

Major Richard's eyes darted around the group, the confusion clear to see, as he tried to grasp what had happened to his friend.

"Hang on, when you say he came back for you, with what?"

Linda interrupted his questioning, her hand still outstretched.

"Look Major, I appreciate you've got questions. But that phone and this computer contain sensitive material and evidence crucial to proving what the Russians are up to. We've already sacrificed a lot of good people to make sure it's made it back here safely. I must demand that you hand it back immediately. Must I remind you that I'm under orders directly from the Chief of the Defence Staff..."

He looked at her, her naming of the CDS caused him to nod in understanding as to its importance as he handed back the phone. His questions would have to wait for now. Looking up he waved over to two of the RMP's pointing to the computer.

"You two, see that this is loaded onto the transport along with the others. It's highly important so handle with the utmost care. Don't let it out of your sight.

With infinite care they carried it over to one of the trucks, lifting it up as the group began to say their goodbyes.

Patty smiled, the grin more of a grimace as one by one they all came over to shake his hand, thanking him for the past four days. He stood dazed, thinking to himself had it only been four days? It had felt like they'd been out there for weeks. The engineer team wished them all luck, sharing some banter with the others, one of them giving Reaper the finger and laughing at some private joke between the two of them as he walked away. Patty didn't feel like smiling, he felt numb and detached, somehow disconnected from everything going on around him. He shook Arnie and Catherine's hands, wishing them both the best. Although they were smiling, he could still feel their anger that Patty had helped Mike to drag them away. He felt a flush of anger himself, thinking, who were they to judge him? They hadn't seen what he had, only three people truly knew the horror of what had gone on back at the facility. He watched them turn to go, the final person standing there was Linda who could see the effect that Catherine and Arnie had on him. She opened her arms to hug him, her smile thin lipped as she came close, both sharing a look of understanding as she whispered into his ear.

"Don't you worry Patty. I'll make sure that by this time tomorrow the whole fucking world see's what we saw. They'll understand why Mike did what he did. We at least owe him that."

Patty kept her close, enjoying the feel of having her close by as he struggled to fight angry thoughts, trying to keep them suppressed. After a few moments he felt calm enough to let her go. Nodding and smiling at her, surprised to see her welling up. He'd always thought of her as cold and calculating. Now here she was, showing everyone, she did indeed have emotions, and they weren't always about herself it appeared.

Realising she'd let her mask slip, she quickly wiped away a tear, firing back with,

"These damn bloody little flies! Always going for your eyes when you least expect it."

Patty smiled, deciding not to ruin the ruse, as she turned to the tall RMP sergeant behind her, who cleared his throat to indicate they were out of time.

"Sergeant, what's your name?"

"I'm Sergeant Mahony Ma'am. I'm to be your escort. I'm sorry to break up the good-byes but we need to go. Do you have any personal belongings?"

"What you see is all I got," she replied, mimicking a Southern American accent as she indicated for him to lead the way, turning for one final look at Patty, she mouthed the words silently.

"Thank you."

As she walked away, Patty looked over, noticing Spider was standing moodily by the back of the Warrior glaring back at him.

Was he jealous, Patty wondered, remembering the way Spider had been flirting with the journalist. He looked on as Rachel stepped forwards to chat to the Major.

"Sir, am I on the list?"

"Who are you?" he enquired, taking out the notebook again and checking the list as she spoke.

"I'm Corporal Nock, I was sent down on the helicopter with Major Tristan Phelps and Corporal Jackson. I was there with you the night we pulled out of the camp. You left me with the GSM if you remember."

The Major clicked his fingers in recognition and pointed at her.

"Of course! I knew I'd seen you before! Where is the GSM, is he here as well?"

He looked up expecting to see the man.

Rachel looked at the floor sadly, shaking her head. "I'm sorry Sir, but he was killed when we made our escape."

"Oh," the Major replied, looking over to WO2 Yackers. Up to that moment they'd both hoped the GSM had managed to make it out.

"And Corporal Jackson? Where is she?" he asked hopefully.

Rachel shook her head again, fighting to hold back the grief as she replied softly.

"She didn't make it either. We had her buried at a farm."

"Oh," he replied sympathetically, adding, "well I'm sorry, but you're not on the list to go, so for now I guess you stay with Corporal Patterson."

She nodded in reply, walking back amongst the unit as the others watched the lucky few go, looking on as the group climbed aboard the trucks followed by their new chaperones, pulling up the tailgates as the trucks drove off towards the Chinook. Already its rotors were fully spinning, with the engines spooled up, waiting to take them.

The Major stepped closer, looking at the Sergeant Major.

"Over to you, Sergeant Major."

"Right Sir," he growled, turning to the teams behind him, his voice loud.

"Right then, everyone on you go, let's get these vehicles fit and ready for action."

Patty moved away, about to issue orders to his waiting troops when the Major came closer and barred his way.

"Not you Corporal. I've got some questions for you."

Patty looked down at the arm across his chest, feeling the strength and intensity of the man. Even without wearing the rank of an officer, Patty was under no illusion this man wasn't the sort that was used to hearing the word no.

Nodding in acknowledgment he looked over at Changa.

"Lance Corporal Changayaty, you know what to do. Let's get everyone mucking in."

The Sergeant Major looked over at Spider, seeing him standing idly there.

"You there! Corporal, come on man get your arse in gear! Time to earn your pay again!"

Patty held his breath, certain that Spider would kick off and refuse the order. But perhaps it was the fact they were back amongst the military fold, that shook Spider from his stupor. With a deep breath Spider nodded and walked amongst the troops, taking charge again. Directing orders and controlling the crews.

Leaving them to it, Patty followed the Major over to his Land Rover, the Major removing his headdress and laying it on the bonnet before removing a hip flask from his pocket, offering it to Patty first.

Patty smiled in acknowledgement, taking a long hard pull, wincing as the hot whiskey ran down his throat. His voice was gruff as he gave it back.

"Thanks, I needed that."

"So, I see!" the Major replied drily, feeling half the flask now gone. He hadn't expected to see good whiskey gone that fast. He took a long hard swig himself, putting the flask on the bonnet and looking at him.

"What do you want to know?" Patty asked, seeing the conflict on the Major's face.

"Everything" the Major replied, his eyes narrowing.

"I just don't know where the hell to begin *Sir*." Patty replied, looking back at the vehicles, finally taking in the damage to them all as the enormity of what they'd all been through finally began to hit home.

Chris stepped forwards, placing a hand on the Corporal's shoulder, his voice warm and understanding.

"It's simple. Why don't you just start at the beginning."

Over the next hour, Patty told him everything. From how Mike had got hold of the tank, with Bill being left behind, to how the tank and its crew had sacrificed itself on its last-ditch defence against the Russians. Patty was watching the Major closely, seeing the man's face bearing out the story, he looked shocked and angry when hearing how the tank had been left behind, and then amazed and relieved when he heard how Baz had made it out alive and safely back to them after his brave attempt to draw off the Russians. As Patty described the last part of the story, especially what they'd seen in the woods, and the tank training ammunition, he saw the anger re-surface again on the Major's face as he stood up, pacing in front of Patty. Finally, the anger turned to disbelief and shock at hearing all along that the unit on the radio crying out for support was being led by his friend. His angry words from when they'd last met at Bovington were lodged in his mind, he regretted them now, wishing somehow, he could take them back, knowing the chance that he'd speak to his friend again was now gone.

As Patty finished talking, he watched the Major, who looked away into the distance, lost in his thoughts. After a few silent minutes it was Patty who asked the question.

"Sir, what happened? To you guys I mean?"

Chris looked up in response as Patty added.

"The last we heard, you were all leaving for Dorchester. That's where we thought we'd meet up with you again. But as soon as you left the camp, we couldn't find you. Mike...sorry I mean Captain Faulkes thought you were heading to Yeovil. Where *did* you all go?"

Chris stood up, looking around the airfield at the hive of activity, watching as the REME fitters were already preparing to lift the engine of Patty's warrior. He looked over as the REME truck fitted with the crane was driven over, the driver guided into position. Chris turned to look at Patty, his face full of regret. Patty could see something was troubling him as the Major took a deep breath and replied.

"Not here, not now."

The Major stood up, pointing over to one of the metal nissan huts nearby, his eyes narrowing as he fought back to contain his thoughts.

"Hut 34 is yours. When your troops are finished here, that's where you'll all be staying. It's not the Ritz, but I don't think you'll complain after where you've just come from. The Sergeant Major will tell you where the cookhouse is and give you the lowdown on camp rules."

Chris went to walk away, stopping suddenly and coming back, his voice angry.

"I didn't know Patty. How the hell could I have known?"

Patty looked up confused, shaking his head.

"Didn't know about what? Sir, what the hell is it?"

The Major clenched his fists angrily, pacing up and down, Patty kept silent, watching him pace to and fro. Finally, it became too much for the Major, he walked away, shouting behind him.

"Hut 68, be there tonight at 21:00. We'll talk then."

PM's Press Briefing Birmingham City Centre.

The PM tried his best to ignore the buzz of activity as the twenty people worked around him. He looked over at the speech in front of him, checking and re-checking what was written. Sonya, his Chief of Staff was nearby reading the same speech, scrutinizing it and adding input as they both discussed its contents. The PM blinked in irritation as one of the technicians kept re-adjusting the microphone on his suit. Nearby, two of his security detail stood, stone faced and cold, their eyes scanning everyone coming near him. Outside on the stage were another ten of his security detail, heavily armed and ready for anything, backed up by thirty armed police officers. After what had happened these past few days, they were taking no chances, and for the tenth time that day, they checked over the camera equipment and stage. Sniffer dogs, trained to find explosives were running between the seating and auditorium, whilst outside, the worlds' journalists were having their equipment and credentials checked again. No one was going to be causing problems at this press conference. Already the police had arrested five people trying to sneak in anti-monarchy leaflets and banners, the pain from the London attacks still being felt, even as far away as Birmingham. Everyone was on edge, no one knew what the PM wanted to talk about or reveal, all they knew was that he had called this press briefing, and he wanted the whole world to listen.

The PM looked down, pen in hand, looking back at Sonya.

"I don't like this last bit here Sonya, the line that starts with, 'we go forwards together into the dark', that sounds a little too dramatic and theatrical."

She read the lines he mentioned,

"Yes, but we need something with impact. Something that will resonate with the country. When Churchill said his immortal, 'we will fight them on the beaches quote', his own aides urged him not to do it. Imagine history now if he'd never said that line."

The PM guffawed, adding. "So, which is it to be then? Am I supposed to be listening to my Chief of Staff or not?"

She raised her eyebrows indicating he already knew the answer as he smiled in response, conceding the point. Taking a sip of water, he looked down at the header to his notes, reading the highlighted bullet points.

"*Whiskey Three-Zero.*"

The folder marked Whiskey Three-Zero was in front of him. He already knew its contents; the technical team already had it all loaded ready to play on the big screen when prompted. He closed his eyes, breathing heavily as he thought back to reading the report, talking to the reporter Ms Harding, reading the survivor's reports, realising that finally the evidence they needed, the smoking gun, was readily to hand. He was still shocked at seeing the images, especially the video footage, which was heartbreaking to see, reminding him of holocaust footage, except instead of grainy black and white, this was in glorious full colour UltraHD, there would be no denying what had gone on.

He'd already been told not to show the raw footage, to edit it out, but he'd flatly refused, wanting and needing this to be the hammer blow for the world to see, against the propaganda being churned out by both the Government of Tumat, and the puppet government in London.

The whole fabricated story of Tumat's forces being here on UK soil were that they were here for the greater good. He hoped that every high-definition image of desecrated torn bodies and trucks full of unconscious people would chip away at what people believed, until finally the world would see for itself the cold hard truth of what was really happening to his country. The photo of the crematorium truck and the large pile of ash blowing in the wind, he'd save that image for last.

The PM took another swig of water, looking at the clock overhead, already hearing the journalists beginning to file into the auditorium.

He went back to scanning the pages, his eyes flitting over the next highlighted section.

"Temporary suspension of the Capital."

He'd discussed this long and hard with his Cabinet and the King. Already they'd lost the capital city, after the mission to get the King out, the residents of London had now all been turned against the country, believing the tripe that Samuel and his rotten cabinet were sending out. All of London's media, all it's TV and radio stations, even the papers, were now under the quisling governments control, free to spin any story, so long as it worked to their favour. The story had been that the King had escaped, his final order to his security detail had been to fire on the protesters, out of some act of spite or bitter vengeance at being forced to flee. Of course, there had been numerous footage of the attacks, fuelled by the footage of the police giving chase up the Thames, finally resulting in the King escaping on the damaged helicopter. But what of the CTU team that had boarded the high-speed ferry? Why had they all been spared? These were the questions that needed answering. At first there were interviews with them, cameras stuck into faces as they were brought back to dry land, but suddenly, they'd all disappeared, the Met police citing their personal security as to their need for anonymity. The PM knew the real reason, he'd read the after-action report by the rescue team. They'd managed to get the King out without any fatalities, none at least caused by the security services. It had been an outstanding display of courageous restraint and should have been shouted from every roof top and street corner of the country. Instead, the only witnesses to the story were spirited away, no doubt being held in a detention centre until they either changed their story or were silenced forever. Now London was off limits to anyone not towing the puppet government's line, all roads and rail networks in or out were heavily guarded by the Met which had now become a quasi-military police force, bolstered by units loyal to Tumat that seemed to magically appear out of the capital. Now the police were free to act under their own rule of law, arresting anyone on the streets not loyal to the new puppet government. Any members of the armed forces still in London had been rounded up and were all being held under trumped up charges of treason. Some unlucky ones had been caught by the mob, still reeling from the attack with their thirst for revenge still unsated. Jeffery had winced at the footage, soldiers torn apart, their broken bodies being dragged through the streets. It reminded him of a tin pot dictatorship found in a third world country, not the UK. And that was part of the problem for Jeffery, he was the PM, but without the control of the country's capital how could he claim to be? So, it had been Sonya's idea. Move the capital. The Germans had done it, moving their capital Berlin to Bonn after the defeat of World War Two and the resulting years of the cold war. So, if they could do it in the face of Soviet occupation why couldn't the UK? That's how he'd sold it to his Cabinet and the King, and begrudgingly they'd all agreed. So now, tonight, he'd be announcing that from midnight tonight, the capital city of the United Kingdom would be Birmingham, it's government would reside there, and the King take up residence there. Some of his cabinet had asked for how long, and he'd resisted calls to be drawn on a timeframe, something that Sonya had repeatedly told him not to do tonight. Her words of warning still echoing in his ears.

He looked down, his eyes drawn to the final line on the header.

"Future of the UK, United Nations involvement."

This had been a tough one to talk about. It had been 48 hours since the start of the ceasefire, with the words of the American president still echoing in his ears as he'd fought to resist the plan. He remembered the telephone call, wondering if perhaps there had been another way to play it, to change the outcome, but knowing he was powerless to stop it. Thinking back now it had been a masterstroke of play, with NATO now powerless to help, the US had lobbied and coerced the members of the UN, citing the warning that the UK was a nuclear power. If the evidence given by Tumat was to be believed, and the UK was indeed in the middle of a power struggle, then regardless of who was in control, either Jeffery's government or Samuel's, they couldn't risk the threat of a nuclear armed country to go to all out civil war. The risk of one side using the nuclear option against the other was too great. And everyone knew that once nukes were launched, there was no going back from the brink. Therefore, the US had proposed within the UN to send in a monitoring team, to ensure both sides could not, and did not, access the weapons. The government of Tumat was powerless to stop them, and with angry shouts they'd watched on, as the UN security council had voted overwhelmingly to send the troops in. Surprisingly, the only countries to say no to the vote were friends of Russia, with Tumat abstaining from voting. Without saying anything it had been an admission of guilt, and now at least the world was starting to see through Tumat. The beauty of the agreement was that the mandate hadn't specified how many troops would be used for the monitoring teams, therefore there was no limit imposed. The UN task force was headed up by the U.S, and surprisingly had numerous offers from other NATO countries wanting to help. Now several safe zones had been setup, all classed as demilitarised and free from both sides' military forces, policed by heavily armed UN troops. Conveniently, all of the safe zones were setup around the same areas where the UK forces were weak, and now, with these areas guarded by UN troops, the British forces were free to bolster their depleted forces elsewhere. The ceasefire was holding for now, and with Tumat unable to move reinforcements in, it was allowing the UK the time they desperately needed to get their own military ready. Already the fresher British regiments were flying back in from overseas, and by using the RAF's huge C17 transporters, they could fly the armour in, with each C17 able to carry one tank a piece. Although costing a fortune in fuel, it was far quicker than shipping, and already the RAF had landed two squadrons worth of tanks. But, even with the extra troops and armour, it was to be a huge task with almost 200,000 enemy soldiers facing them on two fronts, and almost 40 percent of the UK mainland under enemy control. One thing was for sure, the ceasefire wouldn't eject them, and Jeffery knew that sooner or later, even with the UN mission, they'd be forced to confront them again. For now though, it was all about bolstering the defences. Speaking of defence, the PM thought back grumpily to the CDS. He'd already refused the CDS's permission to resign, needing the stable hand that the old General provided now more than ever. It was bad enough with the Cabinet being fresh faced and new, the last thing he needed was another new face next to him. Instead, he'd prompted the CDS to consider the options, urging him to continue in post for another two years, he'd urged him to at least finish the job first, trying to tug at the old soldier's sense of values. Another sticking point was the Carrier

HMS Queen Elizabeth, she was still stuck in Portsmouth, along with nearly twenty other naval vessels, including the Royal Navy's latest type 45 destroyers. The initial invasion had bypassed Portsmouth, with the ships helpless and stuck, there was no need for the Tumats to go anywhere near them, why waste resources on something that was going nowhere. The UN forces however had taken a different view, and currently the fleet had been impounded and the crews detained. Jeffery was desperate to get back control of the ships, even if only to stop other countries from pouring over them and stealing a lifetime worth of secrets and technology. Allies or not, when it came to securing an advantage, he knew everything was considered fair game.

He was torn from his thoughts as Sonya stepped closer, looking at the clock and hearing the outside noise of the assembled press. He looked at her, she smiled back, her face stern as she then checked him over one final time, adjusting the microphone on his lapel and looking over angrily at the technician who was supposed to have done it.

He looked over to an aide by the steps that led to the stage. The aide smiled and gave a thumbs up. They were ready. Already they could see the flashes of some of the cameras, the Press keen to get the exposure and light levels just right.

He nodded to his security detail who spoke into their hand mikes, as Sonya picked up the file, talking to him as he walked over.

"Remember, concentrate on the highlighted points, do not get drawn into time-frames on the new capital and if you get stuck or lose your train of thought then look over at me. I'll talk you through it."

He nodded as she quickly keyed her microphone.

"Sound check, one two, one two."

"Loud and clear," he replied, smiling.

"This is it," he added, looking up to stage and nodding solemnly.

"Yeah, this is it," she replied, before adding, "you were made for this...Just don't trip on the bloody steps going up."

He smiled, nodding in reply, as outside he heard his introduction.

"People of the world's press and distinguished guests. May I now present to you all, the Prime of Minister of the United Kingdom and her overseas Territories."

Taking the cue he carefully climbed the steps, mindful of his aide's warning and emerged into the spotlight, his face stern and serious, every little detail of his appearance being thought about. He walked to the rostrum, the cameras silently recording as conversations died away, the only noise the flash of the cameras as he carefully placed the folder on the lectern. He looked over at the autocue, seeing it ready to run, the words written on there, 'as soon as you're ready Sir, nod your head.'

He looked down at the water, calmly taking a sip, his arms settling either side of it as he looked up, his eyes scanning the room, seeing the looks on the reporters faces staring back at him. This was it. This was his moment. He looked over to Sonya, nodding his head as the autocue began.

"I'd like to begin if I may by firstly saying to all those affected by the conflict currently ravaging our country..."

16

Battered Pride

Royal Naval Air Station Yeovilton

Patty left his troops getting themselves settled into the nissan hut, a rickety corrugated iron structure, built in the 1950's and yet still serving its purpose now. Full of dead flies and flaky paint, it was where they were calling home for now, and everyone had settled into the familiar routine of being back within a military camp. Thankfully Sergeant Major Yackers had left his troops off the camp's guard shift, so at least everyone would have an uninterrupted night to sort themselves out. Patty's Warrior had the REME team still working on it, fitting the new engine was taking longer than thought, a crack in the engine mounts having been discovered. Given the punishment that the vehicles had been through recently, Patty was surprised that there hadn't been more faults. The REME fitters had decided to stand down Patty's crew, electing instead to complete the work themselves. Now, Sid and Whippet could at least get some well-earned sleep. The Major hadn't been kidding when he said the huts wouldn't be the Ritz but compared to sleeping on the back decks of a vehicle behind enemy lines, they were comfortable enough, and within minutes of being inside, everyone except Spider was fast asleep. As Patty had left the hut, he'd found Spider outside, brooding and looking up at the darkening sky. He'd tried to talk to him, but Spider made it quite clear he didn't want to talk, electing to walk off towards the vehicles. He wanted to be alone.

Time, Patty thought to himself watching him go, he just needs time.

Patty walked amongst the darkened huts, hearing laughter and music coming from the open windows, some of those inside trying to forget the past few days. It appeared that the huts around him were full of officers. He stumbled into a figure leaning against one hut, wearing the rank of a Captain. The figure drunkenly laughing at him as he continued to pee against the huts side, Patty mindful to step away from the growing puddle.

Leaving the Captain to it, he continued to search the numbers on the doors. Finally, after a few attempts he found the hut number he was after, the old rickety tin door creaking as he knocked on it.

"Come!" he heard, opening the door with a creak and stepping inside.

Overhead the single bulb almost blinded him, as he stepped into the spartan interior, devoid of all but the most basic of furniture. A single cot bed with a green army sleeping bag rolled up waiting to be used, a table, desk with laptop and two-fold up canvas camp chairs. The Major was sat in one chair, with a half empty bottle of whiskey on the table next to him. He looked up, smiling in recognition as he saw the Corporal, indicating with his hand that he take the other chair.

Patty removed his beret and awkwardly sat down, wondering what the hell the Major wanted with him. The Major poured a more than generous measure for them both, some of the liquid spilling onto the table. Patty could see he was already well on his way to being drunk.

"To absent friends!" the Major shot out, raising his glass as Patty did the same, the Major downing the drink quickly, as Patty sipped his more reservedly. The Major smiled at him, seeing his discomfort.

"You really think that rank has any place here now?" he asked, his eyes bright with humour as Patty contemplated his words.

"I'm drunk, and after the past few days that you've had, so should you be. So, hurry up and down that drink. We've got lots to talk about. And I'm not sitting here drinking, only to watch you sober, you miserable looking bastard. No-one's here to judge you."

Patty looked at the officer, taken aback what he said, wondering how the hell he knew Mike, or what the hell he was playing at. The nightmares of the past few days came flooding back, the numbness he felt earlier returning. The Major was right, it had been tough.

"Fuck it!" Patty exclaimed, downing the glass and offering out for another, the Major grinned triumphantly.

Within twenty minutes Patty was feeling lightheaded, his earlier reservations gone, as the whiskey began to take hold. The Major kept insisting Patty tell him all about the past few days, which at first, he struggled with, but finding that the more he drank, the more words came flowing out.

Chris poured another measure, listening as Patty began describing the events at the facility, the horror of what he'd seen, the shock at how Mike had left those people behind, knowing they were going to die.

Chris said nothing. Watching and listening, as Patty began to describe details at the facility thinking he'd never be able to discuss them again. Finally, as Patty finished, he looked back at Chris, remembering the real reason he had come.

"Major." he began, stopping himself as Chris raised a warning finger.

"Chris." he corrected himself, the Major smiling drunkenly in acknowledgement as Patty continued.

"What happened back on the airfield to get you so angry? What happened to your unit when you left?"

Chris went to pour another drink, realising the bottle was empty.

Staggering upwards and swaying, he went to the camp bed, pulling from underneath a crate of whiskey. With a flourish he smiled as he produced another full bottle, quickly unscrewing it and throwing the cap to the floor. With a steadier hand he poured another two measures, collapsing back down into the chair and getting comfortable, before finally, with lowered voice he began to tell his story.

"After we'd left the camp, we headed west, the Colonel wanted us to put as much distance between the camp and our unit whilst it remained dark. We heard the gunfire in the distance, I had no idea that it was your unit, let alone I had left the Trooper, or one of our fucking tanks behind."

"You had no ammunition, no way of firing back. To be fair I don't know what use you could have been." Patty added.

Chris nodded solemnly in thought as he continued, the whiskey helping him to talk freely.

"Still plays on the mind though Patty, the thought of leaving people behind, I should have checked, that was on me..."

Both men nodded and each took another drink as Chris continued, his voice sounding increasingly sober as he recounted events.

"We kept pushing on, picking up more stragglers by the hour, our unit growing in size, creating quite the trail to follow. The Colonel was worried that come daybreak our trail would be easily spotted and followed by the enemy. That's when Baz had the idea with the DTT's. I believe he told you already?"

"He did," Patty acknowledged, draining his glass and pouring another as Chris continued, his eyes narrowing as he remembered.

"As soon as Baz left us we cut into the river, the plan being to drive along it, hide our tracks for a few miles before coming back out. It worked for the first few miles, then…"

Patty watched as Chris shook his head angrily at what had happened, taking another long swig before continuing.

"The Colonel was driving alongside the tanks in a Jackal. You ever seen one?

Patty had seen them, thinking back to when he was a young Fusilier, training to drive them. They were big open topped 4x4 wheeled vehicles, with a roll cage running along the top to protect the crew if it rolled over. It had been designed for the hot dusty climates of Afghanistan and he remembered nearly freezing to death when learning to drive it in the cold UK winter weather.

He nodded in reply as Chris leaned in close, his eyes wide as he lowered his voice.

"The Colonel's driver, perhaps he was distracted, I don't know, but one minute they were driving alongside us, the next his vehicle hit the embankment and rolled over into the river."

Chris used his hands to demonstrate what he meant, standing up, knocking over the chair as his voice rose again, his hands pulling at something unseen, only his mind could see.

"It wasn't deep at first, we thought we could pull the Colonel free; his legs were caught underneath. We tried to get him out, but the more we tried, the more the vehicle sank into the mud, and then the water level began to rise. The vehicle laying as it was, acted like a bloody dam."

Chris narrowed his eyes, his voice lowering again as he continued reliving the night.

"The worst bit though was when he knew, when he finally understood this was his end. For the few final seconds that his head was still above water. He didn't scream, he didn't shout, he didn't cry. He just looked at me, with this sad sorry look of pity and said, 'you're in charge, this is your problem now Major. Good luck, you're going to need it.' And that was it. He took a final breath and disappeared below the water."

Chris pointed at himself; a look of confusion etched on his face.

"I remember thinking to myself, my problem now. What the hell did he mean by that?"

Patty kept quiet as Chris went silent in thought, deciding he'd already said enough on what happened to the Colonel. He bent down, picking up the collapsed chair and sitting back down, continued to talk.

"Well, let's just say that within an hour I knew what he meant... After what happened, we came out of the river pretty quickly, still continuing to head west, still following the plan. But with the Colonel dead, some of the other officers began to question my ability to lead. As I saw it, he'd handed command over to me just before dying. Others disagreed, saying his judgement was impaired with the stress he was under. The Adjutant, Captain Norris began to stir up the other officers, trying to sow discord amongst the ranks, saying I wasn't a true officer, I'd never been to Sandhurst, I was merely a glorified Sergeant Major, with no concept of the bigger picture. It didn't take long before others began to question my ability to lead. One of the Engineer Captains wanted to leave, to take her units east, to try to push on to Tidworth. I told her no, we'd stick to the Colonel's original plan. She told me to fuck off. Can you believe that? A Major, told to fuck off by a Captain? Perhaps in hindsight I should have handled the situation better. That wouldn't have happened when I was a young lad, I can tell you."

Chris scowled at the thought, shaking his head.

"It didn't matter anyway. Come daybreak, we found that sometime during the night move, she, along with the Adjutant, had broken away from the convoy with their units, taking some of the Warriors and one of the tanks with them. All told they took nearly 40 percent of our total fighting strength. At least they couldn't take *all* the tanks. That was my unit, *My troops*. They listened to me. All except that bloody fool Corporal Haley. He's the reason we left the tank behind with Bill. He told me that all the callsigns were ready to go, I should have checked of course. But perhaps that fool was better off gone. Anyway, now he'd taken one of the tanks with him, that left us with just eight.

Chris's voice trailed off in thought but still Patty couldn't understand the anger of earlier. Nothing about what he'd said so far had warranted the outburst.

He watched on as Chris took a deep breath, blowing out hard and nodding in thought, looking back at him. Seeing Patty's confused look, Chris decided now was the time to come clean. Suddenly appearing sober, he continued, his eyes watching Patty closely.

"The next night, we were able to link up with the Commandos coming out of Lympstone. They had radio communications back to Headquarters and their orders were to carry the fight to the enemy, do what they were designed to do, raiding supply lines, covert operations. But then, having met us and having armoured support available, they couldn't do that. So, whoever was still giving the orders up top told us to merge with them, become a combined arms battlegroup, our new callsign was called Whiskey One-Zero. Our orders were then to push north, stay out of contact and link up here, in RNAS Yeovilton. Yeovil needed help and we were going to give it."

"I thought we were the only ones on our way to help?" Patty interrupted, cocking his head in thought.

Chris looked at him searchingly, as he added.

"No, that's what HQ wanted you to think. I'm afraid though that you were to be just the diversion."

"Diversion?" Patty asked confused, shaking his head. "No, that's not right, we were sent ammo and drones. And we had the Apache support. They wouldn't have done all of that just for a diversion."

Chris banged his hand on the table angrily, causing Patty to stare at him as he yelled.

"GODDAMMIT PATTY! DON'T YOU GET IT YET?"

Patty saw the anger in him resurface again, shaking his head and keeping his voice low in reply.

"No Sir, I'm afraid I don't get it. Why don't you stop playing word games and just tell me what it is you're trying to say."

Chris took another deep breath, before replying,

"I had units under my command mutiny and leave, led by a Captain, consisting of a mixed bag of armoured vehicles, including trucks, Warriors and a tank."

Patty's mouth opened in realisation at what Chris was getting at, as he continued.

"Then a day later, I'm being told of a unit, being led by a Captain, consisting of Warriors, a tank, and trucks all now positioned in a woodline and asking for ammunition."

Patty's mouth opened in realisation at what Chris was trying to articulate, as he continued,

"I put two and two together and thought your unit was that of Captain Norris and Corporal Haley. I contacted HQ and suggested to them that we should use your unit as a diversion to help get our other units up towards Yeovilton. Use your unit to stir up the hornets nest, to take the brunt of it, so we could move up safely."

"So, we were the lambs to slaughter?" Patty replied softly, frowning and thinking aloud.

"Yes, but headquarters took it one step further, they had this grand plan to convince the enemy you were a far bigger unit, to pull the enemy away from other areas of the front. You might not know this but HQ were broadcasting your location loud and clear for the enemy to find you. You always had a target on your back."

"Jesus Christ!" Patty exclaimed.

"Oh, it gets worse." Chris replied, laughing nervously.

"It does? How?" Patty asked uncomprehendingly.

Chris downed his drink, urging for Patty to do the same. He refused, wanting to try to keep a clear head for what he was being told.

Ignoring him, Chris poured another drink, then looked back at him, his eyes narrowing as he almost whispered.

"Training ammo."

"That was because of you?" Seeing Chris nodding in response Patty stood up, shaking his head, disbelievingly.

"No. Impossible!"

Chris sat silently spinning the glass around in his hands as Patty continued looking down at him.

"You said it yourself; you were miles away. How the fuck could you be responsible for that?"

Chris looked up, his sadness clear to hear, as he replied.

"Once I knew of the plan, I then passed up my recommendation that the tank that was with them, that was with *you*, not be sent live ammunition. I argued that it would be a waste of ordinance. Especially as they, or should I say *you*, were given less than a 5 percent chance of surviving more than an hour. The General's agreed, and that's why you were sent the training ammo."

"Now hang on, if that's the case then why send us the live 30mm ammo? Or all that hi-tech stuff-the Talons and Wasps? Or the Apaches? Why bother sending all that to us?"

"The 30mm was sent to you because we've got loads of it spare. The 120mm for the tank, not so much. As for the other stuff, the tech stuff, I've never heard of anything like that, so can't comment. The Apaches, well my guess is that someone was just trying to increase the odds for you guys."

"WELL, THANK FUCK SOMEONE DID!" Patty shouted, standing up and banging his own fist on the table. "Because otherwise we'd all be dead in a fucking field somewhere, all because your bruised ego wanted vengeance on a few rogue officers."

"It wasn't like that!" Chris shot back shaking his head defensively. "Look, we had other units trapped as well. Four of the tanks were coming in from Lulworth, other units scattered across the countryside. If it's any consolation they all made it back to safety, thanks to what *you* all did. I wanted you to know that. It *was* for the greater good."

Patty stood, looking down at the man and shaking his head. Suddenly he wasn't feeling as drunk as he'd thought.

"Bullshit! the only reason you called me here tonight was to clear your conscience. That's why you didn't have the balls to tell me sober. Well, now you have *Major*. Now you've finally lightened the load. Do you feel better for it? Is tomorrow now going to be a better day?"

Chris just looked to the floor as Patty continued, the drink and the anger making him forget who he was talking to.

"I can't blame you for what happened to us, I'm not that naïve. But did the training ammo have an impact? You fucking bet it did. You might not have been directly responsible for what happened to Mike, but you can bet your fucking bottom dollar your actions didn't help him or his crew. Perhaps with the real ammo, who knows. Maybe they'd have even made it back here. *You* threw him under the bus with that decision."

He picked his beret up, putting it on his head and muttering "Some fucking friend you turned out to be," and was about to leave when the Major shot out.

"We're not finished yet *Corporal*."

"Oh I think we are..*sir*." Patty spat back, walking towards the door. He heard the chair crash backwards, turning to see the Major standing, his eyes full of menace.

"Don't make the mistake of thinking just because I've had a few drinks Corporal that I don't know what I'm doing. Now, like I said, *we're* not finished here."

Patty looked at the Major, realising he was right, drunk or not, he was still the officer in charge of the camp. He exhaled loudly and stepped forwards, slamming his feet to attention, the noise echoing off the hut's floorboards.

"SIR!" he shouted, staring ahead, the light above him seemingly brighter than before as the drink made him sway slightly.

Chris staggered behind the desk, opening one of the drawers, pulling something out and walking forwards, his hand offering it out to Patty.

Patty looked down confused at the Sergeant's rank slide.

"Sir?"

The Major smiled as he put the rank slide into Patty's hands.

"That's right *Sergeant*. A promotion. With everything going on, I feel it only right that you get what you deserve."

Patty shook his head, a look of wonder on his face as he tried to refuse.

"No Sir, not for me, this isn't for me. I've only just recently been promoted to Corporal, and I've fucked that up enough. There must be others. Corporal Webb for instance."

"Now who's throwing their friends under the bus." Chris shot back, shaking his head as he added forcefully.

"No use arguing Sergeant, it's official, so you'd better get used to it. We've got a severe shortage of experienced senior NCO's, what with the recent casualties and such, and now I've just changed that. I've got fresh troops coming tomorrow to bolster your men and I expect you to begin training them immediately."

"You bastard! You're enjoying this!" Patty shot back, the alcohol making him more forthright than he would be normally.

Chris kept his face firm, looking the soldier up and down.

"I'll forget that outburst Sergeant, I'll put that down to the high spirits and the shock of the promotion. Now if there's nothing else."

Chris pointed towards the door, indicating they were finished. Watching as Patty threw up a salute, the shock still on his face as he disappeared into the night. Chris stood watching the darkened door for a few moments, nodding agreeably, he liked the Sergeant, he could see what Mike had liked about him, he wasn't afraid to speak his mind when pushed.

Sighing, he walked back over to the desk, pulling out another rank slide, and flinging it onto the desk, the recently appointed Sergeant's words still echoing in his ears. Chris had tried to say the same thing when they'd told him of his promotion only two hours before. Sat on the desk, waiting for Chris to put it on, was the rank slide of a Lieutenant Colonel.

He looked at the bottle, about to pour another drink. Something stopped him, as sighing to himself he replaced the top, hearing Mike's voice in his head.

"That's not going to help Chris. Come on, let's get this done. Stop feeling sorry for yourself and get back at it."

He threw the bottle over to the far corner with disgust, looking around him to check he was alone. Exhausted, he fell onto the camp bed, tears coming freely as finally he began to let it all out, finally he'd grieve for his friend.

Bovington Camp

Captain Lunyou came out of the offices and into the rain, looking up angrily at the grey clouds that had appeared overhead, matching his mood.

"The summer and it's fucking raining." he fumed, realising that with all his time spent over here, it was still the weather that he struggled the most to get used to. Why does it always have to rain? Why can't you just have winter and summer? he thought to himself letting the rain soak into his clothes. He limped away from the offices, his leg still sore, but electing to leave the walking stick in the office. The last thing he needed was to be seen to be weak in front of the others. He could see in the distance a group of soldiers on the grass drinking and singing, not letting the rain dampen their mood. They were all recently back from the front lines, the survivors of Colonel Golgolvin's unit, all full of brash tales of bravery and action. Impressing the greener troops yet to see action, as they drunkenly staggered about the camp with their tales. Lunyou didn't believe half of it and had put it down to false bravado, after all, if they were that brave, then how did they survive to make it back? Only the brave stayed to fight, and only the brave died on the battlefield. The truth was they weren't the brave ones, they were just the ones who'd managed to run faster than the other cowards. Lunyou had seen some of the after-action reports, stories of flying tanks and lasers. The stuff of fantasy, if only the great Golgolvin had been there. Lunyou could have at least made him the scapegoat, finally with the chance to pay back the humiliation reaped onto him from that first night. Instead, the Colonel was still missing in action, believed to be dead. Perhaps finally Lunyou was rid of him. He lit the cigarette, smiling at the thought of Golgolvin's charred smoking body in a rain-soaked field.

He saw his Sergeant get out of the driver's seat of the 4x4 to open the passenger door for him, then stopping at the noise that sounded in the distance. Lunyou looked up, now hearing the noise, seeing the car in the distance screaming towards them, the sounds of squealing tyres on the tarmac. The soldiers heard it too, looking up and cheering as the Porsche 911 came screaming into the parade square, smoke scrabbling from its rear tyres as it drifted sideways in front of the group. Lunyou recognised it straight away. A crayon grey Porsche Turbo S.

The car began to spin around on the spot, the tyre smoke obscuring it as the drunken group of soldiers were cheering the driver on. Lunyou looked over to his Sergeant, his eyes narrowed.

"Artem, let's go take a look."

With Lunyou leading the way, both of them walked towards the car, being forced to wait for the driver to stop his crazy antics. The car skidded to a stop, the passenger door opening and a soldier carrying a bottle of beer emerged, looking green. He ran off to the side, falling to his knees and throwing up as the driver's door opened and the driver emerged standing triumphantly, one arm on the roof and banging loudly as he waved over to the next waiting soldier sat on the grass. Clearly, he was the entertainment for the group, daring them to ride with him.

The driver looked up, the confident smile disappearing as he recognised Lunyou and his Sergeant approaching. Everyone there knew who he was and who he worked for, and with their Colonel gone, there was now no-one to protect them.

Leaving the engine running the soldier stepped away from the car and stood to attention, his eyes flickering between the group of soldiers and the Sergeant. Even though drunk, the group saw the danger and quickly dispersed, leaving the driver to his fate.

"Nice car." Lunyou said appreciatively, looking down at it.

The driver said nothing, the rain matting his cropped hair as he stood ramrod still.

"Where did you find it?" Lunyou asked, as he pushed past the soldier and sat in the driver's seat.

Lunyou's Sergeant stood menacingly close to the soldier, causing him to swallow nervously as he replied.

"It was in the carpark down the road, in another complex. The keys were left on the back wheel."

Lunyou sat in the car, his eyes looking over the familiar gauges as his hands ran lovingly over the steering wheel. Cars were another passion of his. His collection back home contained twenty models, all exotic and all very expensive. He looked up at the soldier who was now shivering in the rain.

"Say what you want about the Germans, but they do know how to make great cars."

The soldier blinked as the rain ran down his face, looking down at the Captain, seeing the appreciation for the car etched on his face. Thinking his prize was about to disappear, he pleaded.

"But Sir, I found it...I mean, surely it's mine?"

Lunyou looked back up at him, smirking at the soldier's displeasure, before finally relenting and shaking his head.

"Pah, you don't think I'm here to take this from you do you? Back home I've got two of these!"

The soldier breathed a sigh of relief as Lunyou continued to speak, his hands opening the sun visors and glove box as he rummaged around the interior.

"No, the reason I'm curious, is that this car costs more than any officer or soldier earns. So, what *is* it doing here? Who owns it?"

His hands found the forward boot release, with a clunk the boot opened, Lunyou quickly stepping out and opening it.

"And you say you found it down by the complex over the road?"

The soldier shook his head agreeably as Lunyou looked over at his Sergeant adding,

"The ATDU hanger, that's where the tanks came from."

Lunyou opened the bonnet, looking at the black bag sat inside. Quickly he snatched it up, opening the zip and upending the contents. The items fell back into the boot, some clothes, spare socks, and then a white plastic card fell out, Lunyou's eyes were drawn to it immediately. He picked it up, holding it close, reading the words and smiling, before handing it over to his Sergeant, whose eyes lit up with malice as they recognised the photo displayed on the card.

"Looks like we now know who owns the car. Recognise him Artem?"

The Sergeant stood looking down at the photo on the gym membership to Ariel and Ewens gym, recognising that face again. With all the conflict going on in the middle east, and with Ariel and Ewen being Israeli, they'd had no end of activists trying to get in and disrupt the lessons. So out of necessity they'd been forced to increase the security at the gym, insisting all clients have a keycard with photo ID. Mike had always forgotten the pass, so kept it in his gym bag ready to go. In his haste to evacuate out of Bovington, he'd left it in the car.

Artem tried to read the name out loud in English.

"Meekhall Faaalkes!

"Micheal Faulkes." Lunyou replied, laughing at his Sergeant's attempts. He limped back to the car, reaching into the passenger side and rummaging through the glove box, rain streaming off his arm.

Triumphantly, he found what he was looking for, standing back up and smirking.

"Well, well. Look what we have here. The car's insurance paperwork. And here we have the address of one Micheal Faulkes. He lives in Poole! Thank you, Mr Faulkes. Thank you indeed."

The Sergeant frowned as Lunyou looked back at him, proudly holding the paperwork out.

"Artem, what say we go pay a little visit to Mr Faulkes home? Let's see if he has any family."

The evil smirk of his Sergeant told him what he thought, as leaving the soldier standing there they both walked back to the waiting 4x4.

Lunyou put the paperwork into his pocket, careful to keep it dry. Looking up at the rain he smiled to himself, the pain in his leg feeling less and his sombre mood lifting.

"It looks like today's going to be a good day after all…"

17

To Everything There Is A Season

Location Unknown

Mike woke slowly, the blurred images of his surroundings coming slowly into focus. He turned his head slowly, scanning the room as his brain desperately tried to piece together what had happened. Had he been dreaming? Fuzzy images and dark thoughts of earlier danced around in his mind. Had he died? Was this another dream? He slowly lifted his arm, feeling the pull of the cables attached to the drip in his arm. Beside him, the rhythmic beep of the ECG machine continued its steady beat as he wiggled his fingers in front of his eyes, the dream like state of his mind made it hard for him to focus. Clearly whatever drugs were being pumped into him were having an effect. He looked around the room, it was empty, clinical and white, devoid of any furniture less a single white chair near to the bed and a bedside table. Behind him were machines and the drip that he was connected to, all placed on a wheeled trolley. On one wall he could see a single sliding door. The far end of the room was dominated by a large glass mirror, Mike saw it for what it was, a one-way viewing portal. He had no doubt that people or cameras were the other side watching his every move. There were no windows in the room, and Mike realised he had no way of knowing if it were night or day. He couldn't even remember how long he'd be there, or more importantly how he'd got there. His focus began to sharpen as he looked down again at his arms, expecting to feel the chains or shackles tying him to the bed. Surprisingly there were none, and he raised both arms in front of his face, his fingers wriggling in front of his eyes as if performing a mad puppet show dance.

As his senses became more alert he tried to sit up, the effort causing him to flinch as a sharp sudden stab of pain shot across his stomach. He looked down, pulling weakly at the sweat-soaked sheets, exposing his abdomen and bandages that were wrapped tightly around him. They were fresh, recently applied and small red stains covered the bandage's outer edges. He continued to inspect himself, seeing the smaller bandages around his legs, the medication making everything feel numb to the touch. As he raised himself higher, he saw his reflection in the mirrored window, he drew a breath as he saw how he looked, he'd had better days. He could see his head was covered in thick bandages, with a large yellow, crimson stain running down one of them. His nose looked to have been broken and reset, the scar running thick across it, as two fresh black eyes stared back at him from the mirror.

He touched the bandages and his nose, his fingers lightly pressing against the material and the flesh, confirming what he was looking at. He winced in pain as he caught his nose, his body still not regaining its full co-ordination as fresh blood dribbled down his nose from the fresh wound. He leaned over the bed, trying to stop the blood flow as suddenly he felt the urge to vomit. Below him he saw the empty container, clearly for just that. He tried to reach for it, his fingers weakly grasping it, realising he was going to be too late.

He couldn't stop it. With immense effort he began to throw up all over the floor, his fingers resting on his chin, trying to keep his head over the bed's side. Thick black bile splattered all over the clean floor, as he feebly tried to keep the liquid off him. Behind him he heard the door open, two people came rushing in, their plastic shoes squeaking on the floor. Both were dressed in surgical clothing, with masks covering their faces. One pulled him up further onto the bed, whilst the other grabbed the container and held it close to his mouth. After a few moments Mike was finished, but his body was still retching, his stomach now empty of whatever had been in it. He nodded in thanks at the two people, both saying nothing in return, as one lay him back on the bed, the other wiping his mouth with some blue surgical tissue.

With surgical precision they quickly went about cleaning up the mess, one took the container and its vile contents from the room whilst the other was knelt beside the bed, efficiently cleaning it up. Mike tried to look outside the room through the open sliding door, seeing nothing but inky blackness beyond, as the second person stood up, the cleaning materials all deposited into a yellow hazmat bag. The person turned to leave the room and he called out weakly, his voice croaky.

"Thank you."

Whether it was upon impulse or just good old-fashioned courtesy, the person in the mask had turned, Mike could see from the eyeliner she was female as she nodded her head in acknowledgment.

Just like that they were gone. The sliding door closed automatically behind them, and the room went back to its cold clinical state. Mike lay there trying to remember the past, trying to recall what had happened. It was as if a grey fog now inhabited his brain, he knew his name was Mike, that he could recall, but anything else seemed to be just out of reach. He closed his eyes to think, contemplating what to do next when suddenly a wave of tiredness enveloped him.

I'll just rest my eyes for a moment, he thought weakly to himself, the medication making him feel lightheaded again. Then, as quickly as he had woken, he was back to sleep again, the dark dreams and thoughts once again filling his head.

Mike had no idea how long he was asleep for, he woke in an instant, his arms tearing at the sweat-soaked sheets at the nightmare figure of a dead man crawling up the bed towards him. He sat up, breathing heavily, as his eyes searched the darkened room. The lights were off, behind him he saw the faint glow of a reading light still on as a click sounded overhead, the voice coming through a speaker in the ceiling.

"Are you okay Sir?"

Mike froze, hearing the ECG machines beeps slowing down as his racing heartrate began to calm itself. His eyes looked around the room suspiciously, certain he would see the ghastly figure.

"Calm down Mike, it was just a nightmare, it wasn't real," he said softly to himself, as the voice asked again.

"Sir, are you okay?"

Mike looked up to the mirrored glass, the voice confirming his suspicions. He was being watched.

Mike swallowed, his throat feeling like razor blades as he looked over to the bedside table and saw a plastic glass and a full jug of water.

Ignoring the voice, he reached over, his strength and co-ordination still failing him as he fumbled for the plastic beaker, causing it to fall with a clatter onto the floor.

After a few seconds the automatic sliding door opened with a hiss, clearly the person watching had seen enough.

This time the person was dressed in the green scrubs of a hospital porter, they bent down to pick up the beaker, picking it up and filling it from the jug.

Mike took it slowly from their outstretched hand, taking slow careful sips, using the time afforded him to look at the person, recognizing from the colour of her mascara that this was the woman from earlier. He saw on her scrubs she had written in marker pen on one side of her chest her blood group and rank. On the other side Mike saw her name.

"Ramirez, your name's Ramirez," he croaked.

She nodded in reply as she took the cup back, filling it again as he asked,

"Where am I?"

She handed the full cup back to him, watching him sip it as she replied.

"All in good time Sir. For now, we want you to just rest, get your strength back."

Mike emptied the cup again, his throat feeling a little better as with his voice sounding a little more like his, he asked,

"Well Ramirez, can you at least tell me the time?"

He could see from her eyes that she was smiling, as with a Georgian drawl she responded.

"Not having windows will do that to you. It's 2am sir."

He nodded appreciatively, adding. "And the date? What day of the week is it?"

She looked back at the window, as if someone else were watching before shaking her head.

"Like I said Sir, all in good time."

Leaving him alone with his thoughts, the nurse walked back out, the door closing behind her with a hiss. Mike stared at the window for a long time, wondering who or what was behind it before finally relenting. The nurse was right. Right now, he needed to rest and regain his strength, perhaps then his memory would return, and he could figure out what the hell was going on. He closed his eyes again, fearful that the ghostly apparition would return. Within seconds he was out, the darkness once again returning along with the numb sensation as he drifted back to sleep.

Mike awoke to two female nurses standing over him, one was checking the bandage on his abdomen, the other checking the bandage to his head. They looked down, seeing him awake both smiling disarmingly. The one checking his head leaned over to speak to him.

"Well good morning sleepy head. Have a nice sleep?"

Mike shuffled up the bed, one of the nurses reaching behind to plump up a pillow, as the other pulled Mike upright. Mike said nothing, watching them both suspiciously, his mind much sharper than the previous night. He could hear the nurses' accents, so far everyone had sounded American. He knew that was impossible, the last thing he'd remembered was somehow being amongst the Russians. He had questions, lots of questions, but for now, so long as everyone was playing nicely, he'd play along with them.

He looked over, seeing the ECG machine was already switched off and the drips removed from his arms. At least whatever the medication was, he was off it.

Putting aside his concerns he looked up smiling in thanks as one of the nurses leaned in, whispering.

"You feel up to any food yet? I can have the kitchen rustle up some dry toast."

His stomach grumbled in response at the thought of food, causing her to look down and nod as the other nurse began to speak.

"Afraid dry toast is all we can give you for the time being Captain Faulkes."

Hearing his name, Mike shot her a look but kept quiet, thinking to himself, so you know my name at least? What else do you know?

Mike kept quiet, smiling at them as they readjusted and tucked in the bed sheets and left the room. Giving them nothing in return.

Slowly he flexed his arms, looking around the room again, becoming aware of the slightest of movements, a slow gentle rocking motion that he'd felt before in the past when on his boat at anchor. So he was on a boat, that's where he was being held.

Five minutes later and one of the nurses came back in, carrying a plate of dry toast and another jug of water, replacing the one on the side table.

"Thank you." Mike replied, noting his voice was sounding stronger as he took small careful bites of the toast, washing each piece down with water. He swallowed carefully, each piece feeling as if it were made of glass.

Five minutes later and the plate was empty. Mike hadn't had the appetite to finish, having to force the last piece down knowing his body needed the energy. Especially if he was planning on finding a way out of there, his mind was willing, but the body not so. Already the pain medication was beginning to wear off and he began to feel as if he'd just been in a wrestling match with a gorilla. He looked down again, wondering what had caused the injuries, trying to piece together what had happened. All he could remember was a tank, a battle, and a forest on fire. The more he tried to think, the more the grey cloud that filled his brain seemed to darken, until eventually frustrated and with a growing headache, he had to stop.

With a hiss he heard the door open, and two new faces entered. One was a doctor, his fresh green scrubs, pulled over the military uniform still had creases on them where they were fresh out of the packet. The second person was military, the light blue DPM material was the new type of urban digital camouflage that Mike had seen before, worn by the American Forces. Mike recognised the man's rank as that of an Admiral, so was he supposed to be in the American Navy? Mike wondered questioningly.

Mike sat stone faced, watching them enter the room as the Admiral pulled the chair up alongside the bed and sat down comfortably, whilst the doctor stood at the end of the bed, picking up Mike's chart and reading it, ignoring him.

Mike watched on, eyebrows raised waiting for them to speak, wanting to give them nothing in return.

It was the Admiral who spoke first, his voice complimented by the Texan drawl.

"Captain Faulkes, D'ya know where you are? Or who I am son?"

Mike shook his head slowly, trying to picture the man, or think why he should remember him.

Seeing him none the wiser, the Admiral continued.

"Ok, well we're gonna try to fix that now. See, the docs are telling me ya took a real nasty blow to the head. They reckon what you're suffering from is called Post Traumatic Amnesia. Apparently, it can last hours, days, even weeks after an injury. Now they've told me to go easy on ya, any sudden excitement, or trying to push you too hard and it could cause you to black out. So, we're gonna play a lil' game of fill in the blanks. Y'all tell me what you know, and then if there's anything you're not sure of, I'll try jog your memory, help you along, see if we can't get to the bottom of what happened out there."

Ahh thought Mike, so this was the plan. This so-called Admiral was correct, he couldn't remember anything from the past few days, but he *could* remember things he'd learned from the past. He thought back to a film he'd watched; how the Germans had done something similar to captured aircrew in World War 2, in the run up to the D-Day landings. In a desperate ploy to find out the details of where the landings were taking place, injured allied service personal woke up in what they were led to believe was an allied hospital, it had American speaking Germans in there, complete with fictitious newspapers dated four months after they were captured, with other English-Speaking Germans posing as other wounded personnel. The plan being the prisoners would think the war was nearly over, and with the landings already having happened they'd be free to talk about what they knew, thinking they were safe and sound back in an

American hospital. It hadn't worked for the Germans in the film, the prisoners could feel something wasn't right, just like Mike could feel the same now. Something about this just didn't seem right.

The Admiral sat watching, waiting for Mike to say something, his eyes narrowing as instead Mike poured himself another glass of water and slowly sipped at it. Mike watched the doctor step forwards, putting the chart back and grabbing Mike's head painfully, forcing it upward as he shone the bright light into his eyes. Mike blinked against the light as the doctor said without compassion,

"I need you to keep your head still. Look behind me at a spot on the wall and focus on it."

"Bit difficult with you in the way." Mike shot back, his temper rising at the slapdash approach of the doctor.

The doctor said nothing, Mike looked at him, noting the lean hard features, the eyes unsympathetic and full of scorn. Whoever this man was, he wasn't a doctor, Mike could feel the anger radiating off him. For a few moments the doc stared back at him, his head inches from Mike, his eyes boring into his, as if trying to intimidate Mike.

Mike kept his thoughts to himself as the doctor finally nodded to himself, satisfied with what he could see. Mike's suspicions were confirmed when the doc stepped back to the charts, his hand going instinctively for the empty chest pocket that would usually house the pens. He looked down as Mike replied humorously.

"No pen? I thought every good doctor carried at least two."

With a sneer, the doc turned and left the room, leaving just the two of them alone.

Mike turned back to the Admiral who remained patiently sitting there, his own eyebrows raised as if to prompt Mike to begin. After a few moments the Admiral's patience began to wear thin.

"Okay son, what is it? Why ya giving me the silent treatment?"

Mike's eyes narrowed, as he looked around the room, his gaze focusing on the window.

"Admiral, or at least I'm guessing that's who you're meant to be. You'll have to excuse my impertinent tone, but I'm not too sure I totally believe you're who you say you are right now. Granted, my mind's not too great at the moment, but the last thing I do remember was being in the company of Russians. And now, suddenly as if by some miracle here we are, wherever the hell this is, with you asking me to tell you what I can remember. How do I know you're who you say? How do I know this isn't some half assed scheme to extract information from me?"

The Admiral sat back as Mike finished, one leg resting on the other, his fingers drumming the chair as he sat back in thought at what Mike had said. Nodding in understanding, he smiled, his arm waving around the room with a flourish as he spoke.

"Ya think that somehow we're all the enemy? And we're interrogating ya?"

Mike folded his arms across his chest defiantly in answer.

The Admiral leaned forwards, his elbows resting on his knees as he looked at Mike.

"If we were interrogating ya, don't ya think it'd make more sense to keep that there drip in your arm, feeding ya whatever drugs we like?"

Mike looked over at the drip, realising the Admiral had a point. Mike didn't know the names, but he knew that there were drugs available to make people talk. Perhaps the Admiral had already tried. Perhaps with Mike's memory currently on pause, the drugs wouldn't work. Seeing he was still suspicious the Admiral stood up, walking over to the mirrored window.

"Right, let's show him."

Mike watched as the two nurses came back in with a wheelchair. With infinite care they helped him up and into it, quickly covering his modesty as the hospital gown flapped open, his bruised and battered body briefly on display before being covered by a thick, light blue blanket.

He looked up at the Admiral who stood smiling, looking down at him, his voice full of mischief as he spoke.

"Time for some fresh air Mike. Let's see how good ya sea legs are."

He tried to conceal his surprise as they wheeled him out of the room into a brightly lit corridor lined with doors on every side. Mike guessed they mirrored his own room, counting ten of them as they continued down the corridor towards a set of double doors at the end, with the Admiral following closely behind.

He watched as the doors opened, inside were two heavily armed US Marine guards, their cold gaze looking down at him, their eyes looking back up as they recognised the Admiral. Both snapped to attention, ramrod straight and arms razor sharp as they shouted.

"Tenhut!"

"At ease men." the Admiral's voice shot back with authority as he added, "just taking one of our guests topside for a little fresh air. The Captain here thinks we might all be Russian."

Mike noticed both Marines look sideways at each other as the words sunk in before looking back down at him pitifully and shaking their heads as they stepped aside, one of the Marines producing a key card and swiping the door.

With a hiss another door opened automatically and slid to the side, the nurses pushing the wheelchair through as Mike nodded to the guards, who both smiled disarmingly at him.

It was like stepping into another world, as now the white, quiet corridors, were replaced by military grey walls lined with pipework and cables running the length of it. The corridor seemed to go on for at least 200 metres, filled with military personnel wearing all manner of uniforms and all walking purposefully. Mike spotted Air force, Navy, Marines, some Army, all had the distinct flash of the stars and stripes on their arm, and many stared at him curiously as they passed him, as if he were some alien from another planet. He tried to ignore the stares as the nurses wheeled him down the corridor, the Admiral saluting all those who saw him, everyone in the corridor snapping to attention and waiting for the entourage to pass. Mike could smell the scent of the warship, a mixture of gun oil, aviation fuel, sweat, deodorant and diesel fumes. Overhead he could hear the speakers of the ship blaring out to the crew, the voice ringing out with an Alabama twang.

"Attention crew, reminder that the PX on E deck will be closed from 14:00 hours today. Any crewmember wishing to purchase supplies after this time can do so at the commissary on D Deck."

Mike watched as they approached a thick blast door, looking in disbelief as they wheeled him through it and into one of the giant hangars beyond.

It was huge, measuring at least 100 metres in width and seemed to run the entire length of the ship. Inside the vast space were all manner of aircraft. Light grey Blackhawks, huge twin rotor ospreys, sea harriers, and multiple wheeled vehicles. Mike's head was on a swivel, looking around him at the array of hardware. Nearby forty US Marines were conducting what looked like a PT session, the sweat pouring off them as their instructor yelled at them, "Push through it!"

He looked behind him in amazement at the Admiral who said nothing in reply, pointing over to the nurses to indicate where he wanted Mike to be wheeled to. At one end of the hangar was an Osprey, its wings folded up and tied securely onto the ramp, waiting to be brought to the upper deck. The Marine Sergeant, stood at the elevator's controls was waiting for the Admiral, waving in acknowledgment as Mike was wheeled onto the giant elevator. The Osprey towered over the wheelchair as Mike was positioned next to it, looking on as smoothly and quickly the 200-tonne ramp shot upwards, gone was the gloom of the hangar deck, replaced by the sunlit sky and fresh breeze of the wind, as Mike emerged onto the flight deck of the giant ship. Mike winced with the sudden glare, his eyes slowly adjusting as he looked around. Realising the vessel he was on was a smaller version of the US Navy's super carriers. It had a flat top deck and off to the right side sat the island, housing the bridge and superstructure.

Around him, hundreds of people were working, some loading crates of supplies into waiting helicopters, others manoeuvring some of the Ospreys into positions on the deck. Mike watched on, open-mouthed. Above him on the superstructure of the ship, a huge stars and stripes flag fluttered lazily in the wind. Mike looked around him in awe, counting almost twenty warships cruising around them. Nearby he could see the huge hulking shadow of an American Aircraft carrier, with the smaller shapes of its aircraft parked up in rows, waiting to be called into action, whilst the smaller more agile shapes of the destroyers cut through the convoy, their bows easily slicing through the blue calm waters of the channel.

Seeing him taking in their surroundings the Admiral now finally spoke.

"Okay Captain, hopefully now you've seen enough. Now let's try this again. I'm Admiral J.D Stringer, commander of the 8th US Atlantic Fleet. You're currently onboard the Marine Forces Amphibious Ship USS Dorchester, positioned in the English Channel."

Mike looked up at the Admiral who stood facing him, leaning back against the ships rail as he dismissed the nurses.

Mike waited until they were out of earshot before asking, his confusion clear to hear.

"But, I don't understand. How can you be here? I thought NATO were powerless to help?"

The Admiral smiled and cocked his head.

"Ahh so you do remember something. You mean all that cock n' bull about Tumat being a member of NATO? And how two member states at odds with each other can't rely on other NATO members for help?"

"Yes," Mike responded, looking searchingly at the Admiral.

As if to answer, the Admiral pulled out a velcro patch from his pocket, showing it to Mike before putting it on his arm. The blue patch had two letters written on it, big, bold and in white.

"U.N." Mike read loudly, looking away thoughtfully. "United Nations?" Mike asked, his puzzled looks turning to one of recognition as finally he began to understand.

"You're here with the U.N! Of course! That's how you've got around it!"

The Admiral smiled as Mike began to work it out, happy to see the silent and moody Captain finally talking openly. He waved his arms around him at the fleet, raising his voice to shout over the noise of an Osprey coming in to land.

"That's right Captain, welcome to the United Nations 8th Fleet. Our mission is to establish areas of safety in high population centres, to ensure safe evacuation of displaced people and to make sure that both parties of both governments maintain the Law of Armed Conflict and that nuclear weapons remain *out* of the conflict."

Mike shook his head in disbelief as the Admiral continued.

"Between you and me, our President saw fit to play the Russians at their own game. They took NATO off the table, so we went and put the UN on it. Now our UN peacekeeping forces contain most of the armies of those NATO partners they thought to neuter. We've got troops from everywhere ranging from Belgium to Greece, all queuing up to come help y'all. Ya didn't really think we'd leave you all on your own did you?"

Mike smiled in relief, looking around the ships again.

"So, is it over? The fighting I mean?"

The General narrowed his eyes as he added.

"I wish I could say for sure, we've had a ceasefire in effect these past three days. It's holding...for now. In the meantime we've got UN peacekeepers establishing safe routes in and out of the designated safe zones. The Tumat's didn't like it much, but being the junior partner in the UN, they don't get much of a say in the matter."

Mike closed his eyes, feeling the cool sea breeze on his face, suddenly feeling more alive. The Admiral noticing this, hoped Mike was now open to talking more candidly with him.

"You were found in woodland by one of our forward recon teams three days ago. They were scouting one of our UN landing sites, when they came across you and some Russian Colonel, both unconscious. Looked like you'd both been going at each other pretty hard; apparently both having stabbed one another. Wanna tell me about that?"

Mike's hands felt the bandage around his stomach again, feeling the wound tenderly, trying to evoke some thought or memory in response. Nothing came and he shook his head despondently.

"I'm sorry, but I can't remember anything."

"What can you remember?" the Admiral asked, his voice raising as another Osprey flew in low overhead to land on the deck. Mike used the noise to give himself time to think, waiting until the aircraft had landed before replying.

"I remember we were under attack, there was a plane dropping troops, and something to do with people in a truck. I was on a tank, and I think we were trying to get somewhere."

"What about the tank? Can you tell me anything about that?" the Admiral enquired; his eyebrows raised.

Mike's brow creased in concentration, trying to force the memory. After a few seconds he shook his head, his voice full of frustration.

"I'm sorry but I just don't remember. Vague memories are all I have, sorry I'm not much use right now."

The Admiral stepped forwards, looking back over to the waiting nurses and nodding before replying.

"Ok Captain, don't you worry, these things take time. It'll come back to you when it's ready. Meantime, get plenty of rest, get some decent chow inside you and we'll talk some more later."

Mike looked up apologetically and nodded in thanks, wrapping the blanket around him against the sudden cold he felt, as he shivered on the deck.

The Admiral watched on as the cold, feeble figure of the Captain was wheeled down below, waiting until the elevator was out of sight before he strode back along the flight deck and into the superstructure, careful to step over the raised edge of the doorway, which was always waiting to trip the unwary.

Using his extensive knowledge of the ship, the Admiral quickly walked down the maze of corridors and another four flights of stairs, anyone in his way stepping aside and standing to attention to let him pass. He nodded at them as he went, coming to another set of double doors flanked by two Marine guards, who slammed to attention upon seeing him. He merely nodded in acknowledgment to them as he approached, pulling the keycard from the lanyard around his neck and inserting it into the keypad next to the door, before keying in the eight-digit code from memory. After a few seconds the door unlocked with a loud clunk, one of the guards stepping forwards to pull it open for him as he stepped inside. The door led into part of the ship that other sailors referred to as the crypt, only accessed by members of the intelligence services, or members of one of the many clandestine organisations that worked within the military. The door led through a corridor and into another hangar bay, smaller than the ship's main hanger, but still large enough to accommodate five of the latest Lockheed Stealth helicopters, prototypes that were never even considered to have made production. Each helicopter was encased in a special radar absorbing material and their angular design meant they gave off the smallest of radar signatures when flying, equivalent to a small flock of birds. Instead of the standard rotor configuration, atop each one were four large discs, each one on top of the other and designed to counter rotate to the other. All had holes cut into them at seemingly irregular intervals. The Archimedes disc, as it was referred to by its engineers, gave the helicopters' outstanding performance in the air, and was near to silent, the only noise coming from the cutting-edge turbines, which were also soundproofed to be as quiet as possible.

The Admiral walked past the helicopters, watching as the ground crews lovingly worked on two of them, treating them with the same care and affection as if they were their own flesh and blood, fixing the damage from their earlier mission.

He walked over to where a group of technicians were carefully examining items on a work bench, powerful arc lights illuminated the area as others stood close by, taking photos with a camera and writing down notes.

On the workbench were two of the Wasps belonging to Aurora, the technicians carefully unloading the live 40mm grenades still inside the cargo pods. On the hangar floor were the remains of one of the Thumpr's motors, its body charred and dented as it had fallen to earth. The Admiral looked over as the technicians worked, looking up, as the angry doctor from earlier now stood next to him. Gone were the doctor's clothes, replaced now with a military uniform, the badges on the arms denoting a member of the US elite Delta force, as the man wore the rank of Major.

"Did he say anything Admiral?"

"He didn't recognise you Major, if that's what you mean. He's still suffering from the effects of the gas. According to our scientists the memory loss could last days, even weeks."

"Can we hold him that long?" the Major asked, following, as the Admiral now walked up the line of benches.

"As far as the Brits are concerned, he's Missing In Action. For all they know he died in that strike."

The Major winced as he thought back to the inbound cruise missile strike, having been forced to leave six of his team behind in the inferno. It had been a hell of a cost, but from the way the Admiral talked, he'd been assured it was worth the price. He looked up as the Admiral walked up to the remains of the laser, crudely torn from the tank in their haste to escape with the stolen equipment.

"How the hell did they manage to get all of this to work?" he said admiringly, looking about as he fixated on their prized possessions.

They'd been tracking the progress of Whiskey Three-Zero since finding them via satellite, after the second night, watching from afar as three sky birds were tasked from the Pentagon to keep tabs on the British units that had survived the initial onslaught. One of the units, Major Richards, had eventually made it safely back, whilst the third unit, similar in size to Captain Faulkes unit had pushed east, getting as far as Ringwood, before coming under enemy attack as it attempted to navigate through the front lines. The Admiral remembered watching from the Crypt with the Delta operatives, as the tank had been the last to go, managing to hold on for another fifteen minutes against the Russians before finally exploding in a huge fireball as four anti-tank missiles had smashed into it, destroying it in seconds. However, it had been Whiskey Three-Zero that had piqued their interest, when, on the third night, the Brits had sent them a resupply, using equipment that none of them had ever seen before on the battlefield. And then when the satellites began to detect the faint radiation readings from the unit, that's when alarm bells had begun to ring in the Pentagon. Had the Brits just sent them tactical nukes? After a few tense hours the American military scientists had finally concluded it wasn't nukes, but the strange readings were emanating from something, and some of the scientists were beginning to talk of the possibility of fusion reactors, something that up to now, they'd assured the President were still years away from being developed.

Suddenly Whiskey Three-Zero had their full attention, and the Admiral and all the joint chiefs of staff back in the war room had watched on unbelievably, as the unit had burst out of the woodline that morning, with the Talons now identified as the source of the readings. Within minutes the order had come through from the American President and Joints chiefs. "We want that tech."

And that was how the Delta operatives and the Admiral had found themselves planning the snatch and grab raid, whilst the rest of the UN task force were busy preparing to land.

At the far end of the hangar floor, immobile and cold, the Talon was watching them. The Major found it hard to look at, knowing the last mission had almost been his downfall. His twenty-man team had been waiting in the woodline in ambush before the tank arrived. Laying the minefield had been easy, with two tomahawk cruise missiles laying down the air portable mines, it had taken less than thirty seconds, but it was the rest of the plan that was fraught with risk. The plan had been to ride out the battle and wait for Whiskey Three-Zero to be disabled in the minefield, then use VF56 gas to disable anyone left alive. The VF56 gas was cutting edge, odourless and tasteless, it could defeat 98 percent of military respirators, rendering people immobile and unconscious within milliseconds. However, its one weakness was once administered, it would cause acute memory loss. Once both the Russian and British troops had been knocked out, then his team would be free to enter the minefield, steal the tech and drones and be gone before anyone regained consciousness, none the wiser. He and his team had waited in the woodline, wearing the latest prototype in digital camouflage, behind digital ballistic screens designed to mimic their surroundings using cutting edge cameras and displays and suits that would mask the thermal signature of the human body to its surroundings. They were invisible to the human eye and to any thermal camera, or at least that's what they had thought. They'd watched in anticipation as right on cue, the lead vehicle of Whiskey Three-Zero had struck the mine, not catastrophic, but enough to get them to stop. This was it; this was their chance. It had all began to go wrong when the launcher used to fire the gas had malfunctioned, the team member looking on cursing, as he desperately tried to clear the stoppage as the Major watched the crews of the armoured vehicles now pull it safely away. He remembered the anger he felt as instead of driving into the minefield, Whiskey Three- Zero had skirted around it, driving away and out of sight. Now the only way to launch the gas would be up close, and with 500 metres of minefield between them and the tank there was no way they could do it. He decided to abort the mission and was about to get the stealth helicopters to come in to pick them up, when suddenly the tank was back, driving into the minefield! He couldn't believe his luck! They'd watched from afar as the tank had set itself up into a fire position, looking back the way it had just come, 200 metres away. He needed to get closer to use the gas, so slowly his team began to creep forwards, trying to close the gap to enable them to throw the gas cannisters. As they'd moved, he'd watched on his helmet display as the Talons had screamed through from the south, being provided with live feed from the satellites, watching in awe as the robots seemed to be working together as part of a pair. His team were now only 100 metres away, almost close enough to throw the gas grenades, when suddenly the tank began to creep forward and fire. "Oh shit!" he'd manage to mumble as suddenly they'd found themselves in the middle of a battle. Two of his team were crushed as the tank had reversed off, the crew oblivious to what they'd just done as the tank moved into another position. He could only curse at the streaks of red left in the grass, knowing there would be nothing left to bury of his troops. Then they'd been forced to take cover as the woodline around them came alive with bullets, as the Russians and British began to trade shots with each other. Another two of his team were shot as the Russian infantry had poured into the wood, a case of mistaken identity as the screens they'd hid behind had failed after being shot at too many times. He was under strict orders not to return fire, the US was not involved in the dispute, and even though it was tempting, him and his team had been forced to hunker down and take the blows, waiting for the right moment to strike. Then, finally the tank got itself stuck, and the crew were forced outside. It looked like the battle seemed to be coming to an end, at last he could use the VF56. He was about to deploy it when overhead the scream of incoming fire was heard, and he'd been forced to dive for cover as a heavy bombardment saturated the woodline. Remarkably none of his team were hit, and as he'd crawled out of cover, it was then that he saw the robots were back! He'd never get a better chance than now. But something else had then gone wrong, despite the fact his team were wearing thermal suits, and hidden behind camouflaged screens, somehow the robots knew they were there, reacting to the noise of his troops. One by one, his team were hit, the incoming fire hitting the ballistic plates and knocking them back down as they stood to throw the grenades. Finally, he'd lost patience, ordering his two EMP teams to engage one of the robots in the clearing, whilst another began to shoot the drones out of the sky. After a few minutes of fighting, they'd managed to disable one of the Talons and two of the Wasps, as the drones and robots were all pulling back, heading back the way they'd just come. Finally, he had his chance, and seeing no-one was left alive, what remained of his team ran up to the other side of the tank, coming across two soldiers still fighting. Recognising one was the tank's commander and knowing he knew how the equipment worked, the Major gassed them both, deciding to send them both back with the tech.

It was only after the first helicopter had landed, that they heard of the impending cruise missile strike over the radio, giving them less than sixty seconds. They grabbed what they could, loading up the two downed Wasps and ripping the Hornet from the turret, having to sling the heavier Talon under the helicopter, lifting off just as the second helicopter was trying to land to pick up the remainder of the team.

The Major shook his head in anger as he thought of the scene playing out again in his mind, the explosions, the fireball, his troops left to slaughter. The complete cock up of the mission. His anger had got the better of him, and even though he knew they were important, it had been he who had sunk his knife into one of the prostate figures, even contemplating opening the door of the helicopter and throwing them both out. It had been one of his Sergeants who had stopped him, citing their value and importance, the cost already been paid with by the lives of the team.

It had been a tough ride home, and he'd spent the past five hours writing letters back to his soldiers' loved ones, vague on the details, even vaguer on how they died.

"Major!" the Admiral asked again, his voice louder, disturbing him from his dark thoughts.

"Sir!" he looked over as the Admiral enquired again.

"I said, did the other one recognise you?"

"Oh," the Major replied, remembering he'd gone into the Russian Colonel's room, mirroring the pantomime played out with the Captain. Shaking his head, he continued, "No Sir, same as the other one. He thinks I'm a doctor, he's awake, spoke a few words in Russian, but has no recollection of what went on. Wants to know where he is."

"I bet he does," the Admiral replied smirking, adding, "keep him in the dark for now."

The Admiral walked up to the Talon, his eyes admiring the work that had gone into it, remembering the feeling of envy he'd had when he'd been invited by the UK military to visit Aurora, seeing the first prototype. At the time it was rigged up to a battery, a huge thing that had to be wheeled around with the Talon, giving it the power to operate for less than an hour. The Brits had kept quiet about its power source, it wasn't ready in time for the demonstration, hinting at a new revolutionary form of fusion reactor, self-powering with clean efficient plasma. He'd left the demo, being assured by his own team of engineers that the Brits would never get the reactor running. Now here they were, three years later and in front of him was the very thing they said they couldn't do.

"How did you do it?" the Admiral asked admiringly, his fingers running over the cold steel of the robot before looking over at two of the technicians with laptops plugged into the Talons body.

"Well? Is it stable to transport?"

The technicians looked up as one, as the more senior of the two, answered in reply.

"The core's balanced and emitting low peak radiation. Shielding looks good even with the EMP damage. Shame your men had to kill it with the EMP. We could have learned quite a bit.

The Major looked up; his voice full of scorn.

"Well fuck me! The next time I bring one back, I'll make sure the weapons are still working. We'll see how you two feel cosying up to it then."

The Admiral ignored the Major's outburst, continuing with,

"Forget the weapons platform for now, it's the reactor we're after. Is it safe or not?"

They looked at each other before nodding.

"Yes Admiral, it should be fine to transport."

"Good! I want everything packed and documented for the trip home by 10:00 hours tomorrow. No delays gentlemen, we got a lot of very interested people waiting to see this."

The Admiral walked away, leaving them all to it as he walked over to one of the outer hatches, swinging it open, heading to one of the few outside areas of the ship not accessed by any other decks, affording privacy to any of the Delta teams who wanted to be in the fresh air.

He pulled the sat phone from his pocket and dialled the number from memory.

He waited until he could hear the autonomous voice recording playing over the speaker before keying in another six-digit code to encode the call. After a few more seconds, the line became clear again, the voice on the other end asking,

"Jim?" the voice enquired, as the Admiral replied.

"Yeah, it's me, we're looking to have our cargo loaded up and enroute to you by 10:00 tomorrow. Expect arrival around 20:00 hours."

"Excellent news. We've got a lot of excited people here wanting to see this."

"Roger that." the Admiral replied, looking around him out of habit, before speaking again, his voice softer.

"What about our two guests?"

"Have they talked yet?" the voice asked.

"Not yet, they're still having trouble remembering what exactly happened thanks to the gas. The Captain's met me before at Aurora, so I know he's linked to the tech, but I don't think he can remember any of that now. As for the Colonel, he's still dazed, with little or no short-term memory. I think we might be okay for the moment."

"Well," the voice replied, adding in warning. "you still got some of us worried over here about the game you're playing."

"That can't be helped Dave, trust me, this Captain knows more than he's letting on. Did you get the footage we sent earlier?"

"We did."

"So, you've seen it yourself, one tank holding off a whole damn Russian BTG! And then when it shot down those two Mig's Christ, what we could do with that tech. And those robots! God damn, I'd seen them before, but nothing like that. The Russians were overwhelmed by them. Imagine what the Brits could have done if they had another twenty."

"And you think that this Captain is somehow the key to all this?"

"I do. I think that somehow he was in control of it all, and that we need more time to evaluate and interrogate."

"What about this Colonel? Why bother to keep him?"

"I've been told by the scientists that mental trauma can help unlock the effects of the gas. I don't know what went on between them, but the Captain could have got away. I watched him sabotage his escape plan and choose to stay in the fight to get at him. I'm going to keep this Colonel in my back pocket for now, wait a little, then have them both meet up. See if that can't jog a few memories."

There was a pause on the end of the phone as the person was thinking. Suddenly replying with,

"Why not just use Triflorium?"

The Admiral shook his head at hearing the mention of the truth drug.

"We tried that early on, but the trouble with Triflorium is that the subject needs to know he's lying for it to work. Both of these guys are still suffering from the effects of the gas, so all we managed to get out of them was a load of nonsense, nothing tangible. Plus, the danger with Triflorium is if we use it too many times you can end up putting the subject into a catatonic state. Until we know for sure they're lying, I can't risk using it again."

"Ok Jim, well it's your ass on the line if this goes south. For now, observe them. But if you think there's any chance at all of a risk to the operation, then you're authorised to deep six them. Make sure they disappear."

The Admiral sighed, closing his eyes and rubbing his nose as he thought about what deep six would mean. Simply put, they'd both be dropped over the side of the ship at night, never to be seen again.

"Understood. Anything else?"

"No Jim, for now that's it. Oh, and the President sends his regards."

18

Special Relations

UK South Coast

Peter was looking out over the water as the sun glistened on the surface, thinking how tranquil it all looked. On a day like today he should have been with his wife, out on a walk somewhere peaceful, or perhaps on a boat, enjoying the water. Instead, he was in the passenger seat of the Royal Navy Merlin, flying low over the south coast of England, enroute to pick up an old friend. He looked across at the other passenger, Sir Charles, the head of MI5 who was with him, having arranged the pickup after what Peter, and more importantly Wendi, had discovered. Over the past three days Peter had been ordered to use the AI programme more extensively, giving her more time in the real world as she sought out the answers to some of the problems they faced. It was on one of her latest missions that she discovered the information that had led them to now be on a helicopter over the English Channel, enroute to the naval taskforce offshore.

Sir Charles looked out of his window and pointed down as Peter leaned over to look, watching as the two US Marine F35's took station alongside them. Peter smiled in reply, happy to see the taskforce were taking no chances on inbound flights. Ever since the UK attacks, air forces around the world were now relying on the mark one eyeball, rather than technology, to identify incoming aircraft. Until the new threat could be countered, radar was now off limits, and not to be trusted.

Within minutes, Peter heard the engine noise change and felt the airframe shudder as the helicopter began to lose speed and slow down, as the deck of the USS Dorchester came into view. He was impressed at the size of the MFAS, even for a small fleet carrier it dwarfed most other navy's aircraft carriers. He watched on as the pilots' took their cue from the Air Boss, the airman stood on the flight deck with two paddles, using the semaphores to guide them into position as they brought the helicopter in smoothly, landing on the deck and quickly cutting power as the ground crew came running in to chock the wheels.

Peter waited until the lead pilot turned and gave the thumbs up before opening the sliding side door, and stepping out, walking forwards with Sir Charles following behind as they both ducked under the spinning, slowing rotors. Ahead of them, flanked by two Marine guards stood the Admiral with whom they'd arranged to meet.

Peter was the first to speak, extending his hand and smiling in recognition as he approached.

"Brigadier Peter Rawlinson, and this is Sir Charles Lynwood."

The Admiral removed his mirrored aviators and smiled in reply as he shook hands with them both.

"Admiral J D Stringer, welcome aboard the USS Dorchester, gentlemen."

They followed the Admiral and his guards as they walked away from the noise of the flight deck and over to a quieter area, as finally the Admiral turned to talk.

"So, gentlemen, mind me enquiring as to what this is all about? Why would the head of MI5 and the Boss of Aurora be requesting this little here meeting?"

Peter and Sir Charles looked at each other as the Admiral identified who they worked for, making it more than clear he knew all about them. It was Peter who answered first.

"Admiral, I'm not sure if you'll remember, but we met once, during your visit to Aurora when we conducted weapons tests a few years ago?"

The Admiral shook his head, and smiled apologetically in response as he lied, "I'm sorry Brigadier but I've attended many weapons tests in my career, you can't expect me to remember 'em all."

"Oh," Peter exclaimed, as Sir Charles now intervened.

"Admiral, the reason we're here today is that we've been reliably informed that you've got on board two people of interest to us, one, a Colonel by the name of Golgolvin, and the other a British Captain, his name's Captain Faulkes. Do either of these names ring any bells with you?"

Peter saw the Admiral glance up at the two names, probably wondering how they knew they were onboard before the smile returned, shaking his head again.

"I'm sorry gentlemen, but it looks like you've just had y'all a wasted trip. We don't have any Russian or British officers on board. This is an *American* vessel, for *American* military personnel only."

Peter produced his mobile phone, about to show the Admiral something when instead Admiral Stringer held his hands up in defiance, smiling as he continued.

"Look I'm sorry gentleman, but as I'm sure y'all can appreciate, I'm mighty busy, so I'm going to have to ask ya both to leave. Sorry for the wasted trip, perhaps next time a simple phone call would do."

Peter didn't move, instead he held out the phone defiantly, the Admiral sighing in irritation as Peter replied.

"Admiral, could you just take a look please, perhaps you might not be aware they're in the military, perhaps you've got them onboard as civilian casualties?"

Taking the phone, the Admiral made a big show of studying the image, on it was displayed a passport photo of Mike. He recognized the Captain straight away, even without the bandages and black eyes. Showing nothing of what he knew, he handed back the phone, shaking his head again.

"I'm sorry, but we don't have anyone on board matching the description of this person, civilian or not. Like I just said, the only people we have on board are American military personnel."

The Admiral turned to leave, as Peter looked at Sir Charles expectantly, waiting for him to say something. Seeing the prompt, he finally spoke out.

"Admiral, before you go, one other question if you please."

They could see the shoulders slump in irritation, clearly the Admiral wanted them gone. He turned and put his aviators back on, both of them could see their own reflections in the lenses as Sir Charles continued.

"A moment ago you said that you didn't have any Russian or British officers on board, but we only mentioned Captain Faulkes as being British. How did you know Colonel Golgolvin was Russian?"

"What?" the Admiral asked, looking on in growing irritation as Sir Charles continued,

"How did you know that Colonel Golgolvin was Russian? If you've never met the man?"

The Admiral's mouth opened in realisation, as Sir Charles continued,

"Now, our special relationship between our two countries has been built up from years of mutual trust and co-operation. Up until one minute ago I firmly believed that trust to be reciprocated."

The Admiral looked at them both, the corner of his mouth firming in irritation as he shrugged his shoulders.

"Reciprocated? I'm sorry Sir Charles, you've lost me there. Is that the plan here gentlemen? Throw some big fancy words from some gents with a few posh titles at the dumb yank, and hope he bows down to your mighty little empire?"

Both were a little taken aback at the Admiral's sudden hostility as he looked back at them defiantly, adding,

"In case you hadn't yet realised, we're on a US navy warship, in international waters, and you've both insulted a senior US navy officer, accusing me of lying, both a stain on my honour and reputation. And all while we're here *again*, helping you god damn Brits to fight your own shitty little wars. Why I ought to have both your ungrateful asses slung into the brig and kept there till you both learn some God damn respect and manners, sons o' bitches!"

Both of their faces flushed with anger at what the Admiral had just said, when Peter produced his phone again, and seeing what he was about to do, Sir Charles shook his head in warning.

"Peter, you were warned not to do that!" he shot out, as ignoring him, Peter stepped forwards, offering his phone out again to the admiral.

"If these men are not onboard then I'd like you to explain this."

With a look of growing anger, the Admiral took the phone, looking at the images on the display, the anger turning to shock and disbelief as the photo images of the USS Dorchester's own CCTV feeds were playing back at him. On the clear colour images he could clearly see the hospital wards, and rooms, then the screen changed as a vivid shot of both men were displayed, both in hospital gowns, easily identifiable. He was looking at both Captain Faulkes and Colonel Golgolvin.

"How the hell did you get this?" he shot back angrily, the Marine guards tensing at the Admiral's sudden aggression, unsure of how to act as Sir Charles turned to Peter angrily shaking his head.

Peter ignored the hostile stares, looking defiantly back, looking over to the Marine guards still listening in.

"Admiral, if you want this conversation to continue, then I suggest we lose the extra ears."

The Admiral looked over to the guards, taking the hint as he dismissed the Marines. Both looked at each other, uneasy to be leaving the Admiral as he shot back at them.

"I said take a break goddammit! Go get some fresh air somewhere else!"

As they turned to leave, he shot back, "And not a word of this to anyone, I find out you talked and you'll both be working the mail room for the rest of the year!"

With the Admiral's warning ringing in their ears, both Marines walked glumly away, Peter waiting until they were out of earshot before replying.

"Good, now we've got your attention, let's start again. We know you're holding them both, now how about in the interest of both our countries continued *friendly* relationship, you release them to us, and we'll be out of your way."

The Admiral was looking back at the camera feeds, disbelieving that the ships secure servers could have been hacked. How the hell were they doing this, he fumed to himself, thinking through the possible outcomes. What else did they have access to, not the crypt, surely? No that was intricate levels of firewalls and passwords, secure satellite feeds and only the pentagon had the 216 digit cypher key. No way would they be in the crypt. He looked up again as Peter finished speaking.

"So you're spying on us now? Is that what this is about? Allies spying on allies?"

Sir Charles had recovered from his shock at what Peter had done, he knew Wendi was the reason Peter had the footage, the PM and the CDS had specifically forbidden him to show anyone else it's capabilities. Now in his anger, Peter had unveiled their latest weapon, now the Americans knew what the British could do. Keeping his anger in check his eyes narrowed as he spoke.

"Admiral, if there was any deceit or illicit behaviour being conducted, then I suggest you look at your own side first. We know all about Tumat and the secret deals with the Americans, you mentioned you're here to help us fight our little war, but you're only really here to help clean up your own bloody big mess. Now, you're the one who's holding both officers illegally, against the rules of armed conflict, and you lied to us. If anyone should be giving lectures on morals, it's certainly not you!"

The Admiral's face flushed with anger, as he tried to think what to do next. He could have them both arrested, spying on an American warship was a detainable offence. But then what else did they know? These two weren't stupid, they wouldn't have come here without a means of getting away. Seeing the hostile look in his eyes Peter spoke out.

"Admiral, you have my word, if you fetch those two men now, before we leave, I'll tell you how we're able to hack into the ship."

"Oh will you now?" he shot back, unbelieving as to what he was being told.

Seeing the anger, Peter then remarked, "Look, why don't you have a think about it, we're not in a hurry, I'll even let you keep the phone so you can have a look at exactly what we're seeing."

The Admiral looked at the phone angrily, walking up to the deck side, he threw it vehemently into the sea, watching with satisfaction as it splashed into one of the waves, sinking from view.

"Hope that was insured." he remarked drily, wishing he'd listened to the advice of the others back home and just killed the detainees. It wasn't as if they'd gleaned anything from them, the Colonel was just constantly angry, ranting about his men and his unit, wanting to get back to them and the Captain could only remember the events up to the Bovington attack, but nothing more recent. He seemed to have no recollection of the robots, drones, or how to use them and had no idea of any tank battle. He hadn't expected anyone to come looking for them, and now having these two here, with eyes into the sensitive parts of his ship totally un-nerved him. Something about the smug look of the Brigadier angered him, all he wanted was both of them off his ship, in fact he wanted *all* of them off his ship, but didn't feel like just giving into their demands just yet. Quickly he made his mind up, looking up at Peter he demanded.

"Ok, so here's the deal, I give you *one* of them, you choose which, and then you tell me how the hell you're plumbed into my ship. Once you tell me, I'll let you fly off the flight deck. You lie to me, or don't tell me, and I'll impound that helicopter and you're all going stateside for a visit to a holding cell. And I think you both know how that ends up."

Peter was about to reply when Sir Charles stepped forwards, interrupting him and taking back control. "We know how the game's played Admiral, but we're here for them both, the deal is for two not one. And if you try anything funny, if our helicopter has a little accident on the way back home, then our security services release everything we have on your President. If we go down, you're coming down with us."

"Why do you want the Colonel? He's useless to you, he's your enemy.

"Perhaps, but that's not for you to worry about." Peter replied.

The Admiral firmed his mouth in thought, as nodding he replied.

"Ok, agreed. Now wait here, I'll have them both brought up."

Peter watched him walk away as Sir Charles walked over to the other side of the flight deck, pulling his phone out and talking into it. After a few minutes he came back, his face stern. Peter knew he'd just opened a can of worms by showing the Admiral the footage, but he didn't care. He owed it to Mike, they all did, and the thought of him being held a minute longer by an ally angered him. What the hell were the Americans playing at?

After a few minutes, the first figure emerged in a wheelchair, Peter had looked up hoping to see his friend but recognised the face of the Russian Colonel. He was flanked by three heavily armed Marines, who were weary of him, but when they got closer, Peter could see their fears were misplaced. The Colonel's legs were heavily bandaged, he wouldn't be running off anywhere anytime soon. The Colonel looked around at the ship, his eyes opening wide as he saw the vast task force around them. Clearly he'd never been on deck, and he strained in the chair, having to be restrained in place by one of the Marines as he tried to stand to look round.

He looked on in surprise at the Royal Navy helicopter, then looked over at Peter and Sir Charles, as he came closer. The nurse pushing him stopped the wheelchair by the Merlin's open side door, as Sir Charles knelt down to speak.

"Hello Colonel Golgolvin, my names David Fisher," he lied, "I'm from the United Nations. We're here to get you home."

The Colonel looked blankly at him, his eyes narrowing in suspicion as he began to quickly talk back in Russian, Sir Charles smiled, waiting for him to finish before replying in perfect Russian, one of Sir Charles's many languages he'd learned on the job. Golgolvin's eyes opened wide as he heard his own language, looking around him in surprise as finally Sir Charles nodded to the two Marine guards who helped to lift the wheelchair into the helicopter. The load master onboard took charge and began securing him for the flight.

As Sir Charles came back over and stood next to Peter, he asked, "What did you say to him?"

Sir Charles winced against the sun that shone on the water's surface.

"I told him that I knew he spoke English, however if he didn't feel comfortable speaking it yet, I'd happily speak Russian to him. I told him that he was being released into our care, and that he'll soon be back with his men."

"That's it?" Peter remarked, as Sir Charles shrugged his shoulders and lowered his voice.

"What do you expect me to say? Hi, I'm MI5 and we're here to try to recruit you and send you back in a prisoner exchange, hoping you'll help us against your own?"

Peter smiled as Sir Charles spoke, his eyes being drawn to a second wheelchair being pushed out, this one had only one guard following on as the Admiral walked behind them. Peter walked forwards smiling, happy to see his friend again, the smile dying on his lips as he took in the sorry image of what was coming towards him.

Mike was dressed in a hospital gown, his face black and blue, like a panda his eyes were heavily ringed by his black eyes. His nose was offset and broken, and his head wore a bandage, no doubt he'd suffered a head injury. His abdomen was tightly wrapped in bandages, but it wasn't the bandages or the injuries that appalled the Brigadier, it was the way Mike was looking back at him, eyes wide and face offset to the side, drool spooling out of his mouth. Peter looked up in shock as the wheelchair was brought alongside the Merlin, Mike looking on vacantly into space.

"Mike." Peter whispered horrified, leaning down to see his friend looking blankly back at him, with no recollection as to who he was speaking with. Quickly, Sir Charles pushed past him, leaning down and looking into his eyes, seeing for himself what had happened.

"Triflorium." he muttered, looking up at Peter and replying quickly, "Truth drug. He'll need a good dose of anti-serum and quickly. We'll need to move fast if we want to save his mind from permanent damage."

The Admiral walked up to them, pointing to them both.

"Well you've got what you came for, now give me what I want."

"You bastard! What have you done to him?" Peter shot back, Sir Charles having to put out an arm to stop him as the Admiral's face looked back impassively.

"We've done nothing to him, he's merely dosed up with painkillers is all. Now just give me want I want and then get the hell off my ship!"

Peter stared angrily back, as Sir Charles leaned in to whisper, "Peter, we don't have time for this, if you want to save him, we need to go...NOW!"

Shaking his head, Peter looked back, a look of disgust on his face as he looked at the Admiral. Behind him stood the four Marines carrying automatic weapons, making it clear the helicopter would not be leaving without the Admiral's say so.

He took a deep breath and calmed himself, his anger dissipating as he replied,

"Very well, we've had a device brought onboard your ship four months ago, its located in your PX on E deck. Two of your crew members work for MI6, every once in a while, they move the device, so it doesn't get discovered. Find the device, and you cut the link. Simple."

"And these two crew members?" the Admiral shot back, his eyes narrowing.

Peter smiled glumly, looking down at his friend. "For what you've done to him, I think I'll let you find them yourself."

The Admiral looked down at the dribbling figure, pinching his lips in thought before turning to the airboss.

"Get em out of here!"

Peter helped the nurses as they carried the wheelchair on board, the load master looked down sympathetically at the figure, as he made sure the wheelchair was strapped in. He looked down at the growing puddle under the wheelchair, before running forwards and grabbing some paper roll. In a final act of indignity, Mike had just wet himself. Peter sat in shock, shaking his head at the condition of his friend, as finally the loadmaster gave the all clear, closing the side door as the engines began to spool up and the shadows of the rotors began to spin overhead.

Two minutes later and the Merlin was lifting off the flight deck, Sir Charles and Peter waiting with bated breath, hoping the Admiral would see sense, but half expecting to see a missile streaking towards them. It wasn't until five minutes later, when over land that they finally relaxed somewhat and settled down. Peter looked towards the back of the helicopter, the Colonel was staring over at Mike, there was recognition there, Peter could see him trying to piece together how he knew him. Peter didn't understand how they'd been captured, or why, only that by using facial recognition software Wendi had located them both on the ship, hacking into the Pentagon's war room, and then using the ship's onboard CCTV to find them.

Sir Charles leaned over, shouting into Peter's ear to be heard over the sound of the helicopter's engines.

"You realise that right now he's going to be tearing that ship apart looking for your so-called device. And that by naming two of his crew, he'll be tearing them apart, going through all the personnel files."

Peter's face remained impassive as he looked out the window, unable to look over at Mike, too upset in his current state, as finally Sir Charles continued.

"You understand Peter, the problem you've just caused, by showing the Americans what we have with Wendi. They'll work it out eventually you know."

Peter ignored him, not wanting to talk any longer, simply watching out the window as the helicopter continued on its journey.

Another thirty minutes later and they landed at Birmingham Queens Royal hospital, where both Mike and the Colonel were unloaded into the waiting hands of the military doctors ready to receive them. Sir Charles had already radioed ahead, detailing how to counter the effects of Triflorium, having used it before when interrogating suspects of the crown. The hospital already had the necessary drugs standing by, and Peter watched as Mike was carefully lowered to the floor. He wanted to jump out to say something to his friend, but the shame, and the embarrassment he felt for his friend stopped him. He knew Mike, he knew he wouldn't want him to see him like this. Instead, he sat, watching as Sir Charles stood outside talking to the four MI5 operatives who were there to guard the Colonel, to keep him safe and secluded, until Sir Charles could return to question him. Within minutes he was back aboard, and the helicopter rising above the Birmingham skyline, heading back to Aurora.

Now it was just the two of them, as Sir Charles leaned forwards to speak.

"Peter, did I ever tell you about when my grandfather worked at Bletchley park?"

Peter remained tight lipped, staring out the window as Sir Charles continued, "Worked in Hut 6, during the war. Grumpy old bastard, but the one thing I was always proud of was his input in helping crack the Enigma code."

Peter looked away from the window, wondering where Sir Charles was going with the conversation as he continued talking.

"Not long after he'd helped crack the code, he was transferred to Churchill's war room, and became a Special Liaison Officer, delivering the now uncoded messages, called Ultras, for Churchill to read personally."

"Is this really relevant right now Charles?" Peter replied angrily, watching the countryside flashing by.

Unperturbed Sir Charles continued, "One day, my grandfather was given an Ultra to deliver, and he goes into Churchill's bedroom, it's three in the morning and the PM is in bed in his pyjamas, awake and smoking a cigar. The PM reads the report aloud. Coventry is to be bombed by the Luftwaffe in the next 72 hours. Now the PM knows he can stop the attack, he's got the means to evacuate the city, has the means to defend the city, but he also knows that if he does this it will alert the Germans that their highly prized code had been cracked. And if the Germans suspect we'd cracked the Enigma code, they'd change it and then our vital intelligence asset, vital for the winning of the war would be gone. Perhaps with it our chances at final victory."

Hearing enough, Peter quickly interjected, growling, "And instead Churchill did nothing and allowed the City to be bombed, killing hundreds of people and destroying most of the city, but kept the secret of Ultra safe. I'm well aware of the Coventry bombings Charles, I did study history at school."

"Yes, but did you know that my Grandfather lived in Coventry? That his wife, my Grandmother was there? He could have telephoned to warn her, knowing what he did, but he didn't. He kept quiet, knowing to do so could give the game away. He risked his own wife to keep a secret. He put the needs of the nation above his own self-interest."

"Charles, I really don't want to talk about this now."

"As you wish Peter." Sir Charles replied, settling himself in the seat.

Twenty minutes later and Peter could see the airfield come into view as the Merlin began to land. He saw the familiar hangars come into view as the helicopter softly landed on the apron, the pilots shutting down power as the helicopter lowered onto its wheels. Peter knew the helicopter would be taking off again shortly, Sir Charles was needed back at the WOC, so Peter watched on, surprised as Sir Charles followed him out and walked beside him away from the helicopter. He looked over seeing the Warriors of Whiskey Three-Zero parked by the hangars, no doubt the crews were settling into the routine of the airbase. It had been his idea to attach them to Aurora under his command, he'd reminded the CDS that those crews were the only ones who'd tested the hardware and weapons in real combat, so why not now make them part of the unit. Peter had hoped later to get to meet them, no doubt Kyle and David were helping debrief them, looking at any major changes they could implement on the weapons. He turned to Sir Charles, about to speak, when he saw Kyle running across to meet him. Kyle looked flustered and breathlessly shouted,

"They've taken her! They've stolen Wendi."

Peter turned, knowing now why Sir Charles was out of the helicopter. Seeing Peter's angry look Sir Charles quickly explained.

"As I tried to explain on the helicopter, you chose to save Coventry, instead of thinking of the bigger picture. You forced our hand Peter, you made us do this when you pulled that little stunt on the ship with the Admiral. The PM was quite clear in his orders to you. Go and try to get them back, but under no circumstances divulge Wendi's existence!"

"I did no such thing!" Peter shot back, adding, "besides, if I hadn't have used what we knew, the Admiral would have sent us packing, and we both know what he would have done to them. This time tonight they'd have both been dead."

"But by showing him those bloody pictures, you showed him that we were spying on our allies, and worse than that, you showed him we had the ability to do so! We both know he's not stupid, after he realises there's no devices onboard his ship, the Americans will begin to investigate how we did it. In doing so, they could find out all about Wendi and worse, come to take her. Do you have any idea what *any* government in the world would do to have that power? It's too much power for a civilian company to wield, especially one led by someone that we now know can't follow simple bloody orders."

"But Mike would be dead Charles! Christ, can't you see that?"

"So what!" Sir Charles countered, his voice rising as his own anger began to boil over. "Every day I have brave men and women, operatives in my line of work who are selflessly laying down their lives to defend what's left of our bloody country, whose deaths go unnoticed, unpublicised, all for the greater good. So why should your friend be any different?"

Peter remained tight lipped as Sir Charles continued, "And what did we get from the bargain?" What did we get from unveiling what is perhaps this country's greatest ever intelligence asset produced? We get a drooling, half-baked imbecile who pisses himself and will probably spend the rest of his life staring out of a bloody window!"

Both of them glared at each other, as Kyle wisely kept quiet, after a few tense moments it was Sir Charles who spoke first, his anger abating.

"Look, Peter I'm sorry for what I just said, I know we owe a great deal to that man, and I hope to hell he recovers. But either way, you just gambled one hell of a bet, and the risk to our future capability is now too great to simply throw away. Perhaps if this had been a more peaceful time you may have got away with it, but as things stand, with the country in the grips of war. I'm sorry, but the decision's already been made, as of now, Wendi is the property of the UK intelligence services."

Seeing the look of horror on Peter's face, he waved his hand around the airfield, adding, "Just be thankful it's only Wendi we're taking, others wanted to strip you of all this. At least you get to keep your company."

Peter watched on in mute frustration as Sir Charles began to walk back to the helicopter, finally shouting after him.

"I hope you know what you're bloody doing Charles, because once that genie's out of the bottle, it'll be impossible to put back in."

"You let us worry about all that, you just concentrate on making us more of those bloody drones."

And that was it. Peter watched on as Sir Charles climbed aboard the helicopter, fighting the downdraft as he watched it climb away into the sky, disappearing from view.

For a few seconds, he and Kyle stood there, in silence, not quite knowing what to say, until eventually Peter broke the silence.

"Well, that's been an interesting day. I don't know about you Kyle, but I could do with a drink..."

Kyle nodded glumly, both deflated, as they turned to walk back to the hangars. In the distance Peter could see the troops of Whiskey Three-Zero were walking over, drawn out by the noise of the helicopter. They'd all known that Peter was going to pick up Mike, he'd promised them he'd get him back. All stood there, expecting to see him with Peter on the helicopter, all waiting to greet him home. Peter wondered what he'd say to them, did he really want to describe what he'd seen?

Sighing to himself, he shook his head slowly. He couldn't describe what he'd seen, that was worse than thinking Mike was missing. He began to walk towards them, his thoughts already turning to ways he could softly break the news...

19

When Two Worlds...

Three weeks after the ceasefire.

"Everyone off!"

Kate looked up apprehensively at the border guard who was stood in the aisle, her eyes flicking outside the coach window to the tank that was parked menacingly on the side of the road. Some of the passengers were slow to respond, causing the guard to lose his patience.

"Come on! We haven't got all bloody day, I said off! Document check!"

This was the third checkpoint that they'd had to stop for since arriving in occupied territory. Every time it was the same procedure; everyone off, check documents, bag search, numerous questions, then back on the bus to the next armed checkpoint.

Kate stepped off into the cold grey landscape, joining the back of the queue with the other passengers, looking around at the faces of those around her. She couldn't help but notice how clean she looked - a total contrast to the other people. All of them had a vacant look, their clothes grey and filthy, granted the pouring rain didn't help, and within minutes she was as wet and miserable looking as the rest of them. She pulled her summer jacket tight around her, cursing the fact she'd left her heavy waterproof coat back at the hotel. To be fair, when she'd left the UK it had been summer, now it was almost winter. What the hell had happened over here?

As she waited, cold, wet and tired, her thoughts drifted back to how it all came to pass, the day when she'd last spoken to Mike.

Since the invasion started she'd been trying desperately to call home, trying to reach him, her parents, even her friends. No-one seemed to be answering the phones. All she could see on the news was the violence and bloodshed of the invasion, listening to both sides blaming the other. She didn't believe this half-baked story of the Monarchy attempting a coup, and suspected something else must be in play. She had driven the hotel reception crazy with her constant badgering for information, trying anything she could think of to find out what was going on at home. Finally out of options, she'd resorted to hiring a car, driving the 698 miles to the British embassy in Washington, hoping to see the ambassador. But once she saw the hundreds of people waiting to see him, she knew then how bad things were. She'd sat there with all the other concerned people in the embassy lobby, all desperate for news of loved ones back home, all being told the same information. "We have no further updates."

Finally after four sleepless days and nights they'd all heard the news of the ceasefire brokered by the United Nations. Finally the fighting had stopped. Since then she had tried repeatedly to get home, but with the UK's airspace as dangerous and compromised as it was, all international civilian flights were banned. She'd even driven to military bases, hoping to bribe her way onto one of the many military aid flights heading to the UK. But all the US soldiers merely smiled apologetically as she begged them to allow her onboard, feeling genuine sympathy for her as they said no.

Finally, with a heavy heart she resigned herself to having to wait with the other British people all desperate for news on loved ones. Bulletin boards were erected in the embassy lobby showing daily lists of casualties as the two competing UK governments released the names. Every morning a new list of names were added and every morning Kate had to go through the same routine with mixed feelings of dread and hope. She'd repeat this procedure every morning for the next week, walking up to the boards, holding her breath as she read the latest names, finally feeling relief as she walked away knowing her family were not on there. She'd watch on as others would burst into tears and cry out as they recognised names of loved ones. She felt sad for their loss, but thankful that it wasn't her grief to bear. They must be alive, she'd thought, Mike would know what to do, he always did.

By the third week Kate had been so desperate for news from home she would have built a damn plane and flown it herself, her fears of flying taking a firm back seat as finally the news filtered through. Civilian flights were finally being allowed back in.

She'd ran into Washington Airport, expecting now to book a flight, fighting against the throng of people who were also desperate to get tickets. Each person was met with the same disappointing news, although flights were allowed, passengers now needed a travel pass to enter the occupied territories as they were now called. If Kate wanted to get back to Poole, she'd need one of these passes. So it was back to the Embassy, joining more queues of people. Finally she was called forward to the desk, watching on dumbfounded as the clerk warned her of the new name changes to the occupied areas. Over 40 percent of the UK was now controlled by Tumat. Her home county, Dorset had now become the 'New England District' and was under the occupying forces new laws. She was handed the application form along with the warning that her application could take weeks to process. The realisation was dawning on her that this was far more complicated than she had imagined. The chaotic scrum of hundreds of people behind her emphasised they were all in the same position. Filled with a glimmer of hope and desperate to see her family she took the pen and the form, running over to a slightly quieter part of the lobby and filled it in before fighting back through the queues to hand it in.

The clerk checked it over, nodding satisfactorily before handing her a leaflet and replying.

"Thank you, please take this to read, it will explain the new rules for New England District. We'll be in touch."

And with that she was waved away, the clerk's attention already on the next person.

Kate had gone back to her hotel and waited, reading and re-reading the leaflet, feeling anger at seeing the changes in her country. Chatting to others waiting in the hotel, she began to hear rumours about what was going on over there, and the more she found out, the more she knew she couldn't live there. If Mike and her parents were alive, then this wasn't about her going home. It was about her reuniting with them and all getting out of there. Knowing she could be waiting for weeks, she began to use her time to plan her escape, where could they now call home? Her planning had been interrupted only two days later with a knock on her door, a member of the hotel reception handing her the envelope. She felt surprised and relieved at seeing the contents, inside was a one-way ticket to Birmingham and more importantly a 48-hour travel pass, granting her access to her home. More than enough time to get back, get Mike and her parents, and get the hell out. She was in such a rush to get going she didn't even bother to pack, abandoning her luggage in the room, electing instead to take just a few essentials in her handbag.

On the flight back she'd thought through what to say to Mike. Her parents wouldn't be the problem, they'd go with her no matter where, but Mike could be, he was settled there, and what about the house? Could they still sell it from outside of the occupied areas? It was a lot of money to just leave behind, but then she'd thought about those mornings in the Embassy when checking the lists, knowing others had been less fortunate. Perhaps this was just one of those times when money didn't matter and what mattered most was keeping yourself and your loved ones alive and safe.

She'd tried to sleep on the flight, dark thoughts quickly filling her head as the closer to home she got, the more anxious she became, surprised that now her fears were not about flying but the fate of her loved ones. She was drawn to the flash of lights outside the aircraft in the dark sky, seeing the navigation lights of two fighter jets that took station over each wing, escorting them through Irish airspace. People around the world were still on edge, clearly taking no chances.

An hour later they had landed, the passengers quickly whisked through the near empty terminal of Birmingham airport and into the customs desks, the checks taking even longer as military working dogs were called in to search everyone. Kate could see the changes, the way the people looked at her, the way she was spoken to, it was as if the war had tore the very heart out of the British people. She smiled at the Border Force officer as he rummaged through her bag, who in turn ignored her, keeping his face cold and hard. After a few moments he was satisfied, giving her back the bag and indicating with his arm for the next person to come over.

Twenty minutes later and she was on the coach with some of the passengers from the flight. All looked to be heading into the occupied lands. Some of them looked anxious, not quite knowing what to expect as outside the cold grey light of dawn began to appear, the clouds overhead grey and full of rain, eerily matching the mood. Everyone could feel it, the country they had all left, was a far cry from the one they were returning to.

"Miss."

She looked up, disturbed from her thoughts by the elderly gentleman who was gently nudging her, pointing over to where the guard was impatiently waving her over to the guard box.

"Oh..Thank you," she muttered, quickly walking forwards, her feet squelching in the wet mud.

Without any welcome he reached out, his hand taking the travel pass as she tried her best to keep it out of the rain. Thankfully the guard box was dry and the guard had no such problem when reading it.

"Destination?" he barked

"Poole."

"How long you staying for?"

"I'm going home, that's where my family are."

"This pass is only valid for 48 hours. If you intend to stay longer then I suggest that when you get home you register yourself to your district office. They'll have the necessary forms you need to make yourself a citizen."

"I understand." she replied, already knowing she had no such intention of doing so.

"And you do understand that failure to register yourself constitutes an offence under the New England District rules for immigration? If you outstay your visa and are found guilty of such a violation you *will* go to prison."

"I know all the rules, I've read the leaflet."

After a few moments of scrutiny he smiled forcefully and handed back the pass.

"Well, in that case, welcome to the New England District, Mrs Faulkes."

Kate nodded in thanks, trying her best to smile, but looking at the array of soldiers around her, all brandishing assault rifles they were far from welcoming.

"You're not Russian." she enquired, noting his English accent was at odds to his dark uniform and red arm band emblazoned with the black letters N.E.D.

He smiled suddenly, the cold facade cracking as he answered, "Of course I'm not. I was born here in Ringwood."

She looked on confused as to why a local would be helping the enemy as he continued, "There's been a lot of changes around here lately."

"Like re-naming Dorset, the New England District?" she asked.

The guard pursed his lips and narrowed his eyes before replying, "I suggest for your own sake that you keep comments like that to yourself."

She followed his gaze to the soldiers nearby, nodding in thanks at the veiled warning before putting her pass back into her handbag.

Another border guard waved her over to his tent, ushering her inside for yet another handbag check. At least she was out of the rain now. She stood back and watched as for the third time that morning her handbag was upended without care, the contents spilling out over the table before rough hands went through her personal items. The guard looked up, remarking.

"Is this it? You have nothing else with you?"

"No, I'm travelling light."

Within minutes she was back on the coach, watching through the steamed window at the huge queue of people yet to go through the border. She couldn't help but notice some of those from the coach were pulled off to the side, animatedly chatting with the border guards. Clearly not all of them seemed to have the pass that she had. She looked down at it, still unable to read the Cyrillic writing, only the paragraph written in English.

'This bearer of this pass is guaranteed unfettered access to all lands currently under the control of the peacekeeping force of Tumat. The bearer is not to be impeded or delayed. Any delay will be reported as a violation of the UN ceasefire resolution 248.6 Paragraph 6 and those delaying said bearer will find themselves liable to prosecution.'

Were all the passes worded like this, she wondered, looking outside at the throng of people. She had seemed to breeze through the checkpoints with the greatest of ease. She still couldn't believe how she'd managed to obtain it so quickly.

The pass was quickly forgotten about as she saw the empty seats on the coach, knowing it wouldn't be going anywhere yet so instead she settled back and closed her eyes, trying to rest. But she couldn't relax, she was sick with worry as to the fate of Mike and her parents. Were they still at home? Were they still alive? She thought through the plan again in her head, knowing that Mike and her parents wouldn't have the necessary paperwork to get out of the occupied areas by car. The coach journey had already proven that, not that it mattered, her plan was to get home, grab her family, walk the small distance to the marina, get onboard their boat and blast the fuck out of the harbour, watching the problems of the New England District disappear behind them. They were going to escape by sea, they were going to France. She knew the boat had the range and the fuel to do so. She had friends there that she'd already contacted, who were waiting for them in Cherbourg, to help start their new life. She knew the boat had fuel, Mike had a habit of insisting the tanks were left full. The only real problem was that the boat was in bits, halfway through it's restoration, but Kate knew it was all cosmetic, the engines still worked, and that's all she needed, two good engines, a chart, compass and a steering wheel. She could do this, they could all do this.

She heard the coach's engine start up with a rumble as the coach doors closed and it began to pull away. She looked about, surprised that some of the passengers were still not aboard, looking out she could see them still arguing with the border guards. Whatever was happening, they were not being allowed back on. She looked to the driver, seeing his glum look in the rear-view mirror reflected back at her

"Driver, those people haven't got back on board yet."

He ignored her, driving slowly through the checkpoint barrier, as she stood up and walked forwards.

"Excuse me, I said you've left those people behind!"

He looked over at her, shaking his head as he replied, "Look love, I'm only here to drive the coach. So why don't you just sit down and let me do my job. Don't make any trouble for me eh?"

Kate was taken aback by what he'd said, his willingness to be so complicit. He clearly wasn't going to confront the guards. Shaking her head unbelievably, she made her way back to her seat, seeing through the back window the border checkpoint and the passengers dissipating into the distance. Knowing that any doubts she may have had about getting her family out of there were now gone. She'd seen enough, now she was certain, now it *was* time to get the hell out.

She settled down, watching as the rain increased again, the water running in beads down the windows, knowing that finally at last she'd get to see those she loved. She'd see her family..

6th Div HQ Bovington

Lunyou stood watching in the rain, as the twenty soldiers of his unit were loading up into the back of the truck. Nearby another six British police officers stood by their patrol cars, waiting for the arrest team to make its way out of the camp's perimeter. Lunyou sneered at them, angry to have them thrust upon his unit, the General having insisted that with the ceasefire in place, and the world's press now watching intently, it was to be the British police who made the arrests and not his men. "Remember, we're supposed to be here to assist them, not control them." General Terekhov had warned. Ever since Project Houdini had been exposed to the world's population the General had been more cautious, trying desperately to paint the picture of forces of Tumat as liberators, not conquerors.

Assist them, thought Lunyou angrily, remembering the district's latest intelligence assessment he'd seen just that morning, showing a growing resistance within the population that showed no signs of weakening. He knew members of the police were involved, they had to be. How else were the culprits getting away with it? If the FSB were left to their own devices he'd have stopped this growing rebellion in it's infancy.

Fifteen of their soldiers had been killed this week in his district alone, apparent victims of the 'honey trap'. A beautiful woman would approach one of their off duty soldiers at a bar, laugh with him, flirt with him, entice him outside with a promise. The lucky soldier, usually plied with drink and unable to believe his luck, would go outside with the woman, being led somewhere quiet, thinking it was his lucky night. Only to find when they were finally alone, they actually weren't. A welcoming committee was waiting. All part of a resistance movement calling itself the BRF (British Resistance Force). Any information on this new terrorist organisation was vague, all he knew was it was being led by someone the locals had nicknamed 'The Reaper'.

They'd tried warning the soldiers, making the clubs and bars where the attacks were happening off limits, arrested landlords, club owners, even planted their own undercover officers in the bars looking for these deadly beauties. But still more attacks came, these BRF bastards were becoming bolder, more ambitious, growing in popularity. Already, more of their symbols were appearing painted on shop doorways and on the sides of walls. Only yesterday some cheeky bastard had painted the BRF slogan on the side of Lunyou's house. That hadn't been coincidence, and Lunyou knew the more these little attacks were allowed to continue, the worse it would get. He vowed to find those responsible, but first, he had today's business to attend to. Today he would be exacting his own form of personal vengeance, repaying a favour to someone who had caused him so much trouble in the past.

He'd had the house in Poole under surveillance since discovering Faulkes's address three weeks ago, learning that an elderly couple named Roy and Martha Stokes lived there with their cat. He'd found out from the police that they were the parents of Faulkes's wife. Surmising they must have been left behind in the chaos, he originally planned to arrest the couple immediately. However, General Terekhov had forced him to wait, the rebellion that had been growing within the local population had taken priority and required the FSB's full attention first. Instead he'd been forced to watch the surveillance team's footage, observing the couple tottering around the house, thinking angrily to himself, how fucking cute.

Now the latest events had finally pushed him into action, with a new player emerging in the game. He always knew Faulkes had a wife, but she had been safely out of the way in America, well out of his reach. Or so he'd thought. He couldn't believe his luck when his office told him of her application for a travel pass to return to the district. With hundreds of applications, it should have taken her at least two weeks to get the pass, but Lunyou needed her here now, for his own agenda, so he had the FSB fast track her application. After all, he did know her husband, so felt it only fair to assist her return. Now, with her new, 'go anywhere 48-hour pass,' she was on her way home. He knew that Faulkes was alive, but not living at home. He was somewhere up north in a hospital, hiding from prying eyes. But Lunyou had a plan, a plan that would pull that bastard back into his clutches. He'd use his wife and parents as bait.

The parents hadn't left the house for the whole time the FSB were watching, so he could only assume they'd been smart enough to have kept a stockpile of food from before the invasion, with no other reason to venture out. Food shortages were rife in the area, and after the first week of looting and lawlessness shops were still struggling to restock themselves. Now all citizens of the district were required to register for ration cards, handing over any stockpiles of food they had, for re-distribution by the District. Lunyou knew that the couple hadn't done so and was waiting for them to be joined by Mrs Faulkes. Then his team would raid the house, find supplies, plus a few extra items his team would plant there and arrest them all for profiteering in black market goods. That's why the British police were with his team to make the arrests. He wanted the information to be as public as possible. Hopefully the locals would be outraged, how dare this family hoard food whilst others were starving and dying on the streets. The news would filter back to whatever rock Faulkes had hidden under, and undoubtably he'd come back to get them, ever the fucking saviour. Lunyou would be waiting for him, finally able to pay back in kind all the trouble Faulkes had caused him.

He smiled menacingly, already playing in his head the scenarios in which he'd introduce himself to Mrs Faulkes. His evil thoughts being interrupted as his Sergeant approached,

"We're ready to go."

Looking up, Lunyou could see all the vehicles loaded and lined up, the police cars lights flashing, ready to keep civilian traffic away from the convoy.

"I get the feeling today's going to be a great day Artem. Right then, let's go welcome Mrs Faulkes."

His Sergeant smiled, ignoring the rain that poured down him as he opened the 4x4's door for his officer, watching him slowly getting in, the leg wound clearly still having an impact on his mobility. As he closed the door, he noticed the rain begin to stop. Above him he could see the faint glimmer of the sun's rays begin to burst through. Perhaps Captain Lunyou was right, perhaps this was going to be a great day after all.

Poole – Dorset

Thank god the rain had stopped, Kate thought, as she walked slowly along the deserted neighbourhood streets, glancing into people's empty driveways, noticing the apparent lack of cars. She knew some of the people in these houses and hoped that wherever they were they were safe. Some of the houses had their curtains pulled across, some of which she noticed twitch slightly as she walked past, the people hiding behind them clearly not wanting to be seen.

She stared open mouthed as part of the street seemed to disappear into a vast mountain of rubble. As she drew closer, she could see four houses had been totally destroyed, now nothing more than twisted ruins, the only sign of people were the discarded personal possessions in amongst the rubble. As she passed she could see framed photographs, dust riddled clothing, even children's toys thrown in amongst the pile. Under one of the huge piles she could just make out the shape of the front of a car, its wheels splayed out, bodywork mangled. She continued on, seeing in spray-paint the warning scrawled on the hastily placed sign.

'BODIES INSIDE. KEEP OUT. UNEXPLODED BOMBS!'

"Jesus!" she muttered, slowly stepping away, fearful her footsteps could cause an explosion. After a few tense steps she felt confident enough to keep walking up the street, nervous about what she might find when she got to her house.

A few minutes later she was stood at the junction that would take her into her street. Her house was only 100 metres down the road, she could walk it in less than a minute, but something held her there. Suddenly her doubts and fears began to intensify, rooting her to the spot. What if the house was gone, she thought fearfully, what if they weren't there? What if they were dead? What would she do then? After all this effort to get home, she'd be trapped here, alone. Suddenly her bottom lip began to tremble and her eyes welled with tears. She tried to fight the urge, to think of something more positive, but the more she tried to hold back the tears, the more she began to cry, the stress, the anguish, the fear of the past three weeks all beginning to take hold, all of it finally leading to this moment.

Eyeball - One

The surveillance team was watching on as Target Two stopped at the end of the street, almost home. One team member was watching through a high-powered camera lens through a pinhole aperture in the white sheet, the other reporting back to their headquarters over the radio.

"What's she doing now?" the operator on the radio hissed.

"She's stopped. Looks like she checking the street out."

"Fuck! Do you think she's seen us?"

"Not a chance," the camera operator exclaimed, pulling his head away from the camera and checking their cover once again. They'd occupied the empty house opposite Alpha-One, the target house codeword, weeks ago, setting up in the dead of night. Using a wooden frame and white sheet, they'd erected a simple white barrier in the bedroom that overlooked the house, creating a fake wall within the room. Then, using a razor blade, they had cut tiny slats into the fabric, visible only to the camera, which could see out into the street. Now they could remain hidden behind the barrier but observe Alpha-One and were safe in the knowledge of knowing that to anyone outside looking in, it would appear the room was empty. It was the easiest and most basic of surveillance setups, but it was tried and tested, it worked.

The camera operator went back to observing, clicking away on the shutter as he reported.

"She's crying. Looks like she's having second thoughts."

"Agggh," the other replied in mock sympathy, warranting his colleague to look at him with raised eyebrows.

After a few moments the camera was clicking away again as the operator reported.

"Right she's off again, that's Target Two now walking towards Alpha One."

The radio operator relayed the reports as they watched her walk towards her house, wiping her eyes on a tissue she had pulled out of her handbag. She stopped at the main gate, pausing again and looking up the street.

"Come on....come on!" the camera operator breathed, urging her through the gate. They knew that once she was inside their job was finished, then it was over to the arrest team.

After a few tense moments of waiting she finally stepped through the gates and made her way up to the front door.

"Fucking finally!" the camera operator exclaimed, the tension evaporating from him as he continued reporting.

"Right, Target Two now at door of Alpha one."

"She's knocking on door.....Door is opening.....I have visual on elderly gentleman."

"Confirmed, elderly gentleman is Target One...Target One and Target Two are hugging...."

"They're now joined by elderly lady...Confirmed, elderly lady is Target Three."

"I have visual on all three targets."

The radio operator was quickly relaying the messages, both waiting for that all important moment, when she went inside. When that happened, they'd send the code word.

"Okay, she's stepping inside, door closed. RASPUTIN! RASPUTIN! RASPUTIN!"

Delightedly the camera operator punched the air, as the radio operator sent the code word, quickly being acknowledged by their control room. Now their job was done, it would be passed to the arrest team. The radio operator relaxed, removing his headset and lighting two cigarettes, handing one to the camera operator. They had ringside seats to the spectacle about to take place, and having spent three weeks in that house, they were finally looking forward to seeing the fruits of their labour.

Somewhere over Oxford

Mike inhaled deeply as the fumes of the aviation fuel filled his lungs as they flew over the Oxfordshire countryside. He was alone in the Merlin, the only other passenger being the load master who watched him curiously as Mike drew deep breaths.

Mike ignored the stares, closing his eyes and remembering the words of his psychologist back at the hospital.

"Now remember Mike, the brain is a muscle, and like all muscles it loves exercise. So every chance you get from now, I want you to take in your surroundings, every smell, every taste, everything you see and feel. Take the time to take it all in. Hopefully, these sensations will help trigger some of your missing memories."

He had spent almost a week in a coma, the doctors trying to delicately undo the effects of whatever mess others had made of his brain. When he first awoke he could only remember his name, and the odd early childhood memory, which was strange to him as he could recognise items around him. He knew what a pen was, knew what a helicopter looked like and what a television was for. But anything personal, anything about his past after the age of about 12 was a blank. Every day with the psychologist brought more and more questions but never answers. He'd had many visitors, one person called Peter had seemed to know him, and as Mike looked back at him, he saw the flash of something there, some deep form of recognition, but it had quickly faded again, lost in the big dark cloud of his memory. The doctors had said he was lucky to be alive, and that his head was like an egg, it had been broken open, scrambled, and then all put back in the broken shell. There was a lot of work to do, but they told him that with time, his memories would return.

He opened his eyes, frustrated that nothing new had come to mind from being in the helicopter. He still needed more time. He may be finding it hard to exercise his brain, but not his body, that was something he could do with his time. He looked down at his hands, slowly flexing them, feeling the blood begin to pump. He still wasn't back up to his full strength yet, the doctors had told him to take it easy, but he'd ignored them, making sure to spend every hour he could with the physiotherapist in the gym. At first he'd struggled to walk 20 feet from his wheelchair, every step had been agony, filled with pain, his stomach feeling as if it would tear itself open at the stitching. But now, after two weeks he felt confident enough to walk unaided, electing to leave the wheelchair and the stick behind at the hospital. His hands felt under his jacket and t-shirt to the fresh scar, it was healing nicely, within two months he'd have full movement there.

It had been Peter's idea to transfer him, telling him after his last visit that perhaps being around his friends might help trigger some of his lost memories. Peter had laughed when Mike looked surprised at the thought of knowing more people. When Mike had asked how many people he knew, Peter had merely replied, "Wait and see. You're not quite the loner you think you are."

Mike had to admit, he was getting bored of the hospital food and welcomed the chance of a change of scenery. And that's how he found himself now on the helicopter, heading south, destination unknown.

He looked out the window as he felt the helicopter begin to flare, to bleed off airspeed as the landing gear came down with a thump. Looking outside he saw a huge concrete water tower come into view, then the perimeter fence of the camp, then finally the concrete apron. After a few moments the helicopter was settled on the ground, the engines' whining down as the crew chief lowered the ramp and began his checks. A few moments later he was back, giving Mike the thumbs up to exit. Mike went to grab his bag, but the crew chief was quicker, shaking his head and taking it from him.

"Oh no you don't, doctor's orders. No heavy lifting for another week!"

Mike smiled in defeat and followed the load master out into the sunshine, seeing three figures, recognising the one in the middle as Peter.

"Here he is, the hero of the hour!" one proclaimed, stepping forwards and hugging Mike.

Mike grimaced against the term 'hero' ignoring the pain in his stomach as the figure hugged him awkwardly. After a few seconds he released him, Peter stepped over,

"Kyle, just give him some room."

The man called Kyle stepped back, the beaming smile thinning somewhat, as Peter offered out his hand, his own welcome more conservative.

"Damn great to see you Mike, really. You've been missed around here."

"Thanks Peter." Mike replied, his own face a mask of confusion as he looked around. Nothing about the airfield jogged any memories. Seeing his confusion the third figure stepped forwards placing a hand on his shoulder.

"Mike, you may not remember me either, my name's David."

Mike looked the man up and down, staring at his face for a moment, again there was a flash of some familiarity, something from his past. Suddenly his eyes narrowed as he proclaimed, "You were a pilot...you were in the RAF?"

David smiled and nodded. "That's right Mike, I was. Well remembered."

All three grinned at Mike triumphantly, impressed that a memory had been unlocked this early on as Mike looked over to Kyle. "And you're a tech geek, a whizz on computers."

"No, not a tech geek Mike. I'm a computer God!" Kyle replied enthusiastically as Mike smiled, happy with this small victory and felt a level of optimism.

Perhaps Peter had been right, perhaps this was a good idea to be here.

Kyle then added excitedly, "God, Mike, we've got so much to talk about, I want to hear all about it, the tank fight, how the Hornet worked, working with Wendi, being on the-"

"Kyle!"

Seeing the look of confusion growing on Mike's face Peter interrupted Kyles excitement.

"Come on, we spoke about this. Too much too soon, you're rushing him."

"Oh sorry." Kyle replied, looking apologetically back, before putting an arm on Mike's shoulder.

"Sorry Mike, but in case you've forgotten, I've got a habit of talking too much when I get excited, you used to always joke with me about it."

Mike smiled back, trying not to hurt Kyle's feelings as he replied, "It's okay Kyle. We'll get there, and I promise that when I remember you'll be the first to know."

The homecoming was short lived as the loadmaster stepped forwards carrying Mike's bag, David quickly scooping it up as Peter remarked,

"Come on then, let's clear the HLS. Let's show Mike around our new home."

With Kyle taking the lead with Mike, animatedly discussing the airfield, all four walked back towards the hangars. Peter had David deliberately walk slower so they could chat out of earshot.

"Good call keeping the others away David."

David nodded glumly, "They weren't happy about it. Sergeant Patterson was adamant they get to see him. Speaking of which, he's requested a meeting with you later about the new training area, apparently he wants to discuss the range layout."

Peter nodded, quickly thinking through the changes to Aurora since his last meeting with the CDS. Already, Peter had huge orders from all branches of the military for the Wasps and Talons, with the company's production capacity being almost quadrupled overnight. Now factories in Birmingham, Leeds, Cardiff and Sheffield were all working using his designs, churning out the war machines in even greater numbers. Only the Talons highly classified power sources were still being made and fitted on site, still the only part of production that Peter had been able to keep in house. Originally the drones were designed to be dropped into units with zero training, but now the MoD wanted dedicated operators of the drones, especially after seeing the battlefield reports on how well they'd performed, leading to the Operator's Training Programme, (OTP) being introduced. Sergeant Patterson and his troops were being used to train the new drone operators coming in from the military, using their own combat experience on the kit. It had been Sergeant Patterson who had been instrumental in leading the training schedule, developing the two-week programme that was due to begin next week. However, as soon as the soldiers had heard Mike was coming back, they all wanted to be there to greet him. It had been David's suggestion that perhaps today would be the best time for one final sweep of the training area, to get the troops out of camp and out of the way.

Peter remembered the angry looks as they loaded into their vehicles that morning, sensing what he'd done. He didn't mean to be harsh, he just wanted Mike relaxed and not under any pressure just yet. He still had so much to process. As if thinking the same, David asked,

"Mike still hasn't asked anything at all about his wife? No name, no mention? No hint?"

"No, not a peep." Peter replied glumly, adding, "I don't know if that's a blessing or a curse. How can you mourn or miss someone, if you don't even know they exist?"

"I can't believe she was at the embassy all this time, right under everyone's bloody noses." David said angrily.

Peter nodded in frustrated agreement, thinking back to when he'd spoken to Sir Charles about finding Kate. Peter had known she was in America, but by the time Sir

Charles and his contacts had finally got round to trying to locate her, it was too late. They'd traced her from the hotel in Chicago to Washington, and then finally to another hotel before boarding a flight. Peter had expected her to be picked up at Birmingham airport, but somehow in all the chaos and confusion, the border force guards had let her in, stating that her travel pass granted her unrestricted access. To have stopped her could have caused a diplomatic incident. That had been the last anyone had heard of her. Now, silence, not a peep. It was as if she had simply disappeared into thin air.

"But they're still looking for her though aren't they? I mean Christ, we know her name, we know her address. How hard can it be?" David replied in frustration.

Peter nodded solemnly. "I've passed her details on David, but let's not forget, we're all out of favours with Sir Charles. He assured me that they were doing their very best, but don't forget, her house is in the occupied zone. If that's where she's headed then she'll be outside of Sir Charles's influential web."

"Couldn't they use Wendi to find her?"

"They could, but we both know they won't." Peter replied, remembering back to Sir Charles angry outburst when he'd used Wendi to rescue Mike.

Already in the news, China, Iran and Russia were reporting massive city-wide electrical outages as something had disrupted their power grid infrastructure. It was being blamed on Indian Cyber terrorists, keen to stall the industrial might of those economies it competed with. Peter knew it was the work of WENDI, no doubt Sir Charles was keen to flex the muscles of his latest asset to impress his political masters. He wouldn't want the distraction of locating one individual, especially one with close connections to Peter.

"So what do we do? Do we tell Mike? I mean, how the hell do we even do that?" David asked, apprehensively.

Peter watched ahead of them as Mike listened in to Kyle animatedly chatting about the camp before sighing in reply.

"I don't know David, this is all a new experience for me, one that I'm not familiar nor comfortable with. I'm just hoping that he'll realise himself over time, and by then, perhaps, the question would have answered itself."

"And what is the question?" David asked, looking intently at Peter.

"The question is, Kate, where the hell are you?"

Eyeball-One

"Where the fuck are they?" the camera operator spat out, looking at his watch again.

The arrest team should have been there by now. They called in the code word almost an hour ago. What the hell was Lunyou playing at?

He looked again at the house, knowing there should be twenty armed men smashing the door in, searching the house and dragging out the three targets. Instead, it was peaceful, serene and eerily quiet.

He lit another cigarette, exhaling and looking over to the radio operator.

"Fucking hell! Tell them again. Ask them where the fuck the arrest team are."

The radio operator keyed the radio, his voice frustrated.

"Control, Eyeball-One, Rasputin I repeat Rasputin. Now where are the arrest team? We need an update on their ETA."

The voice on the end of the radio sounded as equally frustrated as they replied, "Roger understood Eyeball-One, we're trying to raise arrest team. Still no update on their ETA. For now keep eyes on."

"Fucking eyes on!" the radio operator said angrily. "We've had eyes on these bastards for three weeks! We've done our job, now fucking send someone to do theirs!

"Understand your frustration Eyeball-One, just keep doing what you're doing. We'll keep trying to raise them. They'll be there."

The Camera operator was about to say something when he was drawn to movement at the door.

"Shit! I've got the front door opening on Alpha one!"

The radio operator began to relay again as the camera operator began to report.

"I've got all three targets leaving the house, Target two is carrying a small case and a pet carrier, target one has a backpack. Looks like they're leaving! We're going to fucking miss them!"

Both operators watched on with growing frustration as they watched Target Two lock the front door, checking it was locked with a push before taking the other two carefully by the hand and walking out to the street. All three stood there looking longingly back at the house. Clearly they were not planning on returning, otherwise why take the fucking cat?

"For fuck's sake we're going to miss them!" the camera operator hissed, as the radio operator urgently sent over the radio.

"Control, we have all three targets on the street, they're obviously leaving for good. Do you want us to go down and arrest them on site?"

Both operators pulled their pistols, checking they were loaded and made ready before tucking them into their waistbands, fully expecting to be ordered to apprehend. The camera operator was quickly sucking the cigarette, getting the most out of every drag before throwing it to the floor, expecting to be leaving any second. Below them the three targets had started to move and were walking up the street to the junction. They were not walking that fast, and both operators felt more than confident they could easily catch them.

After a few tense moments finally the Control room responded.

"Eyeball-One, Control, negative, do not detain, remain in location."

"What?" the radio operator remarked, as the camera operator leaned over and grabbed the radio.

"Control, Eyeball-One, did you not hear what we said, all targets have left Alpha-One and walking away. They're escaping on foot. We can detain them now, do we have permission to go down and stop them?"

The voice that came back was a different one, more authoritative,

"Eyeball-One, you will remain in place. Arrests are to be carried out by civilian police and not, I repeat NOT by military forces. Remain hidden and in position. Keep eyes on the house. Arresting forces will be there any second."

"FUCK!" Both operators exclaimed together, not caring about the noise.

The radio operator sat down angrily as the camera operator stepped from behind the screen, looking out the window up the street at the three figures as they slowly disappeared around the corner.

"Three fucking weeks wasted." he muttered angrily, as he looked down and picked up the discarded cigarette, still smoking and angrily took a long drag, watching as the cherry burned brightly. After a few more seconds it was finished, and he stubbed it out on the wall, looking back up the empty street.

And just like that they were gone, Mrs Faulkes, her slow assed parents and a cat. They'd managed to do it, they'd managed to escape the clutches of the FSB.

He turned, watching as the radio operator began to pack up his equipment, collapsing the observation post, already wondering,

Where the fuck was Lunyou?

Somewhere in Dorset.

Captain Lunyou opened his eyes, the blurred images slowly coming into focus as the cacophony of noise filled his ears. He could hear explosions, gunfire, shouts and screams. He looked around, his fog filled brain trying to make sense of what was happening as he felt the raindrops dripping through the 4x4's smashed windows and onto his face. He looked over, already seeing Artem was dead. His cold, lifeless eyes still open as his body slumped over the steering wheel, the huge piece of metal protruding through his side told Lunyou his Sergeant would never be leaving the seat again. He tried to open the door to exit the vehicle, its mangled metal refusing to budge as the 4x4 remained pinned against a telegraph pole. As Lunyou tried to move he felt a stabbing pain in his legs. Looking down he saw the collapsed dashboard that was pinning him to the seat, his legs disappearing in amongst the mangled metal. He tried again to move, yelling against the pain as his hands cut themselves trying to grasp the sharp plastic and metal. After a few seconds he admitted defeat, cursing and yelling out in frustration.

He looked around him, his confused muddled brain beginning to try to piece together what had happened in the events before the crash. He remembered that they had been following the police car down the country roads in convoy, it's blue lights flashing as the water sprayed up from the wet road. Then suddenly his Sergeant had yelled in warning as a Green tractor fitted with forks had approached at speed from a side road and slammed into the car, the forks easily throwing the 4x4 into the air and causing it to roll over down the road, careering towards the telegraph pole. That was how he had come to be here.

Any thoughts he'd had of it being a mere accident were quickly dispensed as he'd heard the explosions and the gunfire, he knew then what had happened. The convoy had been ambushed.

He looked to the broken wing mirror, trying to see what was occurring behind him as the sounds of battle raged on, he could see some of his men were trying to fight clear, jumping out of the truck and diving into cover. Not wanting to be trapped unarmed, he turned to reach for his weapon, cursing when he realised it had been thrown from the vehicle during the crash. He couldn't reach his pistol, it was still in his leg holster, trapped below the remnants of the dashboard. Instead, he saw his Sergeants pistol was ready to be used, dangling uselessly in its holster. He reached over, his fingers touching it, so tantalising close as he tried desperately to grasp it. Slowly, with great effort he managed to pull it clear, his excitement short lived as the pistol fell from his slippery bloody hands into the drivers footwell, far from reach.

"FUCK!" he yelled, in frustration and pain.

Then the gunfire seemed to slow and then cease altogether. Had his troops managed to defeat the ambushers? Were they victorious after all? A silence descended over the area, now the only sound he could hear was the rain hitting the metal roof, it's dripping seeming to increase in volume as he fought to control the fear and apprehension he felt. Looking behind him he could see people approaching from the road, joined by others now emerging from cover in the woods. His confidence began to grow as he recognised the yellow jackets of the police officers joining the figures. His men had won. It was over.

He angrily thought as to how he'd repay the ambush once his men had freed him, looking over to his Sergeant to draw resolve from the lifeless body.

Seeing the figures in the mirror still talking amongst themselves he angrily banged on the roof of the car, shouting out.

"Get over here and get me out! Come on! What the fuck are you waiting for?"

He felt true fear when he saw them walking towards him, the realisation hitting him, they were not his men. They were the enemy! But the police were stood with them, he thought, his confused brain quickly grasping the situation, they *had* betrayed him, he should *never* have trusted them.

His survival instincts kicked in as he reached down again, pulling at the broken metal and plastic, ignoring the cuts and the pain, heaving with all his might, trying so desperately to release himself. He was stopped mid attempt as the figure of one of the men approached him, leaning in through the driver's side, the face smiling in pleasure when he saw him trapped and scared.

"Hello Lunyou."

Lunyou looked up, his face a mixture of fear and shock as he recognised this man. His mind thought back to a farm, to a woman with a shotgun, to a Mr Sam Collins.

He watched as the farmer looked around assessing the situation, opening the driver's door with a creak and loud groan of metal, bending down to pick up the pistol from the foot well. Only once the pistol was safely tucked away did the farmer check Artem, his fingers on his neck checking for a pulse, or lack of one. After a few seconds he sighed disappointingly, "Shame he's dead Lunyou, I really wanted him around to see this."

Lunyou watched on as the farmer walked out of earshot, quickly joined by others, some wearing a mixture of military and civilian style clothing, others like the farmer were fully dressed in camouflage gear, all carrying a mixture of both British and Russian weaponry. There was a discussion amongst the group, perhaps they wanted him alive, perhaps they knew of his father, he thought hopefully. His father was rich, perhaps they were going to ransom him?

He watched on in curiosity, silently hoping that somewhere a Russian unit had heard the sounds of battle and were screaming here to rescue him. He knew then he'd delay them as long as he could, stall for time. There was a chance, a good chance he could survive this, and then he'd make the bastard pay.

After a few moments they'd finished talking, it looked like the farmer was the one in charge, issuing orders as the group dispersed to carry out his wishes. From his limited view, Lunyou watched on as most began to strip the bodies of weapons, whilst one fighter seemed to run in amongst the trees, returning moments later carrying something heavy towards him.

The farmer walked back over to the car, standing close by as the fighter sent over to the woods came closer, Lunyou seeing the object he was carrying was a fuel jerry can. Lunyou watched on open mouthed as the fighter opened the lid and began to carefully pour the fuel through the smashed back windows, the fuel pooling in the boot and between the back seats before pouring forwards under Lunyou's seat. The fumes of the petrol filling his nostrils, dashing any hopes that he may have had of stalling for time.

"If you kill me, there'll be repercussions!" he yelled, trying to shift in the seat to keep out of the fuel.

The farmer remained impassive, his face cold and stern as Lunyou shot back in fear.

"People will die, innocent people will die! Think about it. If you do this, you're killing your own people!"

The farmer stepped closer, his face a snarl as he shot back, "Innocent people have died, and all at your hands. One of them was my Mary."

Lunyou watched as finally with the jerry can empty the fighter threw it into the back seat, stepping back out of the way, leaving them alone. Just him and the farmer.

"Let me go and I can help you, I can help you fight back." Lunyou pleaded, his eyes desperately darting about.

The farmer smiled a thin smile as he produced the silver lighter, holding it aloft with a flourish for Lunyou to see.

"You burned my wife. You burned my farm. You destroyed whatever I had left in the world to love. Now, all I have left is rage."

Sensing his end was near Lunyou became desperate, his voice rising in fear, "WAIT! I HAVE MONEY! MY FATHER HAS MONEY, HE'LL PAY WHATEVER YOU WANT!"

The farmer said nothing, flicking open the lighter and stepping closer.

"PLEASE!" Lunyou yelled.

Sam lit the lighter, watching the flame dancing about in the breeze as the rain fizzled in its heat, his face a mask of silent rage.

"You reap what you sow," he whispered softly.

Then...he threw the lighter.

20

Epilogue

A few weeks later...

Mike watched on from the back of the classroom, as Sergeant Patterson finished welcoming the latest batch of thirty new recruits to day one of the second course of the Operators Training Program (OTP). Already the first batch of operators had completed the course, once fully qualified they were sent back to re-join their units, having conducted two weeks of intense training using the Talons and the Wasps, before finishing in a joint training exercise using troops who themselves were training for war. It had been an instant success, with both the new troops on the ground and the operators impressed at what the robots could offer them on the battlefield. Mike hoped it would help them prepare for what the future had in store for them.

Mike's recovery had been going well, with him having kept his rank of Captain he'd been placed in charge of the OTP course, becoming it's Training Officer. It was something he relished as it allowed him to sit in on some of the lessons. As far as the recruits were concerned he was watching to check the instructors were doing their jobs, but privately he was re-learning how the drones worked himself, making sure he knew the subject fully that he was supposed to be in charge of. After only a few days of sitting in on the lessons he found himself remembering how the Wasps and Talons worked, and spent a day on the weapons range firing them, confirming to himself, and more importantly to the others that he could use them. The more time he spent on the base the more time he'd found his past began to unlock. He remembered some of his life in the Army, his previous combat missions, being in Afghanistan, Iraq, and Kosovo. Perhaps he'd always been in the Army, he thought to himself, perhaps that's why he could only remember being a Staff Sergeant even though he was now a Captain.

It hadn't all been good though as he found the more he began to remember, the more the nightmares would come. It was always the same nightmare, with Mike stood amongst hundreds of people. Almost all were stood silently pointing at him, with each face covered by a white cloth, their bellies torn open, their innards hanging out on the floor in a disgusting mess. One of the figures was stood in black coveralls, Mike could see he was a Trooper and that his face looked familiar, but his body was always ablaze in flame. He'd tried to talk to the figure, but it silently stood burning. And then there was the woman, pretty, familiar, she would stand at the back silently shouting to him. He tried to ignore everything going on around him and hear what she was trying to say, but it was always muffled, always too distant. Every time he'd tried to walk towards her she would drift further away, becoming ever distant until eventually he'd wake covered in sweat. Some nights, without knowing why he'd burst into tears, too scared to go back to sleep in case the nightmare came back. He'd tried to speak to Peter about it, but seeing the awkwardness in him when he mentioned the nightmare, it only made Mike more suspicious. Who was the woman and Trooper, and what was with all those people?

Mike was drawn from his thoughts as the door behind him opened, Mike looked around at the new arrival, seeing it was another member of his training team, Corporal Webb, who was silently beckoning him outside.

Mike quietly stood up, getting eye contact with Sergeant Patterson who nodded in acknowledgement as Mike left the room, joining Spider in the corridor.

"What is it Spider?"

"Sir, sorry to bother you, but the Brigadier wants a word, he's over in his office at hangar two."

"Did he say what it's about?" Mike asked curiously.

"Afraid not Sir, just said to come and get you. By the way, I'd like to speak to you about-"

"Not now." Mike interrupted, before walking off, leaving Spider stood open mouthed in the corridor.

"What the hell happened to you?" Spider muttered to himself, slowly shaking his head watching him go.

Spider remembered the excitement and happiness when the unit had found out Mike was on his way back to join them at Aurora. He'd remembered how everyone had raced back from the ranges to see him, ready to welcome him back. They'd all been warned about the change in the Captain, what to expect, but it was still a shock to see the difference from the man they had all encountered all those weeks ago. Gone was the humour, the spark, the ease at which he'd commanded troops. His experience and confidence that he had seemed to have had by the bucketful had all but disappeared, replaced now with an emptiness that made Mike seem almost cold, robotic, and worst of all, scared. Three times now Spider had seen Mike shy away from confrontation, adopting a more pacified role, relying on others to jump to his defence. Whatever had been done to him, he was not the same person as before, everyone could see that. Spider just hoped that somewhere in there was the Mike Faulkes of old, and that somehow he would return. At least then Spider could get the chance to apologise for hitting him, at least that would be one wound he could heal.

Knowing now was not the time, he sighed to himself and turned to walk back over to the hangars.

Mike was outside the Brigadier's office in a matter of minutes, knocking on the open door he waited in the doorway.

"Come on in Mike, close the door behind you," Peter replied warmly, sat behind his desk overlooking the hangar. Behind them through the glass window Mike could see the Aurora workforce all working hard on their latest project.

Mike walked to the centre of the room, looking around at the newcomer sat on the opposite side of the desk, an empty chair next to him. Mike could see from his rank slide he was a Colonel, and that from his black beret he belonged to the 24th Royal Tank Regiment. On the desk in front of the Colonel Mike could see a large folder bursting with photographs and paperwork.

"Sir, you asked to see me?" Mike asked, glancing between the two of them.

"I did Mike. Firstly though let me introduce Colonel Richards."

Mike turned and looked at the Colonel, acknowledging him with a nod of the head, noticing the Colonel had a serious look on his face, his eyes were scrutinising Mike, the way a boxer weighed up an opponent. Something about the way he was staring at him unnerved Mike. Ignoring his cold hard gaze he looked back to the Brigadier.

Peter stood up from behind the desk, walking over to a switch mounted on the wall. With a quick flick of the switch the giant blinds fitted to the office window began to lower, closing off the office from the outside world. Now it was just the three of them.

"That's better," Peter remarked, "Don't want any prying eyes."

"Brigadier, with all due respect," Mike began, "I've still got the after-action reports to write up, then the armoury checks to do-"

"What a good little soldier!" the Colonel interrupted dryly, causing Mike to raise his eyebrows.

"Excuse me Colonel?"

"You heard me the first time!" the Colonel scowled.

Mike looked over to the Brigadier, confused at the Colonel's tone.

"I'm sorry Brigadier, am I missing something here?"

Peter walked over to his office door, opening it and standing in the doorway before turning to look at Mike, a sadness in his eyes. "Mike, I'm sorry. I hope you'll understand afterwards."

And with that Peter turned, slamming the door shut.

Mike went to walk towards the door when the Colonel growled,

"Don't go running to him for help. You're the one who's got to deal with me!"

Mike turned to face the new threat as the Colonel suddenly leapt upwards out of the chair, his voice low and menacing.

"Sir, I've done the armoury checks, I've done the paperwork, I've got my tongue up your ass...SIR!"

Mike frowned at the Colonel, unsure as to why the sudden aggression. He sized him up, seeing his huge shoulders and arms. Whatever was happening Mike wanted nothing to do with it. He could fear the cold fear creeping up his spine as he began to sweat suddenly. Had the room just became hotter, he wondered. He began to retreat towards the door his arms held up in mock surrender.

"Colonel I've got no idea what the fuck is going on here, but do you want to tell me why you're angry?"

"Why, you going to try to talk me down? Calm me down? I'm angry you gutless little prick, and I want to kick the shit out of something!"

The Colonel walked towards Mike, his arm shooting out and barging his shoulders, knocking him back slightly. Mike kept walking backwards, creating distance from the threat, as the Colonel kept advancing.

"I'm angry because you're hiding out here, whilst other people are fighting! I'm angry because you're a coward, and I want to hit you! What you going to do about it?"

Mike kept retreating, eventually backing himself up against the door. He tried the handle, the door was locked! The Brigadier must have locked them in! What the hell was Peter playing at, locking him in here with this mad man!

Seeing his predicament the Colonel smiled menacingly and advanced forwards, all the while pushing into Mike's shoulders, "And now what you going to do?"

Mike looked behind the man, seeing the only other way out of the room was out of the window, the panicked thoughts filling his head were screaming at him to run, to push past the man and jump through the window. As if thinking the same the Colonel grabbed Mike roughly by the shoulders, pinning him against the wall.

"Please, let go of me!" Mike yelled, the panic making his voice rise slightly

"FUCKING MAKE ME!" the Colonel yelled, cuffing him around the back of the head. Mike was dragged over towards the table, the chairs were kicked over in the ruckus as he was picked up and body slammed onto the table, grimacing as the Colonel began to slap him roughly about the head, his voice snarling.

"You're a fucking coward! Say it! Say it with me!"

"Get the fuck off me!" Mike yelled, trying to break the Colonel's hold.

"SAY IT!" the Colonel kept repeating, "You're a fucking coward! FUCKING SAY IT!"

Mike was petrified, all he wanted was for this man to stop, the panicked voices in his head were yelling at him to say it, but then something changed, another voice seemed to replace the panic, an angrier voice, one more controlled. Mike ignored the hits, concentrating on the voice, closing his eyes, the Colonel's voice drifting into silence as a strange zen like calmness took over Mike. Mike thought to the voice, hearing it over and over, getting louder and louder, drowning out the panicked voices until the voice turned to a face, then to a gym, then to a former IDF soldier called Ewen, his words clearing his mind with razor sharp focus. "Sometimes you may not be able to understand or reason with your opponent. He may not understand you. But he will understand your fists and your feet. So, win that argument first. And then, when you have beaten him, maybe then, he will start to see things *your* way."

Suddenly Mike's eyes opened with renewed clarity, all those years in Ewen's gym flooding back in an instant. The Colonel had his hand cocked back to strike again, with Mike pinned on his back, he was already defensive, limited in what he could do. He lashed out with his elbow, hitting the Colonel in the midriff, watching as the Colonel crumpled in a heap as the air exploded out of his lungs. Winded, the attack stopped immediately as the Colonel slid sideways off the table onto all fours on the floor, gasping for air.

Mike jumped off the table, shaking his head and his shoulders, limbering up, ready for the fight, watching his opponent carefully. Suddenly more memories came flooding into his head, distracting him, the fight briefly forgotten. The Colonel had crawled over to the chair, his arms held up in defeat as he coughed and wheezed and struggled to breathe.

Mike shook his head, the thoughts racing through, his time in the Army, the house in Poole, his Porsche 911, his wife...HIS WIFE! Fucking hell, he was married!

"Kate," he muttered, causing the Colonel to stand up suddenly, all trace of the anger disappearing.

"That's it Mike...That's it, keep going!" he urged, the anger now replaced with a look of hope.

Mike looked up confused at the Colonel, his eyebrows creasing as all the memories flooded back, the battle on the tank, the details of Operation Fools Mate, the death of Bill, the evacuation of Bovington. That's where he knew the Colonel from! His eyes opened wide as he exclaimed,

"You're called Chris, we're friends?"

Chris broke into a huge smile, stepping forwards, his arms outstretched as he embraced Mike in a big bear hug, his voice choked with emotion.

"You son of a bitch! You beautiful big son of a bitch! I knew you could do it!"

Mike pulled back from the embrace, his own voice choked with emotion.

"But if I'm married where's my wife? Where's Kate?"

Chris's euphoria was short lived as he stumbled over how to answer, deflecting, "We can get onto all that in a moment, she's alive though so don't worry."

Behind them they heard the door open as the Brigadier came back in, an apologetic look on his face.

"Mike I'm sorry you had to go through all of that."

Mike looked puzzled as he rubbed his sore shoulders, looking over to Chris who answered.

"Doctor's recommendation, sometimes trauma can unlock the memories. After all that time you spent training with Ewen it was all I could think of to goad you into action."

"So you two cooked up that little ambush hoping to get me back?"

"We did," Peter replied, walking over to his table and clearing up some of the mess. "Hated to do it though, hope you understand?"

"No hard feelings Peter," Mike replied smiling, as Chris joked, "Oh so now it's back to Peter again!"

All three smiled as Mike quickly asked, "What information do we have on Kate, I need to know where she is."

Peter held up a warning hand.

"Calm down Mike, I understand your need to see her. We've got assets looking for her as we speak, but we need to find her first before you can go off and get her."

"So she is alive?" Mike asked, concern etched on his face.

Chris pulled up the second chair, urging Mike to sit as he sat down himself, picking the folder up off the floor as he answered.

"She's alive mate, we've had assets looking for her for a while. As soon as we know exactly where she is, we're going to get her."

"We?" Mike asked?

"Yes, we," Chris replied, "I've been given a week's leave starting today. Figured I'd use that time to help a friend to find and bring his wife home, especially considering the trouble you caused the last time I left you alone!"

Mike smiled and looked down at the folder as Chris began to pull out the contents, a collection of photos and files, organising them on the desk in order. After a moment he replied,

"Right, before we get onto the subject of Kate, let's help fill in the blanks, let me tell you all about your life my friend..."

Somewhere in France

Kate stopped sawing at the wood, taking a moment to wipe her sweat soaked brow as she took a quick break. Removing her gloves, she walked over to where her bottle of water lay on the ground, picking it up and taking a swig before looking around her at the farm courtyard.

Ten other people were all there with her, all working on fixing the giant roof to one of the barns. They had to get the roof fixed before the onset of winter, no-one liked having a leaky roof, especially when they were to be sleeping in it themselves. Emma's farmyard where Kate had finally settled had taken in another four families, all refugees from the UK, all seeking shelter. Now with the farmhouse overcrowded, Kate's friend Emma had been forced to accommodate the other families in the barn. Everyone was pitching in to help, and in a way it all added to the community spirit of the place. Plus the work made everyone forget all about the troubles at home. It wasn't uncommon at night to hear people sobbing into their pillows as the memories of loved ones lost in the fighting re-surfaced. Kate had tried to grieve for Mike, but somehow it just didn't feel right, like somehow she thought he could still be alive. She'd found out about the attack on Bovington and knowing that he had been there, she thought he had to be dead, otherwise where the hell was he? She'd tried to enquire with the New England District, to see if there was any news on Mike's death, but her enquiries were met with a wall of silence, especially since she had spirited away two of its citizens to France. It had been tough going getting her parents over here, halfway across the channel, her mum had suffered a violent bout of seasickness, and her dad had nearly fallen overboard trying to help her. Still, four hours later and they'd been safely moored in Cherbourg. The French authorities had been more than welcoming, almost spiriting the thousands of people there through the checks, and suddenly her friend Emma was there to greet them with blankets and warm cups of soup in hand. And that was how they'd found themselves on the farm.

Kate looked across to her parents, both were sat by one of the smaller paddocks, feeding the smaller lambs. She smiled to herself, even with everything they'd been through, at their age they could still find the happiness in the smaller things. She shook her hands, getting the blood to flow as she began to put the dusty gloves back on, muttering to herself.

"Come on Kate, this wood's not going to cut itself!"

She picked up the saw, about to start again when she felt her pocket vibrating. Her phone was going off, she'd been ignoring it all morning. It felt strange with everything that had happened, the way technology had been snatched from them all to suddenly have a working phone again. In the old days, before the invasion, people would stop what they were doing and race to answer the phone, but now, with phones taking a back seat people would wait. 'If it was important, they'd call back,' was now the phrase of the day.

She continued to saw the wood, all the while feeling the phone vibrating, whoever it was, they were certainly persistent. Sighing irritably, she stopped what she was doing, using her teeth to pull off one of her gloves before pulling the phone out of her pocket. Looking at the screen she could see it said 'Number withheld'

She was tempted to ignore it again, probably someone trying to sell her something she thought moodily.

Eventually her curiosity got the better of her and she answered.

"Hello?..."

Author's notes and acknowledgments

Wow did I really just do that? A trilogy! I think were my first words I uttered when me and my Wife sat down and read the final lines of the Epilogue. But before I continue though, I just want to send out my heartfelt thanks to all those who helped take the time from their own busy lives and help me with the editing and proof reading of the books. Some I've mentioned before, others are new to the series. Firstly to my wife Emily, with whose support, love and guidance helped me to create these books. Then onto Paddy, Victoria and Natalie, all of whom had been with me from the start, their eyes keen and their thoughts and ideas fresh. Then onto our new additions to the series, Nick Burnham aka "Aquaholic" who most of the boating community will know from his excellent boating reviews and boating exploits. if you love boats, or just enjoy seeing people happy to be on them then I recommend you go onto youtube and look him up. Nick had bought the first book back in 2024 and instantly loved the story. So when I asked if he fancied seeing a sneak peek of the third book's draft he jumped at the chance, offering his own keen journalist eyes to proof read the script. So thank you Nick. Also another thank you goes out to one of my fans, somewhere out there is a guy called Frank Moody. Frank had contacted me a while ago complimenting the book and its story. He liked it so much that I thought who better to ask to read the final book and get his thoughts. So Frank was the first person to officially read the book, he loved it, I just hope you did too. So wherever you are out there, thank you Frank.

Now, a lot of my friends ask me why I chose to write this story, perhaps in a way that was a question I'd always asked myself in the past but never thought to answer. One of the reasons was because when I started to write this story back in 2022, I found it cathartic to put my thoughts on paper, a form of therapy, a way to talk of events of the past but in the safety of re-living them through someone else's eyes. Another reason I chose to write the story was because, being ex-military I have an inherent interest in the defence of my country, something I still feel passionately about now. It concerns me when I see how weak as a nation our Armed Forces have become, not through the fault of the brave men and women who serve in them, but due to the constant erosion and meddling of those that have never understood what it is to put on a uniform. The world we live in has never been more dangerous, especially at a time when other allied nations begin to question the strength of NATO as hostile nations constantly push against it. So I guess I wanted this story to highlight how our own country's reliance on others to come to our aid may ultimately prove to be our downfall. In the past we've relied heavily on the United States and other allies to bail us out, who is to say there will be a next time? NATO's article five relies on the political will and stomach of those other NATO members to come to our aid. But what happened after the 2016 Novichok attacks on UK soil? On paper this was a weapon of mass destruction, a biological agent attack on a NATO country. And yet NATO did nothing except a series of sanctions that Putin easily bypassed, and showed such contempt for that he still went on to invade another country. Perhaps in a way NATO's article five is our own version of the French Maginot line, a series of fortifications that were built to stop further German invasions after World War 1. The French believed it to be impassable, a rock on which the German forces would break themselves, therefore any risk of invasion was played down. Imagine the shock of the French people and it's Armed Forces when the invading German Army simply bypassed these defences and went on to subdue the country in a matter of weeks. Perhaps our reliance on Nato's article five is our own country's Maginot Line. So, hopefully by writing about this potential threat to our own shores and highlighting it, we could somehow mitigate against it and put the defence of our own country back into the top tiers of budget spending as it so rightly deserves. There's no point in spending billions on welfare trying to improve people's lives in this country, if we can't protect those very same people from the the gravest of threats from hostile nations intent on controlling or destroying them. Perhaps that's why when I wrote the story of Mike Faulkes, I didn't want him to have the cliche happy ending that some main characters in other stories have, perhaps in a way that's why I chose the ending I did. Not quite the romantic clinch with his wife that some may have wanted, but instead a sort of realistic alternative with the hope that maybe it could be Mike on the phone. I hope as a reader you can forgive me this, but then it is just a story, you, the reader hold the power to decide it's ending. So if you want to imagine Mike and Kate finally get together then that's your story to write in your head. It does seem strange though to think of this story as finished, I keep thinking of what would happen to certain characters had

I continued to write a fourth book, how would their stories pan out, would they go on to see the UK win the war, or would it be destined to remain a broken state, a conflicted nation of two halves, similar to the Korean Peninsular. Perhaps going forward I continue the story, but this time lead off with another character, perhaps Linda the reporter would deserve a book or two, or maybe follow the story of Sam leading the resistance behind enemy lines, or maybe Fletch and his special forces team. Or how about Flight Lieutenant 'Jacko' Jackson, if he were real, I'm sure he'd have an interesting story to tell as to his own Squadrons outcome. Or perhaps I won't, perhaps instead I could start a whole new conflict somewhere else. But then that's the beauty of storytelling, you can have anything and everything all at once.

After all, it is just a story...isn't it?

I'll see you when I see you next...

Thank you

M

Glossary

5.56mm – Standard NATO round – What all NATO assault rifles fire, standardised in size to make logistics easy

7.62mm – Standard Russian Round – Larger than the NATO calibre, able to cause more damage

ADJ – Adjutant – usually a Captain and in charge of a units administration

AGC – Adjutants Generals Corp

AK-12 – Russian Assault Rifle

AN124 – Antonov 124 Russian heavy lift cargo plane

ANPR – Automatic Number Plate Recognition

APU – Auxiliary Power unit

ASACS – Air Surveillance and Control System

ASRAAM – Advanced Short-Range Air to Air Missile

ATC – Air Traffic Control

ATGM – Anti Tank Guided Missile

ATDU – Armoured Trials and Development Unit

Bingo – Codeword used by pilots to describe an aircraft low on fuel

BMP-3 – Russian Armoured Infantry Vehicle – Used to transport troops into combat zones under fire

BV – Boiling Vessel – Square shaped large kettle used on armoured vehicles to heat water and rations

BVRAAM – Beyond Visual Range Air to Air Missile

CAS – Chief of Air Staff – Head of the Royal Air Force

CinCS – Commander in Chief South – Name given to overall commander of Russian/Tumat forces in the South of England

CDI – Chief of Defence Intelligence – Head of UK intelligence agencies

CDS – Chief of the Defence Staff – Head of all Military forces

CGS – Chief of the General Staff – Head of the Army

CNS/1SL – Chief of the Naval Staff/ First Sea Lord - Head of the Royal Navy

Chally 2 – Nickname that crews use to describe the Challenger 2 Tank

CO – Commanding Officer

COBR(A) – Cabinet Office Briefing Room (A) – Emergency response meeting usually chaired by the PM and other senior figures of government

CPO – Close Protection Officer

CPS – Commanders Primary Sight – What the Commander uses to sight and fire the tanks weapons. Also has its own laser to acquire the range to target for the Fire Control Computer

CRARRV – Challenger Armoured Repair and Recovery Vehicle – Used by the REME to assist broken and bogged vehicles

DASS – Defensive Aids Sub System – also called **Praetorian**- provides threat assessments, aircraft protection and support measures to the Typhoon

DTT – Driver Training Tank – Turretless Tank used to train new drivers

DZ – Drop Zone

ETA – Estimated Time of Arrival

EW – Electronic Warfare

EWO – Electronic Warfare Officer

F-35 Lightning – RAF's next generation multirole fighter plane

FCC – Fire Control Computer – Calculates the computations required to help the crew to aim the gun

FSB – Russian Federal Security Services

GCE – Gun Control Equipment

GCHQ – Government Communication Headquarters

Glock-17 – Standard British forces 9mm semi-automatic pistol

Gold Commander – Police designation for the overall commander of a situation or emergency at the scene

GPS – Gunners Primary Sight – What the Gunner on a Chally 2 uses to sight and fire the tanks weapons. Also has a laser to acquire the range to target for the Fire Control Computer

GSM – Garrison Sergeant Major

HORNET – High Optical RadiatioN Emitting Transmitter – Experimental laser system developed by Aurora Defence Systems

HF – High Frequency

IFR – Instrument Flight Rules

IL-80 – Iiyushin II-80 'Maxdome' – Russian Airborne Command Centre, similar to the USAF 'Airforce-One'

Javelin – Portable Anti-Tank Guided Missile System, used by most NATO countries

JNCO – Junior Non-Commissioned Officer

Kaliber 3m-54 – Russian cruise missile – can be launched by sea air and land

Kamaz K-4386 Typhoon – Russian oversized armoured 4x4, air portable with a rapid firing 30mm cannon

Kinzhal – (KH-47M2 Khinzal) Russian hypersonic air launched ballistic missile. Nato designation is 'Killjoy'

L-7 GPMG – General Purpose Machine Gun – Belt fed, rapid firing machine gun

L-22 Carbine – Short barrelled variant of the SA-80-A2 assault rifle issued to armoured crews

L-94 Coax – Coaxially mounted Machine Gun, located next to the Main gun

LIDAR - Light Detection and Ranging - A method of determining ranges and objects using a series of lasers

MBT – Main Battle Tank

MIG-31 – Russian Fighter Bomber

MoD – Ministry of Defence

MP443 Grach – Standard Russian forces 9mm semi-automatic pistol

NATO – North Atlantic Treaty Organisation

NATS – National Air Traffic Services

OC – Officer Commanding

PIRATE – Passive Infra-Red Airborne Track Equipment – allows long range visual identification of a target using cameras, sensors and computer

PSTN – Public Switched Telephone Network – Copper telephone landlines

PM – Prime Minister

QM - Quartermasters Department - Where kit and equipment for vehicles and troops are stored and distributed

QRF – Quick Reaction Force

QRA – Quick Reaction Alert

R-37 Vympel – Russian long range hypersonic air-to-air missile

RAC – Royal Armoured Corp

RAF – Royal Air Force

REME – Royal Electrical and Mechanical Engineers

RMP – Royal Military Police

RSM – Regimental Sergeant Major

RUPERT – Nickname given to officers by junior ranks

RWS – Remote Weapons Station – fitted to tanks that are classed as TES

SA-80-A2 – Standard British Army Assault Rifle

SBS – Special Boat Service

SNCO – Senior Non-Commissioned Officer

Sprut 2S25 – Russian air portable light tank, able to field a 125mm gun

SSM – Squadron Sergeant Major

SU-57 – Russian next gen multirole fighter plane

T-80 – Russian Main Battle Tank

TALON - Tracked Anti-armour Listening and Observation Node - Experimental tracked autonomous weapons platform that had been designed by Aurora Defence Systems. Has cutting edge fusion reactor and uses acoustic and visual sensors to locate, assess and if necessary attack the enemy

TES – Theatre Entry Specific – designation given to the Challenger 2 'Megatron' that has been heavily modified with add on armour, RWS and forward/rearwards facing cameras and other upgrades

THUMPR – Transport Heavy Utility Mobile Platform Remote – Heavy lift drone developed by Aurora Defence Systems

TU-54 Bear – Russian Cold War era turboprop bomber

Typhoon – RAF multi role fighter jet – also known as Eurofighter

UHF – Ultra High Frequency

UN – United Nations

VDV – Vozdushno-Desantnye Voyska – Russian Airborne Forces

VHF – Very High Frequency

VID – Visual Identification

VOIP – Voice Over Internet Protocol – A phone line that is digital and relies on the internet instead of a landline

WASP - Weapons Augmented Surveillance Platform - Experimental flying drone designed by Aurora Defence systems. Allows for airborne surveillance of the battlefield and carries a payload of twelve 40mm modified grenades consisting of six high explosive and six fragmentation

Wildcat - Upgraded version of the Lynx, fast, lightly armed, multirole helicopter used by the British Army and Royal Navy

Winchester – Codeword used by pilots to describe an aircraft out of ammunition

WO2 – Warrant Officer Class 2 – Sergeant Major rank or equivalent

WO1 – Warrant officer Class 1 – RSM or GSM rank or equivalent

WOC – Wonderland Operations Centre

Rank Structures of the UK Armed Forces

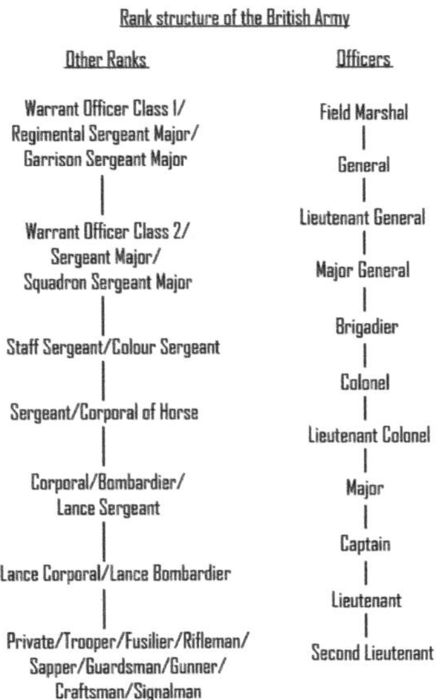

Rank structure of the Royal Air Force
Other Ranks
Non-Commisioned Aircew
Officers
Warrant Officer
RAF Master Aircrew
Marshal Of The Royal Air Force
Flight Sergeant
RAF Flight Sergeant Aircrew
Air Chief Marshal
Chief Technician
Air Marshal
RAF Sergeant Aircrew
Sergeant
Air Vice-Marshal
Corporal
Air Commodore
Group Captain
Lance Corporal RAF Regiment
Wing Commander
Squadron Leader
Air Specialist Class I Technician
Flight Lieutenant
Air Specialist Class I
Flying Officer
Pilot Officer
Air Specialist Class 2

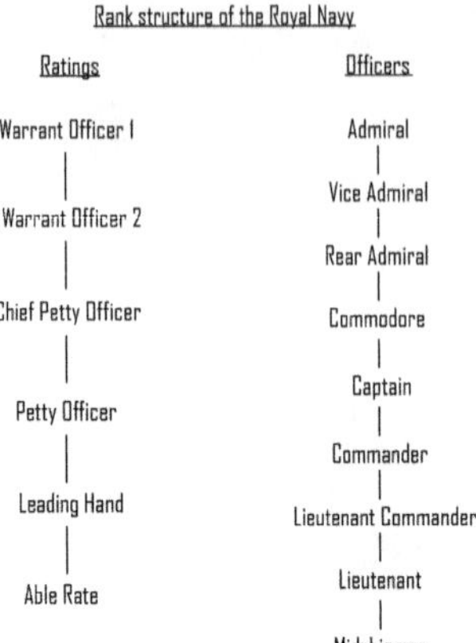
Rank structure of the Royal Navy
Ratings
Officers
Warrant Officer 1
Admiral
Warrant Officer 2
Vice Admiral
Rear Admiral
Chief Petty Officer
Commodore
Petty Officer
Captain
Commander
Leading Hand
Lieutenant Commander
Lieutenant
Able Rate
Midshipman